PREGNANT BY THE COMMANDING GREEK

NATALIE ANDERSON

MILLS & BOON

First published in Great Britain 2019
by Mills & Boon, an imprint of HarperCollins*Publishers*
1 London Bridge Street, London, SE1 9GF

Large Print edition 2019

ISBN: 978-0-263-08276-0

This book is produced from independently certified
FSC™ paper to ensure responsible forest management. For
more information visit www.harpercollins.co.uk/green.

Printed and bound in Great Britain
by CPI Group (UK) Ltd, Croydon, CR0 4YY

PREGNANT BY THE COMMANDING GREEK

For Kathleen,
your relentless perseverance and
efforts are such an inspiration to me—
you rock!

CHAPTER ONE

'WHAT DO YOU MEAN, he wants us to "get rid of it"?' Antoinette Roberts scooped up the small, greying terrier and clutched him close. 'Doesn't he realise that "it" is a gorgeous, living creature?' She glared at Joel, her junior colleague.

'I don't think he does, Ettie,' Joel answered in an agitated whisper. 'He just stormed in here first thing and demanded access to Harold's apartment and started clearing stuff out.'

'You're kidding?' Disgust surged through Ettie.

Cavendish House, an exclusive apartment building in the heart of London's Mayfair, offered full concierge service to its privacy-loving residents, and, as head concierge, Ettie was used to delivering it for her demanding guests; from everyday mundane queries to the most outrageous, extravagant requests.

She didn't just arrange parcel deliveries and make restaurant bookings, she sourced rare first editions of famous novels and cajoled Michelin chefs to cook in a resident's apartment to help create the perfect proposal… And she was proud of the service she worked hard to provide. Until today there'd been no request she hadn't been able to fulfil.

But she drew the line at the euthanasia of a perfectly healthy, beloved pet on a total stranger's *whim.*

'I suppose George let him in?' she growled.

Joel nodded.

That'd be right. George, the building manager, was obsequious to clients, pernickety with petty rules while sloppy with what was actually crucial, and a belligerent bully to the personnel. Ettie spent half her time fixing his blunders and soothing staff resentment when he'd blamed them.

It was her fault it had got this far with the dog. She'd arrived late for the first time in years because she'd been up most of the night counselling her stressed-out sister, Ophelia, who was panicking that she'd flunked her latest physics test. Not that Ophelia had flunked a test in her life. Fiendishly academic, she was away at boarding school on a partial scholarship. Ettie was paying the rest of the fees and Ophelia was desperate to secure a university place. That meant another scholarship, which in turn meant outstanding results in every assessment in this last year of her schooling. As amazing as Ophelia was, Ettie worried the pressure was too intense. But she wouldn't let Ophelia give up her dream. Ettie had sacrificed too much herself to allow that. So, after calming Ophelia, she'd lain awake fretting about how she could better financially support her. Since their mother's death two years ago, it fell to Ettie to make it happen.

But making things happen was what Ettie did. She'd learned and worked for it, making miles-long lists and instituting systems so her sometimes impulsive and distraction-prone self wouldn't forget anything. But today she'd lapsed into her natural disorder. She'd overslept, in her mad scurry she'd missed breakfast, lost her last hair tie and resorted to using an old rubber band, and still missed her train.

When she'd finally raced into Cavendish House this morning, it was to the shocking news that her favourite long-term resident, Harold Clarke, had been rushed to hospital in the small hours of the night. While his passing had been quick and peaceful, his family—the family Ettie hadn't seen visit once in the five years she'd been working there—was already on the premises and clearing out his treasures. Apparently they didn't regard Toby, Harold's small terrier, as a treasure. They'd sent him down for Joel, her junior concierge, to "get rid of".

If Ettie had been at work on time, that nephew would never have made it into the apartment, let alone cast his callous instructions for Toby.

'Ettie, there's something else…' Joel called after her.

Not now there wasn't.

Shock, grief and sheer fury overrode the caution and calm she'd schooled within herself over the years. Ettie tightened her hold on the small dog and impulsively swept to the lift. Appalled by that uncaring request, she'd no time for niceties or other distractions. The family were monsters.

At the slide of the doors, Ettie stepped out onto Harold's floor. His apartment door was open and curt voices echoed along the corridor. She stalked the length of it, unconsciously stroking the soft fur of the small dog. A quick glance into the room showed George on the far side looking as smarmy as ever, next to an older-looking couple. All three were facing a tall man who had his back to her but, given the sullen looks on the faces of the others and the iceberg-thick atmosphere, he wielded the power. His immaculate appearance and crisply clipped hair enraged her all the more. He was obviously loaded because the impeccably tailored suit was clearly bespoke. No off-the-rack number ever fitted so perfectly—lovingly emphasising his height and strength. Though most men didn't have perfect physiques either. One look and she knew he was fit, healthy and wealthy. So why did he need to be so greedy over Harold's assets? Why be so *cruel*?

'You shouldn't be in here.' Ettie didn't hesitate stepping into the room.

How could he not have visited Harold in all this time and yet turn up the second he thought there were valuable possessions to be claimed?

'You don't storm in here and start stripping out Harry's assets and condemning his dog to instant death.' She barely paused to draw breath. 'You want to us to "get rid of" Toby?' Her voice quivered but she stood straight, not letting the tremble in her knees spread to the rest of her.

Because the man had turned around and Ettie was rendered breathless. He was much taller than her and younger than she expected. No older than thirty. But it was his face that stopped her—he had the sharpest, most handsome face she'd ever seen. High cheekbones, a straight nose, a full mouth, a cleft in his chin and a square, relentlessly masculine jaw…and to cap it off, deep brown, unbearably intense eyes. Brown eyes usually held some warmth, right? Not his. She'd never encountered either such beauty or such coldness. He was totally intimidating.

But it seemed he wasn't left as much breathless as speechless. Good. It was obviously time someone challenged him and his appalling instructions. Inhaling sharply, Ettie recovered enough to continue her attack.

'Toby is the sweetest little dog ever, not that you'd know because you never visited him or Harold in all this time…' Her voice trembled as she thought of the quiet elderly man who'd been gentle. And so alone. 'Now it's barely five minutes after…and you want Toby put down? Are you even human?'

George cleared his throat. 'Ettie—'

'You're not going to get away with it,' she carried on passionately, too steamed up to let George and his lack of spine stop her from telling this jerk some home truths. 'I won't let you.'

She became aware Joel had arrived and was breathlessly standing beside her, an appalled but fascinated expression on his face. The older couple present didn't look at her at all but stared at the tall stranger with silent, seething resistance. She knew how they felt.

The man's arctic glare sharpened on her, pinning her with almost visceral force. 'Who are you?'

She refused to quake. 'I think that's my question. You're the one trespassing.'

'I think not,' he said softly. There was a faint foreign tone to his cutting, cold accent.

George was frantically doing some kind of dance behind the arrogant ass's back. But she paid no attention—she was too incensed. The guy needed to be schooled. Tired and strung out and sad, Ettie couldn't hold back her contempt. 'You've never once set foot in this place before now.'

'No.' His quiet confirmation sounded stronger than George's audible gasp.

'You're despicable,' Ettie told him.

'Despicable?' He glanced behind him and caught George midway through miming self-strangulation. He turned back to face her. 'I think what your colleague is trying to convey is that you've made a mistake.'

There was the slightest curl to the man's lips—as if he was deriving some small, hideous pleasure from this moment.

Ettie frowned, not comprehending. She was still puffed from the force of her emotions and her furious dash up to the apartment. 'I'm not Mr Clarke's nephew,' he informed her with brutally cold precision. 'In fact, I'm no relation whatsoever to Mr Clarke.'

Nonplussed, Ettie blinked. Now she took a moment to study him, he didn't look anything like Harold. This man's hair was dark and thick and his eyes were that wintry brown, not blue, and his bronze complexion was more than a summer tan. A wave of relief so strong it was shocking rippled through her. He wasn't an animal-murdering brute?

Then she was hit with a wave of something else altogether. Something from deep inside, so hot and intense that she refused to acknowledge, let alone define it. Because it was *shocking*.

'Then what are you doing in here?' she snapped uncharacteristically. But she was determined to halt the appallingly inappropriate, *intimate* direction of her thoughts. Why was everyone looking at him as if he was ridiculously important? Why was George turning greener by the second?

'You've made a mistake.' His gaze drifted over her uniform in an inspection so quick it was almost insulting. 'And yet I think you're this star concierge I've heard about. Cavendish House's very own Girl Friday.'

She had a sudden prickling sensation that a giant black hole had opened up before her, but that she'd already taken the fatal step. It was too late to stop—the fall was in play and there was no way to backpedal and stop herself tumbling into a bottomless pit.

'My name is Leon Kariakis. And as of close of business last night, I own this building.'

Leon Kariakis? *The* Leon Kariakis? Serious, publicity-averse, wealthier-than-most-small-countries Leon Kariakis?

Ettie stared at him, slack-jawed. Oh, yeah,

she'd fallen into one never-ending crevasse. All she could do was comment stupidly, 'You own…' she drew in a breath and tried to regroup '…and you're not—'

'No relative. This man is Mr Clarke's nephew and I've already spoken to him and his wife about Mr Clarke's belongings. Nothing will leave this building until the executor of his will has been to the premises and itemised everything.'

The other man began to bluster but Leon Kariakis turned and quelled him with a filthy look. 'Is it true you instructed the staff to get rid of the dog?'

The nephew didn't respond.

'Is it true?' Leon Kariakis demanded an answer.

'I didn't mean—'

'Evidently it was very clear what you meant.' Leon cut the man off. 'You will leave immediately.'

'You can't throw us out.'

'I think you'll find I can,' Leon Kariakis replied softly. The atmosphere chilled even more, his physical threat apparent even though he didn't move an inch. If Leon Kariakis wanted to manhandle this guy out of the apartment, he'd do so with ease. And the sorry excuse for Harold's family knew it.

Ettie's heart raced faster than a puppy chasing a pigeon. Since when was Cavendish House even on the market? And to be bought by Leon Kariakis? Even she'd heard of the serious son of the incredibly rich Kariakis holiday empire. His parents owned a number of swanky five-star hotels on the continent, but sole heir Leon had gone into finance, making even more eye-watering amounts of money in an unseemly short amount of time. Apparently buying up exclusive residential apartment buildings was his new hobby. And she'd just called him out—accusing him of animal cruelty and disgusting greed.

'This isn't over, Kariakis,' the nephew blustered. 'You'll be hearing from our lawyers.'

'I look forward to it,' Leon replied tersely. 'I imagine they'll be much more pleasant to deal with than you.'

Ettie bit down on her lip to stop her unbidden smile as the nephew and his wife stomped out of Harold's apartment. They didn't so much as look at her, or the small dog she was still cuddling. But neither she nor Toby were out of the woods yet. All-powerful, super-serious, still scowling, Leon Kariakis wouldn't have appreciated her shouting at him in public like that.

'Everyone else, please leave as well.' He seared her with an icy glance. 'Except you.'

Yeah, she'd just lost her job.

George stepped in. 'Mr Kariakis, I'm terribly sorry for this misunderstanding. Ettie is always—'

'I'll meet with you later.' Leon Kariakis's snappy dismissal brooked no argument.

George shot her an irritated look that she ignored, even though she knew he'd been about to throw her even further under the bus. She was fine. She could handle it. But her heart thudded as her Joel reluctantly left too.

She turned to face the music, disconcerted to discover Leon Kariakis was still watching her and still wasn't smiling. Indignation surged and she lifted her chin at him. She'd been doing her job—protecting her client's pet—and she wasn't going to apologise for that. The silence echoed in the apartment. Even Toby, the dog, didn't stir in her arms, but she stroked him regardless.

'You're Antoinette Roberts,' he said quietly.

'Cavendish's Girl Friday. I've heard much about you and yet…'

She'd disappointed him?

Too bad. Even though she knew she was about to lose her job, she felt a small flush of pride that he'd been told about her. What had he said before—star concierge? Yet she couldn't claim any praise as entirely her own. Joel and the other guys were always willing to help.

'I have a very good team,' she said.

He kept regarding her steadily, but no warmth softened his eyes.

She should probably apologise for mistaking him for one of Harry's mean relatives, but suddenly she couldn't get her voice to work. Awareness trickled down her spine as the tension within her transformed. She'd loathed him on sight, only now…it was another emotion stiffening her spine. And it was just insane. Ettie Roberts did *not* lust after anyone. Ettie Roberts was far too sensible.

But Leon Kariakis was abnormally handsome and the way he was looking at her right now was unbearably intense. It was only that, mixed with relief that he wasn't a cruel tyrant out to murder an innocent animal, that made him all the more attractive in this moment, right? It wasn't *real*. Leon Kariakis wasn't someone she'd ever be interested in and he'd certainly never be interested in her.

A sudden wave of defensiveness let her mouth slip the leash. 'If you're going to sack me, just get it over with.'

There was another moment of profound silence. She burned with a horrible mix of embarrassment, nerves and resentment. She hated how calm and in control he was. Even when she'd shouted at him he hadn't lost his ice-cool composure.

'You don't like uncertainty?' He watched her steadily.

'I don't like being kept waiting.'

His eyebrows shot up. 'I'm taking the time to think.'

'Does it usually take you this long?' She didn't mean to be rude, but it surprised her. He was incredibly successful and she bet he hadn't become so by mulling over trivial decisions about low-level staff.

But wasn't she was doing him a disservice? He'd already stood up to those horrible, grasping relatives before she'd even arrived and he'd had no hesitation in showing them the door. She was finally about to offer a shamefaced, belated apology when he spoke.

'I've found that giving a problem my full consideration, rather than making a snap judgment, results in a better night's sleep for me.' He offered the slightest sarcastic curve to his lips in lieu of an actual smile.

She'd made a snap judgment that he was Harold's nephew, and this was an unsubtle rebuke for that. Yet it wasn't his reprimand that bothered her. It was another ripple of that forbidden feeling slithering down her spine. She did not need to be thinking about sleeping—specifically *him* sleeping—at this moment. And she did not need to be wondering what he'd look like with an actual, genuine smile on his face when he was already this attractive.

He studied her for another long moment and his gaze lowered to the resting creature in her arms. 'The dog is old,' he said bluntly.

'So that means we should just put him down?' she asked scornfully, her outrage torched again. The debate was on and she was fighting for Toby.

'He'll miss his owner,' Leon answered with surprising softness. 'He'll fret.'

The note of compassion from him oddly made her more uncomfortable.

'So we find him someone who can be with him all the time so he has the companionship he needs while he grieves.'

He reached out and petted the dog's head gently. Ettie froze, stunned by the illicit surge in her body at his closeness…the craving.

'He can't go to a shelter,' she added.

She couldn't help staring at Leon. She'd never seen someone as handsome, or as serious, and suddenly he felt more of a danger to her than when she'd thought him to be a heartless brute or when she'd thought he was going to fire her. The unaccustomed response within her to his fierce masculinity was shocking.

She whipped up her resistance. She didn't want to *like* him. Of all the moments for her stagnant sensuality to spark up…

'Would you take him?' Curiosity burned in his eyes.

'I would,' she answered without hesitation. 'Except I'm at work all hours and he'd be lonely. And I'm not allowed pets in my building.'

'Pets aren't allowed in these apartments either,' he muttered. 'Isn't that the rule the previous owner implemented?'

'No resident ever minded Toby. He's lovely and he was around before that petty rule came into force.' She looked down at the dog protectively. She'd disliked that owner who'd wanted to charge more but offer less. He'd employed the awful George to enforce the 'new way'—most of which involved paying the staff less for more onerous rules and rosters, which had led to that festering resentment and feeling as if they couldn't be trusted. Ironically, the rumour was that the absent owner had got into money trouble…and now she was faced with this guy.

'You aided and abetted Mr Clarke in keeping Toby a secret, didn't you?'

They all had. But Ettie lifted her chin; she wasn't about to offer excuses or drag her friends under with her. 'Are you going to sack me for it?'

He remained impassive but she sensed his assessment. And his judgment. 'That depends. What other rules do you break?'

'Just the stupid ones.'

He watched, waiting for her to expand on her answer, but she refused. She was not going to desperately fill the awkward silence he was deliberately leaving. And she was not going to let his stunning looks have a stupefying effect on her brain any longer either. She was here for Toby—for the last thing she could do for old Harold Clarke.

'He needs to be in a familiar environment,' she said. 'Given he's not a nuisance to anyone, you should allow Toby to remain in Cavendish House, don't you think?' she asked with more defiance than deference in her voice.

Because more than anger bubbled within her at his silent appraisal and that stern stare beneath those slightly pulled strong eyebrows.

She tore her gaze from him and desperately looked around Harold's apartment to remind herself of her mission. The old man had been their longest resident. He'd mostly kept to himself, but he'd been kind and his dog had been his world. He'd protected the vulnerable even when he was vulnerable himself. 'We owe it to Harold to take care of Toby.'

'We?'

'Yes.' She lifted her chin pointedly and looked back at him. 'Why can't you take him?' she challenged directly.

There was another moment of total silence, but as she gazed into his eyes, the amber light within them flared. 'No reason that I can see,' he muttered.

She blinked. 'Pardon?'

'Toby will move to my penthouse. You'll take him for fresh air.'

Her jaw dropped. He wanted her to go to his penthouse? 'You want him to sleep in your apartment?'

'It's a temporary arrangement,' he said brusquely. 'On the condition that you walk him. You feed him. I do nothing but provide the space.'

The sizzle she felt was just her, right? She gave herself a mental shake. Just because he was insanely good-looking didn't mean she had to turn into a twittering ditz. She'd pull herself together and get the job done. 'You want me to—'

'Morning and night obviously. Yes.' He turned that cool demeanour on her and dared her to object.

Ettie was so stunned, she couldn't help questioning him. 'Why can't you walk him?'

The coldness that entered his expression now stunned her. 'We'll find a more permanent solution in a few days. In the meantime, there'll be no disturbance to the other residents.'

She was shocked. 'You really want me to—'

'Do I really need to repeat myself?'

'No. Of course not.' She stilled, annoyed with his superciliousness. Usually she'd say 'sir', but she was struggling to suppress her rebellion and tell this guy what for again. He couldn't walk or feed the dog himself? Was he for real?

And yet he'd just offered up his own space to ensure Toby's safety and security, so that the vulnerable little dog could stay.

What the hell had forced that foolish suggestion from him? Leon Kariakis smothered his growl and gritted his teeth. He didn't want anything to do with the dog. The ancient, arthritic creature was most probably incontinent and most definitely going to be a pain. Except he was a sweet-looking thing with the saddest eyes Leon had ever seen, and there was no way he could resist reaching out again to soothe the boy with a gentle pat. As he pulled back, he inadvertently brushed his fingers on Antoinette's arm. He glanced up to her face. Sea-green, luminous, emotion-drenched eyes glared back at him.

Why was she looking so angry again now?

He was the one who ought to be put out. And truthfully he was still oddly angered by her assumption he was the selfish bastard who'd issued the instruction to destroy the innocent creature. Somehow he wanted to make her pay for the conclusion she'd so swiftly, and unjustly, leapt to.

Not *somehow*.

His body knew *exactly* how he wanted her to pay. He wanted her to keep looking at him with those overly emotional green eyes, but not with anger and judgment. He wanted to see hunger and willingness. *Desire*.

Basic instinct roared. Because he knew it was there within her too. She'd studied him anew once she'd realised her error. And she'd responded on the same basic level as he had—the sparkle of awareness in her eyes, the flush in her face, had given her away.

He wanted her beneath and about him. His primal response to her passion shocked him. He wanted her in the most animal, basic of ways.

It was the most inappropriate thought of his life. Lusting after her was wrong. He was staying in the building for only a week or so to understand its processes first-hand before deciding on what changes needed to be made. The last thing he should do was flirt with one of the staff who was literally in his firing line. She was off-limits and he was never that out of control. Ever. This was a situation that required a swift conclusion. Yet he couldn't resist getting involved directly.

'You'll need to bring the dog and all his accoutrements.' He checked his watch and then glanced back at her.

'Yes, of course.' She lifted her chin.

The action didn't make her any taller. She remained a smidgeon shorter than the average woman and slight through the shoulders. Her dark blonde hair was swept off her face into a loose, messy ponytail and her wide green eyes offered unusually clear reflections of her feelings.

She wasn't the sleek automaton he'd envisaged when he'd been told about her. She wore barely any make-up—as far as he could tell, there was little more than a slick of lip gloss. Yet her skin was smooth, unblemished and glowing. The uniform black trousers and monogrammed T-shirt she wore did little to reveal much of her figure, but what they did show was slim and the suggestion of fit. His overall impression was of supple, fresh femininity. He'd been accosted by another of the more elderly residents in the lift this morning who'd been at pains to tell him that Antoinette Roberts was the only reason he'd remained at Cavendish House in recent years.

One look at her and Leon understood why.

But she wasn't his type. She'd spoken to him in a way no one else dared to. Tearing strips off him with blunt, brutal honesty, not stopping to censor herself or having the slightest hesitation in telling him what she really thought. Her heart wasn't just on her sleeve, she was waving it on a flag in front of him.

It was extremely novel. In his life, communicating emotions had not only been discouraged, but also punished. As his parents had ruthlessly taught him, any kind of emotional display was a weak loss of self-control.

Yet he didn't want Antoinette to start picking her words with care now. He liked knowing, without any uncertainty, exactly what she was feeling. And it was her fierce protectiveness that riveted him. Like a lioness protecting a lone cub, she'd held her corner and not given an inch, no matter the possible personal cost to herself. She'd fully expected him to fire her. But Leon knew people made mistakes. He'd give her one chance to redeem herself.

'Be on time. Always. I don't like to be disturbed,' he said roughly.

'I can be discreet,' she answered defiantly.

He simply stared at her. As if she could come into his apartment unseen? Unheard? As if she could ever be anything but disruptive?

A thread of wicked amusement trickled through him as she stilled in the face of his silence. He knew the exact moment she mentally replayed her words and realised an alternative innuendo. The same intimacy-drenched scenario he was imagining. A deep rose burnished her creamy skin—her cheeks, her neck, even the small hint of skin he could see at the vee of her high-collared T-shirt. But then he registered the rebellion in her gaze again—together with her less than subtle attempts to suppress it.

He didn't want her to suppress anything.

The urge to haul this petite emotional tornado close and kiss her into a frenzy of desire almost felled him. Grimly he fought the need to provoke her into taking everything else she might want from him. He knew he could. He saw the awareness in her eyes. Women found him attractive and sex was a fun relaxant. But he'd bet that sex with Girl Friday here wouldn't be as much fun as mind-blowing. If the incandescence of her anger was anything to go by, in bed she'd be unrestrained and utterly responsive.

Sex of the best kind. The kind that was irresistible.

He knew she felt the sparks. They were why she'd flushed over her choice of words. Why she'd trembled at his inadvertent touch before. Why she was looking at him with unrestrained rebellion now. Because she didn't want this chemistry either. And that irritating rejection was precisely why he couldn't resist making what he knew would be a massive mistake.

He roughly pushed the request past the tightness in his throat. 'I want you in my apartment in one hour.'

CHAPTER TWO

'WHY DIDN'T YOU tell me?' Ettie groaned to Joel as soon as she safely got back into the small concierge office, Toby still in her arms.

'I didn't have the chance…'

Of course he hadn't. Ettie shook her head and stopped him, regretting her unfair question. 'Sorry, I know you didn't.'

'Don't you think he's out of this world?' Jess, one of the housemaids, leaned over her desk. 'Chloe saw a model-type leaving his penthouse late last night. She was in the lift. Really dishevelled.' She waggled her eyebrows in a suggestive gesture. 'First night in and he's already—'

'No gossip,' Ettie whispered loudly, but softened her rebuke with a smile at the maid.

The news didn't surprise her. Of course he'd bed models. He was as striking as a model himself. He'd have no trouble getting any woman he wanted into bed. Even she'd responded to him on a purely primal level. He was so handsome it was almost painful. He was extraordinarily uptight, though, and he had a way of looking as if he could see right through her, while at the same time revealing nothing of his own thoughts.

Unabashed by Ettie's warning, Jess just laughed. 'Well, I think he's gorgeous. I'd do him.'

'He's an unsmiling ogre,' Joel grumbled. 'An arrogant jerk who thinks he's special.'

Well, with his obvious physical strength as well as his business success, he was a bit special. He had it all—looks, wealth, women…success.

'He was unfairly harsh with you, Ettie,' Joel added. 'And as for George…'

Yeah, it was no surprise that her boss was nowhere to be seen—hiding out until the dust had settled, no doubt. But she smiled at the hint of protectiveness in Joel's voice. 'He'll be even harsher if I don't get all that stuff up to his apartment within the hour.'

'Do you want help?'

She shook her head. 'We're behind down here already—you get on top of this for me and I'll deal with the ogre.'

She had to go into his apartment. Repeatedly. Her heart beat stupidly quickly at the thought.

The range of inappropriate images that rioted through her head at the prospect of turning up to his apartment early tomorrow morning… Would he be awake or sleepy? She'd bet her life he didn't bother with pyjamas…but what if he had another dishevelled model-type with him? Ugh.

Get a grip and act like a professional.

Somehow she had less than fifteen minutes until the hour he'd given her was up, and she was not being late a second time today. With the dog in one arm and pushing a trolley with all his other stuff, she took the lift. She knocked but got no answer, so keyed in the security code.

'Hello? Mr Kariakis?' She walked into the apartment, but the room was silent.

Was she supposed to leave Toby alone in here or wait with him? Gritting back a frustrated sigh, she popped the dog down and turned to lift all his paraphernalia from the trolley. As she struggled with full arms, she noticed Toby wandering off towards a bedroom. She called to him quickly, dropping his water bowl as she hurried to catch him. And at that worst possible moment the ancient rubber band securing her ponytail snapped, sending her hair flying about her face in a mess of half-curls and straggle. She dumped the dog's gear down in the middle of the room and glanced about for something to use. She spied a pen lying on the nearest table and quickly swiped it up. She twisted her unruly hair into a knot on top of her head and secured it with the pen. Thank heavens perfect Leon Kariakis wasn't there to see her in such a debacle with the dog, basket, blankets and bowls all in a muddle at her feet.

'Ms Roberts.'

She froze. And wasn't that just her luck?

She swivelled to face him as he strode through from the bedroom. Usually it was at this point that she'd offer her first name to a new resident. Something held her back from doing so with Leon Kariakis, however. The grim look of disapproval on his face perhaps?

He still looked impeccable in that charcoal suit. She quelled the smidgeon of disappointment that he might've relaxed a little in his own space; it wasn't to be.

'You're late,' he said.

'Actually, I'm right on time.' She held up her watch and then walked further into the lounge, trying not to let her confidence plummet. Remote and controlled, he relentlessly watched her progress as she self-consciously set up Toby's basket in a corner of the room with a stunning view of the city out of the floor-to-ceiling windows.

'Is that my pen in your hair?'

She froze. Could his voice be any more arctic?

'Sorry, my hair tie broke.' She looked at him and registered the astonishment in his eyes. 'It's a special pen?'

'It can write upside down.'

Was he kidding? She couldn't contain an impish grin at his perennial solemnity. 'You do handstands and take notes?'

Was that an answering glint of humour in his eyes now?

'It's my pen.' He ignored her little joke. 'You stole it.'

'I *borrowed* it.' So much for any chance of a sexy librarian look with the whole hair-tied-in-a-bun thing. The man didn't soften an inch. She sighed. 'You'd like it back right away?'

'If you wouldn't mind.'

Seriously? He was that uptight about a *pen*?

As she took it out her hair tumbled into chaos. She was too aware of his gaze lingering on the unruly mess and then he returned to look at her eyes. Suddenly she felt hotter than when she'd been furious about what was going to happen to Toby.

She held the pen out to him. Wordlessly he took it and put it into the breast pocket of his jacket. Over his heart.

She quickly turned away, wishing he'd just leave her to it. Instead he watched the fall of her hair, and her every other move as she set out Toby's blanket and bowl. Toby padded straight into his basket and curled into a small ball.

Leon leaned against the wall, still watching intently as she gave the dog a couple of soothing pats.

'Is there nothing you can't do?' he asked.

She was unwilling but unable to resist looking up at him. She wasn't sure if he was being sarcastic or not, but she resolved to treat him as she did any other difficult client—with respect and *distance*.

'There's plenty I can't do,' she muttered softly. Keep her hair under control for one thing.

'You've thought of everything.'

She straightened. 'It's my job to think of everything.'

'And you're very good at your job,' he drawled.

She looked him directly in the eyes at that. 'Yes, I am.'

Which was why he wasn't going to sack her for her earlier mistake. Which was why she was going to maintain a professional distance from him now.

Ophelia needed her to keep this job. She needed to remember that. She'd ignore the silent, magnetic pull.

'I assume Security has given you your own access code so it doesn't matter if I'm here or not.' His huskiness somehow built that sense of intimacy in the moment.

She nodded, momentarily fascinated by the discovery that his eyes weren't completely wintry; there were almost amber lights in them. Warm ones.

'This is a short-term solution,' he said. 'Until we can get him rehomed in a more suitable environment.'

'Of course.'

Focus, Ettie.

She looked around the room and then sent him a sideways look. 'Though this environment seems pretty suitable.'

Leon walked over to her and hunched down

by Toby's basket. 'Is he always this subdued?' He patted the dog gently again. 'I wondered if he wasn't well.'

Ettie smiled at him, pleased he was concerned. 'He's old and quiet and missing Harold. He's probably wondering what on earth is going on...'

Leon absently scratched the dog's ears.

'His quality of life is good, though.' Ettie looked at him earnestly.

'Don't worry. I'm not about to summon the vet.'

For a split-second Ettie relaxed, but she was then hit by a flood of intense pleasure at seeing this powerful man almost kneeling at her feet. It was dizzying. 'I'll leave you two to get to know each other, then.' On an irresistible impulse, she teased him. 'Perhaps you could smile at him? Make him feel welcome?' That stupid suggestion had popped out before she'd thought better of it.

He suddenly stood. She'd not realised how near he was. Now he towered over her.

Don't prod a grumpy beast.

'Bare my teeth at him, you mean?' he muttered quietly. 'I'm not sure it's wise to do that to a wolf.'

That low pull tugged deep in her belly—purely physical, animal magnetism that set off a melting sensation deep within. Restless, inappropriate desire. With it came recklessness.

'One wolf to another?' she nudged dangerously. 'Don't you ever just smile?'

Oh, yes, she'd crossed a line now.

He didn't answer other than to stare down at her as if he couldn't believe what he'd heard. As if he was contemplating what kind of retribution he was about to mete out…

He liked to take the time to think, right?

Ettie had forgotten how to think. Or move. Or even breathe. She just stared right back at him for an endless moment. He really was far too handsome. And far too serious. She was utterly mesmerised. 'Thank you for taking care of him,' she whispered.

Something fierce flared in his eyes. 'Contrary to what you thought earlier, I'm not a monster.'

No, he wasn't. And she guessed he was allowed to be as serious as he liked, in his own home and all.

'I'm sorry for that mistake,' she finally apologised. Flushing with heat, she brushed a lock of her rebellious hair back from her face. Again.

He watched her movement as intently and inscrutably as ever. 'Thank you.'

She didn't feel forgiven, she felt flayed.

She didn't know if he stepped closer, or if she swayed, but suddenly there seemed to be no space at all between them. Her breath stalled in her lungs. He was so very close. But he was also utterly, inhumanly, still. He had such intensity of focus—expressionless, but not remote—and having that focus solely on her was more than dizzying, it was like being in the path of a lightning strike. She was going to get burned, but the chance to get lit up…?

Another long moment passed before her brain kicked back into operational mode. Oh, heaven, he probably thought she was waiting for him to make a move. He must get so many women throwing themselves at him. *Models* in the lift, remember? He'd never look twice at her. Mortified, she desperately clawed back her sanity and her dignity.

'I'd better get back downstairs,' she croaked, turned tail and fled.

Leon was hanging on to his control by the thinnest of threads. He'd spent the day determined to forget Antoinette Roberts. And for the first time in a very long time he'd spent a day failing.

She kept appearing in his thoughts—gorgeously fresh, her beautiful, wavy hair shimmering with every turn of her head. He never should have made her give his pen back because now he was beset with the fantasy of having that glorious hair spread across his pillows as the rest of her arched up to…

Leon stalked out of Cavendish House, his body aching. It was late in the evening but he'd not bother with dinner, he'd walk and wear himself out that way. Toby was fast asleep in his basket and too old to keep pace with him. He knew Antoinette had returned earlier to walk the dog and given him food. Leon had deliberately stayed away at the time, but the scent of her lingered in his rooms, sending his brain back into the direction he'd been trying to avoid all day.

Since when did he lose control over his own damn pulse? Ice-cool control was the one thing he always maintained. Antoinette Roberts threatened it with one fiery glance. Maybe it had been too long since he'd taken a lover. He should've taken up that offer last night.

Grimacing, he walked along the footpaths.

The shops were open late and crowds milled about. He glanced sightlessly into the windows as he threaded through the masses. But through one immaculate window display he swore he recognised the gleaming rich hair of the petite woman standing with her back to him.

Great. Now he was seeing her everywhere.

But then he heard her voice as well—her lilting humour as she asked a customer if she needed help. He stared into the store, listening through the open door. Either Antoinette Roberts had a doppelgänger, or she'd come straight here after her shift at Cavendish and was now helping some woman choose a set of thank-you cards.

He walked in, quickly taking in the high-end stationery supplies the shop was stocked with. A couple of minutes later the female customer walked past him on her way out carrying a beautifully wrapped parcel and a satisfied smile on her face.

Leon walked up to the woman behind the counter. 'Ms Roberts?'

It was definitely her. And he definitely couldn't stop staring. Gone was the utilitarian, practical Cavendish concierge uniform and now she was in a lithe little black dress. He could finally see something of her legs and, just as he'd suspected, they were smooth, shapely and gorgeous. He'd known that if she could make those black trousers look sexy, she'd be dynamite in a dress. This one had a slightly scooped neckline, which meant there wasn't anywhere near enough cleavage, but there was skin—creamy, silken-looking skin and the suggestion of sweet curves beneath the fabric. And her glorious hair was freed from that bouncing mess of a ponytail and now cascaded in glossy wild waves down her back. It looked lush, as if it'd be soft to touch and he'd bind it around his wrists—

'Oh.' A blush flooded her smooth cheeks and she licked her lips. 'Mr Kariakis?' Then her wide-eyed gaze narrowed. 'You left Toby alone?'

The beseeching reproach in her eyes made him feel guilty even when he shouldn't. 'You know he ate a good dinner; now he's fast asleep. He's not missing me.'

The inward tension he'd been trying to settle tightened again. He'd needed to get out of that soulless apartment. He'd wanted to exorcise the ghost of her standing there, challenging him with that sassy look in her eyes as she'd flicked his stupid pen back at him. He'd been hopelessly distracted by the memory—but he was thrown back into that whirling web of desire again now.

'What are you doing here?' he asked irritably.

'What do you think I'm doing?' Her tone cooled to match his.

His tension spiked, he released it on her insane workload. 'You've worked all day already.'

She stiffened. 'Lots of people work more than one job. I'm sure you work long hours too.'

But there was a hint of tiredness in the backs of her eyes.

'You're tired.' He refused to believe she wanted to work fourteen or more hours a day.

'Oh, no,' she answered airily. 'Actually as soon as I'm done here, I'm going clubbing.'

'Are you?' He fired with her challenge. 'Excellent. Take me with you—I'm new to town and don't know all the cool places.'

A disconcerted expression crossed her face and he inwardly laughed. He couldn't lie to himself any more. His offer to care for the dog was based in selfish motivation: to see more of Antoinette. He wanted her in his bed. Ideally tonight. It had hit in that first second—lust at first sight. Lust that was only increasing the longer he spent in her company. Perhaps if he satisfied the urge, it'd disappear as swiftly as it had come.

And her reaction to him? He could tempt her.

'I…' She glanced at her watch and that flush across her delicate, high cheekbones built.

It was five minutes until closing and he wasn't planning on leaving. 'You like working here?'

He made conversation to ease her embarrassment. Despite those delicious feisty flashes, she displayed hints of shyness. He found the combination unbelievably tantalising.

'It's nice.' She nodded.

He tensed. 'Nicer than Cavendish?'

Was she thinking of leaving her concierge job? In some ways that would be good—it would free them of any messiness, given their positions there.

'It's quieter than Cavendish, but I don't build the same relationship with my customers as I do there. I only work the late nights here.' She glanced at the counter display. 'It's beautiful stationery.'

'That's why you work here—because you like the product?'

A bubble of laughter burst from her shimmering lips. 'No, if I just liked the product, I'd buy it.'

'So it's money.' He frowned, unhappy at the thought that she was forced to work two jobs. 'We don't pay you enough.'

A wary expression crossed her face. 'It's fine. I have commitments. Most of us do, right?'

He shouldn't pry further but he couldn't help watching intently, waiting to see if she'd say more. Her clear eyes dimmed with faint shadows.

'Saving,' she muttered, unable to help herself.

Unusually for him, his curiosity deepened. But it wasn't his business. He had no right to press further. 'Good for you.'

She nodded awkwardly. 'So did you want anything in particular?'

He bit back the blunt answer of what he particularly *wanted* and made himself breathe first. 'I wanted to see if it was really you.'

'Well.' That impish smile flashed on her lips, flicking away the shadows in her eyes. 'It is.'

'In another uniform.' He couldn't help noticing that damned demure neckline again.

'Black again.' She bit her lip as she quickly glanced down as if afraid she'd spilled something. 'Always ready for a funeral, that's me,' she quipped. 'But it's discreet. Unobtrusive.'

'I would never describe you as unobtrusive,' he muttered quietly.

She'd burst into his life in a blaze of passion and fury.

She met his gaze, silently questioning just how he'd describe her. Unspoken awareness flickered between them, like a gravitational pull.

Her blush returned full force, a ruby tide over her creamy complexion. 'I should get back to work. It's almost time to close.'

She was flustered again. He was fascinated by her unconscious dance—she advanced closer with those challenges, then retreated in shyness. He glanced around the shop, pleased to discover it had emptied completely of other customers. 'Show me the biggest seller.'

'Seriously?' The droll scepticism on her face was a picture.

Entertained by her expressiveness, he leaned closer. 'Why not? You don't think I can afford it?'

She sent him another look. 'Well, I know you don't need a new *pen*.' She lifted an item from the counter and met his gaze with a prim, shop-girl pose. 'But we have an exquisite range of journals.'

'Exquisite,' he echoed dryly.

'Incredibly so,' she emphasised, refusing to acknowledge his soft sarcasm.

'What is it about girls and diaries?' He reached out and traced the smooth leather cover with his finger. 'Do you pour out your soul into one of these every night?'

'What if I do?' She lifted her chin in that irresistibly defiant gesture.

'Would it make for fascinating reading?' He was appallingly curious now. For the first time intrigued enough to want to know all a woman's thoughts, all her wishes, every last secret and deepest desire.

'Sadly, no. I only keep lists in mine.' She reached across the counter and flipped an open book around to show him. 'See?'

'This is yours?' His pulse rate lifted.

'I work on it in quiet moments,' she said. 'I have permission from my boss—it's good to see our products in use.'

Her defensiveness amused him. Was she as discomforted by him as much as he was by her? He leaned closer to read the scrawled list.

'I forget things,' she added nervously. 'I'm naturally disorganised, so I work hard to get it together and nail my job. Lists are the only thing that work for me.' She tried to pull the journal back but he planted his hand down to keep it there. His fingers brushed against her for the second time that day. Skin touched skin. She stilled, as did he.

A millisecond later she snatched her hand back. But he knew she'd felt that current of electricity flow between them.

He turned the pages of her journal, refusing to feel any remorse—she was the one who'd offered it for his viewing. But to his disappointment there were no deepest desires on show inside. Only ruthless organisation, as she'd said.

'Everything in your life is dictated by a list?' There were reminders, shopping lists, ticked-off tasks, pros and cons for other things… 'It's a lot of lists.' He flicked through more pages, wishing there were something far more personal in it. 'And in a rainbow of colours.'

'It doesn't need to be boring. Right? But I'm no artist, so I just choose a different colour for each…'

'I have a planner,' he offered idly. 'But it's online.'

'Online?' She shuddered theatrically. 'I couldn't get all these lists on the one screen. And what if it got deleted?'

'What if you lost your journal?' he countered with the obvious. 'What if someone you don't want to read it gets hold of it?'

Her impish grin darted back. 'That's why there are only lists and reminders.'

'So, nothing too personal or incriminating?' He sighed with genuine disappointment. 'You're not a risk-taker, then.'

Her eyes widened.

'You won't run the risk of someone discovering your secrets,' he explained.

'Perhaps I don't have any,' she muttered.

'Everyone has secrets.' *And desires.*

Silent, she just gazed back at him.

'And I'll bet you're not really going clubbing,' he added quietly.

This time her smile was more sheepish than impish, and she shook her head.

'Have you had dinner?' He didn't give her time to answer. 'I don't think you've had time if you came straight from your shift at Cavendish. You must be hungry.'

He saw her hesitate and spoke again before she could deny it. 'Have dinner with me.'

'No thanks,' she instantly answered.

'Am I that awful?' he shot back, unafraid to challenge her directly. He knew what he wanted. He knew what she wanted too. He was just more honest about it.

She stared at him for a moment, shocked. 'No, I—'

'Well, don't let me down so roughly. It's only dinner.'

Roughly? Ettie narrowed her eyes on him. He was pulling her leg, right? Behind that serious facade there was some humour. 'It's not a wise idea. You're my boss.'

'It's not a date, just dinner. If it makes you feel better, you can tell me about life on the concierge desk. I need to know how the whole operation works. There'll be no repercussions for complete honesty.' He paused. 'Anyway, I'm not really your boss.'

Yeah, right. 'You own the building I work in.'

'But a management company employs the staff.'

'Do you own the management company?' She wouldn't have been surprised if he did.

'They're contracted… I don't own them.'

'So that makes it okay?' Her heart was pounding unnaturally fast.

'I think it creates a technicality we can take advantage of.' He looked right at her. Those amber flecks in his eyes lit up with every word. 'And you like breaking the stupid rules, right? This is a stupid one. Besides, I'm only living in the penthouse while I get my head around the building. Then I'll lease it to a client and move to my next investment, so you won't see me much.'

His message couldn't be clearer. He was saying he'd stay out of her way. That his presence was temporary. That this was just dinner. Just one night.

But Ettie needed a moment.

'You don't ever want to stay in one of your buildings?' She was intrigued by his transitory lifestyle.

'I like projects. I like the excitement and unique challenge of each one, and once I've overcome that challenge it's time to move on to another.'

She suspected he wasn't just talking building acquisition. It was lovers as well. 'You get bored easily?'

A speculative gleam heated his eyes even more. Yeah, he was talking on more than one level. But he answered with that customary seriousness. 'I like to keep busy. I like having problems to grapple with.'

'You don't ever want to just blob out on the beach?'

He cocked his head and considered it briefly. 'It's not something I've ever done.'

'Seriously?' She frowned. 'Not ever?' Didn't his parents own all those hotels in Greece? Wasn't that the ultimate holiday destination? 'You never have holidays?'

'Do you?' he countered.

'I don't have much choice.' She grimaced. 'I work hard but I don't have the same financial rewards, and I have obligations…' Which she didn't want to go into with him right now. 'What's the point in all your success if you don't stop and celebrate it every so often?'

'The point is the success itself,' he answered.

'You don't get tired?' She was flummoxed. If she could take a break somewhere warm and beautiful, she'd be there in a heartbeat.

'Don't worry,' he murmured. 'I know how to relax.'

Yeah, she bet he did. She sent him a reproachful glare and he suddenly laughed. Ettie gaped, stunned at his instant transformation from unsmiling autocrat to hot, buttered hunk. She dragged oxygen into her tight lungs. It wasn't right that a man should be *so* gorgeous.

'It's not what you're thinking,' he said. 'Well, not entirely.'

'How do you know what I'm thinking?'

'It's written all over your face.'

Hopefully not *everything* she was thinking. And hopefully it wasn't obvious how her innards were positively melting. 'So you don't do this often? Pick up women and take them to dinner?'

'No, not often, actually. Does that surprise you?' His expression returned to serious as he studied her. 'You don't believe me?'

'You've been seen with other women,' she said.

His eyebrows shot up. 'When?'

'Last night, apparently.' She tried to play it cool but she was already regretting bringing it up. 'A woman leaving your apartment.'

He'd probably been celebrating his first night in Cavendish House.

Now Leon studied her for another long moment. She knew he was thinking. She just wished she knew *what.*

'You were talking about me.' His lips curved ever so slightly. 'You were curious.'

Before she had the chance to deny it, or to apologise, or to melt in a swelter of embarrassment, he continued softly.

'Was she seen in my company?' he asked. 'I don't think so. The woman who left my apartment late last night had arrived only minutes earlier. She's an acquaintance who'd heard I'd moved in. She came to see me as a surprise but it wasn't something I wished to pursue.'

'You don't like surprises like that?'

What red-blooded man wouldn't want to be surprised by some model-type turning up at midnight with a booty call on her mind?

'I already told you,' he replied. 'I like challenges.'

Surely he didn't see *her* as a challenge?

But she was pleased somehow, that he didn't dally with anyone and everyone who offered.

Leon picked up her journal from the counter

and opened it again to look at the long columns of her lists. 'You could write a list about whether or not to have dinner with me.' He shook his head and snapped her book shut. 'Or you could just trust your instincts.'

Ettie regarded him warily. Her very basic instincts were hell-bent on leading her into trouble and her instincts had let her down before. Leon Kariakis was pure temptation and he knew it. Unfortunately for him, she was determined to remain in control of herself.

But this was a dare and he didn't scare her.

'All right, then,' she decided with spirit. 'Only to tell you all about the Cavendish.'

'Wonderful.'

He waited while she closed up the shop and set the security alarm. She grabbed her coat, but despite the chill in the air she didn't put it on. The thing was ancient and the zip was broken and she didn't want him seeing how worn it was.

'What do you usually have for dinner?' he asked as they walked along the crowded footpath.

Usually on the nights she'd worked late she grabbed a chocolate bar from the tube station on the way home or didn't bother. Tonight had been going to be a not-bother night. But she wasn't about to admit that. 'I might cook a quick stir-fry.'

'But if you were to dine out?'

She shrugged as nonchalantly as possible. Truth? She *never* dined out.

He sent her a sideways look. 'I know a good place.'

'I thought you were new to the area and didn't know any of the cool places.' She couldn't help smiling.

'I asked one of the concierges at my apartment building,' he replied smoothly. 'They offer a superb service.'

She rolled her eyes and kept pace with him along the busy footpath. A couple of corners later he paused outside a beautiful brick mansion.

She shook her head at him. 'No chance. You have to have a booking.'

He shrugged as if he wasn't fazed. 'We won't take up much space.'

It was a celebrity chef's place—the kind you had to make a reservation for six months in advance, which was actually a good thing, as it then gave you the time to save the small fortune you needed just to enjoy an appetiser, let alone sample the full menu. Ettie made bookings all the time on behalf of her Cavendish residents.

But Leon simply walked up to the door, which the discreet security guard immediately opened. The maître d' swept towards them, his wide gaze fixed firmly on Leon and his smile welcoming and wide. Leon didn't even need to utter a word.

'May I have five minutes, sir, if you'd like a drink first?'

'Thank you,' Leon answered with the ease of one born to privilege. 'Champagne?' He turned to Ettie.

'Lemonade,' she replied firmly and caught a gleam of pure amusement in his eyes.

'Definitely not a risk-taker,' he murmured.

'Fine, then,' she breathed. 'Champagne.'

One glass wouldn't do any harm.

They'd barely been given their drinks when the maître d' reappeared to lead them through the busy dining room. Ettie tried not to stare. Several faces were familiar to her but not through personal acquaintance. These were publicly led lives—an actress, a politician. Possibly a minor royal? They stopped at a secluded table in an alcove near the rear of the restaurant. It was quieter than the main dining room, more intimate and far more private.

'You like it?' Leon asked as she took her seat.

'You know the owner?' She hazarded a guess as she tried not to stare at the gleaming lighting and sumptuous décor, but she couldn't hold back her smile. The place was amazing. 'This is really kind of you.'

'No, I'm not really kind,' he corrected bluntly. 'This is pure self-interest. I get a pretty companion for dinner to take my mind off my misery.'

'Misery?' She quirked an eyebrow while battling the warmth she felt at his compliment. He didn't really mean it. He was just adding 'charming' to his repertoire, which was very unfair of him. 'Because your life's so terrible?' Curious, she watched him keenly for his answer.

But he turned the conversation back on her. 'Was it really going to be a stir-fry?'

'No,' she admitted with a chuckle. 'I hate cooking. Generally I exist on grilled cheese sandwiches.'

'There's a place in the world for a good grilled cheese sandwich.' He nodded. 'But not here.'

'Then what do you suggest?'

'I suggest we leave it to the experts.' He nodded at the maître d', who, with a slight bow, left for the kitchen. 'So, why are you working such intense hours?' Leon sipped his champagne. 'Do we not pay you enough to live on?'

She too took a sip and savoured the fizz of bubbles before replying. 'I'm saving.'

'For travel? A house?'

She laughed and shook her head. Was she really here to *entertain* him and take his mind off whatever torments he thought he had? 'I've a younger sister who aspires to go to university.'

'It's just the two of you?'

She nodded and took another sip.

'How old is she?' His gaze narrowed.

'Seventeen. She's away at boarding school up north.'

'You support her financially?'

'She's on a partial scholarship.'

'And you pay the rest?' His mouth tightened. 'But you're not that far out of school yourself.'

'I'm twenty-three, so a few years out. It's her last year, so it really counts.'

'And she's obviously talented.'

'Top of her school.' Ettie beamed with unashamed pride. 'She's amazing. She wants to study medicine. So.' She inhaled deeply. 'A lot of study.' And a lot of tuition and living fees. But Ophelia was worth it and she'd do anything to see her achieve her dreams.

'What happened to your parents?'

'Twenty questions, huh?' She sent him a look but answered anyway. 'My father was never around. My mother passed away a couple of years ago.'

'That must have been hard.'

It had been but she didn't want to dwell on her mother's slow decline with cancer. Not tonight. Not here. She smiled softly. 'We've survived.'

She didn't tell him about the huge mistake that she'd made not long after her mother's death either. The total car crash that had been her love life.

'What's your sister's name?'

'Ophelia.'

'Antoinette and Ophelia,' he said quietly. 'But you're "Ettie"?'

'Yes, fingers crossed neither of us suffers the delusions or disappointment of our namesakes.' She sat back as the waiter appeared and placed dishes on the table. 'My mother was a romantic.' Not that she'd had any kind of romantic luck. Like mother, like daughter. 'This looks amazing.'

She was pleased to have the interruption to the topic. And she realised she was absolutely *starving.*

He waited for her to take a bite, amusement softening his innate seriousness. 'What do you think? Better than a grilled cheese sandwich?'

Ettie couldn't answer, she was too busy salivating. But she finally swallowed her mouthful. 'I've never eaten anything like it. It's to die for.'

And that was all she could say, because she needed more this instant. He probably thought she was an idiot, but right this second she didn't care. This was one of those rare experiences in life that had to be luxuriated in.

'Here, try this.' He pushed another plate towards her.

Ettie tasted what was, frankly, the food of the gods. Conversation turned to flavours and textures. Leon was animated, knowledgeable and entertaining as they debated which dish was the most delicious.

'Do you have room for dessert?' he teased her almost an hour later as she sat back with a satisfied sigh.

'I should say no, because I'm not remotely hungry now…' She trailed off.

When was she ever going to be in a restaurant like this again? With a man like this? It was a once-in-a-lifetime fantasy night and she didn't want it to end.

'What if we share?' He offered her pure temptation.

She flashed a huge grin at him. 'I get to pick, right?' she said impulsively. 'Because you can come here any time.'

He laughed a little beneath his breath. 'Sure.'

'Or maybe you should pick.' She suddenly backpedalled, remembering the guy was all but her boss. 'You probably know what's good…'

There was a quizzical light in his eye and his eyebrows twitched. 'I'm sure they're all good.' He turned and said something softly to the waiter who'd magically appeared with his impeccable service-required senses on full alert.

Ettie narrowed her gaze on Leon. 'You did not just order every dessert on the menu.'

'You don't have to eat them all, just taste.'

Her jaw dropped at the decadence of the suggestion and she shook her head. 'That's wasteful.'

'Then we can take the rest home for later,' he said softly.

Ettie stilled, swamped with heat at the suggestion of intimacy that throwaway comment inferred. Was he assuming she'd go home with him tonight?

Images burned in her brain—of her licking a decadent chocolate dessert while in bed with him. Even better, licking said chocolate dessert *off* him.

'Ettie?' He was watching her closely as if he could read her mind. 'You can take them home and have them for breakfast,' he clarified in a slightly husky voice.

The less than subtle undercurrents between them were unbearably strong and gaining power with every passing second. She licked her suddenly dry lips and decided it was his turn to answer twenty questions. 'Do you have any brothers or sisters?'

He hesitated and for a moment she thought he wasn't going to answer.

But his mouth twisted. 'I'm an only child. Spoilt little rich boy.' His tone was mocking, but the edge of bitterness ran deeper than a mere joke.

'But you built your own business, right?' She

knew his parents had that Greek hotel empire, but he'd gone into finance on his own. That was according to the official bio in his 'most eligible bachelor' blurb in the magazine Jess the housemaid had been flashing around this afternoon at work.

He shook his head. 'I had every advantage—education, health, wealthy parents. While my business success is my own, I can't rightly claim to have done it all by myself when I came from that starting point. Most people don't get that privilege to begin with.'

'But you made the most of your opportunities.'

Of course those schools, those contacts—sure they helped. But in the end, he had to do the work himself. And there were plenty of heirs to vast fortunes who'd frittered their lives away.

A lick of something indefinable flickered in his eyes. 'I like to extract every possible success from every possible scenario. Yes.'

Again that undercurrent swept over her like a blanket of wild dizziness—sensuality of a kind she'd never encountered or imagined. Sexual tension so intense...but it was also teasing, almost fun. Which was surprising, given he was so very serious...and she so very inept at banter.

Two waiters appeared and set six dishes on the table. Six decadent desserts that were miniature works of culinary art.

'They're only small portions,' she said softly, as if that made it better. 'I imagine they're rich.'

'Why don't you take a bite and find out?' That tone was back—dry on the surface, but wicked beneath—daring her to take the risk, to take a bite of something so far out of her league. To taste something miles away from her realm of experience.

She picked up the silver fork and forced herself to focus on the glorious-looking *food*, rather than the man across the table mesmerising her. She took a moment to mentally debate which she should taste first—it was a three-way contest between the chocolate nirvana, the caramel or the raspberry heaven. In the end the chocolate won.

Ettie closed her eyes as she sucked the rich mousse from the spoon.

'Good?'

It was impossible to answer him—the deliciousness too much to express. It was like all the good things in the world had been put together in the one flavour bomb and it had just burst on her tongue.

'Have you tried this?' she mumbled with her mouth full. 'Because I'm not sure I can share after all. And there aren't going to be any left-overs, sorry.'

Leon covered his mouth but she could see deep laughter dancing in his eyes.

'Don't hide your smile,' she scolded recklessly, cross with him for hiding that spark from her. She just knew that had been a gorgeous smile and she wanted to bask in the full impact of it.

'You have great teeth,' she added dizzily as she swallowed more of the silken chocolate. 'Are you afraid I might think you're human? Because don't worry, we all know you're…' She trailed off, suddenly aware she shouldn't complete that rambling sentence.

'I didn't want you to think I was laughing at you,' he said with mock-defensiveness. 'Some women get sensitive about being seen enjoying food.'

Who? Those model-types he hung out with?

'I'm not bothered,' she said honestly. 'I'm utterly unashamed about enjoying this…' She breathed out and surveyed the luscious desserts still before her.

'Well, *I'm* the one offended,' he muttered. 'You don't think I'm human?'

Hmm, unfortunately she had said that. 'I also said you have great teeth.' Which was even more mortifying, but she smiled at him anyway.

'All the better to bite you with,' he answered severely, but she saw the sparkle in those amber-lit eyes of his. No, he wasn't anywhere near as serious as she'd first thought. He was *guarded.* So guarded he'd been wary of letting her see him relax. Why was he so defensive when he had everything?

'Perhaps I deserve a bite,' she acknowledged with a chuckle. 'But you were laughing at me.'

His expression turned sly. 'So are you offended?'

'I'm not that precious. You suit a smile. You should do it more often. If I lived in Cavendish House I'd be smiling all the time.' And if she owned the place, she'd be doing back-flips.

'It's not bricks and mortar that make people happy.'

'Oh, they help.' She laughed openly at that. 'Here, taste this. It'll help too.'

'Oh, am I allowed some now?' Sending her a speaking look, he picked up his fork.

* * *

Ettie's pulse skidded all over the place as Leon escorted her out of the restaurant. She shrugged on her coat just for something to do and turned, ready to walk to the train station. She refused to let her spirits lower now the night was over.

He caught her hand in his. Electricity surged at the firm clasp of his fingers over hers and a new level of intimacy seared. She knew it had been building between them, yet she was suddenly shy, but overwhelmingly she wanted everything she probably shouldn't.

He turned her to face him.

'So, clubbing?' he asked.

She couldn't seem to speak, so she just shook her head.

'You don't want to dance with me?' he asked quietly.

Oh, she wanted to dance with him. Just the two of them. Intuitively she knew he was asking for just that—an *intimate* dance. It was fantastical. But ever since he'd walked into the stationery shop, it was as though she'd stepped into another dimension—an alternative reality where the truths of tomorrow really didn't matter and where the past was irrelevant and where for one crazy night this way-out-of-her-league guy was paying her attention.

He stepped closer, his expression intensifying—even more serious, and *hungry*.

'This is a very bad idea,' he said softly.

'Yes,' she agreed softly. She couldn't quite believe he even wanted to get closer to her, but here he was, leaning in with so much intent.

She'd been working so hard for so long. She'd been let down too many times. She'd been alone for what felt like for ever. What did it matter if there was no future in this? She'd pinned her hopes on a future with a man before, only to be heartbroken. With no hopes, no expectations… there would be no heartbreak, right?

'Terrible.' He lifted his hand and gently framed her face.

She quivered at that lightest of touches. 'Yes.'

She read the sultry promise in his eyes as those pros and cons swirled in her head. What was the worst that could happen? She'd have an amazing experience with a god-like man. And whether he enjoyed it as much as she…well, that was up to him, wasn't it? Couldn't she let that fear go?

'But I want to do it anyway.'

He did? He really did? She smiled and her tummy swarmed with butterflies…but below that, molten heat swirled. 'Yes.'

There was only now. Only this sensation. Only this one chance. And she wanted it.

'And so do you?' His gaze searched hers intently.

'Yes.' *Of course.*

She might be inexperienced, but she wasn't stupid.

'And that's all you're going to say tonight?' His lips twitched.

She stared at him, willing him to smile. 'Yes.'

'To anything I ask?'

She'd not taken a moment purely for herself in such a long time. 'Um…yes.'

His mouth didn't curve into a smile; instead it moved closer. He brushed a light kiss on her lips. Ettie remained still, her face upturned to his, not quite sure this was actually happening. He too was immobile, watching her with that ultra-serious, inscrutable intensity. She didn't want him to watch, she wanted him to *act.*

And then he did.

He cupped her head, threading his fingers through her hair to draw her closer so he could kiss her properly. Not a gentle brush of the lips, but a devastating, can't-get-enough kiss that mirrored the desire clawing deep in her body. That deliciousness in the restaurant was nothing on the sensations shivering through her body now. He devoured her as if she were the best of all those award-winning desserts. She lost track of time and place, there was no more thought, no more doubt as sensation transcended—and overwhelmed—everything. There was only one destination for her tonight and that was right here in his arms, with his mouth sealed on hers and his lips, hands, tongue and heat all working that dizzying magic. He made her tremble, made her want more than she'd ever wanted *anything*.

She moaned, totally overcome. 'Leon—'

He stepped back so suddenly she nearly stumbled. He quickly clamped an arm about her but somehow walked her forward at the same time. He waved and hailed a taxi. Of course one pulled over immediately—he had that way about him. People instantly recognised power, influence, money, and moved the minute he asked.

He thrust a couple of large notes to the driver through the window. 'Just drive.'

He hustled her into the cab ahead of him,

then joined her on the back seat and pulled her in as if he'd been starved of kisses for aeons and was now making up for it. A famished, demanding man now feasting. She was okay with that. So okay. Because she'd discovered her own hunger—her own pleasure in exploring him too. She ran light fingers along his jaw, feeling that hot, sexy stubble—still unable to believe that she was really touching him and he was touching her. She was suddenly super-hot, although neediness made her shiver.

His hand skated over the hem of her dress. His teasing fingers circled, finding bare skin, seeking out more. Ettie quivered but he kept kissing her, and excitement thrummed throughout her body. Who knew kissing could be this erotic? This intense? This incredibly awesome?

She never wanted it to end. Time needed to stop. Because this was *it*. This was her moment—just for her. And he knew—he kept kissing her, increasing the dizzying intensity and turning up the heat with every luscious lick and slide. His teasing fingers skimmed her thigh so lightly it was only a slight tickle. Yet powerful waves of heat rolled over her. Her mouth parted more as she moaned and lifted her hips to quicker meet the delicious, unpredictable stroke of his fingertips. The tease was intolerable. She wanted a firmer touch. She wanted *more*.

He deepened the kiss further still, his tongue wickedly caressing inside her mouth until she was dizzy on the delight of it. He'd unleashed a hunger, a driving need she'd never known. She soared on the sensation, strung higher with that exquisite tension he drew her along with. She couldn't stop the rock of her hips now, instinctively enticing him to touch further, touch harder. His teeth nipped her lower lip just as he skimmed his fingertips higher—all the way to her soft, simple cotton panties. She gasped at the caress. He stilled and lifted his lips a mere millimetre from hers. Then those trespassing fingers stroked once more—so intimately that she violently squirmed, unable to hold back a moan as her fingers curled into fists. *Yes*. That was what she wanted. But he suddenly broke the kiss. Breathlessly she stared up at him. His gaze ensnared hers—his eyes were dark with promise, with satisfaction, with *hunger*.

He growled the address for Cavendish House to the taxi driver, their gazes still locked. Dazed, she read the determination in his eyes, felt the possessiveness of his hand cupping her so intimately, and understood exactly. He wanted *everything.*

If she was going to stop this, to say no, the time to do it was now. But it was also the time to say yes. Was she really going to be another of Leon Kariakis's conquests? His challenge for the night?

Yes.

Now she was in this other world of touch and light and scorching sensation, nothing could stop her from having this. Having him.

Just once.

She'd worked hard to rein in her natural impulsiveness. She'd had too much responsibility to be reckless...but this was only one night.

'Yes?' he prompted in a gruff undertone.

She nodded. She wanted the experience she knew he could give her. He swooped and kissed her again—pure reward, pure promise, invoking that breathless restlessness all over again. But he slipped his hand from beneath her dress and rested it on her breast instead, almost holding her captive. She acquiesced to everything, to the kiss, to the utterly foregone conclusion of this night—and simply drowned in the flood of pleasure his exquisite passion pulled from her.

But as they neared the building she suddenly clutched his wrist and whispered with panic, 'No one can see me.'

'In my company?' He half laughed at her drama and discomfort. 'I've already thought of that, don't worry.' He leaned forward and spoke to the taxi driver again. Moments later the gate to the underground garage slid open, letting them escape the cab unseen.

In the lift Leon pushed a series of buttons on the security pad. 'The lift will go straight to the penthouse. It won't stop on any other floor.'

Even so, she stood as far from him as possible because there was still a security camera in there. She wasn't ashamed but she was protective of her privacy and she didn't want her colleagues knowing that she'd... Embarrassed warmth flooded her and she fixed her gaze to the floor and let her hair fall forward, hoping her face couldn't be seen. At the ding of the bell, the doors slid open to his penthouse suite.

Leon led the way, keeping a little distance as he swiftly shrugged off his jacket and tie and tossed them onto the nearest sofa. 'Toby's asleep,' he said easily.

Ettie took the moment to pause and settle her heartrate. The elderly dog was comfortably curled in his basket and she could see he'd drunk some of his water. She breathed out a little of her tension as she glanced back at Leon. 'Why'd you take him?'

'Same reason you would have if you could,' he answered. 'Why did it surprise you so much that I did? Why think I'm such an ogre?'

Was there a hint of hurt in his eyes?

'I don't think you're an ogre,' she said softly. 'You can just come across as a bit stern.'

'You want me to smile?' He sounded sardonic.

'Yes.'

But he remained as still and as serious as ever. 'Come here.'

His request—command really—was impossible to ignore. She was drawn to him; she had been from the first moment she'd seen him. So she went to him, her heart thundering faster with every step.

'You're sure about this, Ettie?' he asked.

'Just this once,' she whispered. 'Only this once, okay?'

Leon didn't reply. He was so very still, so very serious. She knew he was thinking, she just didn't know what. But she sensed his tension, some kind of warring within. Instinctively she reached out and placed her hand on his chest.

His heart echoed hers—beating with a fierce gallop. The pace reverberated through her palm, up her arm and into her own tightly wired body. His enigmatic gaze glittered down at her.

And then he smiled.

CHAPTER THREE

ETTIE BLINKED, STUNNED again by his instant transformation from moody male model to sinfully arrogant tease. Oh, she was in such trouble. 'What are you thinking about?'

'The best way to begin.'

She swallowed as her poor heart raced even more. But lower down she melted with anticipation. 'Did you need some help with that?' she asked weakly. 'Should we list the options?'

He laughed, which made him all the more heart-stoppingly handsome. But just as she gaped—beyond dazzled—he swooped. He caught her gasp in his kiss, sending Ettie straight back into that intense desire she'd felt in the taxi. Oh, the man could *kiss*. He was playful and teasing—alternating deep, luscious licks with light nibbles that were designed to provoke her to madness. She had more freedom now than in the car, so she wound her arms around his neck and pushed closer, revelling in the press of his hard, masculine body against hers. He was tall and taut and she felt the strength in his core stillness. But his wicked hands wandered again, back to the hem of her dress, back to the silky skin of her inner thigh. She moaned, collapsing against him and letting her feet slide further apart as he trailed those fingertips to the top of her leg, teasing so, so close to where she ached to be teased.

Oh, yes. Please, yes.

But she didn't say it, didn't chant the plea circling in her head. She couldn't—she was too busy being kissed to glorious dizziness. But he must have read her mind, because then he went there—skilfully circling that tight bundle of pure sensitivity. She gasped, breaking the seal of the kiss as pleasure rushed upon her.

'*Oh...*'

He clamped her to him with his other arm, supporting her as the orgasm sent her body into spasms of blissful sensation. Never had she come so quickly with a man. Well, never had she actually *come* with a man.

Panting and suddenly so self-conscious, she pressed her forehead against his chest. He stroked her back but kept that other hand gently cupping her so intimately, soft touches easing her down yet keeping her hyper-aware of him.

'I've been imagining that all day,' he muttered low in her ear.

Really? Breathlessly she laughed as he suddenly switched his hold and lifted her off her feet to carry her through to the master bedroom.

'Me too,' she muttered shyly as he lowered her to stand at the foot of the big bed. So much.

His smile flashed again and it was like being concussed—all circling stars and dizziness, and she really didn't think she could stand for too much longer. She didn't think she could ever get enough of those smiles. But he stepped close and her eyes drifted shut as he kissed her all over again. Vaguely she heard the slide of her zip and before she realised it her dress had slithered to the floor in a sleek heap at her feet.

'Multitasking?' she mumbled in a moment of embarrassment at the simplicity of her exposed underwear. It was black, cotton—no lace or fancy silk and nothing like what any of those models would wear.

But he was still and staring again, erotic hunger stark upon his face. 'You're even more gorgeous than I imagined.'

She crossed her arms and shook her head.

He smiled again but there was an edge of craving to it. 'You don't believe me?' He stepped forward. 'Never mind.' He caught her in a kiss again and then pushed her so she fell back onto the bed. He moved onto the bed too, braced above her, kissing not just her yearning mouth but also down her neck and then lower still. She wriggled but he put a firm hand on her.

'Let me,' he ordered with a low mutter. 'I've wanted to for hours.'

He removed her bra with the skill of a man who'd undone many women. Frankly Ettie was glad as he then kissed his way from one breast to the other, teasing each nipple to a stiff peak of yearning. She quivered as he trailed teasing hands down her ribs to her hips. What was she supposed to do? How could she possibly resist? Her legs had a will of their own and simply spread—earning her a burning glance and then another of those soul-searing smiles. And then he put those lips to even better use.

'*Oh, my, oh, my, oh, my.*' This time she muttered the chant over and over as he teased her. As those hands pulled the panties from her body and his fingers sought out even more secrets. He was kissing her where no one had bothered to kiss her before. It was so shockingly intimate. So incredibly good.

'Leon,' she moaned, half drawing her knees up in rejection as his tongue swirled to even greater intimacy.

She felt the hot breath of his laughter. It tickled and she wriggled a little—half escaping, a whole lot eager.

'You didn't think you were done, did you?' he said, putting a hand on her hip and holding her still.

But what about him? She'd already…she'd already…

But that swirl of his tongue made any more thought impossible. And then his fingers pushed right into her slick heat. She arched taut, locking those talented fingers in place. But even then he teased. His mouth kept up that magic, sucking hard, while his tongue added rough slicks of pleasure. Unstoppable waves of heat rolled over her in a torrent of ecstasy. He growled against her in appreciative hunger as the convulsions started, applying more pressure with his fingers—pumping deeper, pressing harder against her inner walls, and he ate at her like she was the sweetest treat imaginable. Unbearable pleasure tore through her, harder this time as she squeezed on his hold and rode out the crest he'd conjured for her.

'Leon!'

It was a long moment before he answered, sliding up the bed, licking his lips and sending her a smug smile. 'Better now?'

He didn't seriously expect an answer, did he? Because she was still struggling to return to reality, still catching her breath and still desperate for what more that was to come. She wanted *all* of him.

'This is you making the most of opportunities?' she eventually sighed, trying to keep it light even when she was almost buried in need for him.

His gaze turned smoky. 'Yes.'

'Please,' she muttered in total, helpless surrender.

That smokiness flared to fire—pure, burning lust. He thrust back off the bed and pretty much shredded his clothes. He reached into the drawer of the bedside cabinet and retrieved a condom.

'Don't worry,' he muttered. 'I have plenty.'

She trembled with anticipation—her mouth

drying as she watched him. He was very…*well built*, and so highly aroused the sight of him made other parts of her moisten. He knelt on the bed and looked at her. He was a hot, experienced, sexually demanding man and right now he was motionless again—*thinking*.

The sexual suspense was almost killing her.

'How do you want…?' She trailed off. She had such little experience, she had no idea what to suggest.

'You have a list in mind?' he teased with a half-smile. ''Cos I do.'

'You go first, then,' she muttered in a low voice, blushing—and then blushing harder as she realised she blushed all over.

'Oh, *glykia mou*,' he chuckled. 'This first time I'm watching every moment flicker over your beautiful face.' He braced himself over her, running his hand down her side in a manner both soothing and stirring as he looked into her eyes. 'I want to see everything, feel everything…'

She felt a flash of vulnerability but he pressed closer and she could see him too—into those brown eyes that she knew had such depths. Right now, she saw desire and humour and the sharp bite of hunger.

'Then do what you want,' she whispered.

He kissed her into softness and stirring heat again. She couldn't believe this was happening. He overwhelmed her—his size, his heat, his musky scent.

'Breathe,' he muttered, gently probing her tightness. At the catch of her breath he hesitated and gave her a searching look.

'It's been a while,' she mumbled, burning with both desire and insecurity.

Another emotion flared in his eyes—hotter than ever. 'I know.'

He knew? How—because she was so desperate? Because she barely knew what she was doing?

'Relax. Kiss me.'

He lifted her, nudging her legs further apart so she could take him more easily. Then in one smooth movement he kissed her and thrust deep at the same time. She cried out with the shocking pleasure of it and clutched his hips to keep him there.

'Okay?' he growled.

'Mmm-hmm.' She was almost delirious with the delight of it—he felt so heavy, she so full.

And it didn't just feel good, it also felt *right*.

For the first time she actually understood why people liked this so much. He muttered something she didn't understand and crushed her closer.

And *this* was what she'd wanted most of all—him with her as completely as anyone could be. He moved, watching her, kissing her, riding her unswiftly to that point beyond thought. It was unbearably awesome. She gave herself up to complete hedonism, not caring about anything but the demands of her body—driving her hips in the way instinct dictated she must. His breathing roughened, the glitter in his eyes sharpened.

'Ettie.' He huffed her name harshly and pumped harder.

She curled about him more tightly still, screaming as she came harder and longer than she could bear. She heard his roar of need and felt the sudden, full force of his lust unleashed. He slammed into her. Again, then again and again until they collided, interlocked, shaking together for a sublime moment of eternity, lost in that realm of total ecstasy.

She couldn't breathe. Couldn't believe.

'We're doing that again,' he muttered rawly. 'Now.'

* * *

The dog was gone. Rubbing his sleep-fuzzed head, Leon glanced at the empty basket with a frown. Ettie must have woken early and taken him for a walk. Leon wished she'd woken him—he'd have gone with her. Or better still, delayed her a little longer. His body was hard and ready—despite the aches from the full-on, all-night best sex of his life. His curiosity was fully aroused too. For the first time in a long time, he wanted to know more about a woman.

He paced the penthouse, running his hand through his hair again, aching for her return. One night wasn't going to be enough. He'd guessed they'd be good together, but he'd not imagined quite how hot. He grimaced wryly at the condom wrappers littering the bedroom floor. They'd barely bothered with sleep. After that first intense experience, he'd lifted her into the shower and taken his time to soap her up—easing away the last of her shyness and exposing the sly humour he'd seen fleeting snatches of. He'd held off letting her get off until she whispered something she wanted him to do and learned she knew a few curse words too. Hell, in that moment he'd have done anything she asked.

She was generous and sweet and funny and he wanted nothing more than to kiss her everywhere until she came all over again.

Half an hour passed and still she didn't return. A prickle of foreboding slid down his spine. Why hadn't she come back? The full quota of staff would be on shift by now and she hadn't wanted to be seen by any of them.

He stilled, irritated. Was he actually worried about her? And the damn dog?

Disliking the uncertainty, he showered and dressed, but once downstairs he stopped some distance from the concierge desk. Ettie was in her uniform—filling out that crisp monogrammed T-shirt and parading the prim black trousers that on her embodied sexiness. She hadn't seen him; she was too busy pacifying a puce-faced resident.

'I'm so sorry that happened.' She sent the resident her most charming smile. 'Don't you worry, I'll straighten it out with George—he doesn't need to know most of it.' She picked up the box on the desk. 'How about we get Joel to come up and help you lift the dresser back into place?'

It was Saturday. Was she supposed to be working? Even if she was, why hadn't she bothered to wake him and say goodbye? Anger burned beneath his skin, but he turned to leave, fishing out his phone as it pinged with a message.

At the sound of an almighty clatter he glanced back. She'd dropped whatever it was in that box. Now she was flushed in the face and completely avoiding looking in his direction. Which meant she'd seen him. Her obvious discomfort eased the chill in his bones. So she felt awkward? Good. So she should.

She'd sneaked out early this morning and was now attempting to act as if *nothing* had happened. While he could respect her need to keep her private life private, he wasn't going to ignore her. And where was Toby? He almost missed the sleepy thing.

Ettie wasn't butter-fingered. Ever. Yet she'd just dropped an entire box of old cutlery, creating the loudest crash ever heard in the lobby. And Leon Kariakis was here to witness it. Of course he was.

Perspiration slicked over her skin. She couldn't look at him, but she could still see him from the corner of her eye and apparently he was busy scrolling through some vitally important message on his phone. At least he wasn't laughing at her openly.

She'd woken up stupidly early this morning and got hit right in the head with the reality hammer. He was fast asleep beside her—a vision of hot, sleepy sex-god—and she instantly realised how completely out of her depth she was. The one and only other time she'd woken next to a man, it had turned into one of the worst days of her life. Her ex had rejected her in the most humiliating, personal of ways the morning after. And then he'd done it all over again in public. The last thing she needed was to hear even any of that horror again from Leon.

She'd lain there frozen, becoming more and more terrified of the moment when he'd wake and see her in the cold light of day and realise his mistake. Sleeping with the sexually clueless concierge girl?

Her blood had iced at the prospect of the inevitably awkward—*or worse*—goodbye that would ensue. She couldn't bear to have any discussion or polite platitudes.

In the end she hadn't been able to stand the anxious torture. She'd slipped from the bed, wriggled into her dress and run—taking Toby with her before he barked his need to go outside. She'd been terrified of bumping into someone she knew in the lift. Of course, it stopped before the basement, ending her chance to escape to the staff locker room unseen. Jess had entered with her trolley. She'd stared at Toby and then at her.

'You should wear your hair loose more often.' Jess had smiled brightly after a horribly silent moment. 'It looks lovely. I didn't realise how long it had got.'

That was because Ettie couldn't afford to get it cut. And Jess had been lying—it didn't look lovely, it hadn't even been its usual wavy mess, but totally tangled, mussed-up bed-hair. That model had been seen exiting Leon's apartment only the other day in that supposed lift-ride of shame...and now she was doing the same? She pushed away the public humiliation. It wasn't worse than the horror she'd escaped years ago.

But she just couldn't face Leon. Her skin almost blistered with embarrassment at the thought of awkwardly extricating herself from his apartment. Because the last thing she could remember from the night before was his throaty laughter as he'd taken her apart again at some insane hour of the morning and now she couldn't work out if he'd been laughing *with* her or *at* her. She'd been his light relief for the night. And hardly his toughest challenge…in fact she'd been so *easy* she'd almost come in the taxi.

He wouldn't want a repeat. He'd probably been feigning sleep and just hoping she'd leave quietly, right?

But with every step she took, the tenderness between her thighs reminded her of his skilful passion, as did the sensitivity of her skin at her collar from the gentle grazes from his evening shadow…

One night only.

And she was not letting anyone know. Ever.

And she was not going to be able to look him in the eye again either. Ever.

Naturally, it was at that exact moment that he walked up to her desk.

'Where's Toby?' he asked briskly.

She fiddled with the box of cutlery the earlier resident had wanted her to return to the shop he'd purchased it from and just knew the man was *not* smiling.

'Harold's neighbour was away yesterday and only learned about what happened this morning. She's asked to take Toby. She cares for him very much.'

'That makes sense.' His reply was clipped.

'Actually, a number of the residents offered to take Toby when they heard what had happened,' she said meaningfully. 'I think a lot would like the "no pets" rule to be lifted.'

She glanced up then and saw winter had returned to his deep brown eyes. There was no hint of the intimacies they'd shared in his expression. There was nothing at all but cool control.

'Why are you on duty? It's Saturday. Haven't you been working all week?' He fired the questions like bullets.

So that was a no to pets, then. And a no to any kind of smile.

'One of the others called in sick and, as I was here early to check on Toby…' She glanced at Joel, working near by, concerned he could hear them.

'Of course.' Leon nodded. 'Thank you.'

'It really is the best thing, I think,' she babbled anxiously because he had such a remote expression in his eyes and she felt him distancing himself even as he stood there. 'He'll be well cared for. She knows him and…' She licked her lips, dying of mortification, and tried to smile. 'I'll have his things cleared from your apartment shortly.'

He shot her an ice-cool look. 'You'll send one of the porters?'

'Of course.' Nervously she nodded. Because he didn't want her back up there?

Of course he didn't. Could the earth just open up and swallow her whole? *Now?* She'd made the right decision to run.

The second Leon left, Ettie leaned against the desk and breathed out, appallingly weak at the knees. That was it. There'd been no real goodbye. Nor was there any glow of amusement in his eyes—no sense of shared intimacy. If anything she had the odd feeling she'd somehow let him down. But that was impossible, wasn't it? He'd had what he wanted. So had she. And now there was no need to have to talk about it or anything mortifying like that. They could just pretend it had never happened.

It was over.

CHAPTER FOUR

'WHERE'S ETTIE?' THE beautifully clad woman demanded an answer from the youngest concierge. *Joel*—according to his monogrammed shirt.

Leon paused at a distance, unable to resist listening in for the answer.

'I'm sorry, Ms Welby, Ettie is away sick.' Joel offered an apologetic smile.

The woman laughed. 'Ettie is never sick. Just as Ettie never takes holidays. Ettie is simply always here. That's her job.'

'Well, she's not here now,' Joel said firmly.

No, she wasn't. She hadn't been at the desk for the last two days. Leon had noticed. He'd more than noticed; he'd *missed* her—missed seeing her smile and hearing her lovely chat with the residents.

He'd tried to avoid the concierge desk as much as possible initially. Unfortunately, he'd soon discovered that it was the heart of the operation.

He'd pushed back—spending long hours at his office headquarters, taking more meetings. But he'd always glanced over when he'd walked in. And as the weeks passed, he'd walked through the lobby a little more often than was really required. But she still didn't look at him.

And now, even though it had been over three weeks, even though he knew all he needed to, he couldn't bring himself to move out of the penthouse and go home. Ettie still irritated him—rather, the way he kept *thinking* about her still irritated him—and that was a problem, given what he'd discovered about the way Cavendish House was run.

Awareness of her absence—*two days running*—sharpened his curiosity. And a chill of warning slithered down his spine because he saw the protectiveness in Joel's eyes as he referred to Ettie being ill. The young guy was concerned about his colleague. So what was wrong with her exactly, if Ettie was never ill?

'May I help instead?' Joel asked the resident awkwardly. 'Ettie's been schooling me in sorting dry-cleaning, you know.'

But the woman dropped her bundle of clothing on the desk and leaned towards Joel. 'Is Ettie actually okay?'

She'd gone from demanding customer to concerned busybody in a flash. That the woman genuinely was concerned for Ettie underlined everything Leon had learned: that everyone adored Ettie and relied on her completely.

'She should be back tomorrow.' Joel's smile wasn't reassuring enough. 'Let me take this for you in the meantime.'

The woman scooped up the dresses with a laugh. 'Thanks, but I don't trust *anyone* except Ettie. I'll wait for her to return.'

'If you're sure, madam.'

'You know I am.' She turned and caught sight of Leon watching her and her expression lit up with a huge smile. 'Oh, Mr Kariakis, it's lovely to finally meet you. My name's Autumn; I'm in apartment twenty-three.'

Leon nodded. 'Is everything okay for you, Autumn?'

'Well, apparently Ettie is away sick, which is hopeless, because she runs this place, Mr Kariakis; I hope you're aware of that.'

He nodded. He'd rapidly become aware of the fact, as it happened. In every conversation he had with either resident or management, it was Ettie to whom they referred for fixing problems. Which was why the fact that he'd taken her to bed was more of a problem than he'd expected it would be. That and the fact that he still couldn't get her out of his head. 'I'm glad you appreciate the service the Cavendish offers.'

'I appreciate *Ettie*,' she said firmly. 'Ettie is simply the best.'

Yes, she was. He never should have slept with her.

'How long has she been away?' Leon asked Joel as idly as he could after Autumn had headed towards the lift.

'I'm sure she'll be back tomorrow,' Joel said with a valiant defence. 'Ettie's never sick.'

That didn't answer his question, but Leon let it slide. He'd give her until tomorrow to return; if she didn't, then he was going to have to investigate.

He couldn't stop thinking about her. It had only been one night and he'd had many one nights with many women, so why was he stuck thinking about *her*?

Was it simply because she now seemed to be missing? Why wasn't she at work? He disliked unanswered questions. Just as he disliked messy endings and tearful women. They were why he stuck to one night.

Ettie was the first woman who'd left *him*. No tears, no mess, no reference to it at all, in fact. If it hadn't been for the sweet scent of her lingering in the air, he might have imagined the whole thing. Except he dreamed of it every night too.

Not turning up to work wasn't something she often did. Nor were one-night stands. When he'd approached her in front of her colleagues that next day she'd been dying of mortification; he'd just been too annoyed to pay attention to it properly at the time. She was shy. Inexperienced. Sweet. And he was a fool for having lost his head and seducing her. Especially now it had become clear she was the main asset of this entire enterprise and he needed her to take more of a leading role.

A horrible thought hit him: was *he* the reason she was away now? Was she so embarrassed by what had happened she was off hunting for another job? Or had he hurt her in some way and not realised—was that why she'd run off so early that next morning? And how was it possible he felt the loss of that damn dog when he'd had custody over it for less than twenty-four hours?

A sharp memory impinged on his mind. A memory he'd blocked for years—of a tiny puppy he'd adored more than anything else in his life. Only it had been snatched away from him just as everything important had then. He'd been betrayed again by the most important person in his life. He swiftly, curtly reminded himself that pets, like people, were not permanent. The loss of them hurt. Which was why he kept them at a distance.

Emotions—all emotions—were a weakness. He'd learned that lesson long ago and he'd remember it well now. Never admit to them, never show them.

It was barely eight in the morning when he went down to the concierge desk the next day. He'd hardly slept. He wasn't going to rest properly until he knew. That fact irritated him. He didn't allow other people's problems to affect him. He didn't let his *own* problems affect him. He just fixed them.

'Still no Ettie?' he asked Joel bluntly.

'No, sir,' the concierge answered awkwardly.

'But she's never had a day off before in the entire time I've been here.'

Leon spied the battered book open on the desk and recognised Ettie's handwriting. He reached across and spun it round to flick through the pages.

'They're Ettie's lists,' Joel hurriedly explained. 'She designed the systems for us. This is our bible.'

Leon knew exactly what it was. She was insanely over-competent. But basic details were all he needed. A phone number, an address. And, as he'd suspected, Ettie had the staff roster in the back of her book. And, with the roster, full contact details. Feeling like some gumshoe detective—*or stalker*—he employed his photographic memory and left.

The drive took longer than he'd guessed it would. She had to spend a while on the trains in the mornings and evenings, which meant that on those nights she worked her other job she got home horribly late. He climbed the stairs of the rundown housing block, trying not to judge the grime and smell. He knew he was from a privileged background. He was luckier than almost every other damn person in the world. Quelling his concerns for her personal security, he knocked on the door. A few moments later, he heard the locks being pulled back.

'Mr Kariakis?'

Leon tensed. He hadn't been Mr Kariakis when she'd been screaming her pleasure beneath him. But he shoved the resentment aside, because she looked horribly unwell.

'What are you doing here?' She peered past him as if expecting to see someone else. 'Has something happened?'

'What's wrong?' He pushed the words out.

It was a searing pleasure to see her, but he was also hit with a sharp pain at how fragile she looked… Her eyes were huge in her pale face and she was swamped in an ancient woollen jumper, black leggings beneath, warm wool socks on her feet.

'Do you need me back at work?' She looked so guilty and anxious, he felt bad.

'Of course not,' he said curtly, keen to dismiss her guilt. 'Not when you're clearly ill.'

Her eyes widened. 'Did you think I wasn't?'

He drew in a sharp breath. 'Ettie,' he growled. 'Invite me in.'

She didn't want to—that truth was written

all over her beautifully expressive face. But she stepped to the side. The atmosphere intensified as she closed the door behind him. Something was bundled up inside him too tightly and he had to turn away from her.

She lived in a small, dingy apartment. There was no television, just books, and an old laptop on the dining table. He noticed an instrument case on the bookshelf together with a pile of sheet music. The sofa looked old and lumpy. But she'd tried to brighten the place up with a throw and cushions and three little pot plants on the narrow windowsill. It was immaculately clean and tidy. That made sense.

He'd seen the organisation and management systems she'd put in place for the concierge desk. Everything was written up neatly—processes and information. Perfection. No wonder every resident had been asking where she was these past few days.

'You noticed my absence?' she asked huskily.

He'd noticed her absence when he'd woken that morning and found her gone. He'd been noticing it ever since. 'I was concerned you might have been embarrassed about what happened between us. I didn't want that affecting your ability or desire to remain at Cavendish House.'

Her chin lifted. 'I'm not ashamed. And I'm not pining after you, if that's what you were thinking.'

'No.' He almost smiled because hadn't that been one little wish? 'So you're not planning on leaving Cavendish?'

Her brow furrowed. 'Did you think I was off having interviews or something?' She shook her head. 'Of course not. I love my residents.'

He stilled. He should have remembered that about her—loyalty, *passion.* That tension soared. It took everything he had not to take two steps and haul her into his arms.

'How did you find out where I live?' she asked, wrapping her arms around herself in a self-conscious gesture.

'I might've looked at your personnel roster.' He glanced at her.

She still looked shell-shocked and paler than he could've imagined. He had the urge to scoop her off her feet and abduct her. He'd take her back to his apartment, he'd...*what*?

Leon gritted his teeth. Not appropriate. Not allowed.

Ettie swallowed hard, still unable to believe Leon Kariakis was standing in the middle of her tiny flat. It was mortifying. Worse than that, it was…*exciting* in an appalling, illicit way. She'd wondered if she was hallucinating when she'd first answered the door. Now adrenaline surged and she fought not to be driven towards his innate sensuality, fought to settle the sizzle stirring in her blood. Yet her heart beat with more vigour than it had in weeks.

It's not why he's here.

'It was nice of you to be concerned, but it's just a stomach bug,' she said unevenly. 'I think the worst is over now, but you don't want to catch it.'

Please leave. Please leave.

Before she did something stupid like throw herself at him.

'You're sure you shouldn't see a doctor?' He frowned at her.

'No, truly. I just need a little more sleep.'

That customary stillness settled over him as he stared at her. 'Ettie.' His voice was little more than a whisper.

She froze, mentally replaying that soft call to her. Had she heard what she so desperately wanted to hear in his voice? Had there been something more than concern? Had there been longing?

Because of the size of her flat, he was delightfully—dangerously—close. She dragged in a sharp breath, straining to resist. It would be so easy to reach up and kiss him.

You can't.

If she did, she'd be lost. She wasn't cut out to cope with an affair with a man like him. What he'd made her feel that night? She'd be an addict in no time—desperate to have her fix even at the expense of her own well-being. She couldn't afford to be a stupid romantic like her mother—always falling for the wrong guy. The guy who'd never love her back. Leon Kariakis didn't do relationships, he did challenges. Regret swamped her.

If only...

She'd written down the pros and cons and lit a match to send the paper up in smoke. Even so, that lopsided list was burned on her brain. She knew the reality and her responsibility.

'I *need* my job...' She was reminding herself more than telling him. 'I'm sorry to have troubled you. You didn't need to come all the way out here.' Her words were at odds with her secret want. She wanted him to have come here because *he'd* needed—*her.*

'No trouble,' he said stiffly, distance evident in his stance again. 'And you don't need to worry. I'm not about to ask for anything...*inappropriate.*'

He wasn't? Great. Now she was even more mortified by her slight assumption that there'd been any *personal* element to this visit. He valued her more as a concierge than as a concubine. He had no 'best lover ever' award for her—though he'd certainly won hers.

Now he strode to the door, his long pace leashed. He almost looked angry. 'I'll be implementing some changes at Cavendish House. We can discuss them when you get back.'

She nodded, unable to speak because a stupidly large lump had sprung up in her throat.

'But you're not to return until you're fully fit,' he added as an afterthought. 'Everything can wait until then.'

But it couldn't wait.

Because she'd missed her shift at the stationery shop, her boss had released her from all duties there—dismissing her with immediate effect. As she wasn't on contract, just a relief worker, she had little recourse but to suck it up.

The tummy bug had eased—she'd stopped vomiting, though she still felt horrible and horrendously tired. That was too bad. She had to get back to work. Three days off had been an indulgence too far.

She needed the money. And she needed the distraction.

'What's been happening?' she quickly asked Joel as she stepped behind the Cavendish House concierge desk first thing the next morning.

Joel didn't have the chance to reply because Leon Kariakis was bearing down on them both, his expression shockingly thunderous. Oddly his jaw was shadowed, as if he'd not shaved for a day.

'What are you doing here?' His cold, furious gaze sliced right through her.

'What does it look like I'm doing?' Ettie summoned the biggest fake smile she could muster. She was keeping things professional. Maintaining distance. Doing her job.

'You're not working today,' Leon snapped. 'Turn around and go home. I'll hail a taxi.'

Ettie gaped, then glared at him. Had he *no*

thought for privacy? And as if she could ever afford to go all the way home in a cab!

'Excuse me a moment, please, Joel.' She stalked into the small office, not bothering to see if Leon followed her. Because of course he did.

'What are *you* doing?' she threw at him the second he'd closed the door.

'Ettie.' It was a soft growl.

It was the almost irritated look of concern in his eyes that devastated her. She had to turn away from it. But he grabbed her shoulders and turned her back, tilting her chin up. Not so he could steal a kiss, but to subject her to his disapproving inspection. His frown deepened. 'You've lost weight. You shouldn't be here at all today. Not for the rest of the week.'

'I'm fine,' she argued, burning at his touch, at the tension tearing her apart every time she so much as thought about him. Which was insanely often. And to see him? To be this close to him? She was going to have to find a new job after all.

'You're pale. Have you had breakfast?' He interrogated her grimly.

'I need to be here. I need to work.'

'You still look awful.'

'And thank you for that,' she muttered. 'I'm *fine*. It's my decision, Leon. Not your concern.'

An indefinable emotion whipped across his face and then he froze. 'Not my concern?' he echoed with lethal softness.

'You value your independence as much as I do and don't try to argue otherwise,' she said. 'If you needed to work, you would. And I need to work.'

'Not today—'

'I have no sick leave left,' she snapped. 'The stationery shop has given me the boot because I missed shifts this week, and I need the money because Ophelia has unforeseen expenses. I *am* working today and you are *not* stopping me. Nor are you offering to help me,' she burst out, rejecting his offer before he could make it. Because she just knew he would make it now she'd told him all that. 'I don't want any help from you.'

His mouth opened and shut again as he visibly sought for control. But then he lost it. 'Damn your pride, Ettie,' he ground out in a low voice.

He ran a frustrated hand through his hair, his customary coolness evaporating in a swirl of motion. 'There's independent. And then there's stubborn and pig-headed. You're the latter.'

The guy had no concept of talking quietly. He was all orders and commands and shouting. Joel could probably hear him on the other side of the door, and it would be around the staff that she and Leon Kariakis and were alone in the office, arguing like…like…*lovers*.

'Shush,' she whispered furiously.

'Did you just shush me?' His gaze glittered.

'I have to get on with my job. Please, Leon,' she suddenly broke and begged, her voice catching. 'Leave me alone.'

Leon was silenced. And furious. She couldn't be any clearer. She didn't want him around. But he knew she did. He could see the desperation in her eyes now—she was positively drinking him in.

'What are you doing?' Her voice wavered as he stalked nearer.

Behaving badly. Doing what they both wanted. What they both needed. He hadn't slept a wink since seeing her yesterday, his temper was ragged and he'd been under extreme restraint for too long. Her chin was stuck in the air and her 'leave me alone' vibes couldn't hum louder. He wasn't going to linger where he wasn't wanted.

Except he knew he *was* wanted. Very much. He could see it in her luminous, emotion-laden green eyes, and those vibes had a strong bass thrum of desire. But she had irritatingly strong willpower. She didn't want to want him any more. Well, that made two of them. Because he'd never wanted to be held hostage to desire like this. Never wanted to feel this need to know she was okay. To be so shockingly concerned about her appearance.

She was so beautiful. But right now she looked unbearably fragile. Pale and interesting didn't suit Ettie—she was meant to be full of vitality and radiance.

'Leon.' Her whisper wasn't one of rejection. It was a plea.

He was desperate to get her out of his head, the want for her out of his blood. Never before had he wasted time thinking about anything other than work. He'd never let himself want something so much it became a complete distraction. He controlled all his emotions—even desire.

So now he didn't kiss her. He couldn't. Not

when she'd asked him not to. But he'd allow himself just the smallest, gentlest of touches. As he spanned her waist, he heard not just a hitch in her breathing, but also a stifled moan. He felt the ripple of yearning arch through her body and he pulled her closer into his embrace. A hug, right?

But desire burgeoned between them. He gazed into her eyes, watching the searing craving build. Neither could hide it. Nor deny it.

'You don't want any help from me?' he growled at her. 'But you still want me.'

Her soft mouth parted, her lips full and reddened. But her eyes pleaded with him—tormenting him with two vastly different requests. 'That's different.'

It was. And it complicated everything.

She didn't want to want him. Well, *ditto*. With every ounce of willpower he could summon, he released her and stalked out of the room.

Ettie's heart plummeted as the door slammed behind him. She'd *craved* more contact with him. That need had been constant since that first night. No matter how hard she'd fought against it the want simply grew. And now?

She'd banished him for good.

She breathed in and out, trying to steady her pulse and ignore the sharp pain high in her chest. Eventually the adrenaline burst vanished, leaving her overwhelmingly exhausted.

It was so stupid to still feel so tired. She'd not lied to Leon, she'd slept like a log last night, but she just couldn't seem to get enough rest despite turning in as early as she could. She had no idea how she was going to rearrange Autumn Welby's massive walk-in wardrobe right now. Autumn liked her to do it every month and usually it was fine—enjoyable even—to see the dazzling dresses. But this morning the thought of sorting out all those evening gowns made her arms ache and the prospect of Autumn's perfume collection made her gag even more.

'You okay, Ettie?' Joel frowned as she walked from the concierge office to the lift. 'Need a coffee?' He held out a mug.

'No, thanks. I'm fine,' she lied.

In truth she was hot, cold and queasy and the strong smell of coffee almost made her retch. The lift dinged and the doors slid open but Ettie didn't step in. She'd never felt so awful in her life.

'Ettie?' Joel called to her again.

She turned her head to answer him, but then she heard someone else.

'Ettie? *Ettie!*' Leon was shouting.

Blindly she reeled as her body pulsed with regret and *longing*. She opened her mouth to reply but it was too late; nothing came out.

CHAPTER FIVE

'ETTIE…'

It was the merest whisper, but it was that same voice she'd heard in the moment before everything went black.

Leon.

Blinking rapidly, she tried to sit up, but he firmly pushed her back down onto the plush sofa. She shivered at the contact, goose bumps lifting all over her skin. It was appalling how much she wanted that touch.

'Stay still,' he ordered tightly.

He was leaning so close, he was all she could see. Bossy as ever. He'd taken off his jacket, and in his crisp white shirt and dark tie he looked stunning. But it was his eyes that made her all but limp—the potency and depth of the brown and the heat in the amber lights. How had she ever thought his gaze was cool?

It wasn't a ripple of forbidden desire that slithered down her spine now, it was a tsunami. Her body was a disgrace to her—a confused mess. Unwell one moment, racked with feverish lust the next.

'Leon…' She murmured the all too obvious like some brainless devotee. She'd ached to see him again. Then she remembered. She'd fainted at his feet. What an *idiot*.

He looked more serious than ever, which ought to have been impossible. 'I told you, you're still unwell.'

'I've just…' She trailed off.

'It's gone on too long, Ettie,' Leon said decisively.

She struggled against the sneaking desire to lean against him. Instead she made herself look past him. Where was she? Not the concierge office because there was no sofa in there.

'I'm in your penthouse.' Her pulse spiked as she realised.

'Yes.'

'Why?'

'Because you fainted in the lobby.'

'No, I meant… I could have gone into the office.' She moistened her dry lips with her tongue. He hadn't needed to bring her up here. *How* had she got up here? Her heart sank and soared at the same time. He'd carried her. She just knew it.

'Too bad for you.' His tone was cool.

It was too bad, because she still wanted him even when it was impossible. And so damn embarrassing. She shut her eyes to block out the intensity of his impact on her, but somehow it just made it worse. She could *feel* his heat and strength. 'I don't mean to be ungrateful.'

'Leave it, Ettie,' he said softly. 'The doctor's on her way.'

Her eyes flashed open. 'A doctor? I don't need a doctor. I just need another day in bed...'

He was so very near and at her words something stirred in his eyes. Physical weakness sapped her willpower. *His* bed was very near. His bed, where he'd made her feel *everything*.

Her mouth dried as her skin sizzled. Her yearning multiplied to the point of madness. And he knew her thoughts, didn't he? Because he leaned closer, his hand sliding through her hair as he cupped her head and searched her eyes.

'I'm probably infectious,' she mumbled, a final, hopeless defence.

She'd become a little challenge for him again, that was all.

'Too late. I think I've already got it,' he replied grimly. 'Feverish. Sleepless. Loss of appetite…'

Her heart pounded so hard it was a wonder it didn't snap her ribs. 'Leon—'

A loud knock on the door dragged his attention from her and his too rare smile flashed even as he groaned. 'Just in time…'

Ettie pulled herself into a sitting position while Leon answered the door. She heard a concise conversation in Greek and didn't understand a word.

'Ettie, this is Dr Notaras,' Leon said briskly, returning to the lounge followed by a tall, glamorous brunette. 'I'll just be in the study. Call me when you're done.' He said that last to the doctor.

Ettie smiled wanly at the terrifyingly skilled woman and tried to tell her she was fine, but the doctor wasn't all that interested in what Ettie had to say initially. She was too busy taking her temperature and looking in her ears and mouth.

'You've not got any fever,' the doctor noted with a cautious expression. 'And there's no sign of any ear or throat infection. Nothing in the chest. Your pulse is strong, blood pressure good.' She then asked a few questions about her background—no diabetes or history of heart problems?

Ettie shook her head. But what about the nausea? And her sensitivity to some smells?

'Is there any chance you could be pregnant?' the doctor asked blandly.

'N…' She broke off.

There was only one, impossible chance. Although…

She pressed her lips together to stop herself stuttering. There'd been more than one *chance* in that one magical night. Her brain kickstarted into frantic overdrive—desperately searching her memory for dates, signs, *denial*. Finally she seized on the only important fact she could bear to consider. They'd used protection. Every time, right?

'I have a home test in my bag and I can take bloods right now…' the doctor said with quiet efficiency after Ettie's lengthy silence had spoken volumes.

'I can investigate that possibility on my own,' Ettie whispered with a shake of her head. She needed to get away from Leon and find out for herself.

But the doctor searched in her bag for a second and then handed Ettie a slim foil package. She gave Ettie her contact card as well.

'Get in touch if you'd like to see me again. It's truly no problem.' The doctor gave her a professional, but sincere smile.

Ettie had the horrendous feeling it was a huge problem.

'I can come to wherever you are,' the doctor said encouragingly. 'Any time. Leon said—'

'This is just between us, right?' Ettie interrupted swiftly. This woman wasn't about to tell Leon pregnancy was even a possibility, was she?

'Of course.' The doctor nodded and stood.

'Thank you.'

Dr Notaras called something in Greek and Ettie quickly put the slim package into her pocket. She wasn't discussing this with Leon; there was no need. Because it *was* impossible, wasn't it?

She heard more rapid Greek and the lift chime. A few moments later Leon walked back into the lounge alone. He didn't look any less serious, or any more relieved.

'I should get back downstairs.' She couldn't look him in the eye.

'You're staying here,' he replied curtly.

'Leon—'

'If you go back down, I'll cart you straight back up here again even if you scream at me to stop. I don't care who stares.'

Furious at his high-handedness, she determinedly stood in a swift movement. 'I have a job to do and I'm perfectly capable of doing it.'

'What's this?'

Ettie glanced down. The pregnancy test had fallen from her pocket and with his damn panther-like reflexes he'd picked it up before she'd even registered it had tumbled.

'It was just something the doctor…' She trailed off, clenching her fists tightly as he read the print on the packet.

He looked from the test to her. His face had actually whitened beneath his olive-toned skin and his eyes narrowed. 'Is this a possibility?'

She couldn't reply; she was too shocked to see him looking so *appalled*. Her pulse skittered. He didn't want this. He really, *really* didn't want this. Well, nor did she. She breathed in and out, but couldn't think for the noise of her blood pounding in her ears.

'Ettie?' he snapped.

She shook her head. 'We used protection.'

Leon's breath hissed out between his gritted teeth. Her plea granted the smallest peace in his sea of panic. It revealed she'd only him to consider, only that one night. There was no other man in her life and she'd not slept with anyone else in a long time. But then he'd known that the night he'd been with her. She'd been shy and sweet and definitely not especially experienced. The expression of rapture and amazement on her face when she'd come in his arms haunted him. He wanted to make her respond like that again; he'd been aching to do that for weeks.

But now?

The fear in her eyes only grew. 'I just can't be pregnant. Not to—'

'Me?' He frowned. Yeah, even she instinctively knew he wasn't father material. His blood chilled. 'Sorry, Ettie. I know there aren't any other possibilities for the baby's paternity.'

She swallowed but didn't deny it.

'Go and do the pregnancy test,' he ordered. He needed to know. Now.

Her hand shook as she took the package from him. He could all but see her brain processing, frantically remembering dates, the dawning realisation that it might be real. That maybe the reason she'd been feeling rotten wasn't from any infection.

Why hadn't she told him just now? What would have happened had he still been away? If he hadn't been here to see her faint? Would she have told him once she knew? Horror burned. This was everything he didn't want. Flickering memories stirred—of the childhood he'd hated. Of loneliness and lack of power. Everything he didn't want.

He paced the room as he waited. He had to get on top of this situation. *Now.*

She couldn't look at him when she returned from the bathroom. She didn't speak either. She just sat back down on the sofa and drew her feet up until she was in a small ball. An intense pressure built in his chest. But he leaned against the wall and waited, even though he already knew.

'It can't be right,' she said in a whisper. 'We used protection.'

He stared at her fixedly. 'Nothing is one hundred per cent fail-proof.'

'Abstinence is,' she muttered grimly.

Her answer offered a wisp of amusement. 'You know that wasn't an option that night.'

She lifted her lashes, her eyes revealing her distress. 'We're talking lifelong consequences, Leon.'

So she was going to have the baby. One swirling chunk of unease settled within him.

'What are you thinking?' he asked as calmly as he was able. Which was frankly nothing on his usual impassive façade.

She shied away from looking at him again.

'Ettie?' His almost customary cool rose a few degrees. This was so personal, so deeply troubling, he couldn't keep his equanimity. Because it wasn't quite up to him any more.

'I need some space.' She tried to stand up but her face turned grey.

'Sit down.' He was furious with her.

'It'll pass,' she snapped.

And just like that the atmosphere flared, leaping right into dangerous. *Emotional.*

'Most probably. But until it does, you stay right where you are.' He huffed out a tight breath. 'You're not going back to work today.' He threw out a gesture to close down the immediate argument in her eyes. 'Give this today at least, damn it.'

They both breathed out harshly. And then she sank back down to sit on the sofa again.

'It was a night for me,' she muttered fiercely. 'Just for *me*. Just one night. And now this.'

'I'm sorry.' And he truly was. He knew she didn't do one-night stands. He knew she wasn't all that experienced. And the one time she'd let herself go? 'You've got to tell me what you're thinking.'

Because she was thinking—overthinking—if the tight expression on her face was anything to go by. A myriad of emotions flickered in her eyes, but mostly misery.

Finally she turned towards him, squaring her slim shoulders. 'I'm going to have the baby.'

Yes, he'd known that she would.

But then she spoke some more. 'You don't have to…'

A fierce fury enveloped him as she started to negate his input. 'I don't have to *what*?'

Her lack of answer sent him on the attack. 'You doubt I'd want to be involved?'

'You can't even bring yourself to take a dog

for a walk,' she flared up. 'How are you going to meet a baby's needs?'

'I only said I couldn't walk the dog because I wanted to see more of you,' he ground out. 'You know it was my excuse to get you up to my penthouse.'

Her eyes widened and her mouth opened. But she remained speechless. He glared right back at her. She really *hadn't* known that?

He muttered something unprintable beneath his breath. 'I wanted you the second I laid eyes on you, Ettie. And it was the same for you. Frankly, I still want you. Isn't that a good place for us to begin this?'

Her mouth hung open for another moment. Then she snapped it shut and vehemently shook her head. 'There is no *this*. And *that* doesn't last.'

Didn't it? Because it had already lasted longer for her than for any other woman in his life.

He stilled, rapidly reassessing his strategy. He had a highly developed capacity to think through all possible problems, combinations, options in a situation…and he was equally swift to sift and find solutions. An unplanned pregnancy was the antithesis of his life's ambition.

He'd never wanted a child. Never wanted a long-term relationship. He'd never even considered it. But fate in the form of a failed condom was forcing both upon him.

He could barely bring himself to think of an actual baby. It was too tiny, too vulnerable. He wouldn't even know how to hold the thing. He ran a hand through his hair and dragged back his focus. He'd do what he was good at—*management*.

While he could provide many important things—wealth, home, an elite education…those things weren't what really mattered. But he'd ensure it had everything he hadn't had. Safety. Security…

He glanced back up and saw her sitting on that sofa—her arm already curved across her flat belly in an instinctive, unconsciously protective maternal gesture as she watched him with a very wary expression on her face.

For only a second did he brood on those old, darkest of memories. The fear, the pain, the isolation. His mother had hated him and she'd shown it in almost every action of almost every day.

But Ettie would be a good mother. Probably

too good, given that she put everyone else ahead of herself. She did everything within her power for those she loved.

But it was a shame that it had happened so soon for her and with him of all people. Guilt sucked the strength from his bones. He never should have seduced her. He'd been selfish and greedy and now changed her life irrevocably. Because that baby she was carrying was his.

His inner animal wanted to beat his chest and roar. He'd not stopped wanting her in these past few weeks but he'd been determined to do the right thing. He'd kept his distance, respected her wishes…not messed more personally with his latest business acquisition. He'd tried to restore his own control and not break those rules all over again. But this changed everything.

It was very simple now. The baby would have Ettie. And Ettie would have him.

And there was only one tolerable course of action to ensure that: *marriage*.

It would be an amicable, workable arrangement—basically an acquisition like any other. They just needed to hammer out the terms, come to an agreement and settle it.

But, given the way she was freaking out in

front of him, she was going to resist. He was going to have to go gently with her. One thing he'd learned in his business dealings was that in a takeover the acquisition generally loathed being ordered to do something.

'I want to go home.' She glanced at him and defiance shone in her eyes. 'I need some space.'

Leon bit his tongue. Hard. She wasn't staying in that hellhole of an apartment a moment longer.

'This is a shock,' he said after a moment. 'But we're going to figure a way through it. I am trying really hard here not to…'

'Take total control?' she guessed coldly. 'Keep trying.'

He glared at her and made himself draw in another steadying breath. 'I'd like you to live with me,' he said. 'I'd like not to have to worry about you when you're not here.'

'You'd worry that I wasn't doing a good enough job alone?' She got defensive.

He bit back a growl and tried to take even more care over his words. 'You're very good at taking care of other people. Yourself, not so much.'

'I've looked after Ophelia all my life. And

myself. I can take care of it,' she said defiantly. 'It's my baby.'

Her statement of claim sent sparks through his blood. There was the fierce tigress—all passion and protectiveness—but he was every bit as protective.

'Mine too,' he shot back. Screw gentle. 'And *we* will take care of it.'

The look she sent him was pure mistrust and it was so damn unwarranted, it riled him more. 'We're equally responsible, so we'll handle this together.'

She looked away.

He got it. He did. Or he tried to. She was used to taking care of everything by herself. He didn't know much about her mother, but he got that Ettie, the child, had been the responsible one. She'd been the primary carer for her whole little family. But she needed to understand that he wasn't going anywhere.

'I will not abandon you,' he ground edgily through gritted teeth. 'And you're not staying in that damp apartment. That's not happening.'

'It's my home.'

Not any more. 'You'll move in with me. Immediately.'

'You're not even asking now,' she said in an accusatory tone. 'You're dictating.'

'Yeah.'

She stared at him, clearly shocked by his unashamed affirmation of the fact.

'I'm not tiptoeing around, Ettie. Be where you need to be.' He shrugged. 'I'm not going anywhere and nor are you.'

Her fragility frightened him, her resistance frustrated him. His own wants made him grouchiest of all. He wanted her in his bed but he couldn't have that now. He'd have this sorted instead. It was an easy enough fix if they could both keep their cool. He'd tried to reassure her and take it slow, but he was used to giving orders and having them instantly obeyed. 'You're not going to wake up in the morning and find me gone.'

Her skin flooded with colour. Because yeah, that was exactly what she'd done to him. He strode over and hunched down in front of her, striking while he had the advantage. 'We'll get engaged.'

'We'll *what*?' She actually shrank back from him.

'I don't want everyone thinking you're just

my live-in lover or latest affair; I want you to have more status than that.' He drew in another deep breath but it did little to take the edge off the irritation that was festering with her refusal.

'Oh,' she said poisonously. 'Because as your fiancée I'd have *so* much *status*.' Her words simply dripped with sarcasm.

'Ettie,' he couldn't help a half-laugh, 'don't be a witch.' He leaned closer. 'I want this child to be legitimate. It should have its rightful inheritance. This is *my* reputation as well as yours.'

She wrinkled her nose. 'You care about your reputation?'

'I keep my personal life discreet.' His personal life generally consisted of pleasurable screws with swift conclusions. 'I'm seen as reliable for my investors. That matters to my business.'

And he was certain it mattered to her. She was afraid he'd abandon her—well, this was one way of showing he wasn't about to. 'We'll get a ring and announce our engagement—'

'I'm *not* getting engaged again,' she blurted, before blushing beetroot.

'Again?' Leon stilled as her words sank in and a balloon of outrage burst in his gut. 'You've been engaged before?'

CHAPTER SIX

ETTIE SEEMED TO have frozen in place on the sofa. 'We don't know each other at all, Leon. This just can't work.'

'Tell me what happened,' Leon said grimly.

'It doesn't matter what happened,' she snapped.

'Obviously it does, because it's rendering you irrational now.'

'Me irrational? You're the crazy one—insisting on marriage when it's completely unnecessary.'

Actually, it was imperative. The more he thought about it, the more crucial the concept had become.

But she leapt up from the sofa and paced away from him. 'I'm not going through that humiliation again,' she muttered. 'I'm no longer that stupid, naive girl who believed in happy-ever-after.'

Her vehemence drew a smile from him. 'You believed in happy-ever-after?'

She lifted her chin in the face of his amusement. 'Why shouldn't I have?' But then she blushed again and turned away as some bitter memory made her face fall. 'Forget it.'

He considered her words quickly—*humiliation, naivety*. 'He broke up with you?'

She nodded.

He didn't press for more details. Now wasn't the time. 'I'm not promising you moon dust,' he said with simple clarity. 'I'm not declaring undying devotion. We'll have no lies. No false promises.' He drew in a breath as the perfect plan crystallised in his mind. 'Don't think of this as a traditional marriage proposal. This isn't romantic love, rainbows and unicorns, this is a real solution to a real issue,' he said. 'Obviously I'll financially support both you and the baby one hundred per cent. That's a given. But here's my offer. If you marry me, I will pay for all of Ophelia's schooling. Not just the rest of this year, but all her university studies as well. She wants to do medicine, correct? So a decade or thereabouts of training and specialisation? Paid for. She doesn't have to stress about getting a scholarship, she just needs to be accepted onto the course. She can choose any university—hell, any country; if she wants to do some parts of it in the States, Europe…that's fine. All fees, all accommodation costs, living costs, everything. I have it covered. She only has to get the grades.'

He paused, watching intently for her response.

She was motionless, her clear-eyed gaze fixed upon him. 'You can't possibly—'

'Say the word and I'll have my lawyer draw up the contract. I do not enter contracts lightly, Ettie. And I do not break them. This is a legitimate offer. All you have to do is accept it.'

'By marrying you.' Her focus wavered.

'Yes.'

'But we don't love each other.'

'That's irrelevant.' He dismissed the concern with ruthless efficiency. This wasn't about anything emotional, this was about security, practicality, plain common sense.

She swallowed. 'You would expect us to remain married…for good?'

Something stirred low in his gut at her question. He ignored it. 'I don't see why it shouldn't work out long-term. However, if things became difficult between us personally, then we'd find an alternative solution. My financial commitment to your sister wouldn't be broken, however.

Nor to you. As the mother of my child, you will always have a home.'

Ettie reeled. He made it sound like she'd won the lottery. 'Why can't we find that alternative solution now?'

'Because I will not allow my child to be born illegitimately,' he reiterated sharply. 'However, I don't imagine that things would become difficult. We work together well, Ettie.'

Work together? He really saw this as an emotionless, uncomplicated resolution? Obviously for him it was exactly that. Because apparently it wouldn't be the 'done thing' for him to have an illegitimate child with a service worker…

And he was playing on her loyalty and love for her sister to get what he wanted. It was ruthless of him. But she suddenly realised that that was what he did—targeted an acquisition and did what it took to make the deal happen. And he did it damn fast. No wonder he'd made all that money by such a young age.

'You know I can support you, Ettie. I have the finances and the wherewithal to ensure both you and the baby have everything you need,' he said firmly.

The shutters on Ettie's bruised heart closed. 'The baby will need more than financial security.'

She needed more too. Because she knew happiness came from something other than money. But she had the feeling she wasn't about to get it.

'Of course, but the basics in life also matter. Food, clothing, decent accommodation.'

His cold emphasis on the latter irked her enough to spell it out. 'What about emotional security?'

'You already love the baby.'

His simple, swift assertion silenced her and to her horror tears sprang to her eyes. Because in that instant she realised she did. As shockingly unexpected, as inconvenient, as *new* as it all was…it was wonderful. Raw emotion swept over her at the thought of that tiny little being growing inside her. Their baby. Her imagination sprang into overtime, sending her images of a beautiful child—a female Leon, or maybe a mini-me little boy… If this baby had half Leon's looks, it was going to melt every heart.

'Write the list, Ettie.' He was watching her coolly as if analysing her every word, every expression. 'All the reasons for, all the reasons against. Make your decision from there.'

There was no 'decision' and he knew it. The arrangement he'd offered was impossible for her to refuse. Because it wasn't about her. It was about this tiny baby. And it was about Ophelia. Leon was offering complete security for them both. Ophelia could just relax and focus on her studies without the added pressure of trying to get a scholarship. He'd said she could apply to any university and Ettie knew he meant it. It was incredibly generous…

But Leon didn't really want *her*. It had been a one-night-stand—that was all he'd wanted. And she'd lived with the consequences of a one-night stand. Her sister, Ophelia.

She and Ophelia had both been unwanted by their fathers. She'd watched her mother become embittered by the betrayal of the men she'd wanted to love…to the point where she no longer coped with the normal demands of life. And Ettie had been a fool for love too, hadn't she? Flattered by the first man to pay her attention… She'd been such an idiot. And now?

Leon Kariakis didn't actually want anything from her. He had more money than he knew what to do with and he had an endless stream of willing women. He was simply stuck with her and being honourable about it—saying all the right things, attempting to do the right things. But wasn't that only going to lead to resentment in the end? He'd never want to be trapped together for good with her. And his 'contract' was too unbalanced. He was offering a ring and room in his penthouse…and what did she bring to the party? Her overly efficient womb.

'You're offering all this…paying for so much,' she said awkwardly. 'It doesn't seem fair. What do you get out of it?'

His expression smouldered. 'I get what I want.'

Something heavy shifted within her. That low drag deep in her belly that pulled her towards him. But he meant the baby, right?

'Ettie.' That low, irresistible growl sounded.

'Yes.' It whispered out before she'd even thought it.

He was the one who moved, walking towards her until there was too little space between them. 'Let's go and get your things from your flat.' His voice was husky.

She couldn't move.

'Ettie…' He put his hand on her waist. The

amber lights glowed in his deep brown eyes. But he didn't smile. He looked edgier than ever as he applied pressure and pulled her against him until she was in no doubt of his physical response to her.

'Will this be...part of the contract?' She flung her chin up, determined to hold her own with him. Because if she couldn't do that now, she had no chance of keeping him in check.

Something flashed in his eyes. 'I'll be faithful to you and I expect the same in return. But I'm not going to demand sexual favours. There won't be a clause detailing a minimum number of intimacies each week.'

She opened her mouth, shocked at the suggestion. At the appallingly hot response of her treacherous body to such a requirement.

'If anything happens, it's up to us in that moment. Just like normal,' he said. 'No expectations, no repercussions...regardless of what we do in private.'

No repercussions? It was so ironic, but she couldn't laugh. Right now she couldn't even breathe.

He ran his hand down her spine, coming to

rest his palm on the curve of her hip. 'Maybe we should stop negotiating...'

Her body melted. He was seducing her into saying yes. And she knew he could, so easily. Abruptly she pulled out from his hold. 'Maybe you don't try to distract me like that.'

'Maybe that kind of distraction would be good for you,' he countered with a small smile.

Sensation rippled down her spine. 'Maybe we should just go and get my stuff.'

She heard his low laugh as she walked away. She realised too late that he'd manipulated her into doing what he wanted. He'd easily played her...because he knew she was weak with want for him still. She screwed her eyes shut; that was *so* mortifying. Echoes of her ex-fiancé's callousness circled in her head—building her demons of insecurity. She *hated* her inexperience.

'Come on, *glykia mou*. Let's get moving.'

'What does it mean?' she asked. 'That expression?'

Another flicker of a smile curved his lips. 'My sweet.'

'You think that's going to get you extra points?' she asked tartly. But she was breathless beneath the weak sarcasm. It was *really* unfair of him because he didn't mean it.

'I think it's only a matter of time,' he murmured wryly. 'And I think you know it as well as I do.'

'You weren't interested in a repeat,' she said stiffly.

'Because you shut me down.' He shot her an astounded look. 'I was respecting *your* wishes.' And he didn't look all that happy about it.

Her heart thundered. He'd thought she'd shut him down? 'And now?'

'All bets are off.'

Craving curled through her body. Intense, shocking, explicit want. It was desire for contact, right? Physical closeness because she felt alone. It was just an instinctive, basic need that she was determined to suppress.

'The situation is what it is, Ettie,' he added. 'We might as well make the most of it.'

'And in your world "making the most of it" is us sleeping together again?' she jeered bitterly.

'We do it pretty well.'

Pretty well? Great. For him it had been just as average as she'd feared and he was just using *her* weakness for him to get what he wanted.

He suddenly chuckled. 'Oh, Ettie, you're so transparent.'

Before she could argue he turned her to face him and brushed his lips over hers in the lightest whisper of a kiss. Her breathing faltered—all that tantalising promise was only a breath away. But he didn't mean any of it.

'It's not fair of you to tease me this way.' She valiantly defended her heart when he lifted his head from hers.

Because he knew, didn't he, just how overwhelmed she was by his sensuality?

But at her words he stilled. A second after the lift door opened, she found herself with her back against the wall of the lift and he was right there in front of her. Hot, fierce fury unfurled deep and low in her belly at the smoking expression in his eyes.

'I'm not teasing,' he muttered.

Leon slammed his mouth over hers—determined to draw out her spark even if it was only because she was aggravated with him. He wanted her fire. He kissed her hard and deep, plundering her softness with a flick of his tongue. The flare within her was instant. Her hunger took him by surprise and unleashed his own. Hell, he'd wanted this and he'd been too long denied. He curled her arms around his neck so he could haul her closer and grind her against the wall. Her fingers twisted and locked in his hair.

The heady relief at having her in his arms again contrasted with the burning desire tightening his body to the point of pain. He was angry she'd held him at bay when she so clearly craved his touch the way he ached for hers. Now he was mad with her. Now he wanted to torment her. To please her.

She moaned as he cupped her breast with a firm, greedy hand. Her nipple strained against her shirt. Her fingers tightened in his hair. She was so hot he lost his head completely, rushing straight back into that insane intensity of all-consuming lust. He'd suffered weeks of being without this. He didn't know how he'd stood it.

A bell pinged somewhere in the distance. It took him a moment to realise that the lift door had slid open.

'Oh, excuse me.'

Leon froze and glanced down at Ettie, amused to see her turn bright pink. She hurriedly disentangled her fingers from his hair and craned her head to see who it was talking.

It turned out the lift hadn't stopped at the basement. He hadn't even had the brains to push the damn buttons in his haste to touch her. The lift had been summoned by another resident. As a result it had stopped halfway down the building and right now Autumn Welby was staring at them with frank fascination.

'I'll wait for the lift to return. Nice to see you're back, Ettie,' she said breezily. 'I'm so glad you're feeling better.'

Leon glanced again at Ettie, but now she'd gone pale. He tightened one arm around her waist and reached out with the other to push the button on the lift.

'Ettie won't be back on the concierge desk for the foreseeable future,' he said briskly, sending Autumn a dismissive smile.

'Oh.' Autumn nodded. 'Lovely for you, terrible for me.'

The lift doors slid shut again and he looked back into Ettie's face to see nothing but fury.

'For the foreseeable future?' she repeated in a frigid voice. 'Just like that, Leon?'

Yeah, just like that. He wasn't about to apologise and he didn't have the brain to explain it all just yet.

She extricated herself from his arm and folded her own across her chest, all but tapping her foot as the lift swept down to the basement.

'Everyone will know now.' She threw him an appalled look as she stomped out into the garage. 'Everyone will know in minutes.'

'Ettie, we're getting married. You're having my baby.' He followed her slowly, determined to remain calm and get his head around her response to that kiss. 'They're going to find out some time anyway; it might as well be now.'

She drew herself up short and whirled to face him. 'But it's so early…'

A horrible thought hit. Was she worried about miscarrying the baby? Was that even a possibility? A surge of protectiveness—and self-condemnation—welled in him. He shouldn't be pawing her when she needed rest.

'Everything will be fine.' He pushed past the hoarseness in his voice and led her to his roadster. He didn't want his driver for this ride. He needed his own hands on the wheel. 'You're fit, healthy, strong.'

And so damn beautiful that all he wanted to do was scoop her into his arms, toss her onto the nearest bed and pick up where they'd left off before they'd been so brutally interrupted. But he couldn't exhaust her with his selfish lust. He had to put both her and the baby ahead of his own desire. Ettie needed certainty and security. She had too many worries, too many responsibilities. But he'd lift them from her. And while lust might not last, it would get them through this phase until they settled into a long-term arrangement. He could provide her with a lifestyle she'd only ever dreamed about. She'd never have to worry about paying for her own groceries or heating again. She didn't have to scrimp and save for her sister's education. She could care for their baby and breathe easily for the rest of her life. Those key points she could never argue against and never beat. He had this situation won and she knew it.

'You'll have to get another car.' She glanced at the Italian two-seater.

He nodded.

'What about Ophelia's holidays?'

'I have plenty of space.' He didn't tell her he meant his London home. They weren't staying at Cavendish House another night. She was too uncomfortable and he understood that. They needed privacy. She needed the space to let go of her inhibitions—to scream his name as she came.

Cool it, Romeo. He mocked himself. She was exhausted and overwhelmed and the last thing she needed was him making physical demands on her. He'd won already. He could wait a little longer.

CHAPTER SEVEN

IT TOOK ETTIE only five minutes later to fill a small case with clothes and a few very personal effects from her flat. She went to fetch her coat from where it hung over the back of a chair.

'Leave it,' he said. 'We'll get you a new one.'

She stiffened, saddened that he'd noticed how worn it was. She cast a last glance around the room. How was it possible that such a tiny apartment could feel so empty? She'd helped her sister learn to read here. She'd made Ophelia's lunches and cleaned her uniforms. For so long it had been the two of them against the world…

And she wasn't telling Ophelia about this yet. Not until she'd got control of everything—mostly her emotions.

'I'll get the rest of your things boxed up; don't worry about any of it.'

Don't worry?

Her mother had fallen for the wrong man more than once. Ettie had made an almighty mistake putting her faith in a guy already… But maybe Leon's way was right? Maybe it was as simple as writing up the list—the pros and the cons and being cool-headed about it.

He wanted the baby. She came with it. So he'd keep her happy to keep her onside—give her a home, help support her sister. He might even have sex with her if she played her cards right. But even that for him wasn't *emotional.* It was a relaxant—a satisfying physical release. An added bonus to the deal they'd made.

Maybe it could be just fun for her too? Maybe she could be more like Leon? He seemed to have it so completely together…

The irony was that everything had been pretty fine—better than it had in ages actually. She'd been making it work in this final stretch of Ophelia's schooling. But now it felt as if her life had fragmented and all the elements were slipping from her control. She was furious with herself. But she couldn't quite regret it completely.

She watched Leon drive them back into the heart of London. He seemed to enjoy controlling the powerful machine. He appeared as calm as ever. Certain of his place in the world and the decisions he made. It was as if his handsome face had been carved from marble by a master craftsman. Expressionless. Emotionless, he'd locked back into business focus easily. So he really had only been teasing moments ago, while she'd been almost *desperate* for his touch. Now she shivered with a horrible fear she was going to feel even more alone living in his apartment.

'Where are we going?' She sat up and twisted to read the road sign. 'We just went past Cavendish House.'

'We're going home.'

'The penthouse there is your home.'

'No, that's where I was staying for a few weeks while I studied my new investment. *This* is my home.'

They'd turned into a quiet side street in the heart of Mayfair. Her heart ceased beating. It wasn't an apartment in a building, but the *whole* building. She'd known he was wealthy, but this wasn't a millionaire's penthouse; this property was worth multi-multi-millions—a billionaire's mansion in one of the most expensive streets on the planet.

'How many bedrooms?' she muttered.

'Only six.' He walked ahead of her. 'Four bathrooms.'

Oh, was that all? She shook her head after him as he led the way. There was a gleaming kitchen—light, airy, equipped with appliances Ettie wouldn't know how to turn on…

'There's a catering kitchen and staff quarters downstairs.'

She blinked. 'You have a lot of staff?'

'I have a housekeeper; she doesn't live on site but she comes every other day. She'll prep food for us if we want. My executive assistant sometimes uses it if we're working late on a deal.'

'Oh?' She tried not to imagine his beautiful assistant. 'I expect she's very efficient.'

Leon sent her a sideways, all too knowing look. 'He is.'

Ettie stared, overwhelmed by the trio of reception rooms. The home gym and pool and cinema room almost gave her conniptions. It was all beautifully furnished in muted greys and neutrals, with pops of colour—shades of blue in a few rooms, green in another. The curved wrought-iron balustrade of the staircase revealed snippets of the delights of each level. There were both polished wooden floors and plush carpets, and the light fittings sparkled like works of art themselves…speaking of which, striking paintings adorned the walls. The bathrooms were lined with vast marble and gleaming chrome… the entire house was a simply exquisite, designer's wet dream.

Yeah, he'd really been slumming it at Cavendish House. She'd thought *that* was exclusive, but this was a whole new level of luxury.

'Why did you buy it?' she asked out of complete curiosity. What did he need such a big home for?

He looked surprised by her question. 'I liked it.' He glanced around the recreation room. 'Don't you like it?'

She'd have to be mad not to adore it. She thought of the inviting crystal-clear blue of his indoor pool and the spa alongside it. 'You use the beauty treatment room often?'

Grinning, he shook his head. 'No, nor the bar and home cinema much either. You're welcome to it all, of course; this is your home now.'

She didn't think she'd ever feel at home in such an immaculate, luxurious space. It seemed every item in it was unique and priceless.

'Where are the bedrooms?'

He led her up the curving staircase. 'There are a couple of bedrooms on each of these floors.

The study up on the top floor opens onto a rooftop terrace; it's nice on sunny days. But this is my room.'

His bedroom alone was larger than her entire flat. An enormous bed was the centrepiece, but the room was large enough to hold a sofa and an armchair as well as a beautiful wooden cabinet. A wide doorway offered a glimpse of the gleaming marble and black finish of his bathroom.

She cleared her throat. 'Which is my room?'

He sent her a glinting look. 'If you don't want to be in mine, you can choose any of the others. Though I'd prefer it if you were on the same floor as me. For later in the pregnancy.'

No, she did not want to be in his room, or even on his *floor*. He wasn't having everything his own way.

Ettie snatched up her bag and marched to the bedroom furthest from his, knowing damn well she was spiting herself as much as him in this small act of defiance.

'I'm going to run a couple of errands,' he said coolly, following her to the room she chose. 'I'll be back in an hour or so. You take your time and settle in.'

'Okay,' she said.

'Fancy anything in particular to eat?'

She shook her head. 'Whatever you think will be nice.'

He nodded and left.

It took only a moment for Ettie to hang her few clothes—they really didn't suit the designer walk-in wardrobe. With a rueful grimace, she walked around the house again—taking in more details now Leon wasn't here to distract her. It really was incredible. It even had its own garden, which in this space-at-a-premium part of London was almost unheard-of. The whole place was impeccably maintained—that housekeeper clearly had fun keeping it pristine and photo-spread-worthy, with perfectly folded towels at the ready and vases of fresh flowers to give the place vibrancy. All this for one guy?

He came from a completely different world to hers.

But what struck her even more was the lack of anything particularly personal of Leon's on display. There were no family photos, or holiday snaps. The only vaguely personal images were some arty black and white shots of some buildings—buildings he owned, including this one.

It seemed his property empire was everything he cared about.

She returned to the bedroom she'd chosen and walked into the stunning white and grey marble bathroom. She simply couldn't resist that deep-set bath. Not when there was that selection of French perfumed soaps and salts to add to it. Not when she needed to relax so badly. A few minutes later she sank into the gloriously scented, warm depths.

But her raging thoughts wouldn't quieten. That was impossible when her world had been totally turned upside down. Leon Kariakis was insisting they marry. Offering a *contract,* not his heart. But she was going to be okay with that because she was *not* going to make the mistakes of her own past, or of her mother's. She was going to learn from Leon—be businesslike and efficient.

She slipped lower, appreciating the silken slide of the water on her bare skin, and her mind wandered to less *businesslike* imaginings. This bath was definitely built big enough for two.

All thoughts of efficiency fled as sexual frustration suddenly flared. Why hadn't he touched her again since they were interrupted in that lift? That kiss had been incendiary and she ached for more. The nausea that had plagued her for days had dissipated as arousal replaced it. She wanted him to send her into that place where thoughts couldn't impinge, where there was only feeling and pleasure and so much *touch*...

'Ettie?'

She almost jumped right out of the bath.

'Sorry, I won't be a minute,' she gasped. 'I'm just in the bath.'

There was a moment's silence on the other side of the door. 'You must be hungry.' He sounded a little huskier.

Absolutely. But not for what he meant. 'Sure. I won't be long.'

She levered herself out of the bath, wrapped her body in one of the enormous plush towels and quickly dressed.

He was waiting for her in the kitchen. 'I got this for you,' he said without preamble, pushing a small box across the counter to her.

Ettie's heart stopped. Reluctantly, but unable to refuse, she opened the box. She blinked a couple of times, almost blinded. 'Where'd you get it from?'

'Christmas cracker, where do you think?'

'You bought it?'

'Well, I didn't steal it.' He rolled his eyes.

She didn't ask if it was synthetic. She didn't want to give him another chance to look smug.

'You can't just buy what you want,' she muttered, her resistance to him building in a wave of heat and fury. Because it was such a beautiful ring and there was that weak, romantic, *foolish* part of her that would've loved to be given this in another time, another circumstance, with other words… 'You can't buy me,' she added ferociously.

'I know that,' he said softly. 'If there's anyone who knows money can't buy happiness, it's me.'

His reply struck her silent. Unexpected and revealing—had he not been happy? When? She waited, willing him to say more. Instead she watched that expressionless veil slide across the flare in his eyes.

'Just put it on, Ettie.'

It was a flawless square-cut emerald set in a platinum band. A large diamond sat either side of the pale green stone. Simple yet sublime, and so very stunning.

She stalled for time because she was shaking

inside. She'd never touched anything like it in her life. 'You often go out to get takeaways and come back with precious jewels?'

'Every Wednesday. You can set your watch by me.'

Smart Alec. 'I thought this was business.'

'It's personal business.' But there was a glint flicking in his eyes again. 'And it is straightforward.'

How could it be? He didn't think this was complicated?

Was this really just another acquisition for him—a fiancée and a baby? He was so in control and unconcerned and capable. Didn't he feel fear? Didn't he feel anything? Was he really as emotionless as he appeared?

'Stop overthinking. It'll work out.' He walked around the counter, took the ring out of the box and reached out to hold her cold hand. 'For the baby, okay? You want your child to have two actively involved parents. Here you go. A united front. A team, Ettie.'

She sent him a baleful look. She did want that, very much. Because it was what she hadn't had and he knew it. He was counting on that as he slid the ring down.

But people co-parented the world over with perfectly amicable arrangements and weren't married or even engaged. They made it work. There was no reason why she and Leon couldn't work out something just as successful.

Except his argument for marriage was compelling. She too wanted her child to have the security Leon was offering. And she'd nailed being practical at work, so why couldn't she apply the same to her personal life?

Intuition sent a tinge of unease down her spine. The problem was *his* magnetism. He only needed to stand this close, to hold her hand like this, and her heart was racing, sending excitement through every vein, to every cell. Ettie could fall far and fast—make the mistake of believing that, rather than being his "for the practicalities" fiancée, she was his match for real. And that wasn't fair on him. Or on her. Because the same was so not happening for him. He was *only* about the practicalities.

So she had to focus on the same. Keep her guard up, warn off her weak, blind heart.

She hauled together all her emotional strength and pulled her hand from his, tore her gaze from his. She'd accept this for what it was.

She smiled down at the ring. 'It's beautiful, thank you.' Then she turned, desperately commenting on the first thing she saw. 'I didn't know you already had a dog.' She was determined to make things easy and casual between them.

Blinking, he sent her a mystified look.

'The dog bowl on the bench behind you?'

'Oh?' His eyebrows snapped down, forming a frown. 'I ordered those when I thought that Toby might stay.'

Really?

'I'm sorry I said yes to that resident taking him without talking to you first,' she muttered thoughtfully. The sense she'd wronged him somehow in making that choice had been nagging her for these last couple of days.

'Don't apologise; it was best for the dog,' he said crisply.

So he hadn't really wanted him? But she'd sent Toby to that other resident the very next day, so Leon had been super-quick off the mark getting in bowls for him. But that was just his hyper-efficiency, wasn't it? Just as he'd convinced her to agree to marrying him and ensconced her in his home within two hours of learning she was pregnant. It was how he was a billionaire before thirty. Leon Kariakis got stuff done with single-minded, ruthless efficiency and there was nothing emotional about it.

Yet she couldn't look away from him—aware once more of that simmering intensity that his stillness masked. He'd loosened his tie and his shirtsleeves were rolled back and a tuft of hair was still ruffled. She suspected it was from when she'd run her fingers through his hair in the lift earlier. Did he know how tormenting he was?

'You're feeling better.' He changed the subject.

Yes. With every step closer she was to him unfortunately. And she was incredibly curious. He wasn't just a closed book. He was padlocked-and-sealed-in-an-underground-vault private. But they were having a baby together. Getting married. Even in business arrangements, people did due diligence, didn't they? Maybe if she offered information first—broke the ice—he might feel a gentle obligation to reciprocate?

'My father wasn't there for me. Ever,' she said quietly.

He paused and glanced at her.

'So thank you for wanting to stick around.'

He tensed. 'I'm not like him.'

'I know.' The guy was already a better father than what her own had been and what Ophelia's had been by the simple fact he was actually interested. 'My mother got her heart broken a couple of times. It hurt her badly.' She was quiet a moment before summoning courage. 'What about your parents?'

'Absent, mostly.'

Really? She was surprised. 'Didn't they turn up to sports day?'

'No. Are you ready to eat? You must be hungry.'

She frowned, irritated that he'd shut that conversation down so quickly. 'We can't just…start living together and being engaged. We need to get to know each other, Leon.'

He blinked at her again. 'What do you want to know?'

'I don't know. Anything.' Everything. She glanced at those empty bowls on the far bench. 'Did you have a dog when you were a kid?'

'No.' To her amazement his expression became like blank granite. 'Come on, dinner is on the table.'

'Which one?' she asked tartly.

Leon knew he'd been abrupt, but some things

she didn't need to know. Life was for living in *now*, not remembering the miseries of the past. He tried to ignore the prickling at the base of his spine. He was satisfied she was in his house finally, yet he was unbearably aware of her in his space. The mansion was large but her presence seemed to permeate every inch…the scent of her, the soft sounds as she moved about.

He'd had to get out just to clear his head. Sort out the ring as consideration for the contract. Decide on dinner. Check in with his assistant and ensure everything at the office was under control…but he'd listened with only half-concentration and in the end he'd not been able to get back fast enough to check on her.

Stupid to be so concerned. He knew emotions weakened a man—muddying the mind and making decision-making difficult. Isolation and independence brought clarity. There were mergers and acquisitions, splits and divisions, and this was just another. It should be simple.

'Oh.'

He suppressed a chuckle as Ettie came to a halt at the entrance to the formal dining room.

'When did you do this?' She gaped at the table laden with dishes.

'It was delivered while you were in the bath.'

She gazed from the table to the discreet trolley in the corner. 'It's from a restaurant.'

Yeah, as concierge to an exclusive apartment building, she knew how it worked. He paid, the staff delivered. And it was worth it for the privacy.

She lifted the silver cover of the nearest dish and her eyebrows lifted. 'Do you only dine from award-winning restaurants?'

He took a seat and stared at her with all the lazy arrogance he could muster. 'I like savouring perfection,' he drawled.

She rolled her eyes and he laughed in delight.

'You asked for it,' he ribbed her. 'You think I'm pompous? I can eat a wrap on the street from a food van like anyone else, but tonight I want to sit in comfort and privacy and let *all* my senses feast.' He sent her a meaningful look. 'I have a pretty companion to ogle. Besides which, you're tired and you need a decent meal.'

And frankly, her enjoyment of decent food increased his own pleasure in it.

She sighed and sank into the chair opposite his. 'You're so used to doing everything your own way, aren't you?'

'Isn't everyone?'

She laughed aloud, a bubble of genuine amusement. 'The fate of the only child,' she teased. 'You've never had to learn to compromise.'

He tried to smile but his mouth had swiftly dried. It wasn't her fault. She simply didn't know.

'You're very serious,' she continued her judgement. 'Hard-working.'

'It's how I became successful.' He tried not to sound like a stiff-necked ass, but it was true.

'So,' she angled her head to study him, that teasing light brightening her eyes even more, 'not a wild playboy…at least not publicly. You were never the spoilt heir to a fortune who fritters it all away on women and wine and destructive vices…'

'No, that's not me.'

'But why not?' She seemed quite fascinated. 'It's the trap lots of people in your position fall into, isn't it? Stories like that fill the news… Playboy heirs. Dissolute, depraved, who end up broke—'

'Or dying of an overdose; I get the picture,' he finished coldly. 'I guess that's not the way I was raised.'

'So how were you raised?'

He eyed her across the table and she met his censuring look with a radiant smile of utter innocence. Yeah, she knew what she was doing and he knew she wasn't about to let up.

'Strictly,' he muttered.

'You said they were absent.' She looked thoughtful. 'Do you see them now?'

He didn't think of his parents much and he certainly never discussed them. Why would he? But he had to give her something—she was like a dog with a bone. The bald facts would do. 'We have dinner once every six months. It's scheduled—the full year in advance. We discuss returns, hotel occupancy rates, the stock market.'

Her eyes widened. 'Twice a year?'

'Yes.'

'And that's it?'

'Yes.' He could see her mind working overtime.

'Do you ever take a date?'

'Never. It's an obligation on both sides. They never doubted I would do anything other than succeed. And they ensured I was never spoiled by the wealth I was born into.'

He pointedly stabbed a chunk of steak and

shoved it into his mouth. That was enough, surely? She was more curious than a barn full of cats. And the meat tasted like sawdust and glue. He made it go down with a hard swallow. 'Look, I know you're worried about how little we know of each other, but it isn't something that can be forced, or hurried,' he said, closing off the conversation. 'Time will take care of it.'

She still looked thoughtful. And utterly unconvinced. 'Most people wouldn't work as hard as you if they didn't have to.'

'Why not? Don't we all need a purpose? A sense of dignity from a job well done? What makes you think I wouldn't need that too?'

'But to be so driven… When is it enough?' She gestured at the furnishings in the large room. 'What is it you have to prove?'

'I don't need to prove anything,' he growled. 'Perhaps it's just that the goalposts shift. I make a plan to achieve one thing, when it's knocked off I feel like a challenge for something more. Isn't that human nature?'

A shadow crossed her eyes. 'So you're never satisfied with what you have?'

His chest tightened and he laughed and groaned at the same time because her effervescent curiosity was going to be the death of him. But she was irresistible. It was that manner that made her so popular with the residents at Cavendish House. She made you feel like you could confide everything in her and she'd sort it all out for you. 'I'm satisfied,' he growled. 'I just want *more*.'

Right now he was greedy for *her*. She was wearing a thin old T-shirt and jeans that hung a little loose. But she was still flushed from that bath and her skin looked luminous and silky soft. She smelled tantalising and her hair was a wild, damp mess down her back and he just wanted to thrust his hands into the gorgeous length of it and bind her close beneath him.

'I'll tell you something, Ettie,' he said bluntly, shoving those X-rated thoughts to the back of his mind, 'when you come from a background like mine, you swiftly learn that people only stick around because they want something from you.'

She perked up. 'Is that true, really?' She looked at him keenly, a teasing smile flicking at her mouth. 'Aren't there any uncomplicated, nice people out there who just want to be friends?'

He couldn't help but laugh. 'Perhaps I'm too prejudiced to be able to spot them.' He leaned closer and called her out on it. 'Even you wanted something from me.'

'But you wanted the same thing from me.' She wagged a finger at him. 'So that makes us even.'

'I'm as bad as you?' he asked in mock-outrage.

'Possibly worse. Because you took advantage of everything you have to seduce me.'

'And you didn't?' He scoffed. 'With your wild ponytail and passionate eyes?'

'My what?' She looked astounded.

'All the emotions.' He pointed to her eyes, suddenly quite serious. 'Here.'

'What are my eyes expressing now?' she asked, still but breathless.

He stared at her intently—searching those beautifully clear eyes for the signal he'd wanted for so long. And then it was there.

'Your desire for me to take you to bed.' He simply snapped. He didn't want to think any more. Didn't want to try to solve unworkable problems. Damn well didn't want to talk around the issues or, heaven forbid, his freaking past. He didn't want to think of her being hurt by some jerk and her mum dying and leaving her to raise her sister alone. He wanted to relax, damn it. Eat good food and kiss the beautiful woman in front of him over every inch of her delectable body until she arched and begged him to finish her hard and fast. Everything else be blowed.

Her mouth opened, then shut and he could see her deciding how to handle her reply.

'Wow. Impressive.' But her sass was all bluff because what he'd said was true.

He clocked her rising colour, her quickening breath, her widening eyes. And he really didn't want to talk any more. Talking wasn't anywhere near as effective as action. He'd thought he should back off, especially after she'd been so mortified about that woman catching them in the lift. But they needed to clear the air of this tension that kept building. There was only here and now. Together they'd find oblivion.

He pushed back from the table and stalked around to where she now sat bolt upright. He grabbed her hand and tugged her to her feet.

She thought he'd seduced her that night? That was nothing on what he was about to do. He wasn't waiting. He wasn't taking this slow. He wanted her beneath him, about him. He craved the welcome of her soft heat. He pulled her against his body and gazed into her green eyes. For a moment it was as if they'd romped back to that first night—soft laughter, whispered desire, sensual freedom. It didn't need to be anything more than that.

But there was no time for whispered words and soft laughter tonight. His need was too raw. He kissed her, and in that moment it was all over.

Unrestrained, ruthless, he stripped her bare right there in the formal dining room, boldly touching every spot he revealed. The emerald and diamond ring caught the light, sending small, sparking chinks of light onto the ceiling. His pleasure intensified at seeing her wearing it—the time-worn signal that she was taken. For a second he stilled, paralysed by the sudden ferocious anticipation of seeing her belly swell with her pregnancy over the coming months. She'd be softened and ripe with his child. His mark. He wanted to mark her all over—suddenly possessed by a primal, appalling need to stamp her as his. And he gave way to it in that instant, curling his arm around her waist to lift her up and carry her to his bed.

He wasn't making her come in five different

ways before filling her this time. He wasn't letting her come at all. Not until she was unable to bear it a second longer. Not until she begged for mercy. Not until they were both at the end of their sanity. In the cage of his arms he caressed her, alternating with licks, love bites, kisses—he teased and tasted every inch of her glorious body. She was pregnant. She was hot. And she was his.

He laughed roughly as she moaned, her hips circling, her hands seeking to touch him too. He suffered the tormenting slide of her fingertips, the delight of her hard grip, and moved to retaliate. He relished the way her muscles quivered under his onslaught. But nothing pleased him more than the look of hunger in her eyes. She was as willing, as craving, as he.

'Leon, please. *Please.*'

He paused above her, soaking in the moment he'd been aching for.

'Why have you stopped?' she asked, her expression edged with desperation.

'I don't want this over too soon,' he answered with rough honesty.

'I've wanted this for weeks,' she moaned. 'So much.'

Satisfaction and frustration split him. Fire and fury. 'Then why did you deny us?' Why had she put up those barriers? He was making her pay for that. '*Why* did you resist?'

How had she? But he couldn't wait for her answer—the demand of his own body, his own need, was too strong. She moaned in soft, earthy surrender as he thrust hard, fiercely claiming his possession. He arched, his eyes closing as pleasure sent sharp bursts down his back. His body tightened more, wanted more—deeper, harder, for *longer*. But she lost it beneath him, about him, crying out as her sweet body was wracked with the feral convulsions of one hell of an orgasm. But this wasn't over yet. He simply *refused* to let it be over yet. So he held still, his will stretched to the point of pain.

'Leon, it's so intense,' she gasped. 'So intense.'

'All the more reason to embrace it,' he growled, still furious with her for making them wait all these weeks.

'Please,' she begged, breathless and twisting and fierce beneath him. 'Please, Leon.'

It was as much a desperate plea as a forceful command. And now he could do nothing but surrender to both. He felt torn in two by the fierce, unrelenting urges to both master and worship her body.

'Ettie,' he growled. Demanding. Devoted.

The give and take, the push and pull was mirrored in his hard thrusts, in the buck of her fiery hips. He roared as his shy lover responded with that fight. She was that desperate for him. Which he adored because he couldn't get enough of her either. She made him both weak and strong. He was almost rendered unconscious by the ferocity of the pleasure as he pushed her to climax again. Yet her scream was silent, her body so taut with tension, shaking with intense delight, it couldn't render it vocally. The sight of her in that moment stopped his heart. His release came, instant and savage and so intense he all but blacked out.

When he returned to reality and summoned the energy to lift his head, he was horrified to find her face pale, her eyes simply huge and—glistening with tears?

'Are you okay?' he asked warily. Guilt hit him anew.

She was *exhausted* and he'd just subjected her to the roughest of rides. 'Sleep.' He drew the coverings over her, partly to hide the resurgence of his own desire, impossible as it ought to have been. He'd wanted her too much for too long. But surely he could wait until tomorrow before having her again?

Shadows crept into her beautiful, clear eyes. 'I can go back to my room.'

An ice-cold storm brewed in his belly. 'You want that?'

She licked her lips and glanced away from him. 'If that's what you'd prefer.'

Of course he wouldn't. 'What's going on, Ettie? Was I too rough?'

'No.' She wiped her eyes and turned away.

Not good enough. He turned her back towards him and gazed into her eyes. 'Then what?'

Her colour mounted and she seemed to be holding her breath. 'That other night you couldn't seem to get enough…but if you don't really want me any more, we don't have to…'

If he didn't really want her?

'Ettie,' he huffed out a relieved laugh, 'I thought you were exhausted. I didn't want to be too demanding…' He lost his train of thought as he saw the shadows shift to smoke in her eyes. '*Glykia mou.*'

'Sorry,' she muttered, colour flooding her face.

'Why?' He pulled her closer. 'I'm not sorry that my new fiancée is a nymphomaniac.'

He laughed at her gasp of outrage and thrust back the coverings so he could satisfy his need to see her naked beauty all over again.

'We *do* have to, Ettie.' He bent over her uncompromisingly. 'We damned well do.'

He angled her so he could see right into her eyes as he swept his hands over her soft curves and watched the ebb and flow of her tension. To his relief and pleasure, her smile returned. A more feminine, more feline one than he'd ever seen on her. He growled and surged into her—slower this time, tormenting them both to the point of madness. And it was utter bliss.

'I didn't know it could be this much fun.' She almost laughed a long while later.

Fun? Had she thought that was *fun*?

He'd thought it was devastating. But he cleared his throat and pulled his brain back from its fanciful, post-orgasmic superlatives. 'It's supposed to be fun.' And now he was looking, he couldn't tear his eyes from the satisfied glow enveloping her. 'You look better than you have in days.'

'I feel better.' Her cheeks were rosy and there

was a relaxed softness in her expression. She was stunning.

But he cocked his head and aimed to tease them both back to lightness. 'Orgasms for medicinal purposes?'

'Who knew, right?' She giggled.

'What happened with your ex?' The question just slipped out at that most appalling moment. He hadn't meant to ask it—not ever. But the idea that she'd cared for another man enough to want to marry him had grated on his deepest-set nerves. What had been so special about the jerk? Why had he let her go?

Leon gritted his teeth—why did he even want to know? But he did. Desperately.

Ettie was too quiet. He rolled to his side and propped his head up on his hand, studying the return of those shadows. They flickered across her face—resistance, sadness. He hated that some guy had hurt her. He didn't mean to hurt her more by asking about it now. Were the memories that painful? Had the bastard mattered so much she could barely bring herself to speak about him?

'He jilted me just before our wedding,' she finally answered.

'At the altar?' His skin tightened.

'Almost.' She seemed to shrink deeper into the mattress. 'His family had arrived. My friends. Ophelia was so excited about being bridesmaid…it was so humiliating…'

'Why did he do it? Was there someone else?' He couldn't fathom it. What man wouldn't want Ettie in his life? She was sexy, she was funny, she was sweet.

She looked away from him.

'We hadn't been intimate,' she said huskily. 'I'd wanted to wait.'

Leon's brain malfunctioned for a moment. *Not intimate? Wait?* 'You hadn't been intimate at all?'

She shook her head. 'We'd kissed but…' She shrivelled lower into the mattress and tugged the sheet higher. 'I wanted to wait.'

'For your wedding night?' He stilled as a bubble of something hot and fierce and frankly savage bubbled in his gut. That she'd wanted to do that—gift the guy her virginity—made his innards twist.

'I know, it's quaint, right?' She wouldn't look at him.

He shook his head. 'Sweet,' he corrected gruffly.

'I should have known it wasn't right.'

'What do you mean?'

'It wasn't hard for me to want to wait.' She lowered her chin and all but talked into the sheet covering her. 'I thought I had a low sex drive. That it was just me.'

His eyes widened. The woman didn't have a low sex drive. She was the hottest, most insatiable lover of his life. 'But your fiancé didn't want to wait any more?'

'He said it was so close to the wedding…that we should.'

He'd applied pressure and manipulated her innate desire to please. Leon tensed. 'And how was it?'

Her face burned red again. 'He didn't stick around for the wedding, so I guess it wasn't that good.'

So it had been just the once? He had to snap his mouth to keep his jaw from hitting the floor. 'And there's been no one since?'

Her blush built to beetroot, making it easy to read the deep embarrassment and insecurity all over her expressive face. She thought she wasn't sexy, that she didn't know what she was doing. That she'd not been able to satisfy her selfish ass of a fiancé. So there'd been that one let-down of an experience followed by appalling betrayal and rejection after.

And then there'd been him.

'That's why I was so reckless when you… It was so different…' She fell silent, that mottled rosy pink slowly washed from her skin.

He was savagely proud it had been so *different*. 'Poor Ettie. You finally let go enough to have some fun, and then—'

'I end up pregnant,' she mumbled.

One night. Massive consequences. It wasn't exactly fair.

'I guess mindless, meaningless, fantastic sex just isn't for me,' she attempted to joke.

'No, it is,' he replied, utterly serious. 'It just needs to be with me.'

She flushed deeper and her smile faded. 'Is it good for you?'

Was she seriously worried about that? He couldn't keep his hands off her. But that jerk had hurt her, striking an insecurity within.

'There's nothing wrong with you,' he whispered. 'Nothing wrong with what you do, how you respond…' He ripped back the sheet from them both. 'Look at what you do to me.'

She turned her face away but he tenderly cupped her chin and made her look. And then he kissed her—long, deep and lush—and felt that fire between them crackle.

'He was a jerk, Ettie,' Leon muttered, filled with protectiveness.

'He was. I just wanted to please him.'

He hated the bastard who'd had no idea of the treasure he'd had in his hands. He hated the damage he'd done to her. But he had to ease up on releasing that rage. She was more vulnerable than her ultra-efficient, all-smiling concierge persona revealed. 'You left school early and had to work?' He talked, trying to contain his anger and ease the tension gripping his muscles.

'Initially I left because Mum got sick. I needed to care for her and Ophelia.'

But she'd been a kid herself—just a teen. He hadn't wanted to listen earlier, but now he wanted to know everything. 'There was no one else?'

'She was young when she got pregnant with me. She was estranged from her parents—I never had a relationship with them or my father. Ophelia was the result of another doomed-to-failure fling. She'd wanted it to work out with him…'

'But that didn't happen either.'

She shook her head. 'Relationships never worked out for her.'

A chill swept over his skin. 'And you held off having boyfriends.'

'I was too busy to meet anyone,' she said softly.

'No,' he contradicted her. 'You shied away from them.' He understood why—she'd seen her mother's heartache and it had put her off. She'd seen the consequences—she'd lived them. He couldn't resist asking the question that burned in his gut. 'What did he give you that others didn't?' Why had she said yes to that guy?

'I met him not long after Mum died. It was very quick and I was vulnerable, I guess. He flattered me. He made me think I was special.'

Leon hardened inside. 'So he should've done—he was your boyfriend.'

'I wanted someone to love me. I thought he did. But he didn't.'

Leon didn't believe in love. He didn't believe

anyone had it—they had habits and pleasant arrangements. But he could offer Ettie loyalty. 'I'll never betray you like that.'

She looked at him sombrely. Didn't she trust him yet?

'Can we always be honest with each other?' she asked softly. 'Like you said, we're not talking stardust and promises. Don't flatter me. Don't try to soften any blows. Let's just be grounded and honest.'

That fierce savagery clawed at his insides and he finally lost his grip on it. 'Okay, here's some honesty for you: I crave your body, Ettie. I've dreamed about having you again every night for these last three weeks. I adore having sex with you and I want to do it all the damn time.'

Now her smile blossomed. 'Okay.'

She leaned in close and did more than let him. She met him—stroke for stroke, moan for groan. He denied the edge of desperation in his own need for physical fulfilment. He refused to face the fact that he couldn't seem to get enough of her.

All that mattered was that she was here. He'd free her of financial responsibility, he'd give her physical satisfaction, he'd offer her a lifestyle only he could provide…and she'd stay. His child would be safe. As would she.

His plan was perfectly falling into place.

CHAPTER EIGHT

SHE SHOULDN'T HAVE told him about her ex-fiancé. Leon must think she was such a naive fool. She'd done *all* the talking last night—exposed herself and all her embarrassing history. He'd shared virtually nothing, except his fantastic bedroom skills. Had he never been embarrassed? Never been rejected?

Of course not.

He couldn't reciprocate with any humanising stories of his own humiliations, because he didn't have any. And right this second she completely resented him for that. And because he was blocking her from making her own choices. Again.

'You're *not* going to work today.' He was furious.

It was almost nine the next morning. She'd slept in and he was late heading to his office because they were arguing about her plans for the day. As it was, she was feeling unsettled. She wasn't used to having a personal life, let alone everyone knowing about it. Her colleagues, her clients would all know she was sleeping with him. And the massive rocks on her finger were only going to make them even more curious. So she was tense enough without him telling her what she could and couldn't do. Again.

'Are you ashamed of what I do?' she spat sullenly.

'Do you think I'm that much of an ass?' He rolled his eyes. 'Thanks so much. You do honest work. You're good at your job. But do I want a pregnant woman carrying deliveries upstairs? No. I do not.'

'Joel would help me and it's not like I'm huge and uncomfortable already—I'm not even showing. This baby is months away, Leon. What do you want me to do all day?'

The flicker in his eyes irritated her.

'Be your concubine?' she asked tartly. '*Really?*'

'That's your fantasy, not mine.' He practically purred. 'I don't want you working as head concierge of the Cavendish any more. I want you as building manager.'

'What?' His statement undercut her argument

and completely derailed her train of thought. She stared at him. 'You *what*?'

'Building manager. I want you to take over from George. It's obvious who does the work. It's Ettie. Who fixes the orders? Ettie. Who does all the rosters? Ettie. Who do the residents rely on? Ettie. You're doing it all already anyway—you might as well get paid for it.'

She simply sat there, her jaw dropped.

'I can't understand how you've not been promoted already. Actually I can: George has been claiming credit for most of your work. And then tried to blame his mistakes on you.'

Ettie did her best impersonation of a goldfish.

'I've already spoken with the management company,' he continued. 'George has agreed it's time for him to move on to a smaller establishment. And the residents committee have approved it as well.'

'Were you ever going to actually ask me if I wanted the job, or did you just expect me to jump at the chance?'

'I knew you'd jump.' He smirked. But then held up his hands. 'It's no more than deserved, Ettie.'

But she couldn't accept any promotion—not now she'd slept with the new owner.

'What's wrong now?' He released an exaggerated sigh.

'They'll think it's nepotism.'

'Why should you care what they think? The proof is in your ability to do the job. No one who knows you would ever think you *slept* your way into it.'

'Thank you *so* much.' Her blush burned.

He laughed. 'Enough. We've banished that insecurity already.'

She scowled at him. 'If it's more money, then—'

'You're already wearing my ring, Ettie. You're not backing out now. And your "more money" isn't anywhere near enough to cover Ophelia's fees for the next decade.' He brutally shut down her thinking. 'All I ask is that you take the rest of the week to recuperate from the stress of the last few days; you didn't get a lot of sleep last night. Take time to get to know this place. Then go back next week and take over fully from then.'

'You have it all mapped out,' she said stiffly.

Why did that surprise her? She swung her legs

out of the bed, determined to do *something* in defiance of him.

'No. Stay there and rest.' He braced one arm either side of her and leaned over her until she fell back onto the mattress.

Quick and furious and so damned easily he proved his point, leaving her breathless and so relaxed her fight fled and all she could do was moan her approval.

'You keep distracting me with sex,' she muttered when she could breathe again.

'I'm distracting myself with sex too.' He stretched and stood, apparently energised. 'It's a good distraction.'

'But we're not solving this problem.'

'There isn't a problem,' he replied with stubborn simplicity. 'You're making a problem where there isn't one. You don't need to work today, Ettie. You've worked all your life. You've been responsible all your life. Why not take a day to have a break? You're still working—you're growing a little human.'

'I can't sit around doing nothing,' she argued. 'I've never done that.'

'So learn how to relax. Read a book. Watch

TV. Sleep. Anonymously blog about your misfortunes. Whatever, just *rest*.'

She glared at him and then couldn't help laughing, as she knew he'd intended. 'Anonymously blog?'

'Yeah.' He put his hands on his hips, warming to the idea. '*My life as a billionaire's bought bride...*'

She giggled again, but then realised what she actually wanted more than anything was for him to *stay* with her today. She enjoyed his company. But he was off to maintain that millionaire income and she had to keep this as light and 'easy' as he was.

Stay in your lane, Ettie.

'I promise I'll be here for when you return, oh, lord and master,' she cooed. 'In bed,' she added on an impish urge. 'Naked.'

'Hot and wet and ready for me.' He slammed a scorching kiss onto her lips. 'Perfect.'

'I'm getting rid of all the stupid rules,' she informed him when he lifted his head. 'Starting with pets.'

'Oh, I knew that already.'

With a wriggle that was more sexual restlessness than resentment, she threw a pillow as he laughed and left the room.

No way was Ettie spending the day sitting about doing nothing. Not when her brain was fizzing with ideas for Cavendish House. She fossicked through Leon's study, marvelling at his sleek, luxurious stationery supplies. The guy had a thing for fancy fine-liner pens. Smirking, she twisted her hair into a bun and secured it in place with one and grabbed a handful of others. In the kitchen she collected some crackers, cheese and juice. She spread sheets of thick paper over the dining table to brainstorm on. It took her a while to work out the fancy 'smart house' sound system, but she got music playing eventually. Sunlight streamed through the window. She stared at the room for a moment, stunned anew. It was a gorgeous place to work. Then, energised and excited, she got down to it.

'Wow—could you make your lists any longer?'

'Oh!' Startled, Ettie glanced up to see Leon standing on the other side of the table. Her heart pounded faster at the sight of him than from the initial fright. It was impossible not to react to his presence. 'I didn't hear you come in,' she muttered, trying to regulate her breathlessness. 'What time is it?'

'After six,' he said, amusement quirking his lips.

'*No.*' She looked out of the window and saw the changing sky. 'Where'd the day go?'

'Into all those lists,' he answered drily. 'Is there any paper left?'

'Uh, some.' She glanced down. She'd smothered the table in papers, which in turn were smothered in her scribblings. 'What do you think?'

'I think you haven't rested at all today. Have you eaten?'

His concern warmed her as much as it irritated her.

'Actually I've been snacking all day and this *is* restful. I've been perched on this stool the whole time.' She saw him read through her most recent, refined list. 'You like what I've planned?'

'Yeah.' He quickly scanned her bullet points. 'You should set up a meeting with the residents' group. They'll be excited.'

'I've already emailed invitations from my phone.'

'Of course you have,' he murmured. 'That's why you got the job.'

'I can't change everything all at once,' she said earnestly. 'I know I'll need to go slow so they have time to adjust…' She trailed off as his gaze narrowed on her.

She flushed at being the focus of his intensity all over again. Every time, even though he outwardly appeared expressionless, he wasn't remote. It felt as if he was so attuned to her needs, her desires, before she was even aware of them herself. Dizzying, dazzling…*confusing*.

'Sometimes an acute, complete change is a good thing,' he said, his gaze laser-sharp on her.

'Rapid change can also be scary,' she responded pointedly. 'The staff might feel overwhelmed or defensive if they feel it's a criticism of the way things were…'

He considered it for a moment and his rare smile suddenly flashed. 'Go with your instincts; they're good.'

Excitement for her work flooded back. 'I can't wait to get started.'

'On your not-rapid changes.' He laughed and reached out, plucking the pen from her hair. '*Mine*.'

She ran her hand through her messy tangle of waves with a grimace. 'Possessive about your pens, aren't you?'

'You think I was talking about the pen?' That wicked smile flashed on his face again as he fished in his pocket for his phone. 'You okay with Italian for dinner?'

She needed a moment to catch her breath. He was just teasing, keeping it playful. Light and easy. So she'd do the same. 'Are you talking pizza or fancy?'

'How about fancy pizza?'

'Perfect.' She hopped off the stool and stretched out the cricks in her back from leaning over the table all day while he tapped a message on his phone. 'It's Friday tomorrow, then the weekend. Do you actually take weekends off or do you work through as if every day's Monday?'

'You know already.' His answering grin was rueful. 'But we could go to a recital on Saturday night if you like?' He flipped his phone around to show her the promotional information for a concert on at a nearby concert hall.

She read the headliner and stilled. It was an oboe soloist. That was *her* instrument. She looked up and saw his expectant expression. 'How did you know?'

'Saw the instrument case in your flat,' he replied. 'The music book had your name on the front. Why didn't you mention it? You've told me all about Ophelia, but you're reticent about your own dreams, Ettie.'

'*You're* calling *me* reticent?' Her jaw dropped at his temerity. 'I've told you about my ex-fiancé, my mother—'

'But not about your music. Why?'

Because it had been her secret, childish dream and she'd had to bury it. How had he picked up that it had been important—was he some kind of mind-reader? But that was impossible because she *never* thought of it now—it hurt to remember. What he'd exposed was a skeleton shipwreck of a dream that couldn't be resurrected.

'Do you wish you played now?' he asked, still intently watching her.

Her heart ached. Did he have to discover all her secrets? 'It's too late.'

'We could convert one of the lounges into a music room. You could play again.'

'No.' She chuckled softly to hide her sadness and embarrassment. Truthfully she'd been a fool to think she could've made a go of it once. 'I was never that good. I stopped when I took on a part-time job when Mum got ill. I haven't played in years. I never play now.'

'But you were good.' He looked sombre. 'That music was extremely complex.'

'You read music?'

'Sure.' He nodded.

Of course. He probably spoke more than two languages as well, only she didn't yet know it. It wasn't fair that he knew everything about her and she knew so little about him. He hadn't even left clues in his own home—nothing here told her anything more about him.

'So what instrument do you play?' she asked, determined to get an answer.

'Piano. It was compulsory to learn an instrument at school.'

'Boarding school?' She glanced at him sideways, almost afraid that if she faced him he'd fall silent again.

'Yes.'

'For your teen years?' Her curiosity burned. She wondered about everything. What were his parents really like? He had no photos of them at all here. Were they really not close? Did they really only see each other every six months or so? Had he always been this isolated?

'I went there when I was eight,' he said brusquely. 'It was good.'

She waited hopefully but he didn't add anything more.

'It's good for Ophelia too,' she said after a while. 'She gets an education and opportunities she just wouldn't otherwise.' But Ettie missed her sister hugely. If she'd won a scholarship from a day school in town, that would have been so much better. She nibbled her lower lip, thinking about her own child's future education. 'I don't want our baby going to boarding school though,' she realised with quiet conviction. It was too bad if Leon had some schooling tradition going back generations. 'I won't send him or her away. I don't care how good the school might be, there'll be schools just as good here.'

Increasing ferocity fired colour into Ettie's expression, reminding Leon of her passion and protectiveness over the dog the day they'd met. His skin seemed to tighten. He understood why she had mixed feelings about boarding school—she obviously missed her sister. But she didn't know that for him boarding school had been a blessed escape. It had been so much safer and happier than his own home.

'Okay,' he said, needing to draw a line beneath the subject. 'School here.'

He didn't want to think about the years ahead. Right now was tough enough. She'd guessed correctly: he usually worked every day as if it were Monday. But now she was here and yeah, rapid change could be unsettling. His home was altered. Not because she'd brought in a lot of stuff, but because she'd recast the entire atmosphere—with her scent, her laughter, her smile…

Leon hadn't lived with anyone since school. He had no idea how to live with someone. No idea what he was going to do with her all weekend. He could hardly keep her tied to his bed the whole time, as appealing as that thought was. The oboe recital had been a random grasp and mainly he'd been keen to see her reaction because he was insatiably curious about her now. She fascinated him.

He gazed at the colour washing her cheeks and the sparkle shimmering in her eyes. She still glowed with the vivacity and enthusiasm that she'd worked hard all day with. Even when he'd told her not to, he'd known she would. And now that vivacity was enhanced by the filter of pure passion as she fought for something so far in the future it didn't even matter yet. She was so spirited, and so protective of their child's future.

That curling tension tightened—constricting his throat, his chest. He couldn't resist the need to get nearer to her. He wanted her heat, her willingness, her total surrender to his touch. There was something deeper too, something so powerful that he couldn't examine it too closely.

Just want.

He reassured himself. But it was strong.

The weekend plans were irrelevant. Suddenly he had no spare thought for the past, or the future. His immediate need was too intense.

He pulled her against him. He didn't know how else to release the heavy pressure crushing his chest, threatening to cleave him open. He didn't want to be torn apart and have any of this emotion *exposed.* Not memories. Not pain. He wanted nothing but pleasure with her. *Now.*

He slid his hand into her glossy hair and tilted her head back to expose her pretty neck. Her soft lips parted and emotion glittered in her eyes. Emotion he refused to analyse. He didn't know how. He certainly didn't stop to examine his own. He was only seeking her consent—to lose them both in that fiery desire. And he got it—there in her crystal, cloudless eyes.

She might appear vulnerable, but she was strong. He could see her energy pulsing in that soft space at the base of her neck. He bent his head and kissed her hard and deep, releasing all the passion and lust into her, until that weight blocking his chest eased and heat swirled in its place. She was so intoxicating, he sank to his knees, determined to gift her every ounce of pleasure he could. Nothing else mattered. Nothing but now. Here. Her pleasure. Her sighs.

He cupped her full breasts, knowing they were tender and more sensitive, teasing until he felt her need deepening, until he heard her breathy little pleas. Then it was that sweet, wet, secret part of her that he couldn't resist baring, touching, *tasting*.

'Lean on me,' he muttered as he felt her trembling response.

She was hot and lush and he craved every inch, every lick of her. She pressed her hands on his shoulders for balance, her legs spread as wide as they could against the constraints of the panties he'd pulled halfway down her thighs. He revelled in her quivering, in her desperate cries. His blood flowed freely now—warming him, releasing him from that tight, painful pressure. This was what he wanted. He pressed closer still and destroyed her.

Ettie woke late and saw the fresh juice, plain crackers and sliced fruit on a tray beside the bed. She smiled ruefully. Leon was unfailingly attentive and good at anticipating almost every one of her needs. She could hardly bear to think of those insane moments last night when he'd knelt at her feet and made her mad with desire. In that dangerously seductive stance, she'd felt like his queen, as if he couldn't exist in that moment without touching her. He'd made her feel *wanted* in a way she'd never felt wanted before. And he'd made her feel such thrilling, intense pleasure, such total exhilaration, that she'd screamed until she was hoarse.

In the aftermath she'd been so dazed she could barely stand. Her wits had been too scrambled for her to be able to lighten it at all, to even think of *reciprocating*. He'd straightened her clothing and told her to go and tidy herself quick-smart, because their restaurant booking was soon.

Once more, it wasn't just any restaurant and it wasn't pizza. It was award-winning, exclusive and so expensive they didn't bother putting the prices on the menu. There was no choice as to what they got to eat either. That was because the food the world-renowned chef prepared was so exquisite, no one sane would ever think to complain or argue with the selection. Pure perfection. And absolute decadence.

She'd been so tired she'd fallen asleep on the drive home. She'd woken as he'd carried her up to his bed. And once there, she'd realised she wasn't *quite* as sleepy as all that. He'd laughed, indulging her again in that searing, soul-destroying sex. Again. And then again.

Just sex, Ettie. Good sex. Stupendous. But just sex.

But thank goodness he seemed to be as hungry for it as she.

Now he'd gone to work and she had another day to herself before the weekend. Another day to come to terms with the fragile future they were building.

But there was imbalance between them and it

wasn't their bank balances. He knew *everything.* Her stupid mistakes of the past. Even her sorry childhood dream of becoming a musician. Every little secret. Furthermore, he'd done so much for her—the ring, the home, the job…and things so much more intimate than that. He turned her inside out, made her mindless with pleasure. He'd given her pretty much everything.

But what had she given *him*? What had he *let* her give him—other than her body? He didn't open up, didn't let her in. She breathed out and reminded herself it was very early days. He didn't trust her yet and he had a thing about people always wanting things from him—he'd joked about it but there'd been a tiny truth there.

What if she was to give *him* something?

Problem was, it wasn't as if he needed her to *buy* him anything and it wasn't as if she had vast amounts of money to splash out either. And it wasn't about a *thing*, it was about doing something thoughtful, to show that she was invested in making this work the same way he was. That she could be attentive too. But she knew so little, she couldn't think of what to do or get, and she was good at getting things for privileged people.

With a sigh, she got out of bed and returned

the plate and glass to the gleaming kitchen. She caught sight of the shiny new dog bowls sitting uselessly on the counter. She paused, her gaze fixed on them. Leon said he'd never had a puppy, but he'd been surprisingly willing to take Toby. She'd had a feeling that he'd been more keen on that than he'd expressed. It hadn't all been about getting her up to that penthouse in Cavendish House. She remembered how he'd gently patted the dog.

Her heart pounded as she turned over the wisp of an idea in her mind. It would be a huge risk. But instinct told her it would be worth it. It would be right.

Go with your instincts; they're good.

She turned her back on the lists she'd left on the table and ran back upstairs to get dressed.

Ettie Roberts had a mission.

CHAPTER NINE

LEON TRIED TO stay at work. Tried to concentrate. Tried not to think about the weekend ahead. It wasn't that he didn't want her there, he did, but it felt as if the ground was shifting and he couldn't quite hold his balance. In the end he gave up resisting and let the weight coiling within push him home.

'Ettie?' He rolled his shoulders, trying to ease that tension as he shucked off his jacket and shoes.

'Leon?' Her answering call was pitched high.

'Who else?' he asked drily, following the direction of her voice to the kitchen.

He fought to restrain the urge to go straight up and kiss her until the tightness in his chest eased again. Not two nights running—he had more control than that, right? But in the doorway he paused to draw breath. She looked amazing to his hungry eyes—jeans, T-shirt, hair twisted out of the way and secured with a pen again. His again.

'I wasn't sure what time you'd be home… You're early.' Her face was flushed but it wasn't that usual blush of sensuality.

And she couldn't quite maintain eye contact, which initially intrigued, then concerned him. He strolled closer, trying to take it easy, but his instincts were firing. Something was off. 'What've you been up to today?' he asked. 'No more lists?'

The table was scrupulously tidy.

His pulse began to pound. Why couldn't she look at him? Why was she so flushed? Why so silent?

At that exact moment, he heard a strange scratching coming from behind him. Ettie froze, her eyes wide. He cocked his head and narrowed his gaze on her. 'What's that?'

'Hmm?' she mumbled.

'Ettie?'

The noise sounded again and there was no hiding the guilty look in her eyes—her face was far too expressive.

Now she pressed her lips together in an oddly nervous manner. 'I've done something,' she blurted. 'I got you a present.'

He stilled. 'You what?'

'I got you a present. I hope you don't mind.'

Why would he mind? He actually couldn't remember the last time anyone had got him a present. He didn't have a bunch of friends he did birthday celebrations with and his parents definitely didn't send him anything. Not at Christmas either.

There was another scratching sound. And then a high-pitched yelp. Not Ettie. Not *human.*

Leon spun around. 'Ettie?'

She scuttled past him and he watched her hunch down by a box he'd not noticed before because he'd only had eyes for her. Leon couldn't move. It was a big box.

Then Ettie stood and walked towards him and she was holding—

'He was the runt,' she said all in a rush. 'I don't know quite what breed he is…a mix of many, and I know he's not handsome like Toby, but he wasn't going to have a chance otherwise.'

Leon stared at the creature in Ettie's arms. 'You got me a puppy?'

His heart beat too fast; his lungs felt as if they were in a swiftly tightening vice.

'You have space here.' She sounded as breathless as he felt. 'You could train him to go to the office with you, or he can stay here and play in the garden, or he could come to the Cavendish with me…we can make it work. I just thought you'd like him.' She stepped closer and literally shoved the puppy into his arms.

Leon instinctively grabbed the animal but inside he'd frozen.

'You said you'd not had a dog, but I thought you'd quite wanted Toby. I thought…' She trailed off as she finally looked up at him. 'I don't really know what I thought.' She stared into his eyes, her own growing more concerned by the second. 'Do you mind?' It was a whisper.

Leon couldn't move. He couldn't actually breathe. That pressure crushing his chest was too heavy on his lungs.

'He's about four months old, they think,' she said. 'All vaccinated. If they couldn't rehome him they were going to—'

'He's a rescue puppy?' he croaked, determinedly pushing past the immobility to glance down at the puppy who'd settled so quickly in his arms. Small, with bottomless brown eyes that had a heart-wrenching hint of sadness, mostly black hair but with patches of silvery white...he was ridiculously cute.

'Yes.'

Leon cleared his throat. 'Does he have a name?'

She shook her head. 'You'll have to give him one.'

He didn't want to do that. He couldn't.

Memory washed over him. He'd held a tiny puppy like this only once before years ago. It had been small and fragile like this one. It had been his...but only for a little while.

He stilled as past and present blurred and the reality of their future hit hard. He didn't know if he could do this. *Any* of this.

'Leon? Don't you like him?'

He huffed out a hard-caught breath. Of course he liked him. How could he not?

'What is it?' she asked softly. 'Leon?' Her eyes suddenly filled. 'Did I do the wrong thing?'

'No,' he muttered quickly. She was so sweet, she didn't realise. 'No.'

'Then what is it?' She wasn't just sweet, she was astute. She saw right through him.

And he couldn't bear that. 'It's not important,' he snapped, needing to shut her down.

'If it's not important, it won't matter if you tell me, will it?'

He almost smiled at her simple logic, but he was stuck, unable to escape the most painful of memories. 'You don't want my poor-little-rich-boy sob story.'

'Yes—'

'It is what it is,' he interrupted awkwardly. 'I can't change it.'

He didn't want questions, didn't want to remember. His mouth was dry and he felt too big to be holding something so small. He didn't want to hold it close. He didn't want to feel. He needed time to think. But Ettie kept looking at him with those beseeching sea-green eyes and when she did that he couldn't seem to think at all.

'Leon—'

'My neighbour gave me a puppy,' he growled before she could say anything else in that husky, sweet voice. She was so frustratingly curious. 'But my mother got rid of it after a few weeks.'

'Got rid of it?' Ettie frowned. 'You don't mean—'

'Yeah, I do mean.' The words just fell out. A bald, uncontrollable burn of memory. The disappearance. The shocking silence and the absolute emptiness inside him. 'They weren't interested in me—I was their tick-the-box baby. They were busy with their careers. Their affairs. They just wanted a trophy and heir. They didn't want the actual *child*. The actual child was...' He broke off, tearing his gaze from Ettie to focus on the small dog that had nestled so easily into his arms. It was so trusting. But he hadn't been able to protect that first puppy...

He dragged in a harsh breath. He shouldn't have said anything, but now he'd started, ripping open that old wound so it oozed poison and pus. He couldn't stop the truth of it spewing out.

'One child was more than enough for my mother to handle and, as I was a child of privilege, it was her duty to educate me on my duty and ensure I wasn't spoiled.'

'Not spoiled?' Ettie echoed softly.

He looked back into her expressive face and watched as understanding dawned.

'She was cruel?' she said.

Leon couldn't bear the sympathy in her eyes. Why had he said anything? He hated remembering how weak he'd once been. He never wanted anyone to have power over him again. Not physical. Not emotional. Not contractual. Never again would he be that vulnerable. That powerless.

'Leon...'

'I was extremely fortunate.' He tried to plug the information leak, tried to squash all that horror back in the depths of his ribcage. 'I had the best education.'

Never show weakness. Never admit to failure. Always fight.

'But she hurt you. Not just your puppy. She hurt *you*.'

So many times, in so many small ways. He froze but was still unable to think, unable to hold back that pressure bursting within him.

Ettie stepped closer. 'She hit you?'

'Too obvious.' The words escaped, heedless of his battle to keep silent. 'She'd force me to shower in freezing water. Five minutes. Reciting equations, verbs, some poem. Whatever lesson I needed to be drilled in. I had to say it aloud over and over again. That was one of the many...' He paused, drawing in a hard breath. 'Just little things she did to...'

'Torture you.'

'Toughen me up.' He grimaced. 'Cold showers, barefoot runs in the frost, two hours locked in a dark cupboard if I answered back or worse… all things that left no physical mark, but would teach me to control myself. Not cry. Not show weakness.'

Not anger. Not love either. Not any emotions. He'd learned calm instead—to close down, stay still, breathe, *think*. Except he couldn't do any of that now with the way Ettie was looking at him.

'It worked,' he said, stubbornly rejecting what he saw in her eyes. 'I grew resilience. Definitely gained independence. Didn't rely on anyone else for anything.'

'You couldn't tell your father?'

The last sliver of Leon's heart shrivelled. 'He knew.' And he'd done nothing.

'You couldn't tell anyone else?'

There hadn't been anyone else. There'd never been any physical marks left on him. But he had the feeling his old neighbour at their summer house suspected. That was why she'd given him that puppy. Calix had been the runt of the litter, just like this little guy.

His mother had relented too easily—said yes to that nice old neighbour. She'd said yes so swiftly, bubbling with faux gratitude. He should've known it was too good to last. He was to perform. He was to lead. He was to remain in charge of everything. The loss she then subjected him to was to build his fight—the puppy was a mere tool for him to learn pain and to protect himself from feeling it again. Never to lose again.

It hurts when important things are taken from you. The dog isn't important. Our company is.

He'd never trusted again either.

'That's why you were happy to go away to school,' Ettie whispered.

'It was a relief.' Leon wanted nothing more than to freeze back up inside. 'But she'd hit me in other ways. When you're told something over and over and over, you begin to believe it, especially when the person telling you is supposed to be your protector.' She'd shut him off from everyone. Her words echoed in his head.

'*They only want to be friends because of your money. They want to use you. But you haven't done anything to deserve what you have. You don't deserve it.*'

He realised far too late that he'd said it all aloud. Ettie's expression was appalled. He turned away, unable to look at her any more. If he didn't look at her he might get himself back under control.

'My mother was determined to make me strong enough, good enough to take over the specific challenges of a multimillion-dollar empire. To become the tough, decisive boss I'd need to be. I tried hard to please her.' To please both his parents. He'd tried for so long. 'Eventually I realised I was never going to. Nothing would make her happy. So I decided that I'd never be the heir they'd worked so *diligently* to raise. Not by going off the rails—that would have pleased her, I think. It would have proven that I was as "weak" as she'd said I was. So no drugs, no booze-fuelled parties, no threesomes…' He almost smiled. 'I turned my back on that "duty" and rejected the inheritance they offered. I'll never work for the company, or take charge of it. Instead I worked alone and earned more, just to spite her. I worked every holiday and left home the second I was old enough.'

'To make your own way.'

He'd pushed to the top relentlessly—taken huge risks, worked insane hours. Because he didn't want a cent of his parents' money. Didn't want the 'glory' of running their empire. After all, he'd not *deserved* it—so he'd built his own.

He didn't need them. He didn't need *anyone*.

Now he carried the sleeping puppy back to the box and saw the small bed Ettie had got for it inside. He carefully put the puppy in. Why had he said anything? He never talked to anyone about this. Bracing himself against the silence, he turned back and saw her face. His body tightened.

'I don't want your pity.' All that emotion emptied again. He couldn't stand to see the sympathy in her eyes. 'I cannot be pitied. Look at everything I have, everything I've done.'

'Yeah, you're amazing,' she whispered. 'But you don't let people in.'

'Why would I want to?' He turned to look back at the sleeping dog.

Yet he knew he had to—his own child was the game changer. And it was happening *too soon*. He'd never wanted one, but now one was on the way and he wanted it to have everything he hadn't and still didn't have. Self-sufficiency was key to his own existence, yet he was human enough not to want that for his own child. Thank goodness the baby had Ettie.

He tried to be calm, to breathe, to think. But his heart thundered and his lungs hurt. His whole chest was still bound in tension.

Leon stood so still, Ettie almost believed he wasn't breathing. But as she neared, she could feel the vibrations rolling off him. She sensed the power he was exerting to hold back and press everything back down deep. He'd been appallingly hurt and she'd had absolutely no idea. He'd hidden it so well, for so long.

She might not have had a father, but she'd had a mother who'd loved her, who'd at least wanted the best for her. And she'd had her sister.

Leon had been utterly isolated. The witch hadn't even let him keep his dog. His father hadn't stood up for him. The horror of it broke her heart. That he'd been treated as a project, not a person.

While she'd grown up with nothing but love, he'd grown up with everything but. No wonder he was remote and controlled and untrusting. And right now she knew he regretted saying anything at all. While there mightn't have been physical marks, there were definitely emotional scars. Five minutes beneath a frigid torrent of water must've felt like an eternity. Two hours in a dark cupboard for a small boy must've been pure hell.

'Leon—'

'Don't.'

She knew he was withdrawing. Rebuilding his walls to shut her out again. She couldn't let that happen. Not yet.

'Don't think that this is going to change everything just because you've told me a few things,' she said, trying to reach him. 'We're just getting to know each other, that's all. That helps build trust.'

'Don't actions speak louder than words, Ettie?' The strain was evident in his hoarseness. 'Can't you trust me already? I'm not your dad or your ex. I haven't left you.'

Not physically. But emotionally he was walking out of that door. And he was turning the focus from himself to her, to help his escape.

'Leon—'

'Have I betrayed you?' he flared.

'No.' She welcomed the resurgence of his emotion and stepped closer. 'But there's action and there's *action*.'

His default response was to close down all intimacy other than the physical. It was the only way she could think to keep him here *with* her.

'Look,' he cleared his throat, 'you're going to make a wonderful mother, Ettie. I know you'll care for this child in a way I was never cared for. But I can only do what I do.' He frowned as if he was struggling to think. 'I'm good at taking control in a crisis.'

Yes. Because his whole life had been a crisis. He'd been locked for ever in a fight for survival, to win, to be free. When had he last taken the time to just breathe? When had he ever let someone else make the calls and shoulder even a little bit of his burden?

'You have to take control because you've never had anyone you could count on.' She placed her hand on his chest.

He didn't reply. The agony churning in his eyes, the blistering beat of his heart beneath her fingers, said it all. He didn't trust anyone. She didn't blame him; she had trust issues of her own. But maybe in time he could learn to trust *her*? Maybe—eventually—they could be a true team?

'Can't you relinquish control to me?' she asked softly, spreading her hand wider and slowly sliding it down his chest. 'Just once?' She felt his muscles tighten beneath her touch, saw awareness flare in his eyes.

'Are you still feeling insecure about your sexual experience?' he asked gruffly.

No. This wasn't about *her*. But this was the language she knew he understood and it could be their starting point, right?

'Don't you know what you do to me?' he asked harshly as she slid her hand to his belt and twisted her fingers to release the buckle.

She shook her head. That was what she wanted most of all—to see him. To know him. 'Let me see.' She lifted her chin and dared him, unfastening the buttons of his shirt without hesitation. 'Let me do it.'

He didn't stop her. But he didn't help. Like a statue ablaze—the tension thrummed from him as she pushed back the two halves of his shirt so she could see—touch—his burning skin.

'Just let me,' she whispered.

She reached up on tiptoe and kissed along his jaw, aching for the years of sufferance and isolation he'd endured. He didn't lower his chin to meet her lips with his.

'I don't want your sympathy,' he growled, rigid and angry.

'Just as I don't want your money,' she answered.

He pulled back his head to look down at her then. 'This isn't about money.'

'It isn't about sympathy either. This is about *caring*, Leon.' She cupped his jaw with one hand, and slid her other over his chest, tracing the strength and heat. Skin on skin. 'This is about you opening up and letting me in. Let me in.'

'You don't need to take care of me.'

'But you get to take care of me? Next you'll try telling me not to breathe,' she muttered back at him. 'Screw your control, Leon.'

With a sudden forceful push, she pressed him against the wall. His eyes widened and his hands automatically spanned her waist.

'I'm taking control.' She kissed her way down his chest. Her own passion was unleashed. She wanted to *truly* touch him. She wanted to show him—

'You think?' He hauled her back up to kiss her hard and deep, his anger igniting.

'I *know*,' she said when she tore her lips free.

A crazy kind of confidence she'd never before felt fired through her veins. She knew what to do. What she wanted. She showered his body with kisses, with light, teasing touches of her fingertips, with swirls of her tongue, before letting her lips slide closer.

Her own heat increased the more she heard his uneven breathing, the more she felt his tension build. She stepped back for a moment to slide her own clothes off. Slowing when she saw the way he was leaning back against the wall, his feet planted wide apart, watching her strip. She was no real beauty, definitely no model-type, but clearly it didn't matter.

Only when she was fully naked did she step forward again. She unzipped his trousers, pulled them and his boxers down. She knelt in front of him as he'd knelt before her only last night.

She heard his growl—of warning, of *want*. She smiled and kissed closer, closer, but she didn't take him in her mouth. Not yet. It was enough to let him enjoy looking. She saw his hands curl into fists, his knuckles whitening. He liked what she was doing. But he was still holding back. She didn't want him to hold back.

She licked up the length of him and then looked up. 'Lie down.'

He shot her a look but complied with her request.

Ettie simply stared for a moment at the sheer magnificence of him outstretched on the floor before her. He still said nothing but his raging erection and ragged breathing were all the encouragement she needed. Her mouth watered and that confidence flooded her again.

She straddled him and ran her hands over his body. He was so still. Letting her. Yet resisting her inwardly. He'd learned such control. He needed to unlearn it.

And she just needed to touch him. She was firm. Gentle. Reverent. Then rougher. As she released her grip on her own desire, her pace picked up, her intentions deepened, her need coiled. Her breathing shallowed, her heat spiked.

He was so strong. So alone. So worthy of so much more. And now she was angry. He should have had everything. She would give him everything *she* could right now. With a blind kind of fury, she ached to make him feel the way he made her feel—*wanted.* So. Damn. Much.

She slid up the length of his body, desperately kissing him, stroking, sucking him hard and then grinding her heat on him, until he flipped—literally holding her to him and flipping them both so he was above her…within her.

'*Yes*,' she cried out as he thrust to the hilt.

But he stopped—straining—his eyes closed, his jaw clenched as he fought to regain his control.

'Don't stop,' she ordered, gazing up at him. 'Don't shut me out.'

His hands gripped her thighs deliciously hard. She knew he couldn't resist this for much longer. He shuddered as she moved beneath him sinuously, easing her own ache, enticing him to complete abandonment.

His eyes opened. 'I don't like losing control of my emotions, Ettie,' he grated.

'Is it losing control of them?' she challenged him. 'Or is it just expressing them?'

He was still for a searing moment more. Then she saw the flare and felt his sudden shift. He snatched the pen securing her hair—freeing it into a wild tumble around her shoulders. He wound thick hanks of it around his wrists—literally binding her to him and cradling her head in his fingers so he could see into her eyes, so he could devour her mouth. The tug was strong, but not painful as her head tilted back at his pull—exposing her mouth, her neck, her breasts to his ravenous, rough kisses.

'I like it,' she admitted with low, savage hunger. 'I like touching you. I like seeing you like this. I want you like this.'

'On the edge?' he growled, twisting his hands again to shorten the tie between them.

'Over it,' she said brazenly. 'With me.'

He swore bluntly and drove into her, again and again. Ruthlessly, out of control, he claimed his place in her very core—pushing harder, faster, deeper. This wasn't fun or easy or light. It was the most bared, the most touched she'd ever been. The lump in her throat ached. She'd been alone too. She'd been alone so long, but right now—he was here, right here, literally bound to her. Inside her *totally*. Her eyes stung because she was exposed—vulnerable and shaking and so damn needy of *this*. His kiss, his possession. She felt the wild emotion storming through him and into her, only to transform again into something wonderful that they then rode together. He growled again as she arched, pressing herself closer still, wrapping her legs and arms tightly around him, holding him so they were utterly inseparable. His kiss devastated her. Unleashed emotion rippled between them like electricity—a power surge energising them both into frantic, clawing creatures seeking oblivion in this dark, magic world they made together. She gasped as he thrust harder and harder. He was so powerful. And she so complete. All thought was gone, all words. There was only animal sensation, animal sounds…and then screaming, orgasmic agony.

Leon flinched, suddenly wide awake. It was completely dark. Despite the warmth of the soft woman curled next to him, he was freezing. His heart was pounding as if he'd been sprinting for his life. He'd woken like this so many times in his youth and he hated it.

Despite the pleasure he'd had with Ettie tonight, he was now tossed back into that old torment. That stupid talk had stirred up thoughts. Memories. Feelings.

Fear.

He should have kept it in, resisted his own damn temptation. But that gift, Ettie's sweetness, cracked him open. Now he tried to empty his mind again but those malevolent memories swirled, relentless. They'd been woken.

He'd kept it all buried for so long—had hidden that dark, incomplete side of himself from everyone. Living alone it didn't matter, it was easy. But in marriage?

He didn't want to poison her with it. He wished he'd never told her. To complain of a little punishment? Of loneliness? He'd been as weak as his mother had warned. What he needed was his control back.

He slid out of bed silently so he didn't wake Ettie and quickly checked the small puppy. It was fast asleep and warm in its little bed. Leon opened up his laptop in the lounge and tried to work. But his mind was fragmented and he'd achieved little by the time dawn finally began to lighten the dark.

He showered, standing for a long time under the steaming jet—trying to relax. He'd get through the weekend, he'd fall back into bed with her…

But he hadn't even made it to Saturday before falling apart. Having her this close was confusing, constricting…those stirred-up memories still prickled like thorns in a blood-splattered bouquet in a damn low-budget horror film. Reaching out, he flicked the faucet to cold and suffered the pelting icy droplets. They were like little knives, pinkening up soft skin. Those memories surged.

He braced. He'd beaten them a long time ago. Banished them. And he'd banish them again now because he was not that boy any more. He had control. He flicked the faucet back to warm. Yeah. He had *power.* And he would make this work.

He'd talked about it with Ettie—told her far more than he'd ever intended. Surely he'd satisfied her infernal curiosity at last? So now it was done and behind them for ever.

He'd get this back to the practical, responsible arrangement he needed it to be.

He breathed in and quietly walked to the bedroom to grab some clothes. Then he got back to his computer. Focused. Calm. Ready.

But Ettie walked into the lounge an hour later, looking like sunshine in a simple denim skirt and white T-shirt. One look and he felt that hard-wrestled-for control slip again. Every time he so much as looked at her it was like that thing bound tightly within him was loosened. But it was something he didn't want released. Not ever.

'You're working already?' she asked.

He nodded, fighting the urge to reach out and touch her. To use sex as his distraction again, as she'd teased the other day…

But last night—how good she'd felt, how intense that had been with her…that hadn't just been distraction. It had been much more than simple, mindless fun. And it couldn't be like that again.

'I've fed the puppy; he's asleep again,' he said after clearing his throat. 'We'll take him for a walk later.'

She nodded and sauntered through to the kitchen looking like the sexiest, sweetest thing he'd ever seen. He breathed out as she left. See? He could resist. She'd claimed control, but he had it back. Just.

Oh, who was he kidding?

Only now he realised the troubling truth: *she* was his weakness—Ettie Roberts herself. His slide into addiction had already started and he hadn't realised because she felt so good. But *she* was what he craved—*all* the time. But he couldn't use her in that way, as if she were his personal opiate. He had to dial it back. He *had* lost control last night and he'd not expressed anything other than pure, selfish greed.

He refused to be all over her. Sure, they'd sleep together and they'd have this baby, but he'd pull himself together properly and remind them *both* that this was just another business arrangement. That was all it could ever be.

CHAPTER TEN

ETTIE WAS ACUTELY relieved when Monday finally arrived. It wasn't that the weekend had been awful... She and Leon had walked the puppy, wandered around the markets, watched a movie rather than go to that concert—her pick. He'd driven her out of town specially to dine at another amazing restaurant... It was as if he was determined they'd be a normal couple—albeit one with luxurious experiences. She knew he wanted to make this work and she knew he'd be loyal. He had his own brand of duty and honour burned in him. He had everything else too—humour, looks, a bank balance big enough to make anyone's eyes water. And he was so attentive, always ensuring she had what she needed.

Almost all she needed.

But there'd been no more mad, unrestrained sex on the floor, in the kitchen, in the lounge... in fact there'd been no touching at all until darkness fell. But then when it did...?

They'd come together with a wordless intensity that neither of them had addressed afterwards. Neither Saturday nor Sunday. But all through both nights that raw, unrestrained passion had been unleashed. That genie was well out of the bottle now. Leon had made her moan and shake, he'd stripped her back to pure nerves and he'd roared with her, riding her hard. Again. Again. Again. Through the darkness they'd clung to each other, almost crazed with need. Neither of them could get enough and neither of them denied it. Until daylight. Then they were returned to that beautifully curated lifestyle of breakfast at a cute deli, a walk in the park, pondering his next art selection at an elite auction house…but no argument or discussion of anything *deep*. And that was why she was relieved by the prospect of work. She needed the time away from him so she could *think*. Because it wasn't quite right—not since that acutely profound moment on Friday night.

Now she shimmied into her uniform and brushed her hair into submission, ready to face her first day in her new position.

'Here…' Leon was in the kitchen, dressed in a charcoal suit, looking more remote and businesslike than ever. 'Something for your first day as manager.'

She picked up the beautiful business satchel he'd pushed across the counter towards her. She saw the gold insignia and drew in a steadying breath. This wasn't some knock-off from the street markets, this was real leather, from a real luxury label. 'You didn't have to—'

'Look inside.' He sipped his coffee and watched her.

She suddenly felt nervous, because his gaze seemed especially dark this morning—the amber glow was absent. She reached for the slim box tucked inside. Pressing her lips together, she lifted the lid.

It was a pen, but not just any pen. The distinctive white star on the cap told her that, as did the intricately engraved gold nib. 'Leon—'

'Now you don't need to steal mine.' His gaze drifted to her hair and seemed to darken some more. 'You can keep your hair up with it.'

She shook her head. 'I'd be too afraid I'd lose it.' She knew it was worth a crazy amount of money. And it was beautiful—feminine and perfect. But she didn't know if she could keep accepting these kinds of gifts.

'Well,' he set the coffee cup down with a slight bang, 'you can use it to sign the contract in the folder.'

'Contract?'

'The sooner it's signed off, the sooner I can organise the accounts.'

Accounts? With a growing sense of foreboding Ettie looked into the soft leather case again and drew out the slim Manila folder. She opened it and saw several pages of neat type. She stilled as she read the title—it was the prenuptial contract between her and Leon. Their *arrangement* in all its ugly glory.

'I'll need to take time to read it properly,' she muttered, feeling a hit of dizziness as she saw the lists of numbers—*remuneration*. She'd forgotten about their 'deal' over the weekend. She'd been too busy trying to breach his defences again the way she had on Friday night. Too busy trying to restore her own inner equilibrium. And she'd failed on both counts.

His lips twisted. 'Sure. Get it back to me later today.'

She frowned as she studied one page more carefully—the itemised list of her *benefits*. 'This monthly allowance…is for groceries and everything?'

'No, it's your personal allowance.'

But it was more than what she was paid for her job at Cavendish House! She looked up to glare at him.

'You need new clothes and things…'

Her fury mounted and he fell silent at the expression in her eyes. Yeah, he knew she was insulted. But what was worse was that she knew he'd done this deliberately to engender such a reaction in her. Well, it had worked.

'And I get an annual bonus each year for remaining married to you?' she clarified with barely disguised rage.

He lifted that damned coffee cup to his lips again.

'You think I'll respond to that kind of financial incentive?'

'Doesn't everyone?' he asked coolly.

After she'd opened up to him so completely? After what they'd shared on Friday night? Hurt swept over her in a violent wave. Yet immediately after it followed a deep resignation—and *regret*. Because she remembered she'd *already* responded to a financial inducement. It was why she'd agreed to marry him in the first place. This was just the painful reminder of that reality—in cold black and white print.

She shuffled the odious pages together and shoved them into the damned gorgeous bag, tossing the pen in too, not bothering with the perfect little presentation box. 'I'd better get to work; I don't want to be late.'

'I'll drop you.'

'No need.' She turned a huge smile on him as she marched out of the room. 'I'm happy to walk.'

To her enormous relief—and no small amount of regret—he didn't follow her. She breathed quick, steadying breaths all the way to Cavendish House but her nausea had returned. And all her horror.

Yet why should she be so angry about it? Shouldn't she take this as the business opportunity it was? He was giving her everything she could ever want, right?

Because he didn't really want this. Not with her.

He'd lifted that curtain and told her about his life and he regretted it. Not just a wince of embarrassment, but an excoriating extent of regret. He'd pretended he didn't, he didn't show any outward emotion, but she'd seen it eating him, she'd sensed his withdrawal as he sought to rebuild walls he thought were weakened. All weekend she'd hoped—but he hadn't opened up again. Instead he'd made it all about *her*. As if he was determined to make her *happy*—as if it was another job for him to entertain her. Despite their intimacy, the distance she'd felt between them wasn't breached. And she knew the effort he'd made was unsustainable. If it was this hard for him now, she couldn't see how it was going to work for long in the future.

And he'd been busy in the background, hadn't he? Working out his damned clinical contract to seal them both into nothing but a seedy money-for-marriage transaction.

To think she'd actually thought for a moment that they might've become something *more*. To think she'd actually had that fantasy of happy-ever-after. That she'd actually had hope that with time…

One look at that contract and she knew there was no chance. His regret was all-consuming. She'd feel sorry for him if she wasn't so hurt. Did he really think so little of her? Think she'd accept money to make their marriage last month by month?

Now she'd never felt as exposed or as insecure in all her life. Not when her mother had got her diagnosis, or when her ex had texted to tell her the wedding was off. Neither compared to the uncertainty she felt now. Her heart raced as if she'd sprinted her way to work. And now she had to maintain the lie in front of her friends—act ecstatic and in love and all that…it was too hard and all she wanted to do was cry.

Work. Be like Leon. Get it done.

She *had* to get it done. She couldn't let that contract ruin her career as well. She'd worked too hard for it. She just needed to find the time to work out what she was going to do about Leon next. She'd have to do that later.

So she smiled with pure determination as Joel held the door to the concierge office open for her when she arrived, and when he bowed as she walked through.

'Stop it.' She tried to laugh it off.

'You're the boss now… I have to bow and scrape.'

'Ettie,' Jess squealed and leapt up from the seat she'd been sitting on, obviously waiting for her arrival. 'You should *hear* the rumours about you.' She pounced on her and grabbed Ettie's hand, her eyes bugging as she inspected the emerald and diamonds. 'OMG, it's true. I'm *so* thrilled for you.' Jess swept her up in a giant hug. 'When you fainted and he carried you up to the penthouse, it was the most *romantic* thing I've ever seen.'

Ettie hid her face in Jess's shoulder. Her friend's congratulations were heartfelt but she felt hideously awkward. Her engagement wasn't romantic at all, but a business arrangement with benefits.

'And you've worked so hard, you deserve your promotion,' Joel said a little gruffly.

'He's pleased because he gets promoted too,' Jess teased Joel with sparkling eyes. 'What you deserve, Ettie, is *happiness*.'

Ettie blinked back the shockingly sudden surge of tears. She'd worked alongside these guys for years and seeing them this happy for her was… overwhelming. And awkward. So awkward. She blew out a quick breath and smiled as Joel and Jess left the office to get on with their jobs. She could hold it together. It was just hormones and tiredness and the horror of that awful agreement that she couldn't think about right now…

The morning went swiftly because it was perfectly, blessedly busy. But just as she'd finally settled into the swing of it, someone called her to the front desk.

'Hey!'

Ettie's legs suddenly weakened. 'Ophelia?'

'Yes!' Her little sister rushed over and pulled her into a huge hug, managing to dance a small jig at the same time.

'Why are you here? Is everything okay?' Ettie's heart thudded.

'Everything is fabulous.'

Ophelia leaned back and Ettie got a good look at her. Her sister, taller than Ettie, was stunning even in her slightly faded second-hand blazer. Her hair was chestnut and shining and her skin and smile just glowed with health.

'I'm in London for a debating tournament.'

'Of course you are.' Ettie laughed at her gorgeous, geeky sister. 'Why didn't you tell me you were coming?'

'I wasn't sure I could get here. I only have an hour and then I have to get back for the next round.'

'You sneaked out?'

'Well, *duh.*' Ophelia laughed. 'Because I'm so excited for you. I couldn't come to London and not *see* you.'

'Come into the office.' Ettie bit her lip and led her sister into a private space.

She'd phoned Ophelia at Friday lunchtime, after her trip to the dog shelter. She'd told her about moving in with Leon and the baby and *almost* everything.

But not quite all. She could never tell her sister the deal she'd struck with Leon. She could never explain the intricacies of that.

'Is he here?' Ophelia asked as soon as the door was closed, her eyes shining so brightly that Ettie couldn't hold her gaze.

'No, he's in his office. He has meetings.' Right now Ettie was so glad he'd moved out of Cavendish House.

'When can I meet him?' Ophelia bounced on her toes. 'I can't wait to meet him.'

Churning hot acid burned up Ettie's throat. This was so much worse than the lie to Jess and Joel. 'He's a busy guy.'

'You have to come up and see me and bring him. Please! You have to come soon.'

Ettie nodded. But she didn't want Ophelia to meet him. She didn't want this to become that real.

'What's wrong?' Ophelia paused, a slight frown forming on her face.

'Nothing, I'm just...surprised to see you.' Ettie summoned a bright smile, but she and Ophelia were close. Too close—because right now Ophelia saw right through her. She had to act as if it were perfect. It was perfect, wasn't it?

'Good surprised or bad surprised?'

'Good—but if you get into trouble for sneaking out from debating, I won't be happy.'

Ophelia smiled but her gaze was still too watchful. 'Do you love him, Ettie?'

Ettie's throat constricted. She couldn't answer that question. She couldn't answer that one even to herself. But her face burned with a blush.

'Are you happy?' Ophelia's smile was so sweet, so caring, so concerned.

This was the moment to lie. The moment she *had* to lie. But she still couldn't get her voice to work. She made herself nod even as a tear spilled over.

'*Ettie*.' Ophelia wrapped her arms around her. 'I'm worried.'

'Hormones,' she croaked and then laughed to cover it all up. 'I'm fine.'

'You're sure?'

'So sure. Come on, let's have a hot chocolate.'

Half an hour later she kissed her sister goodbye and saw her into a cab to get her back to her debating hall. She stood on the pavement and watched until the cab went round the corner, relieved that it had only been a fleeting visit. It should have been such a treat; instead it had been harder than she'd ever have imagined.

Being that uncomfortable about seeing her beloved sister shattered her. Wrong. It was just *wrong*. It should've been nothing but wonderful, but it had been a nightmare. She couldn't maintain lying to her sister—not for more than the few minutes she'd seen her for just now. She certainly couldn't lie to her sister for the rest of her life. She couldn't lie to her child. She couldn't lie to herself.

Her heart ached.

You've worked so hard for so long.

Yes, and she deserved that promotion. She'd known she did a good job.

You deserve happiness… Are you happy?

She should be happy, right? But she wasn't.

She felt trapped and increasingly afraid that her heart was Leon's prisoner. There had to be another way. She couldn't live this lie. She couldn't lie to those she loved—to *none* of those she loved. Not even him.

'Ettie, are you okay?'

She turned to find Joel on the pavement next to her, concern on his face. 'I'm fine, thanks, Joel. I'm just going to take a walk.'

She needed time to think about how things were going to work. She didn't know what the answer was yet, but something had to change. She walked through the streets and saw the station in the distance. On automatic pilot, she caught the train, letting the familiar route soothe her. She'd not intended to go there, but when she arrived she knew it was what she needed.

Her apartment was colder than usual. Almost empty. He'd had professionals in, because all her stuff was in a few boxes. The furniture was being left for the next person who moved in. She glanced at the windowsill. Not even her herbs needed her any more. They'd already died from the few days of neglect. But it was her home. And in it she'd been honest. And happy.

She needed to be honest again and take back some control. She'd let Leon dictate everything until now. She'd been tired and overwhelmed and confused. But she wasn't now. And she knew what had to happen.

She couldn't sign that contract. She couldn't stay with him. She couldn't live that lie for the rest of her life.

It would slowly tear her apart and she couldn't do that to herself. Because her intuitive, immediate answer to Ophelia's question had hit her hard.

Yes, she loved him.

She'd fallen in love with Leon. In love with a man who didn't love her. Again.

But this wasn't like it was with her ex. She'd never loved *him*. She'd not known what love was until Leon. Not love, nor lust, nor laughter and true companionship…for just a moment she'd had a glimpse of what might've been possible if he loved her too.

Now she looked at the emerald on her finger. It was so beautiful, but without heart. It should have heart with it—it was too stunning to be empty. She took it off and put it on the table, turning away to curl up on the old lumpy sofa. She needed to think through how she was going to be able to live with Leon in her life, but without ever having him in the way she ached for. And she was suddenly so tired, so heartsore, she just had to close her eyes and hide.

The knock on her door an hour later startled her. She checked the peephole and got even more of a shock.

'What are you doing here?' She stepped back after letting Leon in, nervously tugging her shirt when she saw his grim expression.

'Joel called. He was concerned about you.'

Why? 'How did you know where to find me?'

'Seeing as you left your phone at Cavendish, I made a lucky guess,' he said in a chilled voice. 'Joel said Ophelia visited you. Is she okay?'

'She's great. Really. So happy.'

'I'm glad.'

Ettie pressed her lips together. He didn't sound glad.

'I'm sorry if I worried you,' she said.

He didn't answer. He'd seen the ring on the table and he didn't lift his gaze from it.

'I'm not signing that contract, Leon,' she blurted, unable to hide her hurt from him any more. 'I don't expect you to pay for Ophelia's fees. I never should have accepted that offer. I can make it work some other way.'

'What are you saying, Ettie?' His expression had frozen.

She clenched her fists and tried to hold herself together. 'I allowed you to make all the decisions. It all happened so fast, I wasn't feeling well…we got carried away on a tsunami of panic and some of this wasn't necessary.'

'Wasn't necessary?' he repeated in cool disbelief, and turned to look at her hard. 'Ettie, you're pregnant.'

'Yes, and we need to make rational decisions.'

'You call walking out of work and coming back to this dump a rational decision?'

She drew in a sharp breath. He was angry with her, unused to being challenged. 'This is my home. I was happy here.'

'You're not happy at my home?'

'You swept in and took command—'

'You were *ill*,' he pointed out icily.

'You tipped my life upside down,' she shouted back. 'It's just been so quick and I haven't had the chance to think everything through.' She needed to slow down because her alarm bells were ringing.

'What do you want?' he exploded. 'I was *trying*—'

'Yes,' she interrupted harshly. 'Trying too hard.'

He sent her a wrathful look. 'I *what*?' he muttered, outraged.

'You don't want to marry me any more than I want to marry you.'

That silenced him.

'You don't, Leon.' She rubbed her arms, suddenly cold. 'It's a calculated decision you think you have to live with. But you don't. And I can't live a lie for the rest of my life. I can't pretend to be happy when I'm not.'

'You've given us less than a week.' He was livid.

'Isn't it better to realise the mistake sooner rather than later?'

'Or maybe you should give us more time. I might be trying too hard, but you're bailing out at the first chance you've got. You've been betrayed in the past and you're letting your fears get in the way of a perfectly fine future. You think I'll walk out on you,' he added coldly. 'So you've left before I can.'

His accusation stole her breath.

'I can't do this,' she whispered. 'I can't marry you.'

She was his choice by default. They were forced together purely by the fate of a failed condom. Sure, he was offering security for her baby. Their child would want for nothing—it would have the adoration of both parents.

'You're a good guy, Leon, okay?' she said unevenly. 'You win the honourable prize. You're a man who steps up and does the right thing. But you don't have to take it this far, okay?'

'This far?'

'I can't marry you. I can't live with you. I certainly can't sign that horrible contract and be *paid* to like you. We can just co-parent. We can make some better arrangement.'

He glared at her. 'You're saying you don't want to sleep with me any more?'

'We're only back together because of the baby. You don't really want me.'

'How can you say I don't want you when I can't keep my hands off you?' he roared and shoved those hands into his trouser pockets.

She gritted her teeth. 'That's just sex. And frankly, we're using it to paper over the cracks in this arrangement.'

'We what?' He dragged in a sharp breath. Then another. 'You're complaining about our sex life?'

'You use it to avoid emotional intimacy.'

He froze. 'And what do you use it for?'

She couldn't answer that. She just couldn't.

He stared at her. 'You read too much into everything. You attach meaning to memories that don't actually matter.'

'Don't they matter? Don't you think they impact how we both choose to live?' She stepped closer, suddenly shaking with emotion, with how important it was to cut through to what was vitally important. And honest.

'Yes, I've been hurt before and I don't want to be hurt again,' she admitted. 'And if I stay with you, I will be. I've tried to treat this like an arrangement, but I can't. I'm not like you, I can't keep my emotions "under control", and I don't want to.' She inhaled a deep breath and forced herself to finish. 'We'll work together to take care of the baby, but being together in an empty relationship isn't right. I can't keep sleeping with you, Leon. It's destroying me.' It hurt her so much to say it, but it had to be done. 'You deserve more than this…facade. You deserve love. And so do I.'

She wanted him to find love. He deserved it after everything he'd missed out on. And she wanted to find real love for herself too. To *be* loved. While she could be everything *but* the one he truly wanted, that wasn't enough for her. She wasn't going to put herself through the heartache of being with a man who didn't really want her. Her child needed to see both its mother and its father, loved and loving. If not to each other, then to significant others when and if they appeared.

She'd tried, but she couldn't be like him. Nor was she the one for him. Because if she was he'd have recognised it already—he would have *felt* it. He would have known he didn't need that contract to bind her to him. He was a smart guy, not slow.

'Love?' he scoffed. 'There's no such thing as love. That's the rubbish of fairy tales and films. There's just reality and practicality. There's lust and there are contracts.'

And that just proved her point completely. Because for her there *was* love. She felt it for *him*. She ached to give him everything she possibly could, but he didn't feel that way for her. She braced tightly against the painful intensity of rejection.

This is the right decision, Ettie. Right, right, right.

Leon stared at Ettie's expression in the silence that followed his outburst. Dread surged in his belly, a hideous whirlpool of horror and regret. He shouldn't have said that. He shouldn't have crushed her dreams with his icy reality. She hadn't deserved that. Yet he'd had to be honest with her.

He cleared his throat. 'We can make this work, Ettie. We *will* make it work.'

'Yes,' she nodded curtly, 'but not the way you want it to.'

He glared, waiting for her to explain.

'You might be prepared to settle, but I'm not.' She straightened. In a blink the distress was gone from her eyes. There was only determination there now.

'Settle?' The chill spread from his gut to his limbs and then—blessedly—up to his brain. Finally he could think clearly.

'I do believe in that kind of love, Leon.' She looked up at him. Emotion shadowed her eyes, but dignity shone clearly from within them. There were no tears, only resolution. 'I've fallen in love with you,' she said. 'That's why I can't stay and why I won't marry you.'

He stared, dumbstruck, as his brain short-circuited. She *what*?

'How can that possibly surprise you?' she asked with a shake of her head. 'How could I not…? But you don't love me and that's okay.'

'You're not in love with me,' he blurted mechanically.

She was confusing it with gratitude. He was the first person to do things for her. Not betray her. Not abandon her. Not take and take and take. And she had such little experience with sex, she didn't realise it was just physical pleasure. He'd rubbed her up the right way, that was all.

'It's the lifestyle,' he said roughly.

Now her expressive eyes flashed—all anger. 'I don't fall in love with *things*, Leon. You insult me. Your contract insulted me. I'd still love you even if you were poor and lived in a cardboard box. That you felt I needed some reward for staying with you…' She shook her head.

That feeling inside roiled and burned but still he rejected what she was saying.

Her expression hardened in the face of his silence. 'You don't get to deny my feelings or my wishes. You don't get to make all the decisions.' She drew in a deep breath. 'You've found out all my other secrets—you might as well know everything. I fell in love with you probably that very first night. But you don't feel the same. You're trying to do the right thing, but it's too much to ask of you—it's obvious you don't really want to when you can't bear to reveal anything of yourself and you can't trust me for more than five minutes. And I get why, I do. You shouldn't have to open up to someone you don't care about. But don't deny what's true for me. It's painful enough. You don't want emotional intimacy with me. Fine, don't have it. But you don't get physical either. You don't get to have the cake and eat it too. You want too much from me. I can't separate it the way you do.'

She did *not* love him. He could deny that and he would. 'You barely know me.'

'I know all I need to know. Who you are is

what you do. And you do loyal. Kind. Funny. Determined. Stubborn to the point of—' She broke off as her breathing hitched.

Yet it wasn't enough, was it? He'd given her everything he could and it still wasn't enough.

'You don't have to feel bad,' she added, her clear-eyed gaze narrowing on him. 'You don't have to pretend any more. You can find someone else.'

Is that what *she* wanted?

'How bloody generous of you, Ettie,' he said scathingly. 'You haven't even given this a chance. You say you love me but you can walk out just like that?' He snapped his fingers as his anger flared. 'Not much of a love really.'

Her face whitened. 'I also love *myself.* I am worthy of that job promotion. I deserve the great sex life you've shown me is possible. *You're* the one who's taught me I deserve more. Not to expect less or settle for worse. And thank you for that. But now I have to protect myself.' She lifted her chin. 'You don't love me.'

'That's not the point.' He dismissed the statement.

'It is.'

He was so furious he couldn't look at her any

more. Wildly he glanced around and saw the herbs on the windowsill had become little more than a collection of musty leaves in the pots. Without her presence and care they hadn't taken long to wither and die. So typical. He felt his grip on himself slip as that monstrous crushing inside threatened to kill every last brain cell he had and render him only capable of...*what*?

Oh, his body knew what it wanted—to prove to her that she couldn't resist him again. Hell, he needed to get away before he totally lost it.

She'd completely rejected everything he'd offered. She'd rejected him.

'At the very least I can house you,' he said icily. 'Not here.' He retrieved the ring from the table. It burned his palm and he shoved it into his pocket. He stalked to the door, needing to leave before he said or did something he'd regret. 'I'll be in touch to make new arrangements.'

CHAPTER ELEVEN

LOVE? SHE WANTED *LOVE*?

Leon was living in a perpetual state of frustration. With every breath he whipped from fury to wrath and back again.

Let her go. Let her stay in her horrible, small apartment. Let her be alone and miserable if that was what she was determined to do. He was happy to have his house back to himself, right? He'd found it hard sharing with someone for the first time in his life. He'd go back to how it had been—how he liked it. Alone, independent, strong, easy.

But he paced the vast, empty space until the puppy got too tired to follow his every step. He sank onto the sofa and scooped the little guy up. The pup immediately curled into a ball on his stomach and began to snooze.

Leon had no such respite. He'd done everything he could for Ettie. He'd given her a far better home. He'd looked after her health and freed her from that financial burden, he'd recognised her worth at work. He'd had her well-being foremost in his mind. What more did she want?

But he hadn't done everything.

The inner voice repeated it—over and over. From a whisper it strengthened in volume and insistence until it was ringing incessantly in his head.

The void she'd left was huge. She'd taken more than he'd realised.

The baby. Right? It was just the baby. He reasoned his way through the bereft sensation. She was taking away his *child*. And with that recognition his anger returned in full force. He railed inwardly at her stubborn selfishness.

He'd been told so often that people would only want *things* from him. Money, mostly. Money and the kind of "doors open" access his privilege engendered. And that wisdom had proven true often enough in the past. But not this time.

He'd given everything to *her*. At least everything that was easy to give—his money, his success, his home. What was harder was what was hidden. What he didn't even want to face himself. The security she craved wasn't financial. What she'd said she wanted—needed—was emotional. And that was impossible. He didn't believe in love. He didn't even know what it was. Yet with every day that dragged, that bereft feeling only built a bigger and bigger hole inside. It wasn't the thought of the baby at all.

He put a security team back on her. He initiated all the paperwork he could think of to secure both her rights and his, ditching that damned contract he'd drawn up over that weekend to try to hold the complications at bay. But three interminable days later, he still couldn't sleep at night. Worry nagged.

He hated thinking of her being alone. He hated remembering her words. But they echoed relentlessly—a melody to his own berating beat—dragging in loss, lust, unbearable loneliness… and at the heart of that hideous mix grew an intolerable, impossible yearning.

I love you, Leon.

It was the first time in his life someone had said that to him and actually meant it. He knew, to his bones, how much she thought she'd meant it. She barely knew him but she believed her words. He'd been unable to. And he'd been right because in the next second she'd snatched them back again by rejecting everything he'd offered.

By rejecting *him*. She didn't love him enough to stay. She didn't even want his damn money. She was so determined to be independent, all because he couldn't what—wail on about his past? Open up to her? Love her?

Didn't she understand that he couldn't? He didn't know how.

He knew she wouldn't deny him access to his child. She'd just denied him access to *her*. She'd taken her company, her attention, her presence from him. And somehow that was the worst. He couldn't stand it. Nor could he fathom *why* it was so horrendous.

So he did what he'd always done: he fought for control. He isolated himself. He worked round the clock. And he avoided all contact with anyone at Cavendish House. They'd be Team Ettie all the way. He didn't blame them. He understood their loyalty.

He also knew Ettie needed to be loved. That was why she worked for everyone—she ached for any kind of affection. She didn't realise that all those people cared about her without her having to work for it; it was because of the person she was—sunny, generous, interested, enthusiastic about everything in life…

And he'd been stupid enough to tell her he didn't believe in love.

He sat on the floor of his home and rubbed the puppy's ears and finally admitted to himself that he was a coward. More than that, he was a jerk. He'd not accepted what she'd offered. He'd not even acknowledged the truth of it.

The fourth morning it was worse. He couldn't stand it any more. The isolation and gaping hole inside widened with every angry second that ticked by and today it was an actual physical pain. And that was when it finally hit—it wasn't *rage* he felt. It was *hurt.*

Deep, incurable hurt. He was so vulnerable. She'd prised layers of protection and defence open and then she'd struck him hard.

Not even the unconditional trust of the little puppy soothed him. The dog just made it worse, because he made caring—adoration—seem easy. Not to Leon it wasn't. He closed his eyes and leaned against the cool window overlooking his immaculate garden.

Ettie had given him the smallest, tantalising glimpse of something he'd never imagined. When she'd said she was in love with him, he'd had that heart-busting vision of a small family filled with fun and laughter and passion. A family that was *together.* The kind of family he'd never had.

In his childhood family there'd been no honesty. No laughter. No love. Nothing but cold cruelty from his mother. And when he'd tried to talk to his father, the older man had shut down. Dismissed his truth. Silenced him.

But hadn't Leon just done the exact same thing to Ettie? Hadn't he shut down and closed off contact? He'd refused to even acknowledge the problem, let alone try to resolve it.

While he'd silenced her, Ettie had never silenced him. She'd let him speak. She'd wanted him to speak more. She hadn't judged him for his words, she'd just accepted him.

Bile rose in his throat. He did not want to be like his father. And he sure as hell refused to be like his mother. Why had he thought any of what that woman had wanted was okay?

Never show weakness. Not anger. Not fear. No tears. No laughter.

Even when he'd learned to bury his emotions, his mother hadn't loved him. Nothing he could've done could have changed that. She'd taught him all the wrong things. And he'd been so busy fighting for those tangible signs of success, he'd not stopped to see how much he was missing. How much his mother had actually *won*—because here he was, living a life so isolated, he might as well be back in that cupboard she'd locked him in.

Ettie was the one who was right. Expressing emotions *wasn't* the same as losing control of them. And even if he did lose control? What then? What was the worst that could happen? The worst had *already* happened.

Ettie had left him.

And now here he was in his huge house—isolated, cold and stuck in the emotional stunting of his past. He'd thought he was over it, that he was free of that pain. But he wasn't beyond it at all. His own beautiful big house offered no more comfort or companionship than that dark, hideous cupboard of his childhood torment.

That constriction inside—the tight-bound hard knot inside him—finally loosened. And it hurt like hell. But he would *not* be an absent father to this child—physically or emotionally. He had to make more of an effort because he didn't want his child turning out like him. He gazed sightlessly over the garden as he fully realised the painful, amazing truth. That knot inside—he'd hardened it, tried to cover it up, because it was more than a crusted nugget of hope. It was his heart.

Ettie had breathed life into it, blowing on old embers to bring back a flame. His inner fire was flickering now but it needed more fuel.

While he'd do anything to protect his baby, what was even more incredible—wonderful and terrifying—was that he'd fallen so completely in love with its mother. It wasn't just the physical contact, but everything she brought with her. Her smile had put sparkle into his life. He simply wanted to put his battered heart into her hands and be with her. And he wanted to care for her in *all* ways. Her words hadn't just unsettled him, they'd also left him raw. She had a power he'd never have believed it would be possible for anyone to have over him. He was still a little angry with her for that. And yet he knew he too had the power to gravely hurt her. He already had. But he'd never do that again.

He thought back to that very first night—to the way she'd run away the next morning, too scared to even look him in the eye. Braced for rejection, for betrayal, she'd been so certain she was going to be hurt. She'd run because he'd not given her what she needed.

But in order to get her back he had to open up in the way he'd told himself he never would, that he'd never thought he *could*. Heartache forced him forward. There was no alternative, no getting over this. The gap she'd left in his life was crippling.

He'd thought he had it all. He'd thought he was invincible. But he had nothing of real value. Now he'd finally realised, he knew he had to do something about it.

There was action and there was *action*.

CHAPTER TWELVE

IT WAS MOVING DAY.

Ettie looked around her little flat. Not much had changed in the days since she'd left Leon and come back to live alone.

He'd been in touch as promised, but only via paperwork. Formal, bloodless documentation offering her an apartment in Cavendish House to make it easy for her to work and be near to his home. It didn't matter how near or far from her he was, he still killed her heart, but she couldn't be under the same roof as him, couldn't sleep with him any more, and that would happen if she stayed at his house. He didn't love her and that was fine, but to remain and give everything of herself would slowly destroy her.

At least Leon travelled for work. She'd have moments of pure respite. Those urges in the smallest hours of the morning, to run to him, to tell him again that she loved him, to try to convince him to love her...she could ignore those. If she ignored them for long enough, surely they'd disappear. Surely she'd done the right thing?

But doubts niggled. Should she have fought harder for him?

Only then she remembered her past. Hadn't she been humiliated enough? The man didn't love her. No man had ever loved her. Not her father. Not her ex. Not Leon.

Snap out of it, Ettie.

The removal van was due in five minutes. She'd had very little to do—just repacked those few belongings she'd got out.

Someone knocked on the door. She checked the peephole. The guy's cap was pulled low but had the removal logo on it. He was early. Of course, anyone hired by Leon would be efficient in the extreme.

She opened the door, knowing the security guard stationed along from her flat would have already vetted him. But it wasn't the removal man. It was Leon himself.

She stared, her tongue stuck to the roof of her mouth. She'd never seen him this casually dressed. She'd pretty much only seen him either in a suit or naked. Now he was in black jeans, black T-shirt—and both fitted him lovingly. The effect of his outfit was...*appallingly inappropriate*. She clenched her jaw and her fists, furious for her basic reaction to him. *Every time.*

He totalled her senses.

'I need to be able to help you, Ettie.' He shifted on his feet and broke the silence. 'Don't you think?'

That's all he wanted to do?

Unable to speak, she nodded and stood aside so he could enter. She had to be stronger than this.

He was holding a tray she'd not seen through the peephole. 'I brought you these.'

A trio of little plants in pretty pots. Fresh herbs to replace the ones that had died.

'Housewarming present for your new apartment,' he explained in her silence. 'I noticed your other ones hadn't survived your absence.'

Of course. He noticed everything. He'd even got the exact right herbs—thyme, chives, basil. Her battered heart burst apart that little bit more. But it was a peace offering and she could be adult enough to accept it, couldn't she?

'Thank you,' she said awkwardly as he put the plants on the old dining table.

He didn't pick up one of the stacked boxes.

Instead he looked across the small space to her, his expression more serious than ever. It should have been impossible.

'I'm sorry.' His words spilled suddenly into the taut silence. Uneven and harsh, like sharp pebbles tossed with piercing aim.

Was that what he'd come to offer? An apology? Her heart cranked open again, seeping pain and pure disappointment. She should appreciate the gesture, but she found she wasn't quite ready to be *friends* with him yet. Too soon. Too sore.

She blinked rapidly, tried to pull herself together enough to offer a polite smile. Could he just shift the boxes now? But he was standing there—as still as still, his expression unreadable, his eyes as dark as his T-shirt.

'I don't know what love really is, Ettie. I only know what it isn't and I couldn't let that happen to you. It's why I thought I should—could—let you go. I never wanted you to be unhappy.'

Yes, she knew he hadn't meant to hurt her. He'd only tried to do the right thing. Now, could he *please* pick up a box?

'Ettie?' He paused. 'Please look at me.'

He asked so softly and she couldn't resist. This

was the problem; she didn't think she could *ever* resist. Not for long. She wasn't ready for this yet.

He was paler than usual. Intense. Rigid. Her eyes filled because he was trying to open up and be honest and she could see the cost of that effort. She could see the desperation in him. Because he knew he'd hurt her and he didn't like that. He might be bossy, but he was kind, and that broke her heart all over again. 'Leon—'

'No. Let me finish. Hell, start. I'm making a mess of it.' He rubbed his hand through his hair, frustration leaping from him. 'It's taken me a bit to realise you weren't rejecting *me*. You thought you were doing the right thing for me. For the baby. And for you. Because you wanted more than what I was offering. You were right to want that.'

Not the money, the lifestyle, the security. No, she'd wanted something far more precious from him.

'I've always been unwilling to share space with anyone, share anything much. I didn't know how.'

He stood still but Ettie could see the faint trembling of his fingers and she waited. She couldn't have spoken if she'd tried.

'I have that massive house because it made me feel free. I thought we'd hardly be aware of each other in there, but somehow you filled it,' he said. 'I didn't know it at the time, but I've never been as scared in all my life as those few days when you were living with me. And then you left.' He puffed out a long, pained breath. 'And now I've finally worked out what it was I'd been so afraid of. It was that. You *leaving*.' He paused. 'Having you with me was like a dream, and I didn't want to wake up and find you gone. Not again.'

Ettie couldn't move, couldn't open her mouth, not even to release the moan building in her chest. She hurt so much—for him, for her. And the fragile hope that was mounting within was too much to bear.

'I didn't recognise what I was feeling,' he said. 'I just didn't know, Ettie. I've never had it before. Never felt it.' He stepped nearer to her, his eyes blazing almost black with intensity. 'You were right. I buried myself—us—in sex. I had this driving need to get closer to you. It's so good, but that's because it's *not* just physical, Ettie.' His voice lifted. 'It never was. I think back to that first day. I've never been as intrigued by anyone. You were passionate and fiery and sweet and kind. But the thing is, you do lovely things for everyone and I doubted that I was all that special—'

'I don't sleep with just anyone,' she interrupted harshly.

'I know.' He lifted his shoulders and then let them fall in a slight, helpless movement of concession. 'You slipped under my armour without my even realising I had armour on. And then I was vulnerable. I didn't like that, Ettie. Uncertainty is hideous.' He dragged in another breath. 'The trouble is, I don't know *how* to give you what's in here.' He pressed his fist to his chest. 'All I knew was that I wanted you to be free and happy, to fly and have all the things I thought you hadn't had… Before these last few days, I never stopped to wonder *why* I wanted that for you but it's since become obvious. I wanted what's best for you, because I've fallen in love with you. I wanted you to have everything…' His voice petered out and he stood there, alone and exposed.

'I just wanted *you*.' Ettie's throat was so tight she could only whisper as her hope overflowed her wounded heart. '*You* were my pick, my special thing just for me. That first night and ever since, all I've ever wanted was *you.*'

The expression on his face crumbled her defences. He looked torn—somewhere between touched and hopeful and terrified.

'I love you and I'm not going to stop loving you.' Her voice shook. 'But—'

'You think I'm only here because of the baby.' He gazed at her, reading her own vulnerability, her own limiting fears. 'No. Our future was set the second I clapped eyes on you. One night was never going to be enough. But you worked for me and you were shy and I was processing how to get around that when we found out…you were pregnant. That changed everything and I think I just went on auto—instinct telling me what needed to happen and what I really wanted… And that's you—*all* of you and *all* the love you have to give.' He paused. His voice was strained. 'I'm so greedy, Ettie. I want you in my life. I don't want to let you go. I'm *not* going to let you go. And I refuse to regret the circumstances that brought us back together. I can't wait until we meet our baby. I love you.' He shook his head as he repeated it beneath his breath.

She put her hand on his lips and stopped him.

'You deserve to have all the love.' Her eyes watered.

'But how do I show you? How do I make you happy?'

His admission—letting her see his vulnerability—touched her more than anything.

She shook her head. 'You just do—just *you*. Listening to me, laughing with me, loving me. It's not pity. It's compassion. It's understanding.'

He gazed so hard into her eyes it was as though he was drinking her words in and was desperately trying to understand, to believe…

'You don't even realise you're doing it,' she muttered, half marvelling. 'Why do you think I fell in love with you? I took one look and wanted you. Even when I thought you were a heartless brute about to condemn Toby, I still felt that physical pull. But I fell in love with you that night—you let me see your smile, you let me in enough to laugh with me, and it was just magic. You were funny and smart and you noticed what I needed before I realised it myself. You *see* me. You know how to care, Leon. It's innate in you.'

The stark emotion in his eyes melted her.

'You're also completely bossy,' she couldn't help teasing.

He didn't hide his smile then. 'What, you mean I'm not perfect?'

'How boring would that be?' She cupped his jaw, reading the tension lingering in his eyes. 'Just talk to me—about anything. Nothing. Everything. I don't need grand gestures, Leon, or fancy dates. It's the everyday things you already do so well.' She pointed at the herbs. 'See? You notice. You care.'

He frowned and put out a dismissive hand. 'That was just—'

'Thoughtful,' she interrupted. 'You did it because you were thinking of me.'

'I think of you all the time,' he muttered huskily.

She stilled because in that moment she truly, finally, completely believed him. It had been the simplest, most heartfelt declaration she'd ever heard.

'Why are you crying?' He pulled her against his chest as her face crumpled and she sobbed.

'Because I'm happy.' She clung to him, needing to feel his heat and strength. 'I love you, Leon.'

He was here. And he was hers.

'I love you too.' He cradled her gently, stroking his hand down her back as she cried out the days of loneliness and heartache. 'I want everything with you—laughter, love, babies, puppies.'

She gurgled with watery laughter but hugged him hard. 'You were right too,' she said softly. 'I was afraid of going for what I wanted—of making a mistake again—so I ran. It's been so awful. All I wanted was you. And I was terrified that you didn't want me.'

Despite all the kisses that had gone before, this felt like their first. In that magical moment just before contact, when breath mingled and eyes locked, that was nerves and excitement, happiness and wonder. Ettie understood his stillness for what it was—the remnants of fear, anxiety and loss leaving them both. This time their sensuality wasn't to avoid emotional intimacy, but to enhance it. And so swiftly, it flared. Incandescently.

'*Glykia mou.*'

He pushed her clothes aside. Kisses touched skin the second it was bared. When she couldn't stand any more he took her down to the floor, into his embrace. He lifted her onto his lap so she straddled him. Face to face, eye to eye. Back in the light where there was no hiding anything. He held her, helped her slide on him until he was buried as deep as possible. More tears trickled at the sudden, exquisite fulfilment. Sealed tightly to him, staring deep into his eyes, she'd never felt this close to anyone. Never as secure…

And never as *hot*.

A glint of amusement sparked in his eye as he slid his hand down to lightly stroke right where she was most sensitive.

'I'm trying to slow down,' she complained with a moan of delight, and leaned closer to kiss his gorgeous mouth.

'Why?' he muttered against her with pure temptation. 'We can always do it again. We can love each other like this every day for the rest of our lives.'

Every nerve curled in unendurable elation. She trembled in his arms as her physical and emotional reaction to his promise consumed her. He loved her so hard and she loved him right back.

For a long time, they remained breathless in the blissful safety of that loving embrace.

He reached out a long arm and grabbed his jeans from the heap of clothes on the floor and pulled something sparkly out of his pocket. 'Is it too soon to put this back where it belongs?'

She stared at the ring and then back up at him. Her heart galloped faster than it had only moments ago when she'd been recovering from the most intense orgasm of her life.

'We can always get another if you don't like it, but I thought the emerald matched your eyes… you probably didn't notice.' His voice trailed off and he fell silent.

She felt the acceleration of his heart beneath her hand. 'I noticed,' she breathed.

'You did?' His face lit up.

Heart overflowing, she lifted her hand so he could slide the ring back on her finger.

'Will you marry me, Ettie Roberts?' he asked unevenly.

'Yes,' she whispered as she stared into his eyes. 'It's beautiful.' And now it had heart; now it glittered even more brilliantly than before.

'It's for real, Ettie,' he promised, husky and true. 'It's for always.'

Bathed in love, she laced her fingers through his.

'Let's go home,' he said. 'Basil will be wondering where we are.'

'You named the puppy Basil?' She leaned against him and laughed with pure, infectious joy. 'Yes. Let's go home to him.'

Together.

* * * * *

A GUIDE TO *modern* MANNERS

ANNE DE COURCY

with 25 illustrations
by Chic Jacob

THAMES AND HUDSON

For advice, help, comment or insight, I would particularly like to thank the following: Maria Aitken, Kingsley Amis, Jill Bennett, Charlotte Bingham, Terence Brady, Peter Cadbury, Nick Chapman, Vernon Coleman, Michael Fish, Bruce Fogle, Elizabeth Hartnell-Beavis, David Johnson, Norman Lonsdale, Anthony Lubran, Tony Morris, Roger Mugford, Matthew Parris, Fiona Penman, Michael Proudlock, Michael Sampson, Nona Summers, Christine, Lady Vavasour, Leonard West, and of course my publisher and friend, Stanley Baron.
I owe a special debt of gratitude to Adam Jacot de Boinod.

Printed and bound in Great Britain

CONTENTS

INTRODUCTION

Once, etiquette meant knowing when to wear white gloves or medals, how long to remain in your hostess's drawing room after a luncheon party, and how to address an envelope to the wife of an earl's younger son.

All this implied a lateral division of society, a series of strata rigidly defined by birth, background or money. If you could master the mores of the class immediately above you, ran the theory, you stood a good chance of climbing into it.

Today, it isn't so much class that moulds behaviour as category.

The social kaleidoscope has been well and truly shaken; increased divorce, multiple marriages, shifting economic forces, the rise in prestige of the professions, the use and misuse of the searchlight of publicity, have all helped to produce an entirely altered pattern.

Thus attitudes, tastes, customs, even phrases and fashions of dressing, permeate whole groups whatever their social background; shared experience creates the strongest bond of all. A boy from Eton and another of the same age from a comprehensive share far more with each other than either does with his respective parents: being young implies a whole way of life. So does being newly-divorced, much-married, gay, or tailored into one of the more individualistic professions – spotting an accountant, a BBC television producer or a politician, for instance, is relatively easy, while the more thrusting Oxford graduate carries with him for life the voice that cut effortlessly through everyone else's conversation during his undergraduate years.

In the world of natural science, this form of grouping by similarities is known as cladistics. Social cladistics sees a shared pattern of behaviour as arising from common experience, each 'species' posing different problems of etiquette or manners. How, for example, do Body People know when it's true love? When should you wear a labrador? What is the politest reaction when a female acquaintance suddenly strips off on the beach beside you? What makes your doctor dote on you?

Sociologists say that a code is defined by its breaches: much of the new etiquette becomes visible through gaffes. In this book, I have tried to define some major social groupings together with pitfalls unknown to earlier manuals of correct behaviour – in short, to write a Guide to truly Modern Manners. Which, like good manners everywhere, are based on true consideration for others.

Never mind the father's social background, young lady! Is he upper, lower or middle management?

1.
THE ART OF SOCIAL DEFLECTION

In everyday life, the most desirable form of social expertise is the knack of avoiding the difficult, awkward or boring without either appearing bad-mannered or hurting other people's feelings.

This enviable attribute is best summed up as the Art of Social Deflection, and is based on the premise that you can get away with murder by a combination of speed, niceness and giving them something else to think about – in short, deflecting attention away from your own motives or behaviour.

In more leisured days, when most social communication was via the written word, speed was not the essential it is on the telephone. Today, adept Deflectors realize instantly when they have to grasp the conversational initiative.

Saying straightway, 'I can't talk now, the taxi's waiting at the door,' conveys an unassailable sense of urgency rather than any hint of rudeness. Whereas interrupting a woe-filled saga after ten minutes with the words, 'I have to go now as I have people to lunch,' succeeds in offending both your caller ('Is my disaster less important than a trivial social pursuit?') and your guests, who have been sitting watching the soufflé go flat as you murmur, 'Oh no – how *frightful*,' at five-minute intervals.

Exactly the same principle applies if caught in a boring backwater at a party, although here, I need hardly remind you, a convincing excuse for leaving in mid-conversation is *de rigueur* (or in the case of bores, de rigor). All the world is indulgent to an ex-lover: try 'Good Lord – there's someone I was mad about ten years ago. Excuse me . . .'

It is slightly more difficult when trapped at the dinner table. Once, seated between a man with a mesmerically horrific stammer and a non-stop talker, I passed a nightmare evening surrounded by the strangulated gasps and croaks on my right and the ceaseless flow of banalities on my left. Alas, I did not then know the Social Deflector's ploy of Giving Them Something Else to Think About – tipping over a wineglass would have broken me into the conversation opposite, for example. Nor had I met the Bradys.

For two who have perfected this aspect of Social Deflection are writers Terence Brady and his wife Charlotte Bingham. Fortunately, there is a literally flourishing excuse to hand in their conservatory dining room; nevertheless, this is Social Deflection in its most classic form, with all the elements combined in the hands of a master practitioner. When Terence is bored, says his wife, he gives a sweet smile at the borer and exclaims, 'My God – I forgot to water the geraniums!', upon which he springs up, seizes the watering can kept for the purpose in the corner of the room, and wanders hither and thither sprinkling various plants.

'By the time he's come back to his seat even the most insensitive leading lady has stopped droning on about how her part in our next TV play should be made more important.'

There is, although both the Bradys are too polite to mention it, a secondary moral here; never offend a writer or you may get written out of the series.

The most incontrovertible proof of the efficacy of Social Deflection can be found in the Catch-22 situation of backstage congratulations after a First Night. On these occasions, whatever you say is likely to be wrong – if you don't rave, the actors think you hated it, and if you do they don't believe you. Nor is it any good ducking out of the whole thing by not going backstage at all because then, quite naturally, everyone from star to stagehand thinks you found either the play, their performance, or the standard of scene-shifting too appalling even to mention.

The only solution is the Social Deflector's friend, irrelevance, topped with a lavish dollop of sympathetic charm. Rushing into the highly charged post-performance atmosphere of the star's dressing room, you say warmly, 'Have they STILL not given you a lampshade for your dressing room? How MONSTROUS! and only a 15 watt bulb – you'll have to speak to the management!'

Whereupon the actor, enraged, says, 'You're absolutely right!' and afterwards, despite the fact that you haven't mentioned the play once, tells his friends, 'I do love it when Amanda and Jeremy come backstage – they always say the right thing.'

Parrying awkward questions is another field where practised Social Deflectors come into their own. The most basic deflective weapon is, of course, a smile – something which makes offering nothing but silence to an intrusive or impertinent question perfectly polite. Occasionally, though, it isn't quite enough . . . and here one of the Great Mentionables will almost certainly get you off the hook.

The Great Mentionables, I should explain, are those topics certain of fascinating anyone within earshot, distracting them from whatever else they may be talking or thinking about into listeners anxious only to chip in at the first moment's pause with their own riveting experience. As the name implies, most of today's Great Mentionables started life in the opposite corner, as the forbidden subjects of previous generations. Take but three: sex, money – and childbirth.

Throw the word 'epidural' across any Fulham dinner table and the air is instantly rent with competing sagas of parturition. No detail is taboo; the description of a complicated episiotomy will hold the table spellbound, while husbands will contribute wherever they can. 'Amanda wanted to wait until the pains were regular but I said, "Darling, now the waters have broken it's grab your panic bag and we're off."'

It's the same with sex and money. For mixed company, sex works the best; money (how you spend it, what you paid for this, that or the other) needs roughly similar starting points to allow for effective comparison and thence the inevitable undercurrent of competition which gives such conversations their edge. Like weight, money is a perfect single-sex Great Mentionable.

Even to the most skilled Social Deflector, however, some situations provide an almost insuperable challenge. One of the most difficult is if a new mother starts breastfeeding her baby at a dinner party. Admirably natural though this may be in theory, in practice it is almost always a conversation-stopper. Saying, as does the father of one friend of mine, 'Good heavens, he's not going to drink all that, is he?' may hint at surprise but the only real answer is speedy, firm action. The hostess, or even the host, must take the girl to the bedroom, picking up her coffee cup, wineglass, etc., on the way, so that any argument about staying put is pre-empted.

To cut themselves off from the crowd painlessly, chief Social Deflectors make use of the new technology; if Denis Healey can use his Sony Walkman as acoustic airwick, so can anyone else. A bedside computer terminal ('Must just check in with our New York office') makes an even more effective excuse.

One note of warning, though: clothes must subliminally convey a message of important business beyond your control

rather than a simple desire to be somewhere more amusing than with the present company. A pinstriped suit suggests your Walkman is feeding back the first draft of Saturday's constituency speech and that you are retiring to the bedroom solely in order to punch the latest figures through to Wall Street, whereas jeans signal pop music and video games.

Another mark of the experienced Social Deflector is the skilled use of body language.

Here I should warn that it is vital to get the sequence of action and verbal ploy in the right order. First smile and wave, *then* say, 'Oh, there's Amanda!' Doing it the wrong (reverse) way round simply indicates an insulting anxiety to be off rather than an instinctive response to the sight of a friend.

This technique is unrivalled for making it appear that only reluctantly are you being torn away. Indeed, in the hands of the true professional – and I mean hands – the actual words used become almost irrelevant.

Do tell him to start, amanda, before it gets cold!

Watch one of these stars move through a room, here pressing an affectionate kiss on a cheek, there clasping a hand or arm while murmuring smilingly, and it is clear the dazzled victims are listening enchanted to the singer, not the song.

As for finally leaving the party, body language is unbeatable for making a quick getaway. With the departure of the old, rigid conventions on departure time for any given social occasion (the old Lord Home, Sir Alec's father, invariably threw the master switch at The Hirsel at 10.00 p.m. sharp, thus plunging the entire place, including any leftover guests, into Stygian darkness), there is a gap in modern manners at goodbye time that many people find difficult to plug.

The result is those ten-deep groups which cluster like swarming bees around host or hostess, those on the perimeter anxiously awaiting their chance to step forward but unable to bring themselves to interrupt the long and vivacious conversation going on at the centre.

Body language cuts through this tedium in a way that is both brisk and acceptable. Insinuate yourself determinedly into the inner ring, and at the first hint of a pause – a mere intake of breath will often suffice – move smoothly into the Clinch Sequence. Swiftly, but warmly, embrace your host(s), then follow with the verbal ploy – in these circumstances, keep it as brief as possible. '*Wonderful* party,' you say, 'I'll telephone you tomorrow.' And you do.

2.
ACCEPTABLE LYING

Acceptable Lies are those which both parties tacitly conspire to agree are the truth – or if not that, at least in the main interests of one or other or both of them. Socially, this usually means a method of either saving face or cloaking an unpalatable truth. But whatever category it falls into, it is now radically different from the days when a muslin-capped parlourmaid could declare to a caller, 'Madam Is Not At Home,' in the teeth of Madam's silhouette on the drawing-room curtains and all three would accept this as a perfectly satisfactory reply.

For there are fashions in lying as in everything else; today, socially speaking, we are in the Age of Disclosure.

It is, for instance, no part of modern manners to lie about sex. Women no longer fake it, and the sentence, 'Eight month babies run in our family, you know,' is seldom if ever heard. The only exception to this rule is that it's still acceptable to lie, either up or down, about the number of people you've slept with. The Acceptable Lie has shifted away from what you do in bed to another equally angst-ridden area. Work.

Here, *suppressio veri* if not *suggestio falsi* is permitted over everything from the size of your salary cheque to your achievements or intentions; in many careers (politics is but one example) exaggeration or hyperbole gets you everywhere. More relevant, work and the demands of one's professional life are recognized as of paramount and all-conquering importance, taking precedence over every other consideration; a result underscored by the effects, in terms of career competitiveness, of feminism and the Sex Discrimination Act. Hence the fact that the Acceptable Lie is socially at its most effective when work-hinged – not so much white you might say, as a stylish shade of filing-cabinet grey.

Thus no one says, 'Darling, I've got a headache,' any more, but, 'Would you mind awfully, Amanda, if we didn't tonight? I'm still jangling from that awful encounter with Bullington-Smith over the Nu-Bic account.'

Staying Late at the Office has given way to Going over Some Figures with the Company Secretary (who, since the Act aforementioned, is just as likely to be a flame-haired temptress as old Parkins from Accounts), and 'I'm sorry I forgot your birthday' to 'Dammit, my secretary forgot to roll my desk calendar on.'

In other areas of out-of-office life, the work-hinged excuse is not only perfect modern manners but also the kindliest of Acceptable Lies.

Much the best way to quell for ever invitations from those you don't want to become involved with is not by a series of ever-lamer put-offs culminating in either a transparently hurtful excuse or unwilling acceptance, but with a firm Acceptable Lie. 'Since Amanda was made Creative Director, we've had to make it a rule never to go out on weekdays. And at weekends, alas, we always slip away to the cottage.' Note the flattering implication of a high-powered lifestyle; this, coupled with regret, will make your victim eagerly swallow the impossibility of your acceptance.

If you do not wish to commit yourself at once and delaying tactics are in order – who will be there? could it be more fun than it sounds now? – try another Acceptable Lie from the same stable. 'Can I ring you back on that one? I don't know what my secretary's got down in my office diary.' (Always mention your secretary: an anonymous third party neutralizes any impression of personal choice and implies the matter is out of your hands. MPs have been doing this for years, only in their case the magic words are Party and Constituency.)

But the real beauty of the work-hinged excuse is that you can always renege on it if the occasion or the people are exciting enough. And with a clear conscience; once above a certain level of importance people can automatically be classed as Work and therefore a priority, whether under the heading of valuable contacts ('It's vital for Amanda to get to know people in her line of country') or as a chance for self-promotion ('I've always wanted to meet the Chairman as a *person*').

Hence the open-endedness of the Acceptable Lie in the hands of an expert. 'There's just a chance I could cut the Standing Committee and be with you after the Division Bell.' For to be Acceptable, even social fibs today must never be disprovable, the golden rule being: Never get yourself in a position where you won't be believed if you say No.

It only remains for me to add that the best all-purpose, 24-hour excuse I know for getting yourself out of any untenable situation, be it a boring luncheon or a bad choice of bed partner, is, 'Heavens, is that the time! Must rush – I'm meeting someone at the airport . . .'

3.
The First-Name Phenomenon

Once, using someone's Christian name was a sign of family links, acceptance or long acquaintance, a goal for the would-be suitor, a mark of best-friendship, let alone a social signal that you yourself came from the same or a superior rank. In closed societies where interdependence had to combine with hierarchy, nicknames achieved the necessary closeness without overstepping the bounds of proper formality (hence the innumerable Buffys, Tigers, Sandys and Boys found in inter-Wars regiments); otherwise, honorifics were the rule. Children as well as tradespeople called their father 'Sir'; maids and footmen were Christian-named while cook and housekeeper, as senior servants, were entitled to call themselves 'Mrs' (irrespective of whether or not they were married); and in every office, even the most junior clerk was 'Mr' – especially to the typists.

Today, all such criteria are largely obsolete. Christian names are no longer a benchmark of intimacy but the norm. The precepts in all those business manuals of the Sixties ('Smile – and Remember their Names!') have seeped out to nourish a whole generation, wrapping business conversations with the illusion of chumminess and putting a gloss of instant bonhomie on just about any showbiz, pop or media encounter.

Television producers in particular are adept at this style, frequently checking in their kindly way not only that they have got your name right ('Anne – it is Anne, right? – we're going to have to do some rethinking here, aren't we?') but also, doubtless, that they are still talking to the same person. In fact, the nearest anyone in most of the trendy, media-oriented professions gets to formality is to throw in your surname as well. 'Dear Anne de Courcy,' writes the producer's unknown secretary, 'Jeremy has asked me to contact you . . .'

Nevertheless, a few areas of doubt remain, quicksands in the general firm terrain of assurance. When do you call your friend's parents, your boss, the cleaning lady or a peer of the realm by their Christian names? Should you always wait to be asked, or do you jump straight in if you like them?

In my experience, the two categories who never have any hesitation in telling you where they want the line drawn are cleaning ladies and parents. (But few today would react like the late John Betjeman's father-in-law, Field Marshal Sir Philip Chetwode. 'You can't call me Father and you certainly can't call me Philip,' he mused. 'I suppose it had better be Field Marshal.')

As for any of the aristocracy from non-Royal dukes downward, where there is no 'Oh, do drop that "Lady" business – my name's Amanda', the best rule of thumb is to be guided by where you met.

If this is common social ground like a friend's house, modern manners dictate that you behave exactly as you would with anyone else: *i.e.*, after the usual initial 'you' period – shorter or longer according to age, approachability, etc. – switch to Christian names when it feels natural. With peers in business, however, the converse holds good: instant Christian names – if only because part of their value to advertising agency or catering establishment lies in the thrill felt by unsophisticated clients in treating a lord just like any other Thomas, Richard or Henry.

With first names from the moment of meeting now the rule rather than the exception, it is probably not surprising that in recent years an even speedier method of assuming intimacy has emerged. I refer to the use of Christian names *before* either of the parties has met.

'Is that you, Anne?' trills the voice on the telephone. 'You wouldn't believe the difficulty I've had getting through to you, Anne. I thought you'd like to hear some extracts from our new brochure, right, Anne?' For one salient characteristic of the intimate-stranger squad is that they invariably repeat your name with obsessive frequency. Hence the unreasoning surge of irritation that I for one feel when, as almost always, Pamela from Pushy Publicity Ltd gets it slightly wrong. 'Is that you. Anna? I've just had a thought. Why don't we have lunch one day next week – I always like to put a face to the name, don't you, Anna?'

To which even modern manners permits the response through gritted teeth: 'Not if it's the wrong one.'

4.
Kiss Kiss

In most major metropolitan centres, the kiss has virtually replaced the handshake as the social *ave atque vale* of our times.

True, there are still outlying pockets of formality, found mainly in the country and among those of a certain age or who do not have the good fortune to count a few friendly media folk among their acquaintance, where cheeks are not automatically proffered and pursed lips denote only a sudden urge to whistle.

Otherwise, kissing is ubiquitous and, it sometimes seems to me, incessant.

Male actors kiss each other on the cheek, male musicians and foreigners embrace. Lipsticked girls peck the air with cries of 'Darling!', and boys and girls who are great friends but not just-good-friends kiss each other on the mouth.

Social climbers kiss with their eyes open; politicians and café-society hostesses grasp your hand while kissing so that they can heave you briskly past if they spy a better face over your shoulder.

Most favoured embrace today is the double kiss – here the rule is: aim first for the left cheek, then the right – although in some circles it is already being replaced by the triple kiss. In Manhattan they kiss on the lips – turning the other cheek to a New Yorker could be interpreted as a snub.

Whom is it etiquette to kiss? After a party, everyone kisses the hostess (whether or not they've actually met her), and the host kisses everyone he fancies. Advanced clergymen institute the Kiss of Peace among their congregation in the service; at weddings you kiss everything that moves. Publishers kiss lady authors fondly while keeping a tight hand on their contracts, lady account executives bare their teeth and leave a perfumed trace on the cheek of the unwary male into whom they plan to put the boot. Footballers kiss while leaping in the air, the prettiest girl in the room gets picked for the Kiss of Life demonstration, jockeys kiss their horses. At TV-AM, kissing means another 'resignation' is in the air.

Between men and women who like each other a kiss has become so much the natural salutation that men who take strange women out to lunch for the first time invariably kiss them goodbye. Today, the only person who doesn't kiss a woman on the first date is another woman.

Social pitfalls (1)

'We must have lunch some time' (once memorably characterized by Jilly Cooper as 'London for goodbye') has a firm place in modern etiquette as an all-purpose sign-off line. But never be gauche enough to whip out your diary with an eager 'When?': the correct riposte is 'Love to – I'm in the book.' If they mean it . . . they'll look you up.

Social pitfalls (2)

How you introduce two persons living together but not married is much-covered ground; a more subtle social dilemma is presented by the woman who is married but well known professionally under another name.

The trouble is that while feminists opt unflinchingly for sticking to the latter, professional women themselves disagree. While some want to keep a personal identity at all costs, others prefer to leave their work persona behind at the office, sliding after hours into a wife-and-mother role and sheltering behind the nom-de-broom of Mrs X just like any other housewife. 'I want to be liked for what I am, not what I do,' is a comment often heard.

Finding out first is the obvious answer, but two gaffes should be avoided at all costs. Never say, 'This is Mrs X – of course she's better known as Amanda Y,' or the unfortunate woman will feel, as one put it, 'as though I ought instantly to break into a song and dance routine.' Worse still is 'This is Amanda Y and her husband Jeremy.' If he's called by her surname, the poor man will feel even more of a shadow . . .

Sandwiched between the secretive, subterranean existence of the teens and adult life proper comes a period known as Young Adulthood. Sociologically speaking, it is unique to our own times: in all previous centuries – as in this one until, roughly, the Sixties – you were either a child, an adolescent, or grown up, entry into the latter state usually being formally marked by anything from the handing-over of the family latchkey to a bar mitzvah or a Coming Out dance.

Young Adulthood starts any time between the ages of 17 and 20 and usually lasts for three or four years (though some Young Adults enjoy this stage so much they manage to remain stuck in it until outward signs like baldness, childbirth or increasing girth force them out of the chrysalis).

What primarily distinguishes Young Adulthood from all other stages of life is its narrow focus: almost the only people Young Adults see – let alone know well – are other Young Adults. 'At no other time in life do we spend less time in the company of people either older or younger than ourselves,' says the psychologist John Nicholson. 'It is also a period of unparalleled social activity.'

Like any close-knit, semi-secret society living within a wider world, Young Adulthood has developed its own specialized codes, rituals and taboos. The crucial dimension is the presence or absence of parents; and the final demarcation line the first steady job.

5.
YOUNG ADULTS

Much of the Young Adult's etiquette is a sexual gambit of one form or another. Flowers, for instance, are never sent, as in the ordinary world, to say thank you; instead, they are taken along to ingratiate or when forgiveness is needed. 'Women can't resist them,' is the belief of the Young Male Adult, 'and girls in flats like showing them off.'

The strong sexual consciousness underlying the Young Adult's code of manners is the reason why, paradoxically, two Young Adults of the opposite sex can quite often be found sharing a flat together platonically (something that rarely happens in ordinary adulthood). Because everyone knows exactly who is sleeping with – or as Young Adults put it 'going out with' – whom at any given moment, sexual boundaries are so sharply drawn that the general business of living can be got on with in a purely practical fashion.

Once inside the Young Adults' dwelling place, their social code continues to differ from that of fully fledged adults. Most Young flats are tips, for their owners haven't the time between the exhausting round of temporary job or tutorial, telephoning, going out, and coming back and telephoning again, to do more than put dirty plates in the sink before sinking gratefully into their unmade beds.

In girl-owned flats, the main hazards to the unwary are the piles of clothes left around everywhere; these, however, facilitate the constant borrowing that is a Young Female Adult social norm. Boys are slightly less chaotic and usually better cooks. Once a month, when the owner can finally bear the room no longer, a precious hour is sacrificed to tidying up; quite often, there is compensation when many a buried treasure given up for lost comes to light.

If sex is the backbone of Young Adult etiquette, the telephone is its spinal cord. Normal telephoning time runs up to midnight with even the most casually met of other Young Adults, while close friends can be rung at any hour of day or night. No Young Adult would knowingly ring a house with parents in it after 10.30, but mistakes are occasionally made: hence the gasps of horror sometimes heard at the end of the line at 3.00 a.m.

On the telephone or off it, the main conversational topics are sex and scandals, preferably involving close friends – it is, of course, etiquette to pass on any titbits as quickly as possible – but incidents that an ordinary adult might remark on often pass unnoticed. Turning up at a party with your shoes or clothes disintegrating or getting drunk while there, for instance, raise little comment; and so rich is the emotional life that comforting someone crying in the corner of a crowded room is part of every Young Adult's experience.

Much of Young Adult social life is geared to some form of entertainment, usually under the amorphous heading of 'a party'. This vague approach tends to spread right through (the only exception is another favourite pursuit, filmgoing, with its need for a certain degree of punctuality).

Thus, only if knowing numbers is essential does a Young Adult actually reply to an invitation. 'Unless it's a birthday dinner, you'd be very odd to reply to an invitation from someone of your own age group,' is the consensus. If the invitation has come from parents, however – even if on behalf of their offspring – ordinary adult behaviour takes over and a reply is laboriously written and posted.

Similarly, thank-you letters are written to parents, but come as a pleasant surprise to other Young Adults. Here again, sex creeps in: while girls often write them to other girls because they know the trouble involved in giving a dinner party, boys write them to girls they wish to impress (and never, almost needless to say, to other boys).

As for arrival time, this too is '-ish'. Young Adult dinner party-givers say 'Come tonight at eight-ish. If everyone turns up we'll eat ten-ish, then maybe go on to the late film, midnight-ish.' Hence Young latecomers need no excuses of the 'terribly sorry my watch is still on New York time/I was stuck in a tailback from Kensington Palace to here' variety. Nor are they embarrassed if they find everyone else has started eating.

Occasionally, it can be good form to turn up on the dot. Here, too, there are faintly sexual overtones: girls quite like to have one male guest arrive early to provide real or token help – even if it is only to provide an excuse to open the first bottle for a much-needed drink to soothe the hostess's nerves.

Again, the presence of parents polarizes the somewhat grey area of entertaining into sharp black and white. Boys turn up on time and in a suit, with outstretched hand and the words 'Hello, Sir!' on their lips. Convinced non-conformists go over the top the other way, putting on torn shirts, keeping their hands firmly in their pockets and emitting only a casual 'Hi!' to either parent. Girls play safe and wear skirts rather than trousers.

A strengthening trend is pop music played throughout dinner: not so much a question of eating to the beat – it has to be *soft* – as of a kind of acoustic Polyfilla plugging the conversational gaps. Among the classics, Vivaldi is the safest choice.

Everything is even more '-ish' at Young Adult cocktail parties, including arrival time. Anything up to 10 p.m. is acceptable, the only consideration being whether the most amusing people will already have gone out to dinner if you leave it *too* late.

A useful accessory with which to arrive at any party is drink. If invited with a phrase like 'I'm having a party on Saturday, do come,' it is a must. At a pinch two girls who plan to arrive together can share a bottle, but boys, in this as in other matters, are not expected to do things by halves, (Beer, incidentally, doesn't count as a bottle, unless you bring half a dozen.) For dinner parties, male guests bring a bottle but female guests don't. Thoughtful boys ring up to find out whether red or white goes best with the food.

Ringing up is also advisable if several girls are collaborating to give a drinks party: they may be planning some money-saving concoction based on white wine. At boys' drinks parties, the mixing of drinks takes place in a different way – by moving on briskly to supermarket plonk when the whisky has run out.

Never bring a bottle if the invitation is pasteboard or comes from parents.

At private dances or ticket balls, the prevailing mode is that of ordinary adult behaviour. Nevertheless, Young Adult guests still manage to achieve certain points of difference: for instance, the convention of dancing once with every woman at the table has no place in the male Young Adult's etiquette book. Although well-mannered boys still see that their hostess has a good time, every other consideration, from courtesy to tact, takes second place to dancing with the current fancy. Thus sticking to the same partner all evening only becomes a subject of gossip on the post-party telephone link-up if neither of you had previously met.

And while private parties are relatively safe, no sensible Young Adult ever leaves things lying around at a ticket dance. It is finders keepers for opened bottles and cigarettes, and even an untouched bottle will disappear in seconds if left on a momentarily unwatched table. ('Hooray! Henry's found some champagne!')

Going home is another fraught area. Few girls expect to be taken right to the door if it means negotiating a tricky one-way system; prudent female Young Adults carry a fail-safe in the form of a fiver for taxi fare.

Otherwise, when two or three are gathered together for a lift down to darkest Devon, there are only two guiding rules for the travelling Young Adult, both – for once – nothing to do with sex. All should chip in with the cost of petrol, and the one with the longest legs gets the front seat.

Crashing In and Crashing Out

Two major differences between Young Adults and those outside the charmed circle can be summed up as Crashing In and Crashing Out. Let us take Crashing In first . . .

For most people, going to a party is a simple matter of either accepting an invitation or buying a ticket. Quite often, however, Young Adults omit either or both of these formalities. Hence the social artform known as Crashing.

In its purest essence, say cognoscenti, gatecrashing is rising to one of life's most irresistible challenges. Thus for highflyers the Belgrave Square Fair is 'just a straight hop' and the real testers May or Commem Balls; here artistry and a sense of initiative (not to speak of the thought of saving £120 on a double ticket) are what count.

Since College porters, say the experienced, are a tough and heard-it-all-before body of men whom it is very difficult to get past – though occasionally they have been known to soften towards a girl getting hysterical because she has 'left the tickets in London' – physical measures of a more dramatic kind are usually needed. At one recent May Ball, where a four-figure sum had been spent on security, the few successful crashers crossed the river in wet suits, and one landed by balloon.

Crashing a private party is generally held to be poor taste, although there is a fine borderline between crashing and being asked along, however vaguely, by a friend. Few experienced crashers feel any qualms about public or ticket occasions. One of them has said:

'Although there are times when climbing through a window works, daylight robbery still wins. Walking straight through is the best way. You have to give a solid impression – your feet should seem much weightier than they feel.

'You shouldn't have to open your mouth, but if you do, stick to one constant theme. There's no point in being rude or aggressive – this is where amateurs go wrong – and absolutely none in trying to put down the bouncer.

'Basically, you measure up the opposition. Usually the only trouble I have is that, when I've got in, I start to feel sorry for the people who've paid.'

Crashing Out . . .

For Young Adults, attending parties is a vital activity with which neither distance nor lack of time, money or transport should be allowed to interfere. One common solution to the problems evoked by any of these is a row of sleeping bags on the drawing-room carpet, often amid the debris of the night before. As parents tend to flutter about suggesting clean sheets, soap in the basin, and trying to limit the number of guests to the number of spare bedrooms, they are often only told about their unexpected visitors the next morning.

On a planned visit, however, parental presence or absence is generally the governing factor in sleeping arrangements. An acknowledged Young Couple invited to stay by another Young Adult will be put in the same bedroom if the host's parents are away; if not, it's separate bedrooms even if they've been sharing a sleeping bag all round America. The only parents who put them in the same room are the sort who get their children to call them by their Christian names.

6.
THE OXBRIDGE GRADUATE

Academic is a word often used by parents to describe their own Young Adults, usually in a negative sense – as in 'Camilla's not very academic, so she's learning to cook directors' lunches.' Those with the right number of A-levels and an urge towards further education generally go through the gate marked UCCA into Universityland . . . and an even more specialized form of Young Adulthood.

Of all our major universities, Oxford and Cambridge – followed to a lesser degree by Exeter, Bristol and Durham – have the most immediately recognizable social profile, and thus a highly idiosyncratic style in both manners and mores. Only at Oxbridge can you get a quarter Blue for Tiddleywinks, meet token punks with triple-barrelled names, idly watch five gardeners mowing a croquet lawn, and overhear a snatch of conversation beginning 'And twelfthly . . .'

Oxbridge makes its mark on you from the word Go, imposing its exotic behavioural patterns almost before you arrive. 'There I was over from Belfast for my interview,' said one undergraduate, 'and I met this girl I'd known from home. She asked me if I fancied coming punting and of course I said Yes.

'It was a sunny day, full of potential, and she turned up in a long summery dress down to her ankles. I'd just been told I'd got into Pembroke, and in Cambridge Pembroke Street leads into Downing Street, which I thought was a good omen for someone wanting to get into politics. So I was feeling on top of the world.

'We punted down the river and as we swung round a bend she pulled a branch from a willow tree. We floated along with her waving this branch and reciting Rupert Brooke. To someone whose only experience of women before that had been, "Can I buy you a drink, doll?" or "Do you come here often?" it was all slightly traumatic.'

The same could be said of The Gap, peculiar to Oxbridge, whose undergraduates are divided into those who take the Oxbridge exam before their A levels (and who often go up the term after these have been successfully passed), and those who take it in the autumn term after A's, which means that they go up the following October, and therefore have a Gap of nine months between their respective stages of education.

Not only are this 20-odd percent a year older and more sophisticated, they frequently trail with them the prestigious aura of a well-spent Gap, which some claim is a sure-fire indicator of later academic distinction. Distance is not the only criterion – India and Kathmandu no longer rate, though China carries a lot of weight – but a premium is still put on originality. 'If you walk the Inca way you're on for a first,' comments one undergraduate. 'Argentina is either a first or a third, Canada and Australia too obvious to be anything but a second, but

Scunthorpe or Ireland score well. Africa is still Darkest where the Gap is concerned – anybody who brings back a Masai woman will undoubtedly get a starred first.'

The freshman undergraduate is plunged straightway into the peculiar, heady Oxbridge atmosphere, with its inescapable sense of history and continuity, its implication that because you have achieved the right to study here you, too, are special. So powerful is the effect of the ancient buildings that many people feel they have to adjust to the stone around them. Just as Oxbridge architecture is not only aesthetically pleasing but also well-endowed, reflective of privilege and introspective – unlike other universities, which face their campuses, Oxbridge colleges look inwards towards their beautiful courts and quads – so all these qualities can be found in Oxbridge undergraduates, most of whom spend a lot of time creating images.

Most begin with their clothes. Oxford and Cambridge are probably the only universities where tweed coats and ties are everyday wear – the bow tie especially being intellectually okay – and in the summer blazers. For women undergraduates the question can be fraught: both university towns are filled with typing schools, all of whose nubile young trainees want to be asked to a Commem or May Ball and have no scruples about playing the most glamorous cards in their hands. Faced with this competition, the new girl at Girton has to decide whether to fight back or rise above such things.

The result is sharply differing styles of dress instead of the usual student uniform of jeans and sweaters. (At Exeter and Durham this is worn with the addition of ancient Barbours and gumboots, giving rise to the expression Green Wellies to describe the public-school Jeremies and Carolines among the undergraduates. Those who ape them but get it slightly wrong are known as Green Wallies.)

Clotheswise, it only remains to note that the Oxbridge undergraduate who wears a T-shirt emblazoned with the college name is likely to have little to offer socially.

Oxbridge talk is also utterly different from ordinary conversation. 'Frenetic' is probably the adjective that best describes it; lamp posts get walked into a lot. Although there is a higher-than-average quota of pregnant pauses, the general tendency is to cut in and put someone down; often, half an hour passes before anyone manages to complete a sentence.

So strong is the sense of competition that in an attempt to compensate many people develop speech impediments or affectations. A well-carried-off stutter can be the basis of a reputation as a raconteur, while the Woy Jenkins lisp is particularly popular, lending itself to the effective rendering of phrases like 'weally wavishing!' Loud voices are commonplace – shouting shows you think what you are saying is worthwhile – but girls are allowed to be much quieter.

The Oxbridge profile shows up just as sharply in transport. All students have Athena posters but only Oxbridge undergraduates have bicycles. Indeed, Oxbridge could be called Bicycleland: you have bicycle registration numbers; people go to parties not only bringing a bottle of wine but with a bicycle lamp in each pocket; beautiful girl undergraduates are seen cycling along, singing Italian arias with a glazed look on their faces; bored policemen endlessly write down in their notebooks the make of bicycle spotted going the wrong direction down a one-way street with no lights on.

But even in bicycles the prevalent Oxbridge ideal of Young Gentlemanhood persists. 'Anywhere else they'd want a BMX or a racing bike,' said one boy; 'here it's a basket and a squeak.'

Behind all the veneer, and in part accounting for its specialized behavioural code, Oxbridge is, as one social luminary put it, 'an incredibly stressful place. There is such a premium on success in whatever you are attempting – work, acting or giving the best parties. Nine out of ten are here to grind, in one way or another.'

Everyone knows that being editor of *Isis* or President of the Union is the royal road into journalism or politics, just as everyone knows that for genuine acting talent Oxbridge is more of an Open Sesame than RADA. (Though Cambridge is bigger at acting, Oxford has the telly people down, thanks to being nearer London in every sense and also to the Oxford mafia at the BBC.) Yet what made them gods in their final term at school – the fact of getting to Oxbridge – makes them ordinary again when they arrive. Student mental health centres are full of undergraduates who cannot cope with the sudden plunge from celebrity to mediocrity.

Oxbridge sport also has its own peculiar flavour: there are Boaties and the rest.

Boaties hang around together, saying things like, 'We're going to pull some water,' as they charge off to their £2,000 boats. 'Let's chuck him in the water!' is the correct Boatie reaction to anything from getting a First, falling in love, falling out of love or, of course, winning or losing a race. Less hearty or more soft-hearted Boaties often allow the victim to take his clothes off first while they are finishing their pint – Boaties are famous beer drinkers, 'More ale! More ale!' being another Boatie chant.

An alternative to the water treatment is breaking someone's door down, usually with the object of replacing his room in exact detail on the College front lawn. 'Getting your oar in' is the all-purpose Boatie expression for being included in anything that's going, from an evening's drinking to the favours of the female you have your eye on.

Girls, incidentally, are referred to as 'crumpet' or 'pieces' by Boaties; all other undergraduates call them 'women' and news about them travels like wildfire. 'There's a ravishing woman in the Rare Books Room,' goes round nearby streets like a breeze rippling a field of corn and within minutes the place is thronged. Thus, almost instantaneously, certain girls become queens of their year, known far and wide through the university and inevitably picked for photographs when the glossy magazines make their annual foray into undergraduate life.

Student liaisons often last a long time, splintering only when the couple leave the charmed circle of university life for the world outside. Most take on the character of the university: at Exeter, Bristol and Durham, for instance, where well-heeled undergraduates share remote and often squalid farm cottages amid the hills and valleys of the surrounding countryside, this is known as playing houses. Although no Oxbridge couple has ever found true love as a result of being snowed up together for a fortnight in a rural slum, the authorities take a tolerant and sophisticated view of overnight visitors.

While sexual success is a universally recognized yardstick, for the Oxbridge undergraduate food and drink also offer opportunities for a further burnishing of the image; competition extends even to the taste buds. Boys and girls who have never thought beyond a tepid mug of Instant metamorphose quickly into a coffee society, discussing the merits of high roast v. medium, Abyssinian beans v. those from Kenya, Egypt or, for those for whom food is also loaded with moral implications (another one-up ploy), Colombia, Guatemala or Chile. Only in Oxbridge could a joyous shout of 'I've got a new filter!' refer to coffee-making rather than cameras.

For Oxbridge women, tea can be even more important. Oxbridge beauties who dispense Lapsang Souchong or Orange

Pekoe at weekly tea parties create their own *salons*; after Oxbridge, graduates seldom lose their taste for chocolate éclairs, *mille feuilles* or Florentines as found in the patisseries whose mainstay is university custom.

Oxbridge dining and drinking clubs are famous for the amount and cost of alcohol consumed. It only remains to add that while most undergraduates buy a bottle each of port and sherry in their first week, only by dons is it used as a signal. 'How long should I stay?' is a question often asked by nervous undergraduates the first time their tutor asks them to tea; as A. N. Wilson once memorably remarked, 'When they offer you a glass of sherry it's time to bugger off.'

Social pitfalls (3)

With an Answerphone, no man need be an island any more. Answerphone etiquette – still minimal at present – revolves around one cardinal point: say something, *even if it's only 'Jeremy speaking – I'll try later.' Nothing is more irritating for the owner of one of these mechanical message-takers than to arrive home to a series of anonymous peeps, followed first and immediately by the sound of a receiver being replaced and three weeks later by the phrase, 'I've been trying to get you for* ages.' *For the true anonymous caller, incidentally – the one with the heavy breathing and the obscene vocabulary – switching on the Answerphone is an invaluable deterrent.*

Social Pitfalls (4)

Once there were strict rules of etiquette on what should be worn when. Now, ambiguity reigns, as in: 'Shall I put on my jeans, or do you think they dress up?'

*Although most people's instinct is to play safe (*i.e., *underdress), good manners actually demands the opposite. Dressing up implies a compliment to your hosts, while dressing down shows you don't have any great expectations. Besides, who notices someone in mud-coloured Terylene up to the chin?*

7.
GOING SOLO

Going Solo is life after divorce, a whole ethos of launching out rather than clinging to the wreckage. The essence of Soloism is the embracing of radical change. Hence virtually all are women: men left floundering after a breakup tend to stay in the same jobs and are taken in hand by old friends at whose houses they meet and marry women extraordinarily like their first wives.

Solos, though surprisingly untough, are survivors, projecting an image of glamorous independence. Most have a low boredom threshold. One sign of a Solo is when, like Soraya Khashoggi, they continue to be known by the same name whoever they subsequently marry. Today there are more and more Solos around. The prototype is probably Jackie O.

The first thing many women notice about Going Solo is how little they understand the basics of life. In particular, money.

For many, the initial shock is the post-divorce solicitor's bill, huge because it covers not only legal services but listening time. Emotionally distraught, beset with practical and psychological problems, and unused to the male-world concept that time is money, the embryo Solo pours out her worries and anguish to the comforting father confessor at the end of the line without realizing, as one wryly remarked: 'Every time he picks up the telephone the meter starts ticking.'

She has broken the first rule of life as a Solo: 'If in doubt, don't talk – listen.'

'Keep your manoeuvrability' is the second. No sensible Solo wants to lock herself into a long-term emotional or financial commitment before she has had a chance to adapt to her new and changing life. However wretched she may be feeling, however tempting and overtly suitable the offers of masculine protection she receives, the mark of the true Solo is the urge to stay loose until she knows where she's at.

Hence the fact that in the chrysalis stage many Solos are to be found in fairly spartan surroundings, giving their first parties in a room furnished only by telephone, drinks cupboard, one lamp in the corner and the sort of sofa that looks as if it will grow up into a casting couch.

The guest lists of these parties are never the same twice running. Partly this is deliberate, partly it just happens – a sort of unconscious yet intended testing of the social waters. Says one established Solo:

'One of the things you have to realize is that everything from where you live to your appearance, friends, and even how you think is going to change. Give a party for fifty five years after a divorce – and you'll find that only about five of the guests from your previous life are there.'

But even before sending out change-of-address cards, the new Solo will job-hunt. For all Solos *do* something – indeed, this is one of the ways you can recognize the species. Davina Phillips deals in property, Margaret Jay is a television reporter, Patricia Rawlings stands for Parliament, Marcia Falkender writes a political column. Other Solos run shops, magazines, agencies and their own PR companies.

It is always etiquette to ask the successful Solo about her job, which often surrounds her person like an invisible aura – no

Yes, I am a solo...
Yes, I do have a profession...
No, It's not the oldest one.

Solo is *ever* mistaken for a secretary – and invariably spills over into her private life.

But do not think her existence is all work and no play. Although as one Solo points out, 'You have to learn all over again how to send out signals,' this is more than counterbalanced by the improvement in her looks. Sometimes this is because of the removal of the strain and tension caused by a marriage that is going wrong; invariably the inner excitement and satisfaction at finding that she can cope has something to do with it; there is, too, a return of the urge to experiment, change, improve, spend, partly, of course, because meeting men is another area to which the Solo inevitably turns her attention. But this time round, there is more style to it.

Even the pick-up is subtle enough to be missed except by a sharpish man. One Solo, staying at the George V, liked the look of a fellow guest who came into the bar where she was enjoying a pre-dinner drink.

'I saw him notice me, so I gave him one longish glance, then called for my bill.

'This told him three things. That I was English, alone – and about to leave immediately.' The next moment, she recalls, the waiter came over bearing a note and a bottle of champagne; what could she do but ask the generous giver to join her in a drink?

In the early stages of Going Solo, when vulnerability may be increased by loneliness or misery, it is all too easy to make a mistake; and a nasty scene can ensue if the wrong type of man homes in. (This is known as a *faux* pass.)

Here Rule Two of Solo life should be borne firmly in mind: never let him move in with you. It is far more difficult to get rid of a reluctant man than to walk out. Says one sadder but wiser Solo: 'If you reach the stage of throwing his clothes out of the window, always remember suitcases too. Otherwise he has an excuse to come back.'

Dramatic and over-the-top though this sounds, as all successful Solos possess an independence of spirit recognized by those around them, they are allowed extremes of behaviour that would be considered impossible in anyone in a steady couple relationship. Some get away with murder: the late and much-loved Rachel Roberts had a standard letter of apology for sending out after the previous night's excesses.

There is, however, one notable sticking-point: Rule Three of Solo life is 'Never pinch another woman's man.' Indeed, the more successful a woman is as a Solo, the more stringently this ban operates. Solos do not like being Other Women; one notably successful Solo comments: 'If you can't be seen in public with your man, don't get involved. I always stick by the women.'

This philosophy of female solidarity is enshrined at the heart of Solo etiquette. Indeed, all over London at this very moment there is a network of Solo women who, far from competing, are helping each other in the chase. For in this, as in other aspects of their lives, there is a tacit conspiracy among women that simply doesn't exist among men on their own.

The Solo woman's girl friends not only know whom she is interested in at any given moment and arrange little dinner parties where she can 'accidentally' meet the object of her choice; they are also gifted with the knack of telling from a single glance across a crowded room around which of the men present the invisible 'Hands off!' barrier has been flung.

Though most Solo women structure their lives around independence, occasionally a couple team up, setting up a business or partying together. Actresses Maria Aitken and Jill Bennett even pooled their own experience of love, marriage – five divorces between them – and their own real-life close friendship into a TV series ('Poor Little Rich Girls'). They describe the two great needs in Solo friendship under the same roof as reticence coupled with total emotional support when needed.

'When one is down the other helps her up. Both of us are terribly emotional but we've learned over the years that other people are upset and embarrassed to be caught in an emotional storm. So we distance ourselves from each other very deliberately – but in a crisis, we can ring each other up at four in the morning wherever we are or whoever we happen to be with.'

They also sum up the common Solo finding that being alone is marvellous when you're working but terrible when you're not. 'If you're alone, when things go wrong in a steady stream you can get paranoid, and drone on for hours about an imagined insult. That's when you need a friend to say "Oh, come *on*!"'

It is here we come to the crunch of life as a Solo: the imperative, almost obsessive need for true friends. Increasingly, these are other women. No matter how many men fill her life in one way or another, the Solo more than any other woman recognizes the merits of her own sex. Now that she has reached this stage in her own life, says full-fledged Solo Maria Aitken, she is steadily more and more fascinated by women's potential as companions, wits, friends. 'But when I was younger, I never knew they existed. I only saw men.'

8.
THE SECOND TIME MAN

After the introduction of the 1974 Divorce Reform Act, hailed as a 'Casanova's Charter', the divorce rate soared, as predicted. But unexpectedly, it was found that women *were instigating most marital breakups. The old picture of the pathetic, abandoned wife has had to be drastically revised; now, it is the husband who is walked out on.*

Today, exactly half of all divorces take place during the first ten years of marriage. The result is the appearance of a new breed of man, someone who contrary to all his plans finds himself more or less suddenly on his own again. Though usually youngish, he is out of practice with courtship rituals; though basically anxious to return to the married state, he is wary of false leads. Long gone is the gay effrontery of bachelorhood; this is no predator leaping joyfully back into the jungle but a creature yearningly circling the fold of domesticity. With an eye to a happy ending, let us call him the Second Time Man.

The Second Time Man's first emotional relationship after divorce is usually with a laundry. The sheer business of organizing the daily clean shirt – a matter to which he has seldom given much thought previously – offers a certain distraction from his misery. There are the decisions, quite as fatiguing as any involved in romantic pursuit: shall he drop the whole week's load in at a launderette and if so who will iron it

for him? If he opts for a delivery service but is out for the evening and possibly night as well after their midday call, will the previous box still be there next morning? And is there not something that offends against all the economic theories on which he has so far run his life in paying a regular £1 a week for several years to clean a shirt that only cost £15 originally? Compared with the *angst* of finding a suitable laundry to which to plight his troth, post-divorce blues sometimes seem minimal.

Shopping for food is not nearly so difficult. Most Second Time Men tend to patronize small Indian establishments, partly because these are open all hours but mainly because supermarkets hold too many memories of wheeling a trolley round with the ex-loved one among all the other couples. More, there is the danger of encounters with friends or neighbours – in couples, naturally. The Second Time Man imagines he can see pity in every smile and that they are only waiting for him to disappear towards Cooked Meats before saying to each other: 'Hasn't poor old Jeremy gone to pieces since Amanda left him?'

The shopping itself is cut to a minimum, the common denominator for all Second Time Men being pragmatism.

The Second Time Man will teach himself to like black coffee to avoid the bother of putting a note out for the milkman or will survive on a check list of four items only, buyable at the kiosk opposite the underground station, in order not to strain his memory – instant coffee, eggs, crumpets and black pepper is a fairly representative combination – although one thing he finds no difficulty in keeping stocked at its former level is the drinks cupboard.

Many Second Time Men live on a kind of permanent breakfast; others believe it is only possible to eat healthily in restaurants. Although plenty are good cooks, few make the essential connection between the purchase of essential raw materials and what appears on the table; if on dining terms with a Second Time Man, it is therefore good modern manners to offer from time to time to buy the food – if only to ensure you both get a decent dinner.

One of the things that stands between the Second Time Man and starvation is, of course, the number of invitations he gets. Old friends ask him round to take pot luck (most women rather like having an extra man at the kitchen table while not being so keen on stretching the stew for an ex-wife). He is frequently asked as a stopgap to dinner parties; the Second Time Man who is celebrated, witty or well into his stride, is a key social unit.

In the early stages, though, the Second Time Man is torn between feeling too depressed or tired to go out and the unpleasantness of coming home to a cold and empty house. 'Even now, after five years, I still hate coming back to a house that's dark', says one. Especially, he might have added, when it is a house of shared memories.

For unless forcibly evicted by lack of cash or the claims of his ex-wife, the Second Time Man tends to stay in his old abode or, failing that, in the same neighbourhood. Whereas All Change is the motto of his ex, he prefers the comfort of the familiar rabbit runs, the carefully built-up rapport with garage and bank; often, those he encounters on the waystations of his daily life – postman, newsagent, the girl in the dry cleaners – learn about his marital debacle long before he gets round to mentioning it in any detail to friends. One abandoned husband told me he remembered haranguing the window cleaner for half an hour about how his wife had left him, but saying practically nothing about it to friends. 'I even told my neighbours she'd gone away on holiday – I felt too ashamed at first to admit she'd left me.'

Inside, the house is either a cross between a shrine to memory and a dump, or preternaturally tidy (frequently both in succession).

Photographs are stuffed into drawers, occasionally being pulled out for a nostalgic wallow. Otherwise nothing is changed. Not only does the Second Time Man develop a curious new loyalty to the woman who has walked out on him, he also fails to realize that by not altering anything in the house, he makes constant painful reminders of happier days inevitable. As self-pity increases, so does the dust.

Sometimes, the impasse is resolved when the encroaching squalor finally rises above some indefinable mental plimsoll line: this usually occurs when the surface detritus of old newspapers, frayed sweaters, half-eaten packs of cornflakes from the Second Time Man's new way of life is equal in volume to the hard-core debris left from the marriage. Many ex-wives seize the opportunity afforded by a flit to clear out their wardrobes preparatory to starting afresh, leaving behind the clothes they don't want, thus lightening their packing and incidentally ensuring a potent and disturbing reminder of their presence. Most men can't bear to touch all this junk for some time; and, while cleaning women usually remain loyal to their male employer, after his wife has departed they frequently stop any actual cleaning, reserving their energies for plumping up the cushions and lining up the spice jars.

The point where the Second Time Man has the sensation that the whole infrastructure of his life is crumbling round him is the moment of truth. 'When I was down to a single light bulb that I had to carry from room to room, I made a conscious decision to lead a more ordered life,' was the way one expressed it. 'I realized my professional life was being affected by my lack of routine and I was being distracted from my work. I set up regular relationships with the grocery store in the next street and a couple of cleaners – if you have two, you introduce a useful element of competition.'

Often the urge towards symmetry includes the Second Time Man's sex life. Many, when first abandoned, believe they walk around with the words 'I am an inadequate lover' stamped across their foreheads; and the first woman to convince them otherwise frequently inaugurates a period of wild promiscuity. After the fidelity of marriage, the world seems suddenly full of possibility ('all those *women* out there . . .'). Often, the first move is made by the ex-wife's friends.

One abandoned husband told me that about nine months after the split he had calls direct from friends of his wife's asking him out. 'They would say, "Why don't we get together?" It was the first time women had asked me out. They were single and independent and I was pleased and flattered. I thought at first they were just being kind – I hadn't fancied them or anything when I was married.'

The emotional numbness of the new Second Time Man means that an affair can start up almost without his realizing it ('I got the shock of my life when we wound up in bed together,' is a fairly common reaction). Being propositioned, say most, is a strange experience, exhilarating in terms of confidence but also rather embarrassing; such liaisons tend to make the Second Time Man feel rather as if he had bought something fallen off the back of a sexual lorry – pleased with the bargain, slightly guilty at having acquired it and a touch dubious as to its provenance.

As the months pass, the Second Time Man learns the etiquette of these affairs. On the rare occasions when a flat turn-down to unexpectedly offered sex is necessary, it is good modern manners at least to save the girl's face, even though she may not be feeling so particular about other parts of her body. The most courteous way to do this is through the fiction of another girl friend: 'Beautiful Fiona, I should tell you that a week ago I met someone – it wouldn't be fair to her if I didn't give it a try.' All women understand the claims of the first comer.

One valuable addition to the Second Time Man's life is something he often never knew he needed before: a few close women friends. 'You can't ring up another man and blind on about your emotions,' one of these new singles explained to me. Here it is good modern manners for the kindly and sensitive female to recognize the throat-clearing telephone call that begins, 'Did I leave a book in your house, Amanda?' as a cry for help from the walking wounded.

As for non-platonic friendships, most Second Time Men

develop antennae that tell them when a woman is becoming serious. Many salve their consciences by making a Declaration of Non-Intent at the beginning of the relationship – these are the ones stunned to find at the end of two years' close companionship that the woman concerned is thinking of marriage. – 'But Fiona, only two months ago I told you this wasn't serious. Surely you remember? It was that night we went straight to bed after watching Dallas.'

Once this kind of crunch comes, the Second Time Man instantly abandons any kind of manners and cuts the tie, often leaving himself open to sensations all too familiar from his divorce of a few years back. No longer unconfident but still terrified at the prospect of the recurrence of his major dread, loneliness, he is now at his most vulnerable. For deep down underneath it all, what he really wants is a wife. Or rather, to find himself once more in the married state.

Here he faces a dilemma unknown to the carefree bachelor he once was: 'Ultimately, you're reduced to two sorts of women. There are the fascinating bitches, who will probably do to you what they've done to other men. Then there are the nice girls – but if you've been through the mill yourself you're frightened of the damage it will cause to both of you if it doesn't work out.'

Often, of course, it does: three-quarters of all the divorced remarry, the majority happily. Nevertheless, no woman should be misled by the apparent tractability of the Second Time Man into assuming that a long-term romance is in the offing; his insistence on cooking a nourishing breakfast for his partner of the night before is simply good modern manners. For if there is one thing the Second Time Man has learned from marriage, it is the importance of afterplay.

9.
MULTIPLE FAMILIES

Like it or not, the old pattern of marriage as a lifelong, two-by-two institution – two partners, two sets of in-laws, two and a bit children – is disappearing. Already, one out of every three or four marriages disintegrates although the concept of fidelity still remains: by the end of the century the way of life known as serial monogamy will no doubt be the norm. In its train will come a network of new relationships, complicated financial adjustments and, above all, a new code of behaviour.

Will come? In some social strata, not only second but third, fourth and even fifth marriages are considered almost routine. The age of the Multiple Family is already upon us.

The most immediate way to recognize members of Multiple Families is by their constant and unvarying use of Christian names rather than expressions like 'my husband' or 'my mother-in-law'.

Sometimes this is to remind themselves to whom they are actually married at the moment; sometimes because a 50-year-old chief of industry finds it impossible to work out the relationship with his new wife's new stepmother's five-year-old brother in a split second – let alone refer to him as 'Uncle'.

You too should follow this first rule of Multiple Family etiquette. Even if it is some time since you have seen a couple together, never – as in ordinary life – hide behind an anonymous pronoun for fear of making a gaffe.

Asking 'And your lovely wife – how is she?' will only make matters worse, causing an awkward pause as your questionee wonders momentarily not *how* but *who* she is; the eventual answer 'All right' tells you nothing.

Whereas saying 'How's Julia?' is polite, tactful, and guaranteed to give you a flood of the very information you are so cautiously seeking. In the Multiple Family, names are trigger as well as label.

'Oh, Julia!' comes the eager response. 'I'm seeing her and Charles next weekend when Mibs and I go down to Jamie's half-term. You know I let her keep the Old Mill? We may all meet there for Christmas.'

Those who are not natural Multiple Family material might think these chummy little get-togethers of the recently parted unnecessary and unnerving. But when changing partners is an accepted and frequent way of life, the social semblances must be maintained: blood feuds and the Fourth of June simply do not go together. Hence a major part of the Multiple Family code of manners is devoted to the tricky art of Staying Friends.

Staying Friends is what allows husbands and wives separated by many a moon – honeymoon, that is – to share the same front pew when their mutual offspring wed (Multiple Family etiquette demands that the most recently acquired spouses lurk discreetly behind a pillar), to tackle headmasters jointly, or to give a daughter a Coming-Out dance without coming to blows over the bill. Staying Friends, in short, is what keeps the social wheels whirring.

Some people are notably better at Staying Friends than others. Princess Margaret and Lord Snowdon are constantly snapped in smiling converse; when writer Quentin Crewe

Father of the Bride's first wife is up front.
Second wife is Chief Bridesmaid.
Third wife discreetly out of sight.

entertained the Princess recently he asked his first wife Angela Huth rather than his third to act as hostess; Kingsley Amis lives in a totally respectable Multiple Family version of the *ménage à trois*, with his own rooms in the house of his first wife and her third husband.

But one false move can destroy the whole delicate ecosystem. If families are riven and old alliances shaken to the core, something very dreadful happens: the financial bedrock on which the whole complicated structure rests is shattered. The corrosive effects of a really acrimonious divorce can cause even the largest fortune to crumble away.

The secret, say veterans, is never to allow matters emotional – let alone fundamentals like finance – to reach the courts. Once dirty linen is washed in public, either out of vindictiveness or a desire to make a case sound better, it is all but impossible to patch up a relationship.

Hence that favourite Multiple Family maxim: 'If there is a rift in the lute, widening the rift will cause the loot to disappear.'

'You have to avoid bitterness right from the start,' says Peter Cadbury, who has managed to remain on excellent terms with both his ex-wives, 'and this really goes back to how you decide to part.

'In both my cases we decided amicably – well, rationally – that our marriage wasn't working and we would part.

'No one else was involved, on either side. So there was no question of jealousy or bitterness over the new partners we both later met and married. Now, I'd call Jennifer, my second wife, probably my closest friend.'

Without the involvement of a third party, Staying Friends is of course easier. But even when regrouping is a triangular affair, sometimes a radically straightforward move can short-circuit a potentially messy situation. One woman who has quite a way with Gordian knots told me, 'I think it's vital to make a friend of the first wife. Once my husband had broken it to his first wife that he was leaving her for me I thought we should meet.

'But men are naturally possessive about their women – they like their separate territories – and my husband wouldn't introduce us. So, trembling, I called her myself and said "Let's have lunch." Both of us had a bit to drink to give us courage, we got on very well, talked about everything, and needless to say, demolished *him*.

'A few months later we met in Switzerland. The room was crowded and the faces of all those who'd been saying "What will happen if they run into each other?" expectant. But because we

were already on terms we laughed and chatted quite normally – much to their disappointment!'

In those with Multiple Family tendencies, unexpected meetings between wives and their possible successors occur all too often. Here public opinion is – as long as she keeps her head – all on the wife's side: what is needed is dignity and a smooth withdrawal.

Stick to the commonplace, is the advice of one authority (think of the Queen Mother's all-purpose remark for everything from airport receptions to dinner table silences, 'How lovely the flowers are!'), and glide smoothly to the door with an enigmatic,

discomforting smile. There is nothing to be had out of vituperation.

Should self-control prove impossible, try and focus wrath in the right direction. Striking an erring husband is at a pinch understandable (even, in some cases, a successful sexual ploy) but going for his girl friend loses sympathy at a stroke – particularly from other men. 'If she behaves like that, no wonder he left her,' is the near-universal reaction.

One basic rule for the outsider involved in these tense Multiple Family situations is: Stay unaligned. For those attempting to manoeuvre their way through the quicksands of shifting marital allegiances, taking sides is social death.

Enabling others to avoid this misfortune is in part the responsibility of the prime movers. Friends usually sense when a marriage is under strain but, says Peter Cadbury, if they ask you outright, always deny there is a problem. One sensible precaution is never to leave the house immediately after a row.

'If you meet a close friend while you're still simmering you'll probably say something sharply critical of your partner. And it's terribly important not to be hostile – it almost always rebounds.'

Sometimes not taking sides requires a certain mental discipline in order to curb the natural instincts towards both comforting and curiosity. It is all too easy, as a girl friend sits sobbing at the kitchen table, to listen to her pouring her heart out while murmuring sympathetically at intervals: 'I never knew Nigel was such a brute!'

But presto! Three days later she and Nigel have made it up and neither of them is talking to you; the one because you are privy to his most intimate and unappealing secrets, the other because she feels guilty at having spilt them.

The sophisticated solution is an adroit use of the Theory of Social Deflection (see Chapter 1). Open a bottle of champagne, suggest going out for a theatre, film, meal, drink, *now*, right this minute – anything to stop the secrets pouring out, while you are at the same time being supportive and sympathetic.

You must, of course, be able to recognize the signs of imminent disclosure. Women bend their heads forward, gulp, chew their hair, literally wring their hands and grope in their bags for the packet of Kleenex they have usually had the forethought to bring with them.

Men are just as giveaway but, as usual, there is less foreplay. 'Fiona has left me,' they blurt out, only a few seconds after averting their faces and beginning to fiddle with the bottoms of their wine glasses. (These are sure signals that it is time to start evasive action.) Any excuse will do, from gastritis to a suddenly-remembered telephone call; but the most effective is a nosebleed.

Tilt your head back, put up a handkerchief, speak in a muffled voice, and it is a bold man who will force further confidences on you. Moreover, once the moment is passed, men, unlike women, will seldom bring the subject up again.

But even the most strategically handled partings can go wrong for lack of one vital ingredient.

The financially ruinous nature of divorce is too well known to require elaboration from me; to join successfully in the game of Happy Multiple Familes you should either pick future exes with plenty in the bank or be loaded yourself. Only with a champagne income can you, too, afford *mariage à la Moët*.

For Multiple Family life frequently means multiple family expenses. At Christmas, for instance, people like Baron Heinrich von Thyssen (five spouses to date) frequently invite all their exes, children and new friends to one vast, fortnight-long house party.

Multiple Families, you see, are very keen on family occasions. In part this is guilt – even the most dedicated mover-on agrees there is nothing very Family about splitting up – in part it keeps the adrenalin flowing as the ex-wives sniff assessingly round each other; but primarily, as everyone agrees, it is for the sake of the children. For although Multiple children may not always be too clear about whom to call Papa, they invariably know a Father Christmas when they see one.

Social pitfalls (5)

It is all too easy to be jealous of an ex-spouse's new partner. But whatever your views of him or her, never allow an unkind word to pass your lips – especially in front of the children. Let good manners prevail and, if you must, put the boot in only by careful presentation of the facts. 'Dear old George!' you comment fondly. 'Yes, he's her fourth. Luckily, she's very young, so I'm sure she'll quickly learn to adapt to his funny little ways. I don't wonder he fell for her, she's so incredibly glamorous – never a hair out of place and those marvellous *clothes!' Now you have managed to depict your husband's new wife as a hardened little man-eater who thinks of nothing except her appearance, on which she will expect him to spend a bomb, and who will undoubtedly leave him the instant she is faced with the trying domestic habits that only your saintlike patience has been able to cope with. And all without uttering a word that isn't flattering.*

Social pitfalls (6)

An increasing hazard these days is the social question that turns out to be a time bomb. One of the commonest is detonated by an idle enquiry after the health of a partner. 'Nigel has left me,' comes the flat reply.

What is the correct response? For acknowledgment there has to be to a statement of such magnitude, whatever the time, the place, the company avidly listening, the fear that the victim will burst into tears or the fact that you yourself have a train to catch. The demands of British Rail have no place in a life that is falling apart.

One answer definitely out is the derogatory. Saying, 'I'm not surprised, I always thought he was a bastard,' or even a sympathetic, 'The brute – how could *he?' has the immediate effect of calling into question the victim's own taste in choosing the erring spouse – and personal criticism runs counter to all the demands of etiquette. No, good manners dictates concentrating solely on the plight of the abandoned one. 'Oh,* poor *you. How rotten!' followed if possible by an immediate invitation which will show that friends, at any rate, are still true.*

Apart from Society's grand set pieces – and even at Royal Ascot the champagne lunches are a notable feature – the consumption of food and drink is pivotal to most social gatherings; small wonder that etiquette and therefore manners are at their most salient where eating and drinking are concerned. When this takes place in public, the element of ritual is even more overt. Today the major public food forum is the restaurant; and restaurants split roughly into two groups – places where you go to eat, and places where you go to see and be seen.

10.
RESTAURANTS

See-and-be-seen restaurants are full of fun people who are so label-conscious they drink designer coffee for breakfast. The men wear soft suede shirts open over hand-loomed chest wigs, belts that break the £100 barrier, and this year's Rolex. Their beaten-up Armani leather jackets are never handed over to the hat-check girl (who nevertheless receives a large tip on the way out) but slung carefully over the backs of their chairs.

The women wear tans, black in summer and white in winter, Kamali track suits or Edina and Lena sweaters – nobody would dream of turning up in anything as banal as St Laurent – and lots of glossy well-tended hair. Dark glasses are of course *de rigueur* for both sexes.

Since the clientele are divided between those who come to look at other people and those who can't get enough of themselves, one sign of a see-and-be-seen restaurants is the number of mirrors involved in the decor. These will be sited on two distinct levels: near the entrance, at the height where that morning's blow-dry can be surreptitiously checked or openly admired before going on public view, and above any banquette seats along the wall – this is so that while appearing to gaze deeply into your partner's eyes, you can check out the rest of the room.

One sure mark of the lunchtime mecca is that all the waiters actually look like waiters – black trousers, white shirts, hair that is cut rather than styled. The reason for this is that even when, as often happens, customers and their favourite waiters are embracing fondly ('Franco! darling!' 'Signora! It's four days since you've not been in!'), other customers can immediately tell which is which. There is no point in wasting good staring time on a member of the staff – nor, indeed, in paying an enormous bill if you are going to be mistaken for one.

There is plenty of floor space in all See-and-be-seen restaurants, so that customers can swoop on each other between tables. For people like Marie Helvin, Michael White or Anoushka Hempel this takes the form of a Royal Progress; sometimes half an hour passes before Franco or Gino finally manages to seat them at their table.

As See-and-be-seen customers are often delayed – to put it politely – the bar is not so much a resort for serious drinkers as a small vestibule through which new arrivals have to pass. This extra viewing potential helps considerably towards taking the wanting out of waiting for those who fear they have been stood up.

Although the food in See-and-be-seen restaurants is frequently good – despite the fact that deep-frozen giant prawns, salads and omelettes are the overall favourites – the real genius lies in the seating.

This is so arranged that visibility is near-perfect – on a clear day you can stare forever – while nobody can hear what you are saying.

In practice, this means that the tables in the centre of the room are round, so that every chair is set at an angle to those at the nearby tables. Favoured customers are put in the optimum viewing position, sometimes holding court at the room's centre, sometimes in a regal, front-facing niche that is the cynosure of all eyes. Near the door, there is invariably a tableful of glamorous blonde models who serve as an equivalent of the house flag.

See-and-be-seen restaurants always allow pets, recognizing that these are either security blankets or part of the customer's public image (see Chapter 20). The fuss made of the pet is in direct proportion to the importance of its master or – more likely – mistress. The commonest phrase in any See-and-be-seen restaurant owner's vocabulary is '. . . and Patrick Lichfield comes here a lot'.

At the other end of the gastronomic spectrum are Foodie restaurants, an equally clearly defined group. Here the Taste Bud is God and everything from the length of the menu to hours of opening is dependent on the *diktat* of The Chef.

Foodie restaurants are not for the impromptu eater. An expedition to one of them has to be as carefully planned as an assault on Mount Everest, for they are invariably booked up weeks ahead: it is only, they imply, by an untold stroke of luck combined with momentary softheartedness on their part that you can get in at all. Even the very words they use, when allowing that yes, they have a small table next to the kitchen door free in a couple of months' time, smack faintly of the patronizing. 'We can let you have a table at 7.30 sharp,' say Foodie restaurants, instead of the usual 'For two? At 8.30? Certainly, Madam!'

Once its unobtrusive doors are passed, the Foodie restaurant is recognizable by the air of command emanating from most of the staff, who move like a well-drilled *corps de ballet* between tables jammed as tightly as human ingenuity can contrive.

This, a grave mistake in any ordinary restaurant where the fascination of listening to the next-door table's conversation is only outweighed by the fear of your own being overheard, matters not one whit in Foodie restaurants. For here there is no chance of remarks like 'And if he kept a whip under the bed I can assure you I would be the first to know' reducing the whole of one wall to silent, expectant curiosity: all Foodie customers ever talk about is the Food. 'A memorable sorbet!' they murmur wistfully – would that they could take the whole meal from the top again! – as they wipe the last crumbs of *toits d'amande* from their lips. In Foodie restaurants 'A great sole!' is a tribute to cooking, not character.

The finest distillation of Foodie customers' table conversation is of course Foodie Prose. Here it is worth noting that the strong link between sex and food, as remarked on in numerous articles and visually underlined by films like *Tom Jones*, is rather more subliminal where Food is concerned. Nevertheless, a quick glance at the adjectives chosen by Foodie prose-writers shows it is undeniably there. 'An undemanding platter of smoked fish,' they intone, or 'an ultra-orgasmic sherry trifle', even 'a randy little Stilton'.

Foodie customers know better than to argue with the Maître d'. But it is perfectly in order – indeed, part of the game – to engage him in long and abstruse discussions hinged around the menu: the merits of Loire versus Scotch salmon, say, or the ineffable flavour of a particular kind of dill grown on the Swedish foreshore and plucked only when the barometer is falling. What all Foodie restaurateurs hope to be able to say is, 'Paul Levy comes here a lot.'

In between the See-and-be-seen and Foodie restaurants comes a whole gastronomic gamut, ranging from the sort of place where everything from the whitebait to the Wiener Schnitzel is in an advanced state of batter fatigue to those upmarket eateries where the tone is one of studied indifference – at Gavvers, for instance, no one except her table waiter pays any attention to Princess Margaret. Along the way come the ethnic or specialist establishments, like Blooms (so determinedly Jewish it is often known as kosher nostra).

Then there are those establishments where every waiter seems to have a mission to explain, chanting the day's specialities as you endeavour to read the menu; the type of steak house where all the customers hold their knives like pencils; and everyone's favourite – Italian. Restaurants at the top end of the price scale are characterized by one notable fiscal peculiarity: whatever you choose, the bill comes to roughly the same.

What customers look for in restaurants varies enormously and is often ill-defined. To restaurants, however, customers cast a much sharper shadow.

'You can tell what sort they are the moment they walk in,' says one restaurateur. 'You know at once whether they're going to spend a lot of money, complain, ask which item on the menu contains the least calories, or cause aggravation.'

Women are the most adventurous orderers – men tend to go for what they know – but don't spend much. 'Some people need to spend money, to impress,' says one restaurateur. 'Girls don't, because they're not trying to prove anything. Also a lot are on diets, so they won't be drinking any alcohol.'

The other immediately recognizable poor spender is the Hooray Henry. 'You can spot them by their necks,' says the owner of one currently popular Henry watering-hole. 'They've all got these long necks sticking out of their pinstripe suits which they swivel around as they look out for their friends. Many of them can make a piña colada and a plate of peanuts last the whole evening. Or else they sit there and their girl friends pick up the tab. To be fair, the reason they don't spend is because they haven't got much money – their average age is 22.'

The business lunch is signalled by a dark suit and briefcase (businessman) or fisherman's bag (photographer or, if untidy, an architect). The more upmarket the restaurant or the deal, the later the hard sell. The alert restaurateur spots this crucial moment – the time to zoom in for a hefty order of liqueurs – by the production of executive toys like cigar cutters, little pads with gold corners and Economist diaries as lunchers stall for time or juggle for position. The female equivalent is to glance at the shoes and line up the vitamin pills with the Perrier water.

A sure sign of the big spender is plenty of gold glinting from various parts of the person; men who flash jewellery are also ostentatious with their money, runs restaurant lore. When members of the Gold Chain brigade are accompanied by their blonde girl friends, the fivers really fly.

Most difficult of the big spenders to spot at first sight are the ones best categorized as Upmarket Scruffs – well-off ex-public schoolboys for whom it is a matter of pride never to wear a pullover without a hole in it. Despite their statutory uniform of jeans, undone sneakers and an ancient shirt from Cole's, many restaurateurs consider them the best customers of all: they never give aggravation, don't mind waiting for a table, spend a fair amount on alcohol and, if they like you, come in constantly. Another bonus is that they eat the same food every time – two Bloody Bulls, eggs Benedict and chips is a typical Scruff menu; hence the theory that they are practising for the gentlemen's clubs to which they will graduate in another twenty-odd years, where the only conversation permitted a club servant is, 'The usual, Sir?'

Perhaps the truest overall indicator of the profitable punter is a leisurely entry that takes the customer to the bar rather than direct to his table. Watching the clientele sitting and having a drink while perusing the menu is what warms the cockles of a restaurateur's heart.

Even here, though, the sheep are pretty swiftly separated from the goats, who are given to making loud remarks like 'They do marvellous Di-queries here' before ordering a glass of Perrier. Sometimes they call for the cocktail list and spend a quarter of an hour of the barman's time finding out how each drink is made before ordering a bottle of the House White to be divided among their party of eight. These are the ones determined to get their money's worth whatever – if it helped they would lick the plate – demolishing every peanut within sight and pocketing the After Eights from surrounding tables to take home in their kiddybags.

Potential complainers make their presence felt even quicker. 'Is my table ready?' they demand loudly even before the door has been shut behind them (complainers never close doors themselves). Once seated, they start to grumble in earnest. 'Why can't I have that table over there – what do you mean, it's reserved?' They don't want to sit by the door, the lift, the window, upstairs, downstairs, in the middle of the room, in the corner, at a table for four, near the kitchen, airconditioning, music, overhead light or behind the palm tree. When the food comes they ask their companion menacingly, 'Is yours all right?', saying about their own, 'THIS is never calves' liver!'

The less sophisticated give themselves away by ordering steak Tartare and adding, 'I'd like mine very rare,' or asking, 'What year is your Dubonnet?' Complainers tend to wear matching ties and handkerchiefs, and add up the bill on their pocket calculators; they shut up instantly when any television face walks in.

Large parties develop a character of their own. On stag nights twenty-four men come in and behave as though they hadn't seen a woman for years; adulterous affairs are launched at huge post-cocktail dinner parties of the middle-aged under cover of the general chatter; groups of 40-year-old executives entertaining their opposite numbers from Bremerhaven behave like 16-year-old schoolboys as they flirt outrageously with any waitress who is faintly personable. For the restaurateur, age is the deciding factor; says one, 'Anyone under 25 with a lot of alcohol on board is a potential headache – with twenty or thirty kids together there's always bound to be one who tries to get away with murder. If we know it's a young party, we read the Riot Act before they come in and sit on any trouble instantly.'

The technique for this is simple but effective: lure the offender, or the person who made the reservation, to the manager's office on the pretext, 'There's a call for you upstairs.' There they are told to behave, control their party, or leave.

'You never tell them in front of their friends – losing face only makes them argue. But if you lecture them in private there's a good chance they'll feel a worm and then go down and tell everyone else to shut up.' While all-male parties invariably drink too much, the sign of those from a good home is apologizing even while they're being sick.

Other customer sins range from 'stiffing' (not tipping when there isn't a service charge) to quarrelling. Although the occasional lover's tiff, with a beautiful woman bursting into tears over her soup, can lend a certain interesting *frisson* to the atmosphere, sheer anger is destructive. But there is little the restaurateur can do until the decibel count rises to the point where he feels entitled to request the quarrellers to keep their voices down. Worse still are those who pick on staff, usually as a way of showing off.

One consolation in the restaurateur's life is that he always has the last word. For every restaurateur worth his *gros sel* knows the answer to the ultimate threat, 'And I'll tell my friends not to come here either!' is a civil, 'Please make sure you do.'

11. EATING

Today's etiquette is concerned not so much with *how* you eat – if you are in doubt over which fork to use, asking your neighbour causes no more of a flutter than enquiring the time – but rather with the food itself. That is, where to find the best raw materials, how much or little you can get away with eating, and above all, how to cook it.

The polite-society rule against talking about what you are at that moment consuming disappeared through the serving hatch a long time ago. Now, it is not so much a *bêtise* to comment on the succulence of the steaks, the subtlety of the sauce, as rude not to: think of the time and trouble lavished on what is in front of you. So '*Incredible* Bearnaise, Amanda!' you cry – to be met, more often than not, with the response, 'Well, basically, that's Jeremy's department'.

For now that cookery has been raised from its previous chore status into an art form, it has become an acceptable male preoccupation. Men who would once have regarded a request to scramble an egg as a threat to their virility now rush to compose – 'cook' is far too mild a word – dishes of the most exquisite sophistication. The more complicated, in fact, the better: the three-day marinade is a sure sign of the male cook.

These esoteric dishes, of course, frequently require special equipment. Just as dishwashers made washing-up a permissible activity for Real Men, so fish smokers, sukiyaki pans and above all barbecues, with their connotations of the Great Outdoors, are the prerogative of the macho cook. In some kitchens, wives need a wok permit before they are allowed through the door.

All this expertise breeds a healthy sense of competition, with the ultimate accolade being a request for Jeremy's superlative venison gravy. Mostly, these magic formulae are passed on like talismans to best friends only; thanks to this secrecy, yoghourt pudding will suddenly blossom at five out of six consecutive dinner parties. But so predatory do certain social chefs become that occasionally the whole business is conducted on chop-for-chop lines, with recipe-swapping parties where everyone throws a wooden spoon into the centre of the table and goes home with someone else's specification for gazpacho.

Side by side with this open greed ('Amanda, darling!

chocolate cake *and* passion fruit sorbet – how amazing!') runs an equally strong countertrend. Weight – that is, losing it – has become a national obsession, spawning in its wake a thriving industry covering everything from sugar substitutes and pill boxes in which to put them to slimming publications and the most obvious manifestations of all, an endless stream of diets.

Whether they choose the pineapple path or follow the great white-meat way, dedicated diet fanatics are easily recognizable, not so much by the fact that they take their food in minute, homeopathic doses as if to ward off further infection, as by a constant self-reassurance amounting almost to a nervous tic.

'Bitter chocolate has fewer calories than milk,' they say as they reach for the After-Eights, 'and anyway I'll work it off by walking to the office tomorrow.' Nor does finishing off the last scone at midnight count: what isn't eaten in public or admitted to the self has not actually passed the lips. Dieters have cardboard files stuffed with discarded regimes, start guiltily at the word 'Scarsdale', buy clothes a size too small because they know they will be able to fit into them by next week, and are the only people to get drunk on white wine.

Both the greedy and the abstemious share common ground in the two basics of cookery: recipes and raw materials. Where to obtain the freshest ginger, authentic ewe's milk cheese, or the right olives to complete the definitive *salade niçoise* is a matter of no small moment. Just as important are the recipes, invariably known as receipts by the older generation of skilled cooks and those coming or pretending to come from a grand country-house background (and hence, by definition, by upwardly socially mobile Foodies).

Here, the new chic is not a shelf full of glossy Elizabeth Davids varied with the Illustrated Good Housekeeping for jam-making, but the little-known and the traditional – up to a certain point, the older the better. Having the receipt for drop scones as made in 1890 by the wife of a Yorkshire shepherd is the ideal (for preference, the shepherd should either have worked for your great-grandfather or even have been your great-grandfather).

It's my Great Grandmamma's receipt for workhouse gruel.

Lucky couples will discover spidery handwritten instructions for ptarmigan pie in the fly leaves of old cookery books; these give a splendidly one-up start to the dinner party conversation and, if there are enough of them, can even be elegantly produced within hard covers to feed the ever-growing number of cookery book readers.

It should be noted, though, that one extra ingredient is needed to sell these compilations: some specific to give the imprimatur of authority. The simplest is a title. Here the grander the prefix not only the better but the less relevant to ordinary life need be the contents: e.g., 'Condiments My Family Have Used by the Duke of Ayrshire'. As usual, the aristocracy have quickly cottoned on to this phenomenon: today Lady Chatterley would be visiting her husband's gamekeeper not for love among the pheasant coops but to gather material for her manual on Game Cookery on an Open Fire.

12.
DRINKING

In any guide to modern manners, Drink Etiquette (that is, the code of conduct of those who drink to enjoy themselves rather than to give the effect of partaking in some arcane ritual) must play a prominent part.

The most important rules are those dealing with the persistent and the pretentious. Many a pleasant dinner party has been ruined when the host, a captive audience at his table, holds forth endlessly on vintages, temperatures, shippers, storage, and the incredible little wine merchant he has discovered in Wood Green with a stock of fine wines being sold at knockdown prices.

Mr Kingsley Amis, novelist, poet and spirits connoisseur, has a characteristically brisk and pungent way with Wine Bores: 'The moment one of these starts telling you that the '77s are coming on very well, you say, "Shut up, everybody, and listen to

Percy – you may learn something." Very few of them are equal to carrying on in the face of a silent table.'

Sometimes the Wine Bore can be countered with a tall story of your own. The art here is to make it just the wrong side of believable, which dares him to challenge you; as in 'Some of these chaps are really amazing. Do you know, I met a man the other week who could tell which end of the vineyard a bottle came from because they always harvest their grapes from north to south.'

Some of the worst Wine Bores are the sommeliers in restaurants which combine the chichi and the expensive. Mercifully, they are free of the usual major Wine Bore fault – verbosity – but they make up for it with an equally unpleasant superciliousness. These are the ones who say, 'Number *21*, Sir?' in an incredulous tone of voice loud enough to attract the attention of all the surrounding diners. There are several ways of dealing with these pests. Sometimes simply saying, 'Yes, nice and full,' when shown the bottle will do the trick.

If your host is a Wine Bore in cahoots with the waiter you must resort to stronger measures – mutual admiration societies, of whatever description, are invariably the toughest defences to breach. Once again, Kingsley Amis's advice can scarcely be bettered:

'Try saying, "Jolly good, jolly good,' bluffly and very quickly, as though that's what you always say, whatever you may think of it.

'Or more drastically, when invited to taste, say, "Yes, just what I though it would be like. Yes." Then spit it out discreetly but visibly.'

Tasting, incidentally, is quite unnecessary: it is perfect etiquette for a host merely to smell the sample poured out by the wine waiter, and then nod. A corked bottle is not only

Tesco's –
Walthamstow –
Southern side!

unmistakable but so rare that most people will go through a lifetime without meeting one.

In pubs, the action shifts largely to beer and spirits. Here several curious paradoxes emerge.

While it is bad manners for anyone offered a drink to ask for a double (always euphemistically referred to as a 'large') whisky or gin, it is nevertheless what they expect to receive. Only the ungenerous host orders a small (translated as 'single') measure unless specifically asked to do so.

With beer, on the other hand, the opposite applies: anyone who wants a pint has to say so, as asking for 'a glass of beer' just produces a half.

'It used to be established practice that a person already in a pub would buy the latest comer's first drink,' says novelist Guy Bellamy, in whose books most of the action centres round the hero's favourite bar. 'But now that a round for half a dozen can cost a fiver or more, automatically buying other people drinks is rather in a decline. Today more and more people buy their own.'

Nevertheless, the convention of the round system still largely holds sway. One of its effects is to speed up most people's drinking.

In a round, the drinking tempo of even the most leisurely is accelerated to match the fastest in the group, as everyone is anxious neither to miss out on the next round nor to forfeit his own turn to order (a black mark in Drink Etiquette).

According to experts, the best time to make a move is when most people have about a third left in their glasses – if you leave it any later, someone else may get their round in first.

It is also very much against Drink Etiquette to press the reluctant; equally, no one should be too shy or too ashamed to say No in the face of persistence. This is partly a matter of courtesy, partly because nothing cuts a Drinker to his quick more effectively than seeing someone accept and then waste a perfectly good drink by either leaving it or getting rid of it. The late Lord Butler once disposed of a glass of brandy he couldn't bring himself to refuse by tipping it surreptitiously into his shoe; and there are those who say this illustrates exactly why he never became Prime Minister.

Social pitfalls (7)

Being stuck holding open the door of a department store as shopper after shopper surges through without so much as a glance, let alone a thank-you, is one of the most irritating pastimes known to man or woman. How can one prevent the natural and civil gesture of holding the door open for the person following from turning you into doorman for several dozen?

Letting the door simply slam into the next comer's face is, though a sore temptation, clearly not Good Manners; shouting 'It's been lovely but I have to go now' requires a commanding voice and more nerve than most of us have got. Far better to avoid the whole issue by following one simple rule: never touch a store door with your hands.

In the eyes of a certain breed of shopper – or cinema-goer, exhibition-visitor or whatever – anyone who grasps a door is deemed to have taken on the responsibility for keeping it open until the next sucker comes along. To avoid this game of Holders' Keepers, push it open with your elbow, prop it with your shoulder or hold it with your foot, and the next person will then take over automatically – and who knows? even a thank you.

Social pitfalls (8)

In eighteenth-century polite society, the man who rose from his chair at the approach of a lady detained her in conversation for a few moments, still standing, before offering her his seat. This was to allow time for his body warmth to evaporate from the chair seat: even so tenuous a contact with a strange male body, ran the theory, would offend delicate female sensibilities.

Compare such a refinement of etiquette with this January 1985 letter to the Times:

'Sir, Travelling recently on a London bus I get up and give my seat (although I am nudging 80) to a lady. At that moment the conductor comes down from the top deck and shouting "No standing" throws me off.

'Annoyance is then further aggravated when the bus queue, which only a minute before I had been heading, says unanimously 'Back of the queue!' Yours with disillusion . . ."

Guidelines in this particular area of courtesy are more than usually blurred. In a straightforward race for the last seat on train, bus or underground, most men will still – just – let a woman win; yet rows of pinstriped ostriches with their heads buried in newspapers in order not to 'see' the woman laden with shopping straphanging in front of them are a common sight. The gallant gentleman who offers his seat to the nearest standing female is quite likely to be sent metaphorically reeling by an outraged glare and the words, 'What makes you think I'm so feeble?', while the only people who offer a seat to pregnant women seem to be young girls.

Yes, offering a seat today is a chancy business. Apart from obvious candidates – the old, the fragile, the handicapped – is it still part of good manners in the age of equality?

So varied are attitudes that etiquette is certain only on one point: what is not *good manners is refusing ungraciously. Publicly turning down the courteous offer of a seat with a blunt negative, or even an unadorned No Thanks, without adding a word or two of explanation ('I've been standing all day/I get out at the next stop') leaves some would-be-considerate person feeling foolish and awkward. And far less likely in the future to make the same offer to someone else who might need it more.*

Many professions produce their own stigmata: an unmistakable blend of outward form and professional ethos that serves not only as brand but imposes its own expectation on those who come in contact with it. For most of us, among the professional men and women we are most likely to meet in their professional capacity are doctor, dentist, solicitor, accountant and – though frequently by proxy – our representative in the Mother of Parliaments.

13.
ACCOUNTANTS

Pretty soon after your first meeting with an accountant one thing becomes obvious: he is a member of an extraordinarily specialized and single-minded breed of men (the female accountant is still something of a rarity), a true twentieth-century phenomenon whose years of training coupled with natural facility have enabled him to master and memorize vast tracts of some of the most incomprehensible legislation ever devised.

Much of this accountants can quote at will; and at parties they frequently do – two or three can often be seen in a corner, slapping their thighs over the proviso to Section 223 (2) (c) (ii) of 'the Act'. In the office, this technique is a powerful weapon: a well-chosen extract from the Employees and Workpersons' Fiscal Remuneration Rules 1978 can silence even the most obdurate client, and sometimes even produce a state of docility comparable to that of a hypnotized chicken.

Not surprisingly, Accountant Language is a very special form of communication, larded with terms like top slicing, back duty or accruals, that few people can understand. Indeed, accountants can often faze other accountants with a well-chosen phrase or two dug out of some particularly esoteric audit report from Company Accounts. Most accountancy phrases, like Historic Cost Convention or the classical Goodwill Arising on Consolidation, should really be sung to the tune of *Men of Harlech* and accompanied by a moving background of the wilder and greener parts of Wales.

Accountants see things in black and white, whereas for their clients life's landscape is usually tinted in shades of grey. Accountants deal only in fact, backed up with receipts, dates, reasons, times and if possible the phases of the moon; for clients, a vivid imagination is often a more useful ingredient.

The accountant's professional life is centred almost entirely on two focal points: The Client and The Revenue (as the income tax authorities are invariably known). All three perform a complicated orbital dance, rather in the manner of moons circling a planet which revolves round the sun (played, it goes without saying, by The Revenue). Like the moon, clients tend to keep the darker side of their doings hidden.

The parallel between The Revenue and the sun is not inapt, because all accountants have a rich and full relationship with this vast, amorphous body, treating it with the same mixture of awe, cajolery, propitiation and constant, watchful interest as savages do the sun. Certain sacrifices are needed to keep this great Being happy ('I wouldn't charge for a housekeeper *and* a cleaner, if I were you') and to ensure that its gaze falls benevolently on the Client's immaculately presented accounts. Clients revolve round the accountant, and must at all costs be kept from dealing directly with The Revenue; fortunately, most accountants have long-established telephone friendships with some of the Being's High Priests (Inspectors, to the outside world), and often a quick word or two can divert or dispel gathering storm clouds.

Clients, on the other hand, regard The Revenue as an enemy to be outwitted rather than as the ultimate authority. Some carry this attitude to extremes, like the man who told his own long-suffering accountant, 'Every time I have to write out a cheque to The Revenue I regard it as a personal affront.'

Most, however, take a more sporting approach to the slow but

..and salary for my live-in chauffeuse.
ACCOUNTANT

remorseless encroachment of The Revenue, looking on the various forms, delaying letters, postdated cheques or rebates as the ploys and countermoves in some kind of elaborate game – a fiscal version of a cross between hide-and-seek and chess. But however far-fetched or fanciful – to put it politely – the ideas clients put forward for reducing the size of their taxable income, it is an accepted truth among accountants that no clients ever regard themselves as dishonest, even while the phrase 'Do you think we can get away with this one?' is rising to their lips for the umpteenth time. Any accountant will tell you that a client who behaves with scrupulous honesty in the rest of his life is perfectly capable of attempting to set the wages of his jobbing gardener against the expenses of his office. ('Well, someone has to water the window box!')

Amid this quaking morass of truth, near-truth, exaggeration, self-deception, wild fantasy and, occasionally, the deliberate painting of a false picture, the accountant has to pick his steps carefully, treading a narrow and often barely perceptible line between The Client's interests on the one hand and full and truthful revelation to The Revenue on the other – the course to which his own instincts, let alone the ethics of his profession, incline him. Fortunately, the truth does not always mean the whole truth. As one accountant sums it up:

'Our position is that we believe what our clients tell us. We hate being told something that is patently untrue because, while there is no onus on us to be snoops, we *are* obliged not to conceal any impropriety. In other words, if we know something, we have to come clean about it. That's why I always tell my clients, "If there's something I shouldn't know about – don't tell me."'

Whatever they do or try to do to deceive The Revenue, says the same man, 99 clients out of a 100 never see their behaviour as in any way culpable. 'And it is only fair to say that if left to their own devices most people find their own level – that is, if surrounded by honest advisers, they tend to behave honestly themselves. All the same, the occasional client of scrupulous integrity comes as a shock.'

Accountancy is not as boring as it seems to the outside world. Invariably there is an accountant near the heart of any great financial power – and in line for all the financial goodies that go with this (and, not infrequently, the move into the shoes of Numero Uno himself). The accountant who has become Managing Director or Company Chairman is a common phenomenon. On the flip side, accountants are almost always involved somewhere in cases of large-scale City fraud, frequently occupying the pleasing role of detectives, as the only ones able to spot, through the maze of transactions, calculations and paper debits and credits, that something funny has been going on. On the very rare occasions when the accountant himself is the defrauder, his tracks are even more difficult to follow.

With private clients, there is plenty of human as well as compound interest to fascinate. 'After they've stopped talking about figures they start to tell you about their love lives,' said an accountant with a whole stableful of private clients drawn mostly from the acting profession. Said another: 'I reckon we know as much about the lives of our clients as anyone. A lot of women find us cheaper than hairdressers.'

The reason behind this wholesale unburdening is the simple fact that the prevalence of divorce among the clients of accountants is far higher than the national average of one in three.

'While lots of single or married people don't need us, anyone who is divorcing and can afford to go to an accountant does so,' said the senior partner of a respected firm. 'Indeed, many of our clients have been divorced several times, so that we find ourselves accounting for two or three lots of alimony payments to former spouses.'

Fortunately, this particular cloud has a lining of the purest silver. Before you can say 'Decree Nisi!' your accountant will have briskly pointed out the great opportunities for tax savings that now lie ahead of you, thanks to your 'unfortunate circumstances' (accountantspeak for death, being caught out by The Revenue or, as in this case, divorce). One thing, of course, leads to another; as one specialist remarked, 'Once you have pointed out the various options to a client, the conversation usually widens to embrace the less monetary aspects of divorce. It's usually the women who pour it all out.'

Men conferring with these financial father confessors tend, conversely, to be reticent about their emotions while extraordinarily forthcoming about their actions. Many a philandering husband, while gazing bootfaced out of the window, has discussed with his accountant the possibility of putting his new mistress's car on the farm expenses.

One common difficulty for both accountant and client is attempting to create two completely opposite financial impressions at one and the same time.

In the words of one expert, 'People who want to get a mortgage need to be able to demonstrate their ability to repay to the bank or whoever is lending them the money, so they want to look wealthy. But for The Revenue, with whom they may have to deal the very next day, they want to be poor – and using the same accounts would bring the inspector down on them like a hawk on a vole.'

Finally, a brief historical note. It was not Marie Antoinette but an accountant who said, 'Let them eat cake.' Cake, you see, in certain circumstances (when accompanied by an authentic receipt and offered to encourage a transaction in which the payment will be in foreign currency) is tax-deductible. Whereas bread is the staff of life – to The Revenue.

14.
SOLICITORS

Solicitors enter almost everyone's life, if only over making a will or buying a house. In these bread-and-butter basics, as in the more complicated litigation that provides him with a steady flow of honey (the one thing all other professions agree on is that solicitors charge too much), the solicitor is quite clear about Client Etiquette.

It can be summed up in one phrase: telling all. This means pouring out all the facts in a neat stream, regardless of whether or not you think they are relevant. What solicitors dread is the client who says, 'The way I see it is . . .', 'Well, of *course* I didn't mention it – it wasn't at all important,' and 'But I never keep letters or receipts, they just clutter the place up.' Solicitors call these people the muddle classes.

In order to encourage painless self-disclosure, solicitors spend a lot of time assiduously cultivating their image. The desired effect falls somewhere between a kindly but ageing uncle, a tough man of business ruthless in the pursuit of his client's interests and the Governor of the Bank of England.

To achieve this air of discretion and trustworthiness overlaid with the professional chastity of Caesar's wife, solicitors who cycle to work hurriedly change their jeans and T-shirt in the office loo for the obligatory dark suit (in the spring, younger solicitors sometimes rather daringly sport mid-grey). Women solicitors wear simple up-to-the-neck clothes and nothing distracting in the way of scent or jewellery.

As in politics and the higher reaches of the medical world, it's a great professional advantage to go silver at the temples early on in life. (What's really needed is a kind of Grecian Minus 2000.) A pair of spectacles with well-chosen rims for peering over can also work wonders. Younger solicitors often disguise the distressingly youthful appearance that causes clients to ask for 'someone more senior, please,' with beards or spectacles containing clear glass. No solicitor would dream of throwing away a natural advantage by wearing contact lenses.

Traditionally, solicitors have cramped offices in tall formal houses, if possible on the ground floor. (It is a rough rule of thumb that the more lucrative the clients, the more likely they are to have left their stair-climbing days behind.) Here, certain niceties of life – to indicate a regard for the old-fashioned values, trustworthiness, discretion, etc. – combine with an acute discomfort designed to prevent the client from lingering too long.

Hence there are endless cups of tea or coffee served in flowered china and frequently accompanied by biscuits, flowers on the mantelpiece, pictures chosen by the senior partner (*Fly Fishing on the Avon* or *A Cotswold Landscape in Winter*, according to the location of the senior partner's weekend cottage), numerous bits of old leather on everything from blotters to bound volumes of the Law Reports.

Divorce solicitors keep a large box of man-size Kleenex behind the framed photograph of their family on the side-table.

All this subliminal reassurance is so potent clients seldom notice that while the solicitor is sitting with his back to the light

in a comfortable chair, they are in the direct line of draught from the door, and perched on an ancient wooden upright that is the nearest thing to a stool the solicitor can find. 'Give them an armchair and they'll be there all afternoon,' is the consensus among solicitors, or, as one of them put it, 'Hard chairs encourage brevity, which is in everyone's interests.'

One of the reasons behind this tendency to prolong visits is that all clients think the solicitor is handling nothing else except their affairs. This also leads to solicitors being blamed for much that goes wrong, notably delays. If the High Courts are choked up so that the client's litigation is postponed for months on end, or a building society holds up the mortgage on a house, the client complains to all his friends about how slow the solicitor is being.

Because they look so trustworthy, solicitors have a reputation for omniscience and are frequently asked to advise on career or emotional problems as well as the legal ones that drew the client in the first place. Of these, the commonest are caused by neighbours. Says one solicitor: 'Nothing gets as heated as a boundary dispute of one kind or another – putting up a trellis on a fence, altering the position of a gate, building a conservatory or house extension that blocks someone's view. Noise, from yapping dogs or parties, is just as bad. The protection of property is at the heart of most litigation, and the slightest infringement outrages the Englishman's deepest instinct.'

Word processors could have been created for solicitors. The whole profession is enmeshed in paper – drafts, revisions, two copies of every letter sent out and of course endless, endless files. Offices in old houses stuff the basement and coal cellars under the pavement with paperwork. Quite a number of those firms who throw nothing away have had to buy old warehouses along the Thames to contain their decades of correspondence, family papers, deeds, depositions, and doodles by the senior partner.

Contrary to the theory that all solicitors are born with their hands in the steeple position, most don't decide on their profession until some time during their university career (the normal healthy boy thinks of being a Concorde pilot rather than an articled clerk). The moment of truth usually occurs when they are struck by the sudden twofold realization that the next step in their lives is to find some kind of employment, and that redundant solicitors are very, very rare indeed.

This halcyon state of affairs may change at any moment. The

solicitors' Sword of Damocles, in the shape of the abolition of their monopoly on conveyancing, has finally fallen on the profession's collective head. The ones most at risk are assistant solicitors (salaried solicitors who hope, later, to become partners).

The most junior members of the profession – probably the last refuge of the fagging system in the adult world – are articled clerks, who not only learn their trade but rush about collecting one senior partner's tickets from the Palladium, meeting the plane of another at Heathrow or Gatwick, and buying a bottle of sherry from the nearest off-licence for a third.

At parties, the younger and more approachable-looking solicitors become just as much a target for free advice as doctors. They quickly learn that everyone has a legal problem: 'The commonest are motoring stories – how they've been wrongly charged with a driving offence or fined for parking, or lost their no claims bonus – then comes something to do with the house. They ask you what to do if the paint's peeling and the landlord takes no notice, or if it's illegal to paint barbed wire. When you've told them, they go on to ask, Shall they buy the boat they've got their eye on? Now when I meet strangers, I usually pretend to be a racing motorist.'

Barristers, on the other hand, like nothing better than to hold those around them spellbound with details of their latest case. Most are great party men, tending to drink a great deal (being an advocate involves a high degree of tension and a lot of hanging about). Their wives attempt to hold each other spellbound with details of their husbands' fees ('Jeremy won't *look* at a brief under £10,000') in a loyal effort to out-hype the opposition. Barristers' wives, incidentally, are certain of never having the last word, though such is the graceful formality of the language used in Court it takes many of them six months before they realize that 'with the utmost respect' is simply a euphemism for 'Rubbish!'

Unlike solicitors, who are close-mouthed, prone to negative answers, and apt to consider the matter from every aspect before giving an answer to 'What's the time?', barristers are dashing, articulate, talkative and indiscreet, given to telling scurrilous tales about each other – unfortunately, quite often within the privacy of their Inn of Court or Circuit mess.

They are generally regarded as the glamorous end of the profession, and the solicitor often envies them not only the drama of their appearance in court but also the fact that when they make a complete muck of a case they can walk away to the next forensic triumph with a devil-may-care smile on their lips and a song in their hearts, leaving the unfortunate solicitor to explain to the client why a seemingly watertight case has been lost to the tune of several thousand pounds. Even more galling, whether the client stumps up or not, the barrister is always sure of his fee because the solicitor has to pay it. Nevertheless, the solicitor has the last laugh: all barristers, including the grandest silks, have to take their instructions from solicitors.

15. DOCTORS

Should you give your doctor a present at Christmas? Patient etiquette is uncompromising on this point. Yes.

It is equally important to devote a little thought to presentation. Always write your name extremely clearly on the card so that he registers who it is from – and never, of course, give money. Even though that is what most doctors would like best, it would tip the whole balance of the relationship in the wrong direction.

Best bet is a bottle of something, which the doctor can share with his family on Christmas Day, no doubt raising his glass to 'Absent Friends' (see Drinking).

In stylish urban practices, such liquid gifts tend to be burgundy or claret of one of the better vintages, whisky (if the doctor is male) or gin (if female). Those giving sweet sherry are liable to have it offered back to them next time the doctor gives a drinks party. In country districts, presents vary from parsnip wine left on the surgery doorstep by old Miss Heppelwhite to a brace of pheasants from neighbouring landowners. Many a doctor's wife has a better-filled deep freeze than Bejam's.

The main aim of such presents, however, is not to make the medical Christmas pleasanter, or to fill you with the joy of giving. No, its function is altogether more deep-rooted and important: the subtle bolstering of the doctor's self-esteem.

This vital quality is in a constantly fluctuating state, owing to the sharp contrast between the deferential treatment doctors are accorded at hospital and the knocks and worries of ordinary life which make them feel perhaps they, too, are mere mortals. Gone are the days when the dedicated practitioner, secure of his established niche in the community, was regarded as halfway between father confessor and miracle worker.

Today there is a third element: the anxiety that even the present ambivalent status quo is about to be swept away. The rise and rise of complementary medicine means that no doctor is ever free of the suspicion that his patient might be happier – might, even, do better – with a homeopath, acupuncturist, reflexologist or herbalist than a conventional medicine-man such as himself.

BILL

Hence anything you can do to reinforce a godlike inner image and dispel lurking insecurities is more than welcome. Judicious flattery makes a good start.

When you meet socially, always ask solicitously after the doctor's own health. You will make an instant impression: the reaction of most normal people is to pour out their own unique and fascinating symptoms the moment they realize there is a captive medical audience in the next chair.

As for asking your own doctor to dinner, there are two distinct schools of thought here – among doctors. One lot invariably accepts; but younger, less case-hardened practitioners often feel they could not handle the possible embarrassment of examining someone's piles in the morning and facing them over the boeuf Stroganoff in the evening. These prefer to dine only with the patients of other people. ('People' in a doctor's vocabulary means other doctors; the rest of the world, including Everest climbers, long-distance swimmers and Daley Thompson, are patients. Hence the phrase, 'I had dinner with a patient of yours the other day.')

The only exceptions are gynaecologists and doctors so grand they are always known as Mr: provided you are not likely to fall into their abstruse specialist field of inner ear, tropical diseases or nervous disorders of the pharynx, you will always be Someone Else's Patient to them.

Halfway through a meal most of them can be persuaded to recount details of their more hair-raising cases (to a Mr, the outside world consists of cases rather than patients) which will either release a flood of questions from the other guests or stun the table into silence.

Gynaecologists are frequent dinner table guests at the houses of their patients because of the subconscious female assumption that any man who has seen them a) naked and b) at their most unappetizing physically must of necessity be an intimate friend.

In the hospital the opposite applies: the rule is respectful distance. As a patient, you keep quiet and don't ask questions; it may be your body but it's their disease. The greater the entourage around the doctor – the most important consultants never go on the wards without a comet's-tail of students – the more obsequious you must become.

The alternative to grovelling is to be outrageous, at which everyone will be able to laugh and, with face saved, the consultant can indulgently treat you as a special case, a harmless eccentric who is to be humoured.

Equally important is knowing what not to talk about. Never tell your doctor you know someone in the Regional Health Committee, higher echelons of your local hospital group or the Department of Health. Most doctors have a natural hatred of authority combined with a dread of bureaucracy and, far from putting pressure on him, the knowledge that you have a link with the enemy will do more harm than good. Much more effective from your point of view is discovering what your doctor's hobby is and then letting slip casually that you, too, are fascinated by ecclesiastical architecture or skin-diving.

The patients most disliked by doctors are a peculiar product of today. 'You won't find anything to worry about with me, doctor,' they say, a statement that all too often means they are treating themselves – with sleeping pills, laxatives, tranquillizers, vitamin pills, stimulants and, for all the doctor knows, pollen tablets and suppositories to maintain sexual vitality. All this type want is their prescriptions renewed automatically; the conscientious doctor, aware of the dangers of the Valium Society, is also uneasily conscious of the unholy rumpus that will follow from a refusal to hand out the precious piece of paper.

Another sentence every doctor dreads is, 'I didn't want to

trouble you' (one practitioner remarks bitterly that he is having it put on his headstone), because it is usually heard at 3.00 a.m. on the doctor's first free weekend for two months. It comes from the lips of the patient who has devotedly nursed husband or child through a hacking cough during the whole of the week's working hours, only to give in to her fears at a time when the practitioner is supposedly unavailable. Few GPs have an answer to this one: 'If you're fierce, you only confirm them in their fear of bothering you. If you're not, they're happier about doing it next time.'

It is also part of modern patient manners to remember certain minutiae of the surgery. Wearing zips instead of buttons or laces makes undressing and therefore examination speedier; talcum powder is out because it gets on the doctor's cuffs. And when you are given a prescription, try not to say, 'My sister had those, and they didn't work.'

When changing doctors, it is never etiquette to disparage the last one; the one in your sights will think you are a complainer. What creates a good impression is the frank admission that any lack of rapport was probably your fault, followed by (remember?) a little flattery. 'I've heard such wonderful things about you, doctor,' nicely combines the eulogistic with the imprecise.

The same rule applies socially, though for slightly different reasons. If you meet a strange doctor at a party, never complain about your own unsatisfactory practitioner, or your new friend will be torn between professional loyalty and the urge to agree with you. Jealousy is as endemic to the medical profession as to those of actors, barristers and writers, and for the same reason – the insecurity mentioned earlier.

Though few of them will admit it, doctors are very susceptible to the aura of money. Even the starriest consultant will be that little bit more attentive to the few patients he thinks are richer or grander than himself.

Doctors are also – though they pretend not to be – extremely conscious of class. While the overall dedication of the medical profession is beyond praise, there is at the same time no doubt that elegant patients littered round a Harley Street waiting room do a lot for the image of a rising young specialist, just as word-of-mouth recommendations among the rich do for his bank balance.

Hence it is good modern manners for patients to bedeck themselves in the signs of affluence on their visits to the sacred square mile centred around Wimpole Street, both because of the flattering implication as to your man's status, and to ensure he does his best for you. There is no need to be discreet about it, either; despite the fact that fashion has moved on to the anti-chic, doctors are still very impressed by labels. So borrow a Rolls, wear a mink (the more obvious the signal of wealth, the more easily they will recognize it) and, above all, wear Janet Reger next the skin.

The specialist, in his turn, does his best to create an atmosphere so rarefied that the patient does not like to bring up the question of fees. Often, these are substantially higher than expected.

Once again, fall back on your trusty ally, flattery. 'Oh, gosh, I'm afraid that's way beyond my pocket. And I did *so* want to have the best. . . . Is there anybody else – not as good as yourself, of course – you could suggest who you think I might be able to afford?'

At this point, he will either descend abruptly from the mountain top and say, 'Well, what can you afford then?' or give you another name. Either way, it is a triumph for Patient Etiquette.

16.
DENTISTS

One of the dentist's greatest problems is what to wear. His consulting room is crammed with sophisticated equipment: probes hang from dangling steel arms like indoor cranes, instruments steam and hiss in the dental equivalent of a pressure cooker, an X-ray machine looms black and ominous in a corner. Even the simple human operation of spitting out a mouthful of pink rinse activates a complicated sequence of sucking, hissing and gurgling.

Surrounded as he is by gleaming stainless steel, spring-mounted black leather and an imposing array of instruments, the more imaginative practitioner is terribly tempted to dress the part. But operating gowns and white rubber wellies are, to say the least, counterproductive. The patient does not think: 'Here is a man whose goddess is Oral Hygiene dedicated to bringing my mouth up to the required state of perfection in the most scrupulously antiseptic of surroundings with every aid that modern science can supply.'

No, what passes through the patient's mind is an incoherent stream-of-consciousness that roughly assembles to the following: 'This man is planning a full-scale assault on my mouth. When he has me strapped down and defenceless, his drills will relentlessly probe that unbearably tender spot on my left back molar. *And he's wearing that white coat to protect himself from MY BLOOD!*'

So how should the thoughtful practitioner garb himself to convey an impression of hyperefficiency wrapped in tender care?

Admittedly, the late Drummond Jackson, pioneer of analgesia, walked around his surgery in ordinary, everyday clothes, but that was before the days when it became accepted that every item of dress signals a message about the self-image to the alert observer. Now, any amateur psychologist – and who isn't when entering a dentist's waiting room? – can tell you that corduroy trousers on a dentist signify he would have been more suited to a career in veterinary surgery, while it is impossible to think of jeans and asepsis in the same breath. As for the clinical-looking and convenient white coat, worn by the medical or paramedical the world over, the older it is the less hygienic it looks, and the newer – well, the more inexperienced will seem the man who is about to tap the side of your aching tooth with a tiny hammer.

The answer as always is a compromise: clothes that look informal but vaguely sterile. In other words, white – but without the hospital overtones. Although this still carries the faint risk that any patient who fancies himself as a wit will cry cheerily, 'Anyone for tennis?' when he sees you, it is true to say that, clotheswise, a white T-shirt is a dentist's best friend.

Dentists, too, can tell plenty about patients from *their* clothes (in fact, in few other professions do semiotics play such a large part). 'I can suss out what someone's mouth will be like before they even open their lips,' says a fashionable Knightsbridge orthodontist. 'The giveaway is the amount of thought and care they've put into their presentation of themselves, whatever form it takes. The image-conscious almost invariably have well-kept mouths.'

Psychologically, patients fall into four recognized categories.

Group One is every dentist's ideal – charming individuals who are always terribly grateful for everything from a ten-minute scaling upwards and who would suffer extraction without anaesthetic rather than let a word of complaint pass their lips.

Group Two is an extremely fastidious bunch, determined to exact the highest standards. But when satisfied, they too are profuse with their thanks. These two groups have been described as practice-builders.

Quite another mug of mouthwash are Groups Three and Four. Three, to put it briefly, are grumblers; nothing is ever right and whatever the dentist does somehow has the effect of putting him in the wrong: 'Save a tooth through an hour of difficult root canal work and you're told you've made them miss their train.'

Many Group Threes have perfected an aggressive technique that tends to demoralize the less experienced practitioner to the point where he makes some minor mistake, thus offering incontrovertible proof that they were right to doubt his competence in the first place.'Are those instruments clean – I mean, *really* clean?' they will say, looking at a tray of steel probes and instantly conjuring up a doubt in the wretched man's mind. ('Was it this tray or the other I sterilized half an hour ago?') After a Group Three patient has remarked, 'My friend says scraping your teeth only loosens them,' he or she will ask the dentist to change the mouthwash. 'I only like to use it fresh.'

Group Four consists also of grumblers, but with more reason: they are the large number of elderly people brought along by relatives, usually for dentures they don't actually want. A warning signal here is, 'But Mum, you've *got* to have some new teeth – the old ones don't look natural.' These two last categories have been classed as practice-destroyers.

All dentists quickly become familiar with patients' excuses. Those who have not put a toothbrush near their mouths for thirty years invariably explain that this is due to lack of time.

'I'm in too much of a rush in the morning to clean my teeth, and by last thing at night I'm too tired,' is probably the commonest way of phrasing this.

At the other end of the scale are the hyper-meticulous, or incisor fetishists, as they are known in the profession. These are the people who settle down for half an hour at a time with their collection of brushes, paste, floss and a series of gadgets like miniature bottlebrushes. After every meal they rush quickly to the nearest running water so that they can not only give their mouths a thorough overhaul but clean their equipment as well.

Often, this is because their teeth have cost them so much – in which case they are probably American. For in the land of the free, dentistry is a major life investment. Says a British practitioner a trifle enviously: 'The American dentist's whole training teaches him to look at the patient's mouth and quote for the complete and ultimate treatment.

'Now, in anyone's mouth you can find an awful lot of teeth where, for instance, a gold inlay could technically be the best treatment. But you wouldn't suggest it, because it's not absolutely vital – and it's horrendously expensive.'

No such inhibition troubles the American dentist. Fortunately, the American face is the perfect showcase for his work. What is known as bi-maxillary protrusion (where both jaws are somewhat prominent and the teeth correspondingly sizable) is fairly common among the US public; the effect is to expose all the teeth in a wall-to-wall smile – Farrah Fawcett Majors is a good example. Sometimes actors or actresses without bi-maxillary protrusion who wish to blend into the prevailing Hollywood stereotype have their teeth capped in the familiar shape; here the effect is of Tombstone Gulch.

There are approximately 20,000 dentists in Great Britain, and one commonly held view is that at least half are Australian.

And what do you do, Bruce?

Fosters

This is partly because of the fact that Australians are naturally gifted at making their presence felt, and partly because most of them are on the move, thus creating the illusion there are several times as many of them. Australian dentists tend to combine the practical benefits of acquiring experience in the great British teaching hospitals with an urge to bum around Europe. After eighteen months of superb attention, you are likely to find your practitioner has disappeared up the Autobahn in a battered minibus (often with his receptionist), handing his surgery over to a husky replacement from Brisbane. Once home again, a lucrative practice awaits these nomads.

Although dentistry does not have the same glamour aura as many branches of medicine, one compensation is that it offers less of a conversational opening to the dedicated hypochondriac – if only because it is difficult to describe a filling in the same breathless and esoteric detail as an operation. All the same, dentists are often cornered at parties and told about inexplicable twinges amid the bicuspids. 'I always say, "Show me",' says one long-suffering toothman, 'and I ask them to close their eyes as you can open your mouth wider that way. Then I walk away and leave them.'

17.
MPs

London and Home Counties MPs can frequently be recognized by their hunted expression. Not only do their constituents expect them to attend every semi-official engagement to which they have been invited, from the Rotary Club Dinner to the

Sewage Workers' Annual Dance, and throw in a witty impromptu speech that took a week of precious spare time to compose; they also expect to saunter round their MP's place of work when the mood takes them.

Teachers bring the A-level Social Sciences group, all of whom are bursting with interested and tricky questions about voting procedures or little-known Committees. Local Councillors bring businessmen they want to impress, Trade Union delegations make special, solemn trips south. Women's groups find a tour of the House of Commons combines nicely with a trip to the Sales on their Day Return ticket, Christmas shoppers feel it is worth enduring the historical chat for the chance to load up with boxes of the special House of Commons mints or bottles of sherry afterwards.

As few of the younger MPs have the nerve to bark, like some of the older generation, 'What you require is a tour guide, Madam!', those neither fortunate nor sagacious enough to secure a constituency at the optimum distance from London (80–100 miles is the ideal: accepted as too far for evening engagements or casual droppers-in but accessible by the MP himself for weekends or special parties) are at constant risk. To get hold of an MP, all you do is go into the Central Lobby and send out a Green Card requesting the Member's presence.

But this, I must emphasize, is not good constituent behaviour. While the young, inexperienced or kindhearted MP may respond to the call of the Green Card, giving an impromptu caller a guided tour nevertheless takes a two-hour chunk out of his day (I say 'his' because the number of women MPs is abysmally low). Popular Honourable Members from fashionable London constituencies have been known to break off in mid-conversation and dart into the nearest lavatory when a card-carrying messenger is seen approaching.

Nor is it Constituent Etiquette to sulk if your MP does not instantly provide a dozen tickets for the Parliamentary debate you fancy getting up a party for. Tickets for the Strangers' Gallery are not always easily available and the maximum is two at any one time, though constituents do not always appreciate this. In cases where disbelief is open, the Honourable Member should bring his own counterploy into action. Always tell constituents that their political instinct is faultless ('You have chosen the most interesting debate of the *entire* session'), as proven by the fact that the Cabinet and both Front Benches have pre-empted all seats for their most influential supporters.

The MP is even more available to his constituents in his surgery. Here, roughly four out of every five vigorously transgress what the MP regards as Constituent Etiquette; the two points all their questions have in common being that they are nothing to do with politics nor is it remotely within the MP's power to do anything about them.

The Constituent feels that the drive outside his house ought to be maintained by the County Council . . . can the MP help? The Constituent fears the extension to his garage will not be approved by the District Council . . . will the MP use his influence? The Constituent is upset because the Town Council does/does not intend to build a lavatory in the eighteenth-century Market Square . . . the MP must immediately overrule them. The Constituent is certain that a particular traffic warden is persecuting him . . . what is the MP going to do about it?

One MP tells the story of a constituent who arrived with his girl friend, and announced that they were living in a tent because their parents had thrown them out and they had nowhere else to go. 'Ah', said the MP, 'You want to get on the Council Housing List? Perhaps I could write to the Council for you?' No, they were on the List already, but they hadn't got enough points, so they were trying to have a baby. 'But *she*', said the young man, looking angrily at his girl friend, 'isn't getting pregnant. So we wondered if you would tell us what we were doing wrong?'

Grander constituents view the surgery somewhat as paying patients view the National Health – they expect the MP, like the doctor, to attend *them*.

Letters arrive describing the iniquitous and totally unjustified rate rise the Constituent has suffered after installing his fourth bathroom, the need to reroute the new bypass 200 yards farther away from his tennis court, or the habits of tourists who relieve themselves into his front garden . . . will the MP come to tea next Tuesday to discuss this?

A variant of this technique is buttonholing the MP at a Party fund-raising cheese and wine evening to ask why the Council are raising so many trivial objections to the Constituent's plan to erect a second slaughterhouse alongside the first.

All of this disregards the MP's very real power: to help when something is done or threatened by Central Government. A letter from the MP to the relevant Minister ('Dear Charlie, I enclose a copy of a complaint received from my constituent Mr John Bull and would be grateful if you would look into this') is literally a three-line whip curling around the buttocks of the Department. For the Minister's Private Office will put an enormous coloured tag on the missive and send it by hand to the wretched official responsible for the subject, usually with a request for a draft reply and a deadline. The only thing that makes a civil servant hop higher is a similar request from Number Ten Downing Street, with the result that the last resort of an adjournment debate is seldom needed.

But since most visitors to the surgery fall outside this category, the first thing any new MP learns is what to say in response to being treated as an amalgam of Citizen's Advice Bureau, DHSS and Local Council.

Just as Sincerity is the weapon of the American politician, so Frankness is that of the British. Hence most MPs make a virtue of impotence by looking their constituent squarely in the eye and saying, as frankly and openly as they can manage (rehearsal in front of the bathroom mirror is invaluable here): 'I must be absolutely honest with you and say there isn't a lot I can do. It would be *quite wrong* of me to mislead you into thinking I have any power at all in this matter.'

Most Constituents respond sympathetically to Frankness of this kind, feeling that they have not only been let into a confidence but that the MP has somehow been rather good and noble, and they leave the surgery in a warm glow of goodwill.

Others, however, are not so easily fobbed off. Leaving on one side the inevitable minority convinced that the Russians are aiming death rays at the Town Hall or that the Director General of the BBC is peering at them nightly through their television screens (the MP must curb his impulse to say, 'Well, video him for me, then'), there is a group characterized by its persistence. Many of them have, as the MP is unhappily aware, a genuine case; the only trouble is that it is in a field outside his power of assistance, so that when they return Saturday after Saturday, with the identical arguments, in the intervals of sending yet another telegram to the Queen or letter to the Pope, his heart sinks into his boots. The only answer here is to say – frankly, of course – 'I think you should go to the Ombudsman.'

Etiquette requirements vary slightly according to Party. Labour voters expect their Member to be involved in politics, Conservatives want theirs to come to dinner. The Tory MP is a natural social focus, a local grandee fulfilling the same sort of function in his constituency as minor Royalty – one school of thought holds that all Conservative selection committees have the image of the Duke of Edinburgh floating subliminally before their eyes – and it is good modern manners for him to attempt to conform to the ideal in as many respects as possible.

This involves a large house in the country, either in the heart of his rural constituency where his family have preferably lived for generations or, to show his heart is in the right place, as a getaway ('I'm not *really* a Londoner, you know'), and a charming wife who is on the whole brighter than he is. Those who know them well realize that she is the brains of the family and on the whole more politically aware, though less politically interested, than her husband. Nevertheless, she gracefully plays second fiddle, stomping around behind him at election time and deputizing where necessary on platform or playing field while effortlessly steering clear of political discussion ('I'm afraid it's no good asking me – I leave all that sort of thing to Godfrey'). Both of them can open fetes with their eyes shut.

He also has several children. The sons, if old enough, are usually in trouble for drink, speeding or, alas, drugs – but if the MP is the 'right' type, each reappearance in front of the local Bench, far from damaging their father's chances, brings commiserating murmurs of 'Poor old Godfrey!' as the magistrates reflect how easily this could have been their own Hugo, Nick or Nigel. The daughters, on the other hand, are altogether more wholesome, canvassing for their father like mad at election time and rallying round at the Red Cross bazaar, though they usually draw the line at attending Young Conservative dances in the village hall. Their weddings, which take place at regular intervals, are a prominent and enjoyable feature of local life.

Male Tory MPs should be tall (height and the commanding presence given by, say, a spell in the Brigade of Guards makes them Whip material) and have a fund of amusing stories, those based on military, sporting or at least outdoor experience being particularly acceptable. Even more help than a hyphen or two in the surname is a nickname – provided, of course, that it is of the 'Chips' or 'Shakes' variety (anything from the drawer marked 'Grocer' is an automatic penalty point).

There is no real stereotype for the female Tory MP, though someone who could have been an Ambassadress in her own right is probably a rough approximation. And never mind that most Tory MPs today are more likely to be impecunious young barristers living in rented accommodation in the marginal Midlands shoe-town seat they have been lucky enough to win, the Platonic ideal outlined above still hovers at the back of most voters' minds – let alone that of the Selection Committee.

While the Tory MP should canvass in a suit and be what the voters call 'nicely spoken', the ideal Labour member should speak with the regional accent of his constituents. Paradoxically, his offspring should be socially mobile upwards – despite the Dave Spart activists who control selection procedures, the average Labour voter wants to see his own children get on in the world – and personally blameless: not for the Labour MP the sympathetic aside, 'Have you heard that young Gerald has had to go back to the Charter Clinic?'

Labour MPs also have to be careful over sport. Even fishing (or 'angling', as it is known in the Party) is on the verge of becoming regarded as a blood sport just like the terrible Tory activities of hunting and shooting. Many Labour MPs now consider it safest to stick to golf outdoors and anything played on a green baize table indoors. Both give ample opportunity for the favourite Labour sport, hobby and preoccupation rolled into one: plotting.

But since this activity, described by good Party members as strategic rethinking, the forging of new allegiances or therapeutic bloodletting, is apt to be viewed unkindly by the outside world, most Labour Members prefer to keep a low profile socially, confining their activities to smoke-filled Committee rooms. Nor do Labour Members' wives have anything like the workload of their Tory counterparts: not for them the giddy round of officiating at prize-givings, rose shows or Bonny Baby contests. Most live in a kind of political purdah, and it is certainly not good modern manners to ask them, 'Do you enjoy politics?', as telling the truth is one of the weaknesses of these retiring and likable creatures.

From the point of view of social profile the Liberal Party is a ragbag, though exuding a general aura of diffuse high-mindedness, whereas SDP Members tend to resemble dapper Tories with added compassion. One rule of thumb is that the SDP campaign with a more Tory approach in rural constituencies and a Labour one in towns. But while it is etiquette never to offer a Labour Member anything but beer if there are witnesses present (in the more northern seats the straight pint is an article of faith), no such consideration ever troubles an Alliance Member.

Whatever his party, the MP enjoys an assured position more or less irrespective of his birth, education or financial status; nor, despite the slings, arrows and over-ripe tomatoes of outrageous fortune, is his self-esteem ever seriously dented. Even when he is being rabidly heckled, he is at least being *noticed.*

The one thing MPs from all parts of the political spectrum have in common is that whenever anybody learns their profession, the first question they invariably ask is, 'Tell me, what is Mrs Thatcher *really* like?'

Social pitfalls (9)

Few writers start the day without genuflecting nervously in the general direction of Greek Street: finding yourself in Pseuds' Corner is the literary equivalent of the Greasy Spoon award. Politicians, publishers, businessmen and trendy media folk are equally anxious to avoid the piercing scrutiny of Lord Gnome. So what, if anything, do you say to a friend pilloried in Private Eye?

As most of the Eye's victims are drawn from circles where it is virtually required reading, ignoring the reference to a colleague's social, financial or sexual peccadilloes can be almost more pointed than mentioning it; and the conventional 'Never read the thing myself' is useless as a getout.

Fortunately, most of those featured in Lord Gnome's august journal depend in some way on being known by the public and, therefore, on publicity. So it is good modern manners to concentrate on this aspect alone: 'At least they've spelt your name right,' or alternatively 'If they can't even get your name right, what price the rest of the story?' If all else fails, try a disbelieving glance and the words, 'Shome mishtake, shurely?'

18.
The Body Beautiful

With the arrival of the Eighties, a new cult sprang into being. Enemies declare it to be nothing but a socially acceptable form of sado-masochism; devotees can be recognized by their total dedication, preoccupation with unusual parts of the body, specialized clothing, and conversation. I speak of course, of the Body People: those whose goal is some Platonic ideal of absolute fitness, and for whom exercise is a constant obsession. To Body People, The Body is not so much a sex object, more a way of life.

There are Body People wherever you look. More appear every day: the number of those in Great Britain who regularly partake in some outdoor sport is over 11 million and rising; there are 9 million regular swimmers; and you can't walk in any decent-sized park without the risk of nearly being knocked over by the rush of joggers. All of them are Body People and one of their major preoccupations is Body Fuel – I mean, food.

Body People discuss what they used to eat, what they now eat and why, what they don't eat and why, what they're going to eat, what the last meal did to them, how bad they feel after a binge on forbidden foods the night before. 'Oh my God,' Body People say, 'I went out to dinner and I ate a lamb chop.'

For Body People are the new breed of faddy eaters: not so much picky over what they like or don't like as anxious to extract maximum Body Performance from every morsel on their plates. Body People don't think in terms of weight or calories but of Okay Foods. 'Will it build Red Muscle Fibre?' is what they ask instead of, 'Will it settle on my hips?'

Body People consume mountains of brown spaghetti, whole loaves of brown bread, organic vegetables and salads by the gardenful, and complain of a headache if they accidentally down a teaspoon of white sugar. A Body Person in full training has to get through so much of this approved Body Fuel that he or she often finds himself or herself bored with the act of eating. For Christmas, Body People give each other presents of their own homemade muesli; the Body Person's version of the Good Food Guide is Geoffrey Cannon's *Dieting Makes You Fat*.

The influence of Body People is, perhaps, at its most physically obvious in clothes. Body People are responsible for an entire new fashion orthodoxy. When Norma Kamali brought sweatshirting out of the locker room in her now historic collection, she was giving expression to the philosophy that you are a Body Person *all the time* – previous generations only donned their specialist sports clothing when about to perform the sports concerned. But Body People wear Body Clothes everywhere. They truck to the gym in singlets and sweat pants, go out shopping in rara skirts and Nike runners, put diamanté necklaces on their track suits to go out to dinner. A Body Person's idea of really dressing up is to climb into a jump suit and take off the sweatband.

The key point to remember about Body Clothes is that they are basically so unbecoming that only those with perfectly tuned physiques and admirable figures in the first place can hope to get away with them. Only a body of either sex without sag, spare tyre or bulging thighs can look truly good in a track suit; only the slimmest and least flabby bottoms are enhanced by a pair of skimpy satin running shorts; ankle socks and trainers look like hell on short fat legs.

Nor does Body Fashion conceal any exotic surprises. Underwear is stark and functional: French knickers in satin and lace will not be found in the Body Woman's lingerie drawer; she seldom wears a bra unless she goes running (and then only to avert Jogger's Nipple). When a Body Man sees a pair of shapely legs in black sheer stockings and high heels he comments in horror, 'Does she know what she's doing to her thighs?'

Once they possess the wardrobe, Body People have to work at staying in good enough shape to wear it. Unlike other clothes which actually do something for you, Body Fashion means slog, slog, slog.

For most Body People this means the Health Club. For there is all the difference in the world between an early morning run and twenty minutes' aerobics with added arm exercises, or between a workout in front of a home video set and Going for the Burn in a group of twenty.

Once inside these temples to the well-tuned physique, the first thing that strikes you is a change in basic social behaviour.

A Health Club is the one place where you can stare at yourself in the mirror for minutes on end – back view, front view, side view, naked or clothed – without the word 'Narcissus' so much as crossing the minds of any of those around you. All Body People look at, and talk about, their bodies incessantly.

Fundamentally, there are two sorts of Body People, the serious and the posers. Among the serious ones there is heavy though veiled competition in the amount of punishment they can take. One girl will ostentatiously remain in her sweat-soaked leotard after class, saying languidly: 'I'm not changing because I'm doing the 6.30 as well,' to be countered by her friend saying sweetly, 'I think I'll skip it for once because I did an hour's aerobics before work and jogged round the Park in my lunch hour.'

Men concentrate more on muscles. When they get up to H on the Nautilus stomach machine it goes into their diaries in capital letters. Anyone attempting to make such a weight jump at this rarefied level is urged on by the instructors, all of whom gradually gather round him, psyching him on to success. Afterwards, he is toasted in fresh orange juice and, carried away by euphoria, buys the Club T-shirt.

Once an enthusiast reaches a particular height of fitness, it is a point of honour to maintain it, and this, of course, necessitates ever more regular attendance. The more fanatic even resent the enforced absence of their annual holiday. You can always tell newcomers because they talk about their weight; habitués discuss muscle tone. The real aficionados are the ones who visit Fitness Assessment Units every three months, and spatter their conversation with phrases like Maximum Oxygen Uptake.

Clothes are another dead giveaway between the serious and the posers. Posy people (or first-timers) turn up in shiny Lycra leotards with matching shiny tights, several pairs of carefully toned legwarmers worn together, and a sweatband threaded decoratively through their curls.

They wear pink jazz shoes that are totally useless for aerobics and stand about in model-girl attitudes, turning their heads sideways and sucking in their cheeks experimentally. If male, they wear sportswear from Los Angeles and never take their Rolex off for class. Some clubs, it is only fair to say, specialize so heavily in glamour that no one dares wear the same leotard more than once a fortnight.

The aim of every serious Body Person is to look as much like the professionals as possible. Being mistaken for an instructor or a real dancer causes the serious Body Person instant joy.

Instructors' tracksuits are always a workmanlike grey; in fact, grey cotton sweatshirting is the top Body material. No serious Body Person wears pure Lycra; it is always cotton or cotton-and-Lycra for the various layers of clothing.

But that's the same outfit you wore at aerobics yesterday!
Givenchy

Instructors tend to wear more clothes than anyone else. Male instructors wear tights, shorts, leotards, T-shirt, and pull a tracksuit on over the lot the moment class stops; female instructors wear an ordinary basic black leotard and tights topped up by a wrestler's leotard, sweatpants, legwarmers, T-shirt, belt that emphasizes how slim their waist is despite all this, and often a crossover cardi.

The reason for all these layers is that the instructors are so fit they have a lower percentage of body fat (which keeps out the cold) than ordinary humans. Serious Body People wear T-shirts over their leotards to imply that they, too, are down to the magic 13 per cent body fat.

Real dancers are just as easily spotted. All weigh seven stone, have birdlike bones and wear clothing that has seen not just better days but better years, thrown on with an utter disregard for the niceties of colour-matching that are instinctive to most other women. Dancers scrape their hair back and are the only people to put on a sweatband without looking in the mirror.

But all this pales into insignificance beside the whole shoe mystique.

Serious Body People talk about their shoes the way racing cyclists talk about The Bike – where to buy them, which are the best if you have incipient fallen arches, how long they last, whether a retread really works, how anything under £40 is rubbish.

Instructors, who put most of their money into their feet, always have old and tatty shoes because they run so much. Serious runners go for expensive consultations and have special inserts in their shoes to correct faulty action of the left ankle that affects their pace.

In class, the Body People's code of manners is seen at its most stringent. People who come regularly have their own favourite place, known by all the other regulars. If a newie inadvertently stands on this spot its 'owner' becomes upset and there is, says one regular, 'a lot of looking, until the new person becomes uncomfortable. It's quite a power struggle.'

Prime place is near enough to the front to see yourself easily in the mirrors, and a bit to one side so that it doesn't show to too many of the rest of the class if you can't quite manage the hardest exercises. There is an unspoken but accepted rule that only those who are reasonably good stride to the front row.

Rivalry in class largely depends on the sexual ratio: roughly speaking, the more men there are, the greater the sense of competitiveness injected into the atmosphere. The sole exception is men who have been dragged along by their girl friends, and who are looked on with indulgence as clearly being there only for love. 'The men don't like being beaten by women,' says one instructor famous for the toughness of her classes, 'but the women are usually better because they're naturally suppler and have generally been doing it longer.'

Even so, the difference between the Serious and the Posers is still obvious. The latter are expert at pretending to look as if they're working but manage to avoid exercises like mountain climbs or hard floor work. Posers are instantly spottable at the end of class: they are the ones who still look immaculate.

The all-purpose excuse for anyone attempting to excuse idle behaviour is the cry, 'Shin splints!' Shin splints are what happens when you run or jog wrongly, either in the wrong shoes, on your toes, or on unsprung floors (all aerobic work is supposed to be done on sprung floors). But as virtually no new Health Club has a sprung floor because of the expense, and as most instructors have an uneasy feeling they forgot yet again to tell the class to put its feet down flat while it jogged, few of them dare challenge you on this one.

After class, a favourite Health Club activity is gossip. The best is found in the jacuzzi boasted by the more expensive and upmarket establishments frequented by the rich and famous. Here, amid the warm, gently pummelling jets of scented water, reputations are torn to shreds, every detail of the previous night subjected to expert scrutiny, and secrets of every description spilled. No one notices who is in the showers nearby – or even cares.

Which brings us, at last, to the invisible extra in those £400-plus subscriptions. Although serious Body People insist that they don't get the same high from making love as making the Marathon, Health Club sex is the chief attraction for many. Even the most basic of sports centres provide a handy venue for those with the same interests and of roughly similar age groups, while the more stylish clubs have taken over from singles bars as a place to go and meet the opposite sex in an open and well-adjusted way under the approving gaze of the Club's instructors. Indeed, many of those who meet the opposite sex most successfully *are* instructors, who can take their pick of the fitness groupies who cluster round them, eagerly demanding to know the difference between biceps and triceps.

Much of the mystery of courtship is, alas, lost: with a leotard, you can see exactly what you are getting – or in the case of most Club members, hoping to get. Here it is noteworthy that although most men declare they cease to notice individual shapes after the first few classes, they invariably position themselves at the back of the room, a place of particular visual advantage during the more complicated stretch exercises.

Because all bodies are to a large extent similarly clad, women on the prowl tend to concentrate their main efforts on their faces. The female Body Person makes up like a Dallas queen before she goes into class; and in the gym, heavily fringed, sultry glances smoulder across the Nautilus equipment. With luck, the rippling muscled object in their line of sight will saunter over with the nonchalant enquiry, 'Can I help you tighten your lapstrap?'

For despite the instant bonhomie, the all-friends-together camaraderie of class and changing-room, there is a certain ritual over the pick-up. Too crude an approach is definitely out – besides, it would give the Club a bad name.

In the gym, where conversations about flexibility or muscle tone are the norm, it is comparatively easy. Without once mentioning the word sex, you can talk incessantly about each other's bodies until the air around the Leg Extender couch is almost visibly throbbing.

In the outside world, the classic gambit is, 'Why don't we run together on Saturday?', arrived at after the preliminaries have established that both of you are roughly at the same relative degree of fitness. For serious Body People, you see, compatability is matched Resting Pulse Rates.

19.
PERMANENTLY BEAUTIFUL

In some sections of society, a redistribution of sagging facial tissue or unruly contour is as much a rite of passage as the abandonment of fun furs for the high seriousness of the first Blackglama. The only difference is that instead of flaunting it, you conceal it.

For the one thing common to all Permanently Beautiful People is that they want everyone – including and especially other Permanently Beautiful People – to believe they come packaged that way naturally.

The only exception to this rule is rhinoplasty – more commonly known as a nose job -- which is impossible to hide. Thus in Permanently Beautiful circles it is etiquette to get this over at the earliest age the surgeon decrees possible, so that you get the maximum mileage from this rechiselling of bone and self-image. The late teens is a good time for a new nose to make its debut; for girls, it makes an excellent coming-out present. When Susan Hampshire was presented, she already had the pretty retroussé nose which is one of her most famous features, while Christina Onassis had hers done at 16.

Otherwise, cosmetic surgery is shrouded in a veil of secrecy compared to which the CIA's plans for South America are as a well-thumbed book. Men in particular subscribe to this *omertà*: 'I have even known them emigrate to start a new life abroad after a successful facelift', says one top surgeon.

Hence the ambivalence of its etiquette, balanced delicately between the urge to deny all or any retailoring and the desire for everyone to notice the new radiance – after all, if they don't, what is the *point* of spending thousands on all that tautness?

Permanently Beautiful People understand this dilemma only too clearly. 'Darling, how *well* you look!' they cry tactfully after any unexplained absence from the social scene; and never ever would they dream of adding, 'But you look different, somehow.' If an outsider should be so crass as to make this comment, the correct response is, 'Yes, I've changed my hairstyle'.

As in freemasonry, initiates can recognize other Permanent Beauties by certain giveaway signs: the forward-swept curls to hide scars in front of the ears, a hint of waxiness round the eyes,

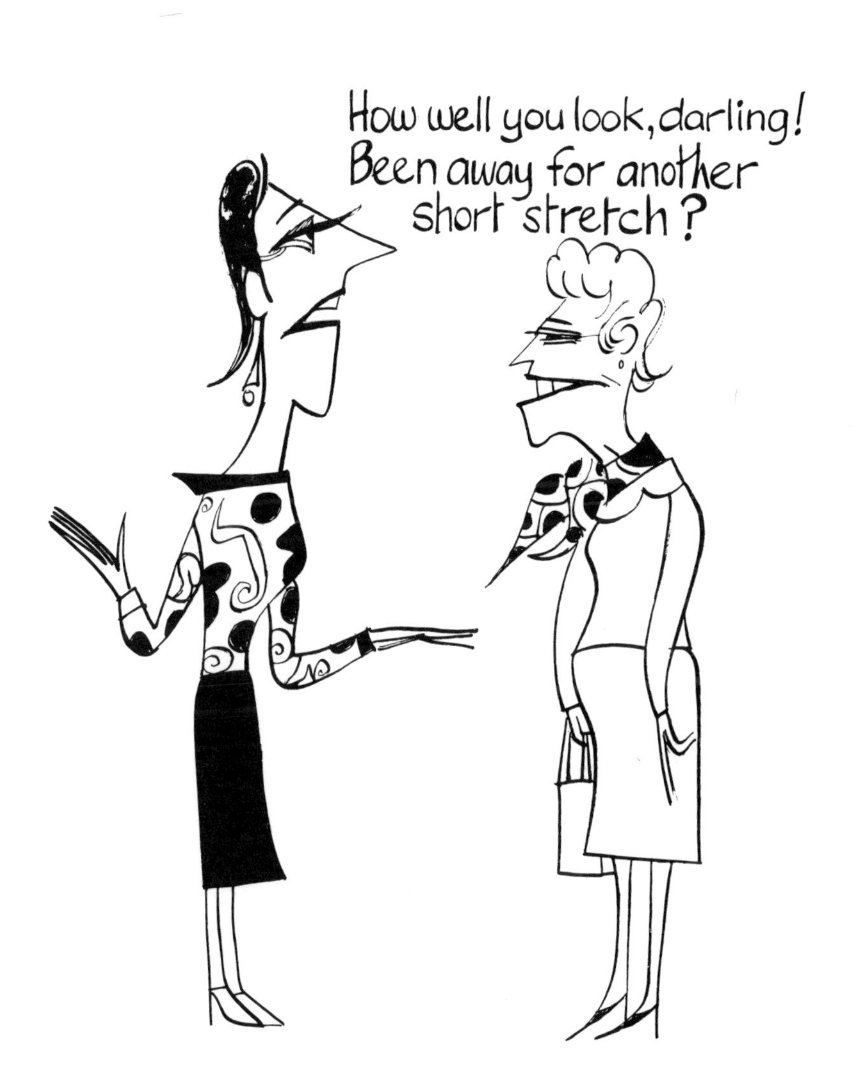
How well you look, darling! Been away for another short stretch?

the faintest widening and flowering of the lips, and of course a sudden sharpness of the jawbone. Those who have submitted to several recontourings can be picked out by one further indication: a curiously transparent complexion (frequent lifting causes the skin to thin).

Other traps for the readjusted Permanent Beauty are baring the body and submitting it to sunshine.

If you suspect an altered bustline, it is not good modern manners to suggest adjourning to the nearest topless beach – all surgery leaves scars, and all scars stay white in the sun. Women with Permanently Beautiful bosoms invariably prefer one-pieces, which are not only becoming but get over the awkwardness of not removing a bikini top when all around are flinging theirs to the winds.

Strong ultra-violet is also bad for those who have had their faces chemically peeled. Here, however, the excuse is ready-made: staying out of the sun for the sake of your complexion is considered sensible rather than surprising. Nevertheless, the dermabraded lady would die rather than say why.

The conspiracy of silence on which the whole of Permanent Beauty etiquette is founded helps the more successful plastic surgeons to maintain their near-monopoly. Because to know much about a particular surgeon is more or less to admit that you, too, have been a patient, only under the blackest oaths of secrecy are the names of these magicians of the scalpel passed on, and then only to best friends of the longest standing. As each surgeon has his own particular technique – why else do you think Nancy Reagan and Betsy Bloomingdale look so alike? – it is often possible to trace close friendships through the prevalence of, say, the Basra eyelid or the Lebon thigh.

Even though only a newcomer would be indelicate enough to ask, 'But where have you *been?*' in the teeth of an uncharacteristic reserve, Permanently Beautiful People always have a set of excuses ready for their inexplicable absences. These range from the recherché, like spiritual retreats or polar exploration, to health farms and visits to clinics for the removal of moles, warts, tonsils, cysts or anything else minor, unprovable, and not too unappetizing.

The more sophisticated combine the whole thing with a trip abroad – fringe Iron Curtain countries are especially suspect – returning bronzed and youthful-looking after a 'marvellous holiday' in their Black Sea, Cyprus or California clinic. You can always tell the second-timers on these excursions, as they are the ones who remember to pack ManTan for the arrival home, and to have ready on their lips the most uncrackable excuse for their new and youthful glow. 'Didn't I tell you? I've fallen in love.'

Social pitfalls (10)

Sometimes a man is talking unsuspectingly to a pretty woman when wham! – he finds he has stepped on a conversational rake. Another Third Stage Feminist has struck back.

While the early militants were instantly identifiable (unshaven legs, unplucked eyebrows, bare faces and work clothing), the Third Stage Feminist carries no warning labels, semiotic or otherwise.

Often, she is as unnervingly chic as any top lady executive – often, she is a top lady executive. She is also quite prepared to chat to women friends about frivolous subjects like clothes or jewellery, and doesn't mind a bit having doors opened for her or her cigarette lit (early feminists, of course, rolled their own); and almost invariably she is living with a man – sometimes she is even married to him.

Frequently, it is her partner's behaviour which reveals the Third Stager. The most obvious sign of men who live with feminist women is the fluency with which they articulate their emotions (often meeting in weekly groups to practise this), and their anxiety not to be role-cast – some will even volunteer to change the nappies of a strange baby. Others do the ironing and make the bed, lying on it only when requested ('I do like a woman who takes the sexual initiative'), make Pill reminder charts for the bathroom door and nonchalantly step into the passenger seat as a matter of course. But now that so many men of all kinds cook (see Eating*), feminist men don't talk about stews but praise their lover's palate for wine.*

As visual identification of the Third Stage Feminist is virtually impossible, it is only prudent, as well as good modern manners towards every woman, to watch your words.

So don't ask her how she manages to cope with all the housework as well as do a job (she doesn't); the proper approach is, 'How do you split the chores?' If she takes you out to lunch, subdue any lingering embarrassment at being paid for by a woman – ten to one it's on the firm anyway – and above all don't bolt for the men's room at bill time.

Don't ever say admiringly, 'You think just like a man,'

God! He's so gauche! You'd think he'd have the grace to mention your marvellous Mouton Cadet before stuffing himself with my pie?

or 'What do girls find to talk about on the telephone?' – this one has two mistakes. Forget 'Has anyone ever told you you're beautiful when you're angry?', 'Of course *I like Amanda – she's got great legs,' or 'Would your husband mind if I asked you out to lunch?' And never, ever mention PMT.*

Dog do's that should be dog don'ts.

Apart from ordinary sensible training, three cardinal rules of good modern dog manners should be graven on every dog owner's heart:

1. If your dog misbehaves on someone else's carpet, YOU must be the one to clear up the mess; whatever the polite insistence to the opposite, disregard it. And if you so much as suspect that youth, nerves or being off-colour may make him pee, don't bring him into the house.*

2. The dog whose incessant barking drowns all greeting or conversation is an unmitigated nuisance. Shut him up – or out – temporarily; then re-train.

3. Some dogs, especially small ones, appear to be totally sex-obsessed. Having one of these creatures humping away at your calf can be embarrassing, not least because there is a natural inhibition at speaking sharply to someone else's pet (dogs usually focus on visitors because their own family won't let them get away with it). If the owner doesn't notice, or doesn't mind, this is one case where you can take matters into your own hand: pick up the dog by its scruff and deposit it on the floor with a sharp word or two. Nobody, these days, has to be a sex object to anyone – let alone a Peke.

*Gerald Ford, when President of the United States, did exactly this: when his dog soiled the White House carpet, Mr Ford would not let an aide clear up the mess, but did it himself.

20.
PETIQUETTE

Etiquette, in the old-fasioned sense of defining which social class you belong to, resides in the small and trivial: one lot raise their little fingers daintily when drinking tea, another never do up the bottom button of what they call their wesc't (the last syllable rhyming, of course, with Asc't). The late Duke of Beaufort once sent his nephew, the present Duke, home for coming out cub-hunting in a polo neck sweater.

It is the same with pets. Hence the anguished cry so often heard on the lips of the upwardly socially mobile: 'When should I wear a labrador?' For it is perfectly true that as well as providing an insight into your subconscious the animal you keep is a guide to status if not class.

Horses, though not exactly pets in the true sense of the word, are the shortest cuts of all to gentrification – membership of the Pony Club is the country equivalent of painting the front door lilac – and not only because of the Royal Seal of Approval; there is a true democracy in the horse world. The only snag is that anything to do with horses invariably costs a lot of money: behind the lawn meet to which the whole county and possibly a Royal Personage come is a run-up of literally thousands in the form of expensive hunters, their keep, the right clothes to ride them in, subscriptions, generous donations to the Wire Fund, Hunt Servants' Benevolent Association and many another deserving cause. All the same, to be greeted by Princess Anne in the competitors' tent at Hunter Trials or Event is a sign you really have arrived.

He's exactly the same out of doors – has this marked preference for oak.

Dogs are an altogether cheaper form of class indicator. Those who wish to brandish their social okayness keep large country-type dogs in their small London flats to imply the existence of another, more spacious way of life at weekends. The two chief gun-dog breeds, labradors and springer spaniels, are the most effective for this, especially if they can be trained to lie soulfully beside the green wellies in the hall. A doggy camp bed, as used in icy country houses where the draughts whistle along the floor, instead of the usual discarded underblanket, is a useful aid to authenticity.

Some small dogs have the same cachet. Undoubted style leader is the Jack Russell; the story of how you had to dig poor darling Benjy out of the badger's sett where he had been stuck for three days after pursing a fox thither is almost as good as membership of the C.G.A. (Country Gentleman's Association, for the benefit of those who don't own a Jack Russell).

Here it is worth noting that many town small-dog owners keep a large dog – labrador, pointer, Weimeraner – in or for the country rather in the same way they have a weekend cottage. Hence the fact that there is probably the highest concentration of Tsih Chuhs in the country around Sloane Square (the New York equivalent is the Cavalier spaniel), while tiny little dogs like chihuahuas or papillons are described proudly by their Ranger owners as 'incredibly sporting' every time they lure their larger, more docile canine companions away on an illicit hunting jaunt. Occasionally, a two-dog owner is thoughtless enough to have pets of opposite sexes; anyone who keeps a dog as a social indicator should get rid of the results with all speed.

Currently, the most fashionable small urban dog is the *bichon frise*, a creature that looks like a poodle gone slightly wrong (poodles, incidentally, were once the sign of an owner gone slightly wrong). Apart from trendiness, bichons' major characteristic is being virtually unhousetrainable, especially when kept in pairs; this perhaps explains why they are usually found in the houses of rich jeans importers with plenty of Filipino domestic help.

In big dogs, the 'in' breed is the Rottweiler – tough. independent and frequently unmanageable.

Rottweiler owners fall into two categories: publicans, who like the feeling of their own A-Team in the background (the usual alternative is an Alsatian), and the highly competent pet owner, able to manage virtually any animal, who wants a challenge – a dog, as one of them put it to me, 'I can really get my teeth into'. Unfortunately, it is all too often the other way round.

One familiar piece of social petiquette, the dog as accessory to the model girl, has disappeared. 'In the early Seventies, all my blonde model clients had blonde dogs – usually Afghans,' says Bruce Fogle, one of London's best-known vets and author of *Pets and Their People*.

Mr Fogle's remark points up a familiar and interesting psychological phenomenon: the pet as projection of the owner's vision of himself – a symbol of what, if he had the courage, he would like to be. (Do not read anything into the fact that your dentist keeps goldfish: watching them swim round produces a hypnotic, subliminally relaxing effect on patients.)

A typical example is the seven-stone weakling who, figuratively speaking, kicks sand in the faces of the other dog-walkers on the Common with his enormous mastiff straining on the leash. Sometimes the name itself is a giveaway.

'If you meet a dog called Brutus, Duke or Rebel, look out,' says Mr Fogle. 'Names like this mean the owner sees it as the free, untamed spirit he himself would like to be – and has therefore given it far less discipline than is good for it. In other words, it bites.'

As for those of liberal, humanitarian principles, what dovetails more neatly with alternative medicine, SDP membership and organic muesli than rescuing a mongrel from Battersea?

Here, as with so many actions done from the best of motives, there is often a sad little corollary: the appealing waif rescued in the nick of time from the canine version of Death Row can bring a few problems with him. Because of their previous treatment, mutts can be very neurotic. The stray dog picked up and taken to a canine welfare organization may have been put out on the street because it grew from a lovable ball of fluff into a large and demanding animal that didn't know how to 'behave' when cooped up in a high-rise flat. If it has experienced this cycle of rejection and rescue several times, it may have many of the same hangups as a child moved from foster family to foster family.

Such dogs, says zoologist and animal behaviourist Dr Roger Mugford, can become overdependent, forming excessive attachments and reacting badly when they feel jealous or think they have been abandoned by their owners – all the problems of an obsessive love affair, in fact, minus the obvious joys.

Here I should point out that sex often plays a large part in the relationship between a dog and its owner – on the dog's side, that is. Bitches often behave better for a man; the male dog who is so possessive of his female owner that he whines, yaps, barks, snuggles, scratches or shoves if anyone else tries to gain her attention is a commonplace.

Often, the owner plays along with this, delivering a fond reproof in a caressing tone (especially if a human male is also present). Many male dogs are so protective of their owner that they mount – and I use the word advisedly – attacks ranging from sexual assault to full-scale biting on anyone who comes too near her.

Sometimes the link between pet and owner's psyche is not so much a meshing of neuroses as an extension of the persona presented to the world. Oriental cats, for instance, are usually kept by people who are very image-conscious and who identify strongly with the stylish, aristocratic aura of their pets. It is hardly a coincidence that the only cat-conscious member of the Royal Family is the charismatic Princess Michael of Kent, noted for her love of Burmese cats.

Behind the steady rise in popularity of the cat lie more general social implications. Once tolerated only as a kind of mobile mousetrap in kitchen or farm, cats are now in a fair way to becoming known as the ideal urban pet. Nor is this solely because they are clean, cuddly, relatively undemanding and need no formal exercise: the cat's native self-sufficiency tunes in exactly with society's increasing fragmentation into ever smaller, more unrelated units.

Those who are or see themselves as loners empathize with the cat's independence. Few cat people like either being bossed around or giving orders to others, preferring instead to go their own way, weaving round obstructions rather than seeking confrontation. A cat staring out over the geraniums means there is someone single at heart if not in fact in the house. The fastidiousness of cats and their air of being in but not of society endear them to gay people (though for a 'married' gay couple the alternative is often a large, beautifully-kept dog). Cats are often a fixture on the desks of writers. For real fanaticism, there is nothing to touch a dedicated cat person.

Pet-owners on the whole are younger and more mobile than the rest of the population (old people are often more vulnerable to pet bans by the local authority or sheltered accommodation); the highest ratio of pets to people is found among media people and actors. Here pets divide up sharply into the minority carried as attention-getters – shoulder parrots, jewel-studded tortoises – and mobile comforters so necessary to their owners' mental well-being that they have even been taken on stage or on to a chat show. 'Many entertainers are so basically insecure they need the extra bit of reassurance a dog or cat provides,' comments Bruce Fogle; and numerous studies have shown that stroking a pet is relaxing, soothing and does wonders for the blood pressure.

'In order to get something out of your relationship with an animal you have to regard it as a person,' says Cambridge zoologist Dr James Serpell. 'And as soon as you think of it as a person, you start treating it as one.' While anthropomorphism reaches its height with dogs – dog wedding dresses, dinner jackets, birthday parties and astrology charts are all commonplace in the U.S. – all pets are supreme ego-boosters. What other friend never complains, criticizes, acts disloyally, grumbles, attempts blackmail, mocks, looks bored, borrows from or gossips about you, or elopes with someone else?

The British pet, moreover, holds one compelling psychological card that is missing from the paw of the average Eurodog or cat. In this country, we are not on the whole a culture of touch – especially where men are concerned. In Europe, men touch anyone within reach as naturally as they laugh or smile; for the British male, permissible touching is confined to his wife and his dog. And on the whole, the dog does better.

Social pitfalls (11)

Unemployment and redundancy are social problems well outside the scope of this book. Nevertheless, one thing bears repeating: it is modern manners of the most appalling kind to sound off about your Caribbean holiday or second Porsche without first ascertaining that your audience is in work.

21.
Baring It

For several weeks each year, visitors to the beaches of France, Spain, Italy, the Balearics, the remoter parts of Greece and, of late, the southern shores of the Mediterranean, encounter a social custom unknown to the etiquette manuals of previous generations. I refer to the quaint Continental convention of instantly baring the breasts at the first sight of a sizable stretch of water or, as it is colloquially known, 'going topless'. For the first-time visitor, it presents a knotty behavioural dilemma which takes one of two forms, depending on sex.

If you are female and in a mixed party of friends, do you bare your breasts as unconcernedly as the bronzed and sinuous girls around you? Or do you feel, 'How can I *possibly* face the Charringtons at church next week? If Joe from the office takes photographs, will he show them around when we get back?' or even, 'What will I do if Jeremy stares? What will I do if he *doesn't?*' . . . and stay covered up.

For men the problem is, so to speak, inverted. As you lie squashed like sardines on some expensive strip of sand, do you pretend not to notice when your cousin's wife nearly knocks your eye out with her nipple – or is it more in tune with modern manners to gaze admiringly and remark: 'I say, Amanda, I never realized you had such super tits. Lucky old Jeremy!'

One of the troubles is that most Britons have no home experience of toplessness to act as a yardstick. While every Continental child old enough to paddle is accustomed to seeing his elder sisters, mother, aunts and even grandmother

disporting themselves in a single brief garment consisting of no more than a few square inches of cotton, British beaches are better known for their acreage of uncompromising Lycra. Only in newspaper photographs does Lovely Samantha Snooks, 18, bare all as she Cools Off In The Surf; and even Brighton's famous nude beach, far from heralding an era of greater exposure, has become simply a mecca for voyeurs.

Then there is the question of the general pallor and sensitivity of the Anglo-Saxon skin. The browner you are the less naked you look (or at any rate, feel), and suddenly baring those parts which have never seen the light of day before often results in bright pink giveaway patches that are not only unaesthetic but so acutely painful as to spoil everybody's fun, including your own.

But both these deterrents are as nothing to one major inhibiting factor: the instinctive conviction of the average British female that there is something badly wrong with her breasts.

'I'm too busty/flat-chested/drooping/shapeless,' she wails, 'and anyway the right one is bigger than the left.' If she isn't terrified people will notice her breasts are too close together, far apart, high or low, she is embarrassed because they wobble, point downwards, have nipples of the wrong size and shape, or appear to wink.

In contrast, she notes unhappily, French girls invariably appear to have firm round breasts like apples above dimpled sexy navels, while Italians swing voluptuously to the water's edge, gleaming black hair brushing deep, bronzed bosoms as they cast occasional smouldering glances across the foreshore. It's true that the Germans, with their strange habit of going totally nude save for tennis socks, sneakers and a nose shield, redress the balance somewhat, but they are so numerous and so rich that whatever they do is greeted with a sigh of weary tolerance; while the Scandinavians, as everyone knows, grow up naked.

Once the plunge has been taken, comes that other great question: when to cover up? Do you stroll nonchalantly to the beach bar in nothing more than a minimal tanga, or do you feel that a surrounding sea of bare breasts could put a fellow diner off his poached eggs? Consensus is unequivocal: cover up when there is no sand underfoot.

Theory, however, is all very well; putting it into practice can take a certain amount of courage. But as with any social innovation, from tobacco to plus fours – or in this case, plus twos – the more it is seen around, the more it gets taken for granted. All the same, so great is the emphasis placed on breasts in our culture that for some women baring them is akin to total self-exposure: hence those bedroom exchanges of the 'Are you *sure* I look all right without my bikini top, Jeremy?' variety, to which the reply is invariably, 'Oh, for God's sake, Amanda!' instead of the desired, 'Darling, you should have been a Playboy centrefold.'

Nevertheless, burning as is the female need for reassurance on this vital matter, this is one case where men other than husbands or lovers should employ a rarely-used piece of social weaponry: the Deferred Compliment.

It is a far, far better thing to remark over dinner that evening at the quayside fish restaurant: 'Gosh, Amanda, you nearly caused a riot on the beach this morning,' than to look stunned at the time and emit a loud 'Wow!' Or even 'Wow! Wow!'

22. GAY GUIDELINES

Long gone are the days when 'gay' meant only light-hearted, lively or insouciant. But as far as modern manners are concerned, the same underlying rule – consideration for others – holds good for gays as for straights. Only, as with all minorities, more so.

It starts with the question of identification. Though some gays are undoubtedly made in Heaven, not all stand around in gay clubs and bars, facing each other in identical attitudes and the same uniform of jeans, T-shirt, leather jacket, sunglasses, moustache and a touch of eau-de-clone behind the ears. Quite a number are shy of self-disclosure.

These may be part-time gays – bank managers who only come out of the vault at weekends, people in Establishment jobs who have painfully built up a façade over the years, others who don't want to come clean because their partner is highly unsuitable, or people who simply want to get on with living their life as quietly, happily and privately as possible. True politeness consists of respecting these unspoken wishes; as with all confidences that might be embarrassing to the giver of them, any disclosure should come freely rather than be extracted by even the friendliest questioning.

Sometimes, of course, there can be hiccups even in such exquisitely balanced judgments. Occasionally, a gay will long to be fancied by women as well as men, and as many of these emotional adventurers seem to possess peculiarly alluring personalities, considerable damage can result. Many a girl has fallen halfway in love with a gay before she realizes it isn't nobility that's holding him back – or alternatively, that she isn't, after all, going to be the one to change him.

Responsible gays disapprove strongly of this kind of teasing. As one of my own friends says, 'It is only good manners to disclose where you're at early on in any acquaintance that promises to turn into a relationship of some kind. When you're still metaphorically being offered a lift home is the time to say, "I hope my better half's up – he'd love to meet you."'

Today, gays are the most affluent minority in Britain, with the homosexual man more likely to be in a professional job, and better paid for the one he's in, than his straight brother. (With female gays, on the other hand, the reverse applies.) The 'pink pound' is a major market force: one recent American survey

estimates that, without family commitments or mortgages, the average gay has around one-fifth of his income free to spend as he pleases.

The result is that gays are not only the first to pick up and follow new trends but also able to enjoy a high standard of living; for many, their homes are a compensation for the families they don't have. When visiting gay friends, therefore, sensitive straights will be extra careful to see that their small children don't knock a wineglass over the pristine white carpet, trail chocolatey fingers along the silk walls, or sweep expensive stereo equipment on to the floor.

The natural creativity of gay people results in a 'gay network' throughout the entire arts, media and entertainment fields. Kindly gays often pass on interesting titbits about impending sackings, promotions or scandals to straight friends who otherwise would not have access to such riveting dramas; another channel of communication is via the 'walker' – the gay who escorts close female friends to dinners, openings and receptions that both enjoy, sharing confidences and giving her an impartial appraisal of what she looks best in and how to wear it properly.

In more formal entertaining, the earlier-mentioned rule of leaving personal disclosures to the person concerned holds good. If they know a friend is gay, and suspect he has a lover, well-mannered straights ask him to dinner with the words: 'Do you want to bring anyone?' Equally, polite gays say to straight friends: 'You do know I'm living with someone?' Gays known to be in stable relationships should *always* be asked as a couple (unless, as not infrequently happens, one half doesn't go out: many gay couples seem to consist of a sparky extrovert teamed with someone dour and anti-social).

If you are set on asking only your particular friend from a couple, the most civilized way is via the stopgap convention, ringing more or less at the last minute with 'Jeremy has got 'flu – could you be an angel and make up numbers?' Otherwise, there's always lunch.

Social pitfalls (12)

Much of modern manners is moulded by issues first made fashionable in the Sixties – racism, the right to free contraception, a vague and benevolent Socialism. The watchful student of human nature will note with relish attempts to reconcile an anguished liberal conscience with the trappings of affluence. Often, these are triggered by a seemingly simple question. 'Do you have a weekend cottage?' not infrequently provokes an apologia on the following lines:

'I am a deeply caring, sensitive person forced by the demands of my taxing profession to seek a few much-needed hours of solitude in the humble cottage I happen to possess in an unspoiled part of the West Country. Needless to say, while I have renovated this internally to the highest standards, the outside remains unchanged save for extensive planting in the small but charming garden. While there are some who claim that the native villagers themselves have been pushed out by the natural rise in the prices of these dwellings, I prefer to believe that by improving and maintaining such properties I am making an important and worthwhile contribution to the country's housing stock. All the same, I would prefer you not to use the words "second home" in future.'

Social pitfalls (13)

Once, strong men blushed if an improper word escaped their lips. Today, stand outside any secondary school at going-home time and the only thing you can distinguish above the general buzz is a steady stream of profanity.

Much effing and blinding disappears as adolescence gets left behind. But a hard core remains, so much so that the question arises: Is not-swearing really a part of modern manners?

The answer would seem to be Yes – up to a point. In grown-up mixed company, the old ban still operates on words to do with copulation. But for anyone under about 30, nouns and adjectives to do with the excretory functions seem to have been not so much absorbed into the language as sterilized of their original meaning. Hence the no doubt apocryphal tale of the young woman stepping on to a dirty Kensington pavement: 'Oh shit! I've trodden in some doggy-poo.'

What are those effing doggies doing, Uncle Noel? Are they developing a relationship?

23.
Country Is Best

In the country, the lines of class are more strongly drawn, time moves more slowly, voices tend to be louder (going Sloane-deaf at an early age is comparatively common) and cats are more frequently feral. People like a feud or two to liven up their lives and the parson – usually through no fault of his own – is often less than popular. Though good manners are good manners whether you live in Mayfair or Mousehole, country etiquette wanders into some curious byways unknown to the town-dweller.

All true country dwellers speak from a position of high if unconscious moral superiority directly correlated to the distance of their homes from the capital. Do not be fooled by a mask of apparent diffidence ('I'm afraid I don't know much about politics/books/fashion – but then, I'm just a country bumpkin'): deep down inside him, the country dweller knows his is the way of life all sensible people aspire to. And the farther away and more difficult of access his castle, manor, cottage or barn, the more he feels justified in speaking his mind on the habits, clothes, behaviour and, above all, place of residence of the pathetic townie. 'I don't know how you can bear to live in London,' with its implicit disparagement of the addressee's choice of job and/or life partner, is a fairly common dinner-party opening from those who would think it the height of rudeness if in your own introductory remarks you wondered aloud why they chose to live in a leaky shack at the end of a muddy lane.

But so deep is the legend Country is Best graven in the English psyche that even the happiest and most successful townies respond cravenly to this overt or implied criticism of their way of life by eagerly remarking that they, too, were born in the country ('So you see, I'm not *really* a Londoner!'), bolt there every weekend, or are only waiting for the day when they can throw up for good the tiresome business of high-earning work, parties and fame to retire to some charming little rural hideaway.

This is not the moment, therefore, to respond to those who blithely carol, 'Do you really enjoy all those crowds and soot? Personally, I'd go mad if I had to spend more than 24 hours in a town,' that there is more than one kind of madness. What is involved here is a simple failure of comprehension rather than a desire to wound, so try instead a civil 'You are probably right.' They can always work out what you really mean later.

Weekenders

Weekenders are often surprised by being given a tough time in the charming little hamlet that appeared so enchantingly peaceful when they first cruised through it in their search for a Friday-to-Monday retreat. The main reason is that their influx tends to split a village, giving employment (good) but forcing up property prices (bad) so that local people can't afford the done-up cottages when the weekenders finally call it a day and return to the rural delights of Hampstead. Hence they find themselves almost singlehandedly keeping the roof on the church, yet not being asked to the good dinner parties; buying the prizes for the village fete, yet not being asked to present them.

One reason for this always-a-bridesmaid syndrome is that townies often offend appallingly without being aware of it. Apart from basic commandments like never leaving undone those gates which you should have done up – anything from small children to cows can get on to a road or into a field to do damage – there are various other taboos and customs. Many are so local that only a period of lying low while closely observing will enable you to act correctly – or rather, avoid acting incorrectly – until you are certain of the ground. Others are pretty well universal in all true (*i.e.*, 80-plus miles from London) country spots.

The main etiquette ground rule is to do absolutely nothing for about a year. In contrast to town life, the average English village is a mesh of complicated, interwoven relationships of all descriptions, with the ever-present possibility of misunderstanding, major row or life-long feud arising from some reference to a piece of ancient history unknown to the newcomer, or the infringement of some invisible boundary. The genuine good neighbourliness – again, in frequent contrast to town life – alongside which all this exists is a further deceptive factor. Only when the main currents of village life have been assimilated can the weekender, tentatively, put a toe in the water. Until then, circumspection combined with the lowest of low profiles is the correct procedure.

Clothes, although a comparatively minor point, can help the beginner blend into the background for the necessary period of observation on both sides. Not that any country person would tell you to your face if you were wearing the 'wrong' garments; nevertheless, the word 'smart' should always be regarded as a warning signal (as in 'Goodness, how smart you are!' while eyeing the brand-new leather patches on a brand-new tweed coat). While waiting to decide on your own specific sartorial

requirements (will you take up fishing? gardening? hunting?), it is possible to survive for months on end in jeans or corduroys, shirt or sweater, black or green wellies. The truly aware have their Barbours run in by someone else.

One of the few exceptions to the non-smart rule is hunting clothes. These should be as perfect and immaculate as the hand of hunting tailor and bootmaker can make them; and flawlessly cleaned and polished (like your horse and its accoutrements). 'Well turned out' is the highest expression of praise.

Another pitfall for newcomers is the question of time. Accustomed to the generous social latitude of town life, they are unaware that when asked for drinks at six, the time to arrive is

Bloody interferers! I likes watchin' juggernauts.
THE BULL AND COW

six. When they turn up at 7.30 their hosts, with barely-concealed impatience, are waiting to go into dinner; the post-mortem in the car going home finds the newcomers baffled by their cool reception. 'I can't understand it, Jeremy – we got on so well the first time we met. I really thought they might become friends.' They will, Amanda, they will – but only if you realize that most country people's lives are geared to the inflexible feeding routines of their animals. Keeping your host's hunter waiting for his oats is much worse than doing the same to your host.

Taking sides

Many country villages are riven by what I can best call the Clochemerle factor. Any proposed change to the environment that could affect the livelihood or visual pleasure of the inhabitants results in the instant formation of two parties with diametrically opposed points of view. This partisanship is seen at its most violent when the issue is local and comparatively trivial – the building, say, of a bus shelter rather than the creation of a bypass. The public lavatory is tailor-made for such a situation.

Those who live well away from main road or square are unanimous in their desire to see the charming 18th-century façades overlooking the green unsullied by the erection of modern toilet facilities; those who live within striking (if that is the word) distance of long-distance coach stops are equally adamant that what the village needs is a catchment area for incontinent passengers.

Etiquette here varies according to length of residence. While it is expected that the village's native inhabitants will be firmly on one side or another – most made their minds up immutably for or against the moment the proposed privy was first mooted – the newcomer or weekender will, if he is sensible, remain silent.

Only if directly involved can he put in his 5p's worth. A newcomer's views on the need to preserve the architectural merits of his adopted village or why it is vital to bow to the forces of progress will cause both camps to wonder, often audibly, what the affair has got to do with him anyway, but a simple plea based on expediency nearly always works. 'My garden is the nearest secluded spot to the coach stop so they troop in there to relieve themselves and now half my lawn is dead,' will gain sympathy all round – if only because it appeals to one of the most fundamental concepts of country life: The Garden.

Gardening

'While gardening this afternoon I heard a faint note which led me to say to my under-gardener "Was that the cuckoo?"' Thus Mr R. Lydekker, F.R.S., in a letter to *The Times* on 6 February 1913, summing up in a phrase much of what gardening is about – love of nature combined with an instinct for the rare, the need to do much of the work in the most unpleasant months of the year, plus the faint streak of dottiness so basic to the English character.

For gardening is not just a pleasant way of passing a few hours on a sunny afternoon; on the contrary, there is a direct link between expertise and poor weather conditions. This is because nothing thrills the true gardener so much as to make a sickly specimen of something that really belongs in the Himalayas flower in a Warwickshire fog. This means that all the most intriguing, rare or difficult plants undergo the most interesting part of their life cycle during blizzard conditions, with the lucky visitor taken to see a tiny bloom of Pharaoh's Eye in the teeth of a gale.

Naturally, gardening clothes are built with these rigours in mind – or rather, the gardener views every garment with an eye to its gardening relevance.

Corduroy is preferred in earthy, not to say mud-coloured, shades; tweed must be of no discernible pattern but able to blend into a background of shrubbery or arboretum at 300 yards distance – rather as shy creatures of the wild 'disappear' into the surrounding scrub or veldt the moment they stand still. There must also be provision for the rolls of twine, secateurs, plantain trowel and gardening gloves that all gardeners carry about with them. 'Wonderful pockets for weeding,' murmured one gardener dreamily, eyeing a loose linen smock. 'But won't books make them a trifle baggy?' replied the bemused assistant.

Gardeners fortunate enough to employ a jobbing gardener enjoy with this treasure a relationship that is almost marital in its knowledge of each other's little whims and idiosyncrasies. Year after year the same battle is fought over whether it is worth growing asparagus in such clayey soil; regularly dear old Jackson 'weeds' the mauve primulas he dislikes so much from the path edge. Overlooking something you can neither prove nor do anything about is a major theme in gardening etiquette.

Gardeners give each other garden books for Christmas, know the Latin names of even the most obscure weed (many gardeners believe this is why Caesar came to Britain), go on the lecture circuit to give or listen to garden lectures, tour the country in coaches to visit famous gardens, know the Open Days within a 40-mile radius by heart, invariably think their own garden is just past or not yet at its best, and are seen *en masse* and in peak bloom at the Chelsea Flower Show (this also sees the apotheosis of the other end of the gardening-wardrobe spectrum, the silk dress and straw hat worn – naturally – irrespective of weather conditions).

Few gardeners have any morals where gardening is concerned, snooping round the *potager* when they know the owner is away, prising secrets of mulching or lawn care from their best friend's gardener, or removing portions of a plant when her (it usually is a her) back is turned. This process is called Just Taking a Cutting – gardeners would be horrified if told they were stealing – and is usually justified by the cutting-taker's murmuring to herself some such phrase as, 'Pruning always helps growth. Besides, she won't notice.'

This activity becomes even more prevalent when any important or interesting (*i.e.*, filled with rarities) garden has been thrown open for, say, a huge sale of plants in aid of the Distressed Gentlefolks' Association. Dedicated gardeners feel that buying a certain number of the rows of pots set neatly out on trestle tables in the stable yard gives them the right to 'adopt' one or two others – a sort of *droit de jardinière*. Hence just as familiar a sight as someone staggering along in the rain under an enormous rhododendron is some variation on the following vignette: two tweed-clad ladies furtively eyeing a superb honeysuckle while one says to the other, 'That's the one! You go and distract the gardener while I get out my secateurs'.

If caught, as not infrequently happens, by the lady owner of the shrub in question – all lady gardeners have eyes like hawks – garden etiquette demands the correct response of, 'You do sell this, don't you?' Placing a slightly higher price on the stolen cutting than on similar ones to be found in the stable sales area, the lady will graciously acquiesce, after which both parties will tacitly agree to forget the whole matter. (Curiously enough, stolen cuttings never seem to do very well; this is known as Percy Thrower's Law.)

It only remains to add that despite all its demands on the time, energy, money and emotion of the gardener, gardening is never seen as in any sense a rival by the non-gardening spouse. But then, unlike the participants met in other country pastimes, flowers never ask anyone to share their bed.

The canine connection

The average Englishwoman, it was once said, would much prefer to give birth to a litter of puppies than to a child. Judging by the number who move everywhere in a cloud of canine companions, a good many appear to have succeeded in this laudable aim. What the anxious newcomer to village life wonders is: Is it rude not to welcome the pack into your house along with their besotted owner?

Dog-owners' etiquette is quite clear here. While town dogs can't be left outside to fend for themselves, no country dog has an automatic right to enter your house. Though the agreeable single dog often gets invited in, all well-trained multi-dog owners expect to leave their pets either at home or snoozing

When sky be grey,
'tis time for rain.
Dinner party
down the drain.
BAH!

peacefully in the car outside; and the truly civil owner waits until well away from a host's property before letting all of them out for a much-needed run. In short, delightful as man's best friend is on a one-to-one basis, pack appeal is something he generally lacks. But then, so does his owner.

. . . good books lately?

Never open a country conversation by asking the views of your *vis-à-vis* on the latest literary sensation. Country dwellers tend to fall into one of two groups. The first lot never read, although copies of *Country Life, Horse and Hound, Stockbreeders' Gazette,*

the local paper and possibly *Yachting World* are to be found prominently displayed in their houses on tables by the drawing room window; all you will encounter here is a blank stare. The second group are as sophisticated as aesthetes anywhere but with the added advantage of having more time to devote to their cultural interests. This lot will make mincemeat of you.

Weather – or not?

In the country, forget the credo current in metropolitan circles that talking about the weather is boring. In any rural area, weather is a constant preoccupation on whose vagaries depend not only livelihoods but most fun; hunting, shooting, race meetings, horse shows, even dinner parties can be cancelled at a stroke if the heavens open or snowdrifts pile up.

Hence one modification to the normal etiquette of greeting. While giving a precise list of medical symptoms in answer to the query 'How are you?' is just as frowned on generally in rural life as in urban, there is one exception. It is perfectly all right to mention those that throw light on any possible change in temperature, wind direction, cloud formation or the possibility of a storm before sunset. Thus 'I had those awful twinges in my shoulder last night – you know it always aches before an east wind,' is not only permissible but regarded as a valuable addition to the information gathered so painstakingly on top of the Air Ministry roof. Needless to say, many country hypochondriacs live a happy and fulfilled life as walking barometers.